Wrath

A John Reeves Novel

Kirkus MacGowan

Diapers, Bookmarks, and Pipe Dreams
www.kirkusmacgowan.info

To my father.
For teaching me what it means to have a strong work ethic.

Wrath

1. The Phone Call

The Phone Call

"Can you start from the beginning again, Doug? I need to make sure nothing was missed." Alan leafed through the pages of the report. Questioning a close friend like Douglas Fincham was never easy, one of the disadvantages of working as a small-town police officer.

Doug lifted his dusty cowboy hat and ran his fingers through his fringe of gray hair. "Again? How many times you boys need me to go over it? I already told them everything I remember." Doug gestured to the other officers around the police department, typing away or chatting on the phone.   .

"I'm sure you did, but we need to make sure we don't make any mistakes. You disappeared for over a week with no memory of it. Not an everyday occurrence. You're a friend, Doug. Heck, you're more than a friend. I'm doing everything I can to make sure something like this doesn't happen again. Besides, you told *them*, not me."

Doug sighed and replaced his hat. "Last thing I recollect is loading Johnny's food in the back of the old Dodge." Doug had named his yellow lab after his brother, saying they were both too loud for their own good. "I remember, because my back was hurting real bad that day."

"From when you fell off the barn?"

The broad shouldered man and his wife invited Alan over for dinner at least once a month. He'd been there the day Doug tumbled from the barn roof. An occasional sore back was lucky considering how far he'd fallen.

"That's right. Always tightens up at the worst times." Doug shifted in his seat. "Anyway, I'm throwing the dog food in the truck, and I get a real bad pain in my back. Worse than normal. Next thing I know, I'm lying in the ditch over by Hailey's farm and getting rained on." His face flushed. "I woke up bare as the day I was born, laying there on my side like I was sleeping."

Calming Doug's wife had been virtually impossible. The case was as crazy as any Alan had heard in his ten years on the Clarkbridge police force. He spent most of his time scheduling shifts, writing speeding tickets, or handing out report and repairs. He'd moved back to his hometown to take it easy, live the life of a small-town officer. Clarkbridge wasn't as small as it used to be, but it was much smaller than Detroit where he'd begun his career.

Alan looked at the stack of papers on his desk and adjusted his loosened tie. Cooper Forbes, a fellow officer, had written the report the previous day when they'd found Doug. "Do you remember the name of the woman who found you?"

"Of course I do. Doesn't it say so in your report?" Doug pointed to the pile.

"It does. Just double checking."

"Fine, fine. I'll play along. Natasha Green. Leslie plays spades with her on Thursdays." He laughed. "I'm not a shy man, Alan, but you should've seen the look on her face when I came up out of that ditch. She slammed on her brakes and almost hit me. You would have thought I was wiggling my willy when she climbed out. Her face was as red as a firehouse. Didn't know a face could turn that red."

Natasha was a regular at Doug and Leslie's for dinner. To say she was reserved was an understatement. "I can only imagine." Alan let out his own laugh.

Sergeant Shaw shushed him, and Gibbs just shook his head—two of the three officers assigned to the next shift.

Alan continued. "She brought you straight to the station?"

"Sure did."

Alan hoped Doug's disappearance wasn't some kind of episode. He'd heard it happened on occasion with people getting on in years. The old farmer seemed to be made of tougher stuff than most, but one never knew.

"One last question, Doug. I don't want you to get upset."

"What's that, Alan?" Doug leaned forward.

"Dr. Howard said he'll get the tox report back to us tomorrow. Will we find anything you haven't told us about?"

The other officers had been too nervous to ask the large man if he'd taken any drugs. They'd asked Alan to do it because of their friendship.

"Tox report?"

Alan adjusted his tie again and smoothed the front of his starched dark-brown shirt. "It's short for toxicology report. That's why we drew blood yesterday. It measures any chemicals you may have in your system, like alcohol or... drugs."

Doug leaned back in his seat and lowered his bushy eyebrows. "Why would you even ask?" His voice took on a menacing tone. "You know I don't do none of that stuff." He crossed his arms and looked away.

I shouldn't have let the chief talk me into taking this case. "I know you don't do drugs. Could you have had a drink or two? It measures things like high levels of allergy meds or pain-killers, too."

"Oh, well, why didn't you say that? I wasn't doing any drinking, but I take them horse pills Doc Howard gave me. Helps with the back pain. I only take them every few weeks or so, when the ache gets real bad. Like I told you, it was extra tight that day, so I'd taken a couple in the morning."

"Do you remember the name of the horse pills?"

Doug drew his brows down, rubbing his fingers through his trimmed white beard. "Valium? No, not Valium. That was Leslie's sister." He stared at the floor a moment. "Vicotron... or Vitridun..."

"Vicodin?"

"That's the stuff. Doc knows how to prescribe them, doesn't he? First time I took one, I slept fourteen hours."

A grin grew on Alan's face. "How many do you usually take?"

"Just one. Sometimes two if it gets real bad."

Alan penned a note about the Vicodin into the report. "Well, that should be it unless you think of anything else."

"I don't think so. You boys have almost run me dry with all your questions."

They stood. Alan offered his hand. Alan was larger than most men, but Doug's hand dwarfed his own when they shook.

"You have my number," Alan said. "Call me if you think of anything, even if you don't think it's a big deal. It might give us a clue as to what happened."

"Will do." Doug pulled the faded tan jacket over his thick shoulders and turned to leave.

Alan sat in his swivel chair, wondering if he'd missed something. *This doesn't make sense. What were you doing in a ditch, Doug? Why don't you remember anything?*

Doug was almost to the front entrance when he stopped. He strode back to Alan's desk.

Alan raised his chin. "Remember something?"

"Kind of. You said to tell you if there was anything else, even if it wasn't a big deal."

"That's right."

"Well... you mentioned the pain killers and it got me thinking. My back doesn't hurt at all. To be honest, it feels better than it has in years. Like I could go out dancing."

He held his arms to the side and tapped his feet in a small jig.

"Really? You think you were kidnapped by a chiropractor?"

Doug let out a raucous laugh. "Wouldn't that be a story to tell? Anyway, that's it. My back feels right dandy."

Alan's phone rang. "I should get this." He tossed the report on his desk and reached for the handset. "You stay out of trouble, Doug. Tell Leslie we're still on for her lasagna this weekend."

Doug waved and headed toward the door.

The man on the phone asked for Douglas Fincham. Alan placed his palm over the receiver. "Hey, Doug. It's for you." He held the phone out.

"For me? Only one knows I'm here is Leslie, and she knows I'll be coming home when I'm done. Maybe she wants me to stop at the store. She's always forgetting something."

"It's not Leslie. It's a man. You want me to ask who it is?"

Doug shook his head, taking the phone. "This is Doug." A short pause. "What was that?" The old man's face went slack. He slowly lowered the phone to the desk.

"Is everything okay?" Alan put the phone to his ear. A busy signal. He sat the phone on the cradle.

Doug's blank gaze lowered.

"Doug? What's going on?"

The old farmer's eyes met Alan's. They peered through him, seeing something a hundred miles away. His skin paled further. He crumpled, sitting down right where he stood. Alan shot around the desk to catch his friend before he went the rest of the way down.

"Talk to me, Doug. What happened?"

No response. Bubbling white foam dribbled from Doug's mouth. His face pinched into a snarl and his body shook, eyes bulging. He reached for his own neck with both hands.

"Shit. Somebody get Doc Howard on the phone." Alan gave Doug's shoulders a violent shake. *God, don't take Doug from me too*, Alan prayed.

Cooper ran to Alan's side and paused; his mouth moved, but no words came out. His buggy eyes flitted back and forth. Sergeant Shaw pounded the numbers on her phone.

Doug's face slowly turned purple. Alan laid him back on the floor. He pried open the man's mouth and peered down his throat, hoping to remove whatever choked him.

Empty.

Even if Alan couldn't see an obstruction, the old man gagged on something. Alan slid behind Doug and lifted his shoulders, wrapping his long arms around his stomach. They barely fit around the man's girth. The Heimlich maneuver was near impossible.

"I got dispatch," Shaw called "We got an ambulance on the way."

"Call Doc Howard, Coop," Alan groaned.

Cooper nodded and turned to use Alan's phone. Sergeant Gibbs kneeled beside Alan, grabbing Doug's shoulders to help sit him upright.

Doug's body convulsed. He slapped at his arms as if they burned, grunting with each smack. Blood vessels popped in Doug's eyes, turning them red. His skin was purple from the neck up.

"This isn't working." Alan clambered up. Doug's leg jerked, knocking Alan from his feet. Sergeant Gibbs reached to catch him, but missed. Alan's head banged on the corner of his desk. He rolled to his back and put his hand to his temple. Sticky blood covered his fingers. Cooper bent to help him up.

"Not me, Coop. Help Doug." Alan pointed to his friend.

Cooper turned back to the old man. Red stained Doug's tan coat sleeves as blood soaked through. "What the hell is happening?" Cooper took a step toward the man on the floor.

Alan held his hand tight over the gash on his brow. Doug flailed and then went stiff. He collapsed unmoving, releasing what little breath he had left in him.

Cooper put his trembling fingers to Doug's neck. They came away bloody. "I can't get a pulse, too much blood."

"Try the wrist," Alan said, as Gibb's helped him to his feet.

Cooper slid Doug's jacket sleeve to the elbow. Long gashes ran up his arm. Dark red lifeblood seeped from each cut. He put his fingers to the old man's wrist. "He's dead, Alan."

Gibbs and Shaw watched in silence, their faces pale. The nightmare had taken less than a minute.

"No way he's dead." Alan let go of his own wound and scrambled onto the large man's abdomen. He pumped with both hands. Red droplets cascaded to Doug's chest with each pump. "Where is the God damn ambulance?" He continued pumping, not waiting for an answer. He counted to thirty and tilted Doug's head back. He tried to breathe life into him. A gurgling noise came from his friend.

"My God," Cooper whispered.

Sergeant Shaw's hand shot to her mouth. She turned away. Alan sat back. Frothy blood bubbled from Doug's throat. Every ounce of air Alan forced in came back out through a gash running almost ear to ear across Doug's neck, as if someone had slit his throat.

Alan trembled with his bloody hands held out before him. "There's no way. I was right here with him the whole time. No way this just happened."

2. Big Man and The Funeral

Manny

John Reeves nodded to his friend standing next to him in the hallway. "If I haven't said so yet, thanks for getting me in on this."

"Oh, just be quiet." Eddy leaned against the wall on the side of the doorway. Sweat beaded on his forehead. "You ready?"

Manny Rodriguez was supposed to be on the other side of the door, armed and dangerous. A neighbor in the apartment across the hall had phoned Eddy about the bounty.

"Ready when you are," John said.

Eddy whispered into the mic on his headset. "Lena, you in place?"

Lena's voice chirped back at him. "Yes, I'm in place, you turd. I've been here for thirty minutes while you two —"

"I get the point," he said, looking to John. "Okay, here we go. Turn your safety off. You don't want to have to do it in the heat of the moment."

"You ever seen a Glock with a safety?" He held the gun up between them.

Eddy gave a sheepish grin and shook his head.

"Thanks, Eddy. I'm pretty sure I know how to use a gun. Are we going to do this, or what?" John said.

Sweat poured from his friend's face, ringing the collar of his gray undershirt. Eddy nodded and wiped the perspiration from his nose with a gloved hand.

John closed his eyes a moment. *Don't let anybody get hurt, especially Eddy. His family needs him too much.* When he opened his eyes, Eddy stood in front of the door, chest heaving. He shot John a nervous smile and raised his hand to knock.

"I can hear you guys out there, man. You coming in or not?" The voice from behind the door had a strong Mexican accent.

John didn't know if it was Manny or not. The only person who might be in the apartment besides him was his girlfriend according to the report.

Eddy gripped the pistol at his side. He stuttered. "Um... this is Edwin Bailey; I'm a private detective from the Bailey Detective Agency. I'm here on behalf of—"

"I don't give a shit who you're here on behalf of. Is your ass coming in here to get me or not? If not, leave me the hell alone. I have things to do."

Eddy's hand still rested on the pistol. John placed his hand on Eddy's wrist, shaking his head. "Be ready, but I don't think you'll need to draw your weapon," he said.

Eddy's eyes grew wide. He hunched toward John and whispered. "What are you doing? He can hear us. Now he knows we have weapons. What if he draws on us?"

"I know he can hear us. I said it out loud on purpose." John reached to the knob and gave it a twist; the door slid open a few inches, hinges squeaking. He patted his friend on the shoulder. "Let me go in first. Stay alert, but stay calm."

Eddy paused. John could almost see the cogs chugging away behind his friend's eyes, debating whether to let John take over.

John pushed the door open with his left hand, keeping his right on the butt of his pistol. He wouldn't need the weapon, at least that's what his gut told him, but his father had forced preparedness into his very being. "Always be ready, John. Even in your sleep," he would say.

The apartment was small, walls pea green, carpet worn smooth in places. Dirty dishes clogged the couch and end tables along with empty beer cans and pizza boxes. The kitchen was to the left, little difference between there and the living room. More dirty dishes and discarded food lay strewn about the counter. A fat, orange cat sat on a fallen box of cereal, lapping at a brownish red liquid on a filthy plate.

Eddy covered his mouth and nose to block the stench. John wanted to do the same but kept his hand free, ready to react. It wouldn't have helped anyway. The smell of old yeasty beer, urine, and... *pork chops?* Whatever the strange mixture of smells came from, they'd be tough to wash from his clothes.

"What you guys doing out there?" the voice called from the room to their right. "You better not be taking nothin. Hey, as long as you're out there, grab me a beer." An insane cackle echoed through the small apartment.

John gestured toward the open door. Lights flashed on the wall from a television, voices from the show barely audible. Eddy moved to the right side of the doorway, his hand clamped tight on his pistol, knuckles white. John unholstered the Glock and held it in front, using both hands to steady the weapon, arms relaxed for quicker movements if needed.

The squeaking wooden planks beneath their feet ruined the gentle steps he took toward the doorway.

"You better have that beer for me, Eddy," the voice called. "I'll be pissed if you don't. You're a guest in my house; you do as I say."

Eddy pulled his eyes away from the doorway to John, sweat falling in rivulets now, eyes bulging.

The things men do for their family, John thought. *He's not cut out for this.*

John shuffled into the room, Glock held before him. Nothing could have prepared him for what he saw. The monstrosity was definitely Manny; though, he looked to be three times the size of the man in the picture they were given to identify him. He sat spread eagle on a king-sized bed wearing only his heavily stained underwear, his chest and face covered in grease from the fried chicken he chomped on. He had to weigh at least five hundred pounds; his breasts hung to his thighs.

Manny's eyes were glued to the flat screen flickering in front of him. "What? You boys never seen a grown man in his skivvies before? Or you two gay? That it?" The remaining bones from a piece of chicken tumbled from his fingers. He turned his gaze toward John. "You want me to do a little dance for you?" The man's body undulated, the bed creaking. "Yeah, that's it, isn't it? You boys like this? Huh?"

Eddy barfed, sausage and eggs spreading across the carpeted floor. John held his eyes on Manny; his body was covered with too many folds. Hiding a weapon would be all too easy.

"We're here to take you in," John said. "You skipped bail and made some people pretty mad."

"Fuck them. I don't have no job. How am I supposed to pay child support?"

Child support? We're picking up a deadbeat dad? Why the hell do we need guns? Eddy sat curled into a ball on the floor. At least his hand came back to his weapon again.

John hadn't lowered his weapon yet, not more than a few inches anyway. Hearing the fat man was a deadbeat father was different than hearing he'd killed his neighbor or committed some other heinous crime.

"Who are you?" Manny said. "You're not Eddy; you sound different."

"Name's John Reeves. I work for Eddy."

Manny's eyebrows scrunched as he looked at Eddy on the floor wiping at his mouth.

"Look, Manny," John said, "We must have some bad information. Why don't you tell us why you're considered armed and dangerous?"

Manny's body shook. He covered his round face with his hands.

"Manny? You okay?"

The man's hands dropped back to his lap. Tears streamed down his plump cheeks. His voice came out high and whiny, like a fourteen-year-old adolescent boy. "I don't know why they would do this to me. I started gaining weight, so I went to the doc, and he told me I have some hormonal thing. No matter how hard I try, I keep getting fatter."

John looked at the fried chicken bucket sitting between Manny's massive thighs. *Doesn't seem to be trying too hard.* John lowered the Glock, holstering it and gesturing for Manny to go on. Eddy stood now, one hand on John's shoulder for support.

"So, Rafaela says she's going to leave me unless I get less fat. Believe me, I tried. Then she leaves, taking my little *hijo* with her when she goes." He slammed a fist into the bed. A half empty bag of chips fell to the floor. "I couldn't take it, so I go to her house. I tell her I need to see my little Belmiro. She says no and comes after me with a hot curling iron. So I hit her... with... a box of donuts that were in my car. They were the only thing I had. I didn't know they would cut her eye like that."

"You hit her with a box of donuts?" Eddy said.

Some of the sadness left Manny's face; his eyebrows sank. "Yes with donuts. It was what I had. I just wanted to see Belmiro. You wouldn't fight for your babies, Eddy?"

Eddy didn't answer.

Manny turned back to John. "The doctors said she may never get her vision back in that eye. She blames me, even though she was the one with the hot curling iron. She talks her lawyers into saying I was too big to hit her with the donuts, like I was some mean, donut slinging machine." John coughed to hide his smile. "They say I attacked her with a deadly weapon." Manny sighed as he slouched. "The only one donuts are deadly to is me," he said, glaring at his massive belly. "Now I can't see my Belmiro no more." His thick hands covered his face, as sobs wracked his whole body.

John pulled Eddy toward the living room. "What the hell's going on here, Eddy? You told me this guy was dangerous. The only thing that should be scared of him is food."

Eddy yanked off his goggles and headset, dropping them into his front pocket. "I really don't know, John." Manny let out a particularly loud wail. "I just deal with the information I'm given," Eddy said.

John nodded, patting his friend on the shoulder. "Well, one thing's for sure. This guy needs help."

Squeaking came from Eddy's pocket. "Oh shit, Lena." He pulled the headset out and hooked it back over his ear. "Lena? You there?"

"Yes, I'm here. What the hell is happening? You ask me if I'm ready, and then I hear nothing. I thought the guy knifed you both and was getting ready to feed you to his boa."

"I'm sorry, sweetheart. Everything is fine here. Well, mostly anyway." He looked through the doorway to Manny still sobbing on the bed, a chicken bone falling from under one of his arms. "We're going to need back up on this one. Lots of back up."

The Funeral

"Are you sure we should show up together?"

"I've already told you, Rita. Chief Burleson can't complain if we don't do anything wrong. Besides, you're my partner. Where I go, you go."

Officer Rita Vasquez was a good cop, only months out of the academy. The police chief, Paul Burleson, assigned her to work with Alan so he'd "keep his head in the game." The Chief's plan worked better than he knew, though not in the way he'd imagined.

Rita leaned across the seat, vest creaking, and planted a kiss on Alan's cheek. "Sorry, partner," she said with a smile. "I don't want you to get in trouble on my account."

"I was thinking the same thing about you."

They pulled into the Hindel's Funeral Home parking lot in their cruiser. Though technically on duty, the Chief allowed them an hour during their shift to visit Douglas Fincham's funeral, enough time to stop in and pay their respects. Alan and Doug's wife, Leslie, were close. He felt guilty working the day of the funeral, but he didn't have much choice. Only fifteen officers worked for the Clarkbridge Police Department. With five on vacation, overtime was almost a certainty.

People milled about in front of the building and on the stone benches outside.

Alan gave Rita a wink and squeezed her hand. "Ready?"

"Are you? I know how much you liked Doug. You know I'm here to talk about it if you want."

"I know, Rita. I'm not ready yet. Let's get this part out of the way."

Alan glanced in the rearview mirror at his thinning russet hair. Rita's glossy black hair—a gift from her Hispanic heritage—made his look even more wispy.

They climbed from the cruiser and headed toward the funeral home, its off-white marble base reflecting the fading sun. Alan hoped to keep it short. Rita was right; he had been close to Doug, so seeing Leslie in this situation would be hard for him. The old couple had been his rock when his wife had passed away five years earlier. They made losing Allie to cancer almost bearable.

Half the city was there. Douglas Fincham had lived in Clarkbridge his whole life and was loved by most. Somber townsfolk, some still dressed in farm clothes, nodded or waved to Alan. He and Doug shared many of the same friends.

They worked their way through the crowd to the main viewing area. Rita looked out of place among Alan's friends. He gave her credit. She was a Mexican female in a city where the minorities could be counted on one hand. As a rookie in a police department where everybody knew everybody else, it wore on her; though she never voiced any complaints.

Leslie stood in a circle of friends, exchanging kind smiles and hugs. When she saw Alan, she broke away and wordlessly gave him a hug, holding him in place. Her tiny frame had always been in sharp contrast to her husband's broad shoulders and thick chest. She felt smaller than ever.

She whispered in his ear, "Thank you for coming, sweetheart. You know Douglas loved you like a son."

Her words cut through his shell, and he almost broke down. There were no words to say how he felt. He just squeezed her again before letting go, wiping away the involuntary tear that had formed beneath his eye.

"We can't stay long, Leslie. I just came to pay my respects."

Her eyes brimmed with tears, too. "I know, sweetie. Just do what you need to do. You stop over if you need to talk."

What a strong woman. Her husband of over forty years had just passed away, and she comforted Alan.

"And I better be seeing you over for dinner next Saturday. Are you bringing Rita this time?" She gave a small wave to Rita who stood just behind him.

"She's my partner, Leslie. I'm not sure how proper that would be."

Leslie wore a knowing smile. Had he let something slip at one of their dinners? He didn't remember saying anything about Rita other than she was his new partner.

"Well, if you change your mind." She kissed him on the cheek before returning to her friends.

Alan nodded to Rita and turned toward the viewing area.

"Are you sure you want me to go up there with you?" Rita said.

He didn't respond.

She nodded and followed.

Doug wore the faded blue flannel shirt and the dirty John Deere hat he wore every day around the farm. *Just like you wanted.* It had been a joke to some of their friends, but Alan knew Doug was serious when he'd said he wanted to be buried in his comfy clothes.

The collar was pulled up close to his neck, and the sleeves pulled down over the arms. Covering his wounds with make-up and wax would have been a monumental task for any funeral home. His face was pale and drawn, the way people always were when laid to rest. It looked out of place on a man so full of life just a few days before.

Alan placed his hands over Doug's and whispered, "Doug, I'm not sure if you're up there listening, but if you are, I'll get whoever did this."

The M.E. said he'd died from suffocation, some type of allergic reaction. Alan questioned him about the wounds on Doug's arms and neck, and he'd just shrugged.

Rita laid her hand on Alan's shoulder. He stepped away to leave. They were halfway to his car when Leslie called his name, having followed them to the parking lot.

"Alan, I need to speak with you a moment."

He handed Rita the keys and turned to the frail woman. "What is it?"

Her mouth worked, but no words formed. She took a deep breath and began again.

"We both know Doug didn't die of an allergic reaction." She waited, and he hoped his surprise didn't show. "I don't know what he died from, but he wasn't allergic to a darn thing. Can you... What are you going to do about it?"

Typical Leslie, putting everything out there.

"Technically the investigation is closed—" She began to protest, but he held his hands up to stop her. "But not for me. I'm not sure what happened, but I was there. I don't believe it was an allergic reaction either."

"Did it have something to do with him losing his memory of the kidnapping?"

"I don't know. At this point, you know as much as I do. I promise, as soon as I learn more, I will let you know."

She marched back toward the ornate double doors of the funeral home. Alan climbed into the cruiser and released a heavy sigh.

"I'm sorry, Alan." Rita ran her fingers through his hair. "I can only imagine how hard that must have been."

He cried for the first time in five years.

3. Krogman

Snark's

"Art! Grab another Guinness for my friend here. He's a little cranky." Eddy barked a laugh.

"Why shouldn't I be?" John growled. "You said we were going after a dangerous man, not a five-hundred pound deadbeat dad."

Eddy took a long pull from his mug of stout. "I already told you I was sorry, John. What can I say? We had bad information."

Arthur Higgins, owner of Snark's Roadhouse, set the pint on the table. John said his thanks. Snark's had been there since John was a kid. It looked the same as when their father brought him and Alan in for buffalo burgers. Dimly lit, except behind the bar where the light reflected on the mirror behind the cache of liquor. The walls—still the unfinished brown wood paneling—added to the dinginess.

"I know what you said." John shook his head. "I just don't like being put in that situation. I went in thinking our lives were in danger."

"They could have been." Eddy waved his beer mug, foam slipping over the edge. "You never know when you'll be shot at in this business."

"Just because you were shot at once by a schizophrenic off his meds doesn't mean you need to wear a vest for every bounty. Enough about the deadbeat dad. You said we have a client meeting us?"

"Sure do." Eddy looked away a little too quickly.

What are you hiding, Eddy? John lifted the icy glass and held it to his nose. Like opening a fresh can of coffee, the rich aroma filled his senses. He placed the pint back on the table, since the foam hadn't settled. "Why are we meeting here? Seems like an odd place to meet a client."

Eddy rubbed his fingers back and forth across his cold mug, looking down at the table.

"What?" John said.

Eddy raised his eyes from the table. "You know her."

"The client?" John asked, and Eddy nodded. "Who is it?"

"Leslie Fincham," Eddie said.

"As in the Leslie Fincham whose husband died a couple weeks ago?"

"That's the one." Eddy raised his mug for another drink.

Alan had taken Leslie on as a surrogate mother shortly after his wife had passed. John hadn't been around to see it happen, but Eddy had filled him in. "What does she need a P.I. for?"

"I'm not sure, John. She didn't say much on the phone. I told you I'd assign a couple cases of your own. This one doesn't involve a bounty, and I thought you could use the work. Plus, Lena has exams next week. She asked for a couple weeks off."

Helena Chandler was a firecracker. She'd played four years of college-level tennis while earning a degree in Tennis Management. Eddy met her through his wife, Sandra, when she'd taken lessons the year before. Lena, as she preferred to be called, had fallen in love with the idea of private investigating, and Eddy hadn't been able to tell her no.

The bell over the door jingled. Eddy looked over John's shoulder and stood. John turned to face the woman.

"Come on over, Mrs. Fincham." Eddy waved her toward their table. "Have a seat."

Leslie Fincham clutched her purse and sat in the seat Eddy pulled out for her. She wore a forced smile.

The owner stopped by the table, wiping his hands on the white towel at his hip. "Can I get you something to drink, Mrs. Fincham?"

"No thank you, Art. I won't be staying long." Arthur nodded and walked back behind the bar.

John and Eddy sat down on either side of the diminutive woman. She held her shoulders hunched.

"Mrs. Fincham, you know John," Eddy said.

"I do. Alan's told us much about you, John."

"I'm not half as bad as he says. Promise," John said smiling.

Her lips twitched in a partial smile. She turned to Eddy. "I'd like to get this over with, Edwin."

"Yes, ma'am. What can we do for you?"

She blinked a few times and took a deep breath. "You knew my Douglas, my husband," Leslie said. Eddy nodded. "He wasn't allergic to a thing. Prided himself on being the healthiest person he knew. I don't remember the last time he had a cold. Other than the back pain, he was as healthy as he was all those years ago in high school." She paused, tears welling in her eyes. "I think there was some kind of foul play. Something must have happened when he was taken."

"Taken?" John said.

"Taken is right. Everybody says he lost his mind, some kind of paranoia or something. But when he came back to me, he was the same as always. The only way he would leave me for a week is if someone had taken him. I want to know who."

"You want us to find out who... took Doug before he passed?"

"That's right." Leslie nodded, her knuckles white from the grip on her purse. She had a challenging look about her, leaning forward and staring into Eddy's eyes, then to John's. She nodded again and opened her purse. "Now, how much is this going to cost? I don't have much, but I'll find however much you need." She held a pen poised over her checkbook.

"There's no need for that, Mrs. Fincham," Eddy said. "Not now."

Her head tilted to the side in a silent question.

"I mean, I'll let you know when we find something. I don't want to take your money when we don't know for sure—"

Her brow drew down. "Know for sure what?" she snapped. "That my Douglas was killed? He was, and he was kidnapped before that. If you aren't willing to find out who did it, then I'll find someone who will." She threw her checkbook and pen back into the purse and stood, her chair scraping across the wood floor.

Eddy stood and placed his hand on Leslie's shoulder. "I'm sorry, Mrs. Fincham. That didn't come out the way I meant. We'll look for anything we can. I just don't want you to get your hopes up. If the police couldn't find anything, I'm not sure we can. I want you to be prepared for that."

"I am prepared."

"Okay, Mrs. Fincham. I'll contact you soon to tell you if we find anything," Eddy said.

She nodded and scurried toward the door, still clutching her purse with a death grip.

"Well, that went over well," John said as Eddy plopped back into his seat.

"You have to understand, John. I get this all the time." He lifted his mug, still half full, and slammed the rest down in one gulp.

"Get what all the time?"

"Widows. Especially the older ones. They always think something happened to their husband. It's worse when they commit suicide. They can never accept that maybe things weren't as good as they tell themselves."

Eddy looked as if he had the weight of the world on his shoulders. His head lowered.

"Why do you do this, Eddy? Take jobs like this I mean. I can see it's hard on you. You could just stick with the accounting."

"I love being a P.I., John. It's the times when we get someone, or find something the police didn't, that makes this all worth it. Catching a cheating husband in the act, or getting pictures of someone out riding a bike when their insurance company thinks they're bedridden. Like I'm making a difference."

"You knew what she wanted before we came, didn't you?" Eddy nodded. "And that's why you passed it off to me."

"I'm sorry, John. I should have known you'd figure it out. You always do. I didn't mean anything by it. It's just that Sandra... we've been..."

John held his hands up. "It's okay, Eddy. Spend the extra time with Sandra and the kids. I'll do it."

Eddy's eyebrows lifted. "You will?"

"Sure. That's why I'm here. I told you I'd work for you, didn't I? Who knows? Maybe there's some truth to what Leslie said. I just hope Alan doesn't think I'm hedging in. He can be sensitive about his job."

"Saying Alan is sensitive is about like saying John Reeves doesn't like women."

"We'll see."

Arthur put the full iced mug on the table between them. Eddy nodded his thanks and pulled it close.

"I'm glad you're back, John. Not just because of this," he gestured around Snark's, "but because I missed you. When I heard you were shot last year, by arrows no less, I was worried I wouldn't see you again."

John winked. "It's okay, sweetheart. I missed you too." He let out the hearty laugh he'd been holding in. Eddy joined in until they were both red in the face. "Now let's show Art we can still drink like when we were teenagers."

Secret Spot

"How can you eat so much and stay so thin?" Alan said, giving Rita a gentle poke in the belly.

"You better not complain. Or do you like your girlfriends on the chunky side?" Rita pooched her belly out, but to little effect. Her vest held it in place. Melted ice cream ran down the side of her cone, and she licked it off with slow, deliberate motions.

"Enough of that or I'll have to leave work early tonight," Alan warned.

They sat by the Branstead River, eating their double scoops of chocolate chip cookie dough. The same place they'd first kissed six months before. Taking their breaks by the calm river was a weekly tradition.

She slid closer to him on the picnic table and laid her head on his shoulder. "I wish we could do this more often."

Alan sighed. He wished they could too. "I know. If we make it until next summer, I can take an early retirement, maybe be a crossing guard for the elementary school."

"You wouldn't be happy as a crossing guard," Rita said.

Alan pushed her back to look in her eyes. "You make me happy, Rita. Did that sound as corny as it felt?"

She smiled and pulled him close for a kiss. They held each other until Rita punched him in the shoulder. "What do you mean 'if we make it'?"

"You caught that part?"

Her eyebrows pulled down into a glare, her tight smile ruining the effect.

"You know, Rita. I'm twenty years older than you. This is great now, but you'll meet some young stud and put me on the back-burner."

Her fake glare became a real one. "Do you realize every time you say that, you're saying you don't trust me?"

"What do you mean?"

"I love you. If you think I'll just leave the next time some good-looking guy hits on me, then you're saying you don't trust my emotions. I'll say it again. I love *you*, Alan. I don't mean right now or just for a while; I mean forever. That's what love means to me."

"I'm sorry, it's just... this scares me. *Us* scares me. Before I met you, I was convinced I'd never be with anybody again."

She pulled him to her chest. "I know this is scary, but I need you to trust me. What we have is real, even if we can't let anybody know about it. I won't pretend to know what you had with Allie or how much it hurt when you lost her, but you won't lose me."

"119 back-up! Back-up! 10-18! Over," Forbes called over the radio.

They looked to the cruiser.

"Alan? Rita? You two there? Um... are you there? Over."

"What's the matter with Cooper?" Rita said. "I thought he took the domestic abuse call."

"He did." It wasn't like Cooper to ask for back-up. Sometimes his nerves got the best of him, and he knew it, so he spent most of his time trying to prove he was a good cop. "Looks as though our lunch break is over." Alan jogged to the cruiser.

Rita called from behind. "You got out of it this time, old man. But we'll talk about this again later."

Alan gestured with a non-committal wave. "This is car twenty-one, Forbes, what's your 20? Over."

"I'm down by Branstead River, at Krogman Tubing, and uh... just hurry please."

Rita climbed into the cruiser and buckled her seatbelt. Alan did the same.

"Everything okay, Coop?" Alan said into the radio. "Do we need to call in another car? Over."

"Everything is definitely not okay. Just get over here; no need for more back-up."

Alan started the vehicle and backed away. He shot their secret spot a longing glance before pulling out.

"What do you think is going on?" Rita said.

"I don't have a clue. But I don't like the way Cooper sounded."

Rita's voice cracked when she let out a small laugh. "For a second there, I thought he was saying something about us being by the Branstead."

"Me too."

Hell's Kitchen

Krogman Tubing was owned by Lonny Krogman, an old friend of Alan's father, Ed Reeves. They'd been on the police force together before Lonny became a prison guard, back when Clarkbridge wasn't as pleasant of a city as it is today. Krogman's was busy in May when the college kids came home for the summer, but the local colleges weren't out for another two weeks. Every couple of years, the police were called in on a drowning, too much alcohol the usual cause.

Probably not a drowning or Coop would have called a bus and the medical examiner.

They pulled into the dirt parking lot next to Krogman's where Branstead River entered Clarkbridge on the north side of the city. Cooper paced in front of the old building. Someone sat on the wooden bench by the front door.

"Put your game face on, kiddo," Alan said. "Time to get to work."

Rita growled. "Oh, shut up. I hate when you call me kiddo."

Cooper jogged over to them when they came to a stop.

"Thank God you're here, Alan. Some crazy shit, er… um, stuff… Oh, my God." Cooper planted his hands over his face. His shoulders shook while he stood there and sobbed.

"Rita, stay with Forbes."

"Yes, Captain," she said.

The person on the bench was Kandi Krogman, Lonny's wife. She held her face in her hands too.

"Mrs. Krogman," he said, as he approached. "Can you tell me what happened?"

Her hands fell to her side, face smudged with dirt and tears. She stumbled from the bench and ran to Alan. She threw her arms around him and squeezed him in a tight hug. "Oh, Alan," she said between sobs. "It's Lonny, he's…" She whimpered and squeezed him tighter. "Oh, God."

Alan loosened Kandi's grip and looked down into her bloodshot eyes. "Listen, Kandi. I need you to go over there with Coop and Rita, okay?" He pointed over his shoulder with a thumb.

Kandi nodded. She crossed her arms and shuffled toward the cruiser, eyes lowered.

"Officer Vasquez," Alan called. "Have Mrs. Krogman take a seat in the cruiser. You two stay with her."

"Wait. Shouldn't I come with you?"

Yes, he wanted to say. That would be correct procedure, but whatever had happened to Lonny had scared Kandi and Cooper out of their minds. He wasn't about to let something happen to Rita too.

"No. I got this one."

He unfastened the clasp on his holster and drew the . 40 Smith and Wesson, placing his finger on the trigger guard. If someone was still in there, he wouldn't let them hurt Rita. Or Cooper and Kandi.

Krogman Tubing was built into the innards of an old barn. The faded red wood slats still graced the exterior, but the Krogman's gutted the inside before turning it into their business with their home upstairs. Alan held his weapon aimed at the ground in front of him, steady as he approached the old building. He nudged the front door open with his foot. He stood to the side allowing his eyes to adjust to the darkness.

He searched side to side. A hand touched his shoulder. He almost fired a shot into the Krogman's front desk.

Rita stood next to him with her weapon drawn. "Sorry, Alan. I couldn't let you go in alone."

"Next time decide a little sooner, would you? You scared the shit out of me."

"Cooper said we should go upstairs, to their home I guess."

"What's up there?" Alan said.

"I don't know. That's all I could get out of him."

Alan gestured to Rita's sidearm. "Be ready."

To their right, a sign hung on the door leading to the upstairs. In hand-painted lettering it read, "Home Sweet Home." He turned the knob. The rusty hinges creaked as it opened. Each worn step groaned as they worked their way up the steep staircase. *So much for sneaking.*

The closer they came to the top, the stronger the stench grew, an odor akin to a freshly gutted deer. They reached the top of the stairs. Alan paused and dropped one hand from his firearm to reach for the doorknob. Dark liquid ran under the door and onto the top step. Alan took a long, deep breath and turned the knob. The scene beyond the door belonged in the darkest pits of hell.

Alan paused at the top of the steps in front of Rita. "What is it, Alan? Why did you stop?"

"Don't come up here, Rita, please. Move to the bottom of the stairwell. Stay there, and don't let anybody else up. And keep your side-arm at the ready."

Rita nodded and turned back toward the bottom of the stairwell. She usually found a reason for banter. Not this time.

Sunlight barely peeked through the shades. Glass remnants of shattered lamps littered the bloody floor. He pulled his flashlight from his belt and placed it under his arm holding the weapon. Lonny Krogman reclined in a sofa chair in front of the television, an over-sized smile on his face. That was as far as the normalcy went.

Blood lay spattered across the entire living area; the television, the couch, the floor, the coffee tables. It seemed too much blood for one body.

The final step into the Krogman living room allowed Alan to close the door behind him. He shined the flashlight into the kitchen to his left, thankful the Krogmans led a plain existence. There weren't many places to hide in the kitchen. Only the card table they used for dinner and two old wooden folding chairs.

An antique mason jar sat in the center of a rickety wooden table next to the refrigerator. He moved closer, his feet sticking to the laminate flooring. Inside the jar was a thick bloody hand with jagged wrist bones protruding from the neatly cut flesh. He turned away and tucked his mouth against his shoulder until the need to vomit passed.

He stepped into the living room. The stench of fresh blood and voided excrement almost overwhelmed him, his sense of smell not desensitizing as fast as he'd like. He shined the light behind the love seat. *Nobody.*

Only one room left, the single bathroom built into their bedroom with its door closed. There was no stepping around the blood. It was everywhere, seeping into the cracks of the wood flooring. The forensics team would have to accept that he had no choice but to plod through the evidence.

Alan placed his hand with the flashlight on the door. It grated open at his touch. With his side-arm still held in front, two quick steps and he was in the room. He shined the beam alongside the bed. Nothing. Nobody could hide beneath the bed; their mattress sat on the floor. Instead of a closet, a metal bar hung from the ceiling on two by fours. A quick glance under the hanging shirts told him nobody hid there.

Checking on Lonny was next. Though by the look of things, he was certain it was a waste of time. Kandi wouldn't have sat there sobbing if Lonny was still alive. Alan put his weapon back in the holster, leaving the clasp unsnapped. He stepped back into the living room and tugged open a paisley curtain. Dust circled through the light shining into the dim room and falling on the back of Lonny's balding head.

The blood was so thick on the floor it hadn't begun to dry. Alan stepped slowly to keep from splattering his slacks. He stopped in front of Lonny's chair. The large man stared forward, smiling that fake smile. Alan reached toward Lonny's wrist to check for a pulse, and paused. The arm came to a pulpy end just below the elbow. Alan moved to the other side. This hand clutched a meat cleaver, blood dripping from the grimy blade. He touched the wrist and the cleaver fell, splashing blood onto his pants.

No pulse.

Alan stepped back for a clear view. The rigid smile still in place, Lonny's neck was a ruinous mess, torn from below one ear to the other. The red shirt he wore opened up just below the rib cage, another long gash from one side to the other, intestines hanging free. Alan covered his mouth again.

He glanced toward the floor. Both of Lonny's legs ended in stumps a few inches above the ankle, the torn flesh looking as it had on his arm.

"My God, Lonny. What happened?"

"Alan, I have a bus on the way," Rita yelled from the stairway. "Chief Burleson is on his way too."

"You can call off the bus; Lonny won't need an ambulance. Just call the medical examiner and see if Burleson can get forensics out here."

4. The Holbrooks

Doug's Drawers

"Wow. I don't know that I've ever tasted better pot-roast, Mrs. Fincham." John wiped at his mouth with the cloth napkin, tossed it on the plate, and pushed away from the table.

"It's just Leslie. You make me feel like an old woman when you call me Mrs. Fincham."

"Okay, Leslie." John smiled.

Leslie picked up his plate. "Are you sure you don't want more? I have plenty, and Alan said he didn't know if he'd make it over for dinner tonight."

Last time John had seen Alan, he'd been almost too skinny. He wondered if Alan was able to keep slim, eating dinner at the Fincham's every weekend. John wasn't a bad cook himself, but he didn't compare to Leslie. *Women her age really know how to cook.*

"I'm so full I'm afraid I'd pop if I squeezed any more in. I won't be able to eat the rest of the day."

"Doug says the same thing, then comes back in for dinner and eats just as much." Leslie's mouth moved as if to say more, but stopped. She nodded and headed to the kitchen with the empty plates.

Twice during their lunch, she'd spoken of Doug as if he were still alive.

John stood and brushed the crumbs from his chest onto the table. If he were lucky, his future wife, if he ever found one, would have half Leslie's cooking talent. Leslie stepped back into the dining area and gathered more plates.

"I'd like to take a look in your bedroom first, Leslie." No use pretending he was here for something other than his investigation. "I'm new to this whole Private Investigator thing, but it seems the bedroom is as good a place as any to start."

She paused halfway to the kitchen. "If you're half the investigator your father was, you will do just fine. I'm glad Edwin picked you for the job. Let me drop these off in the kitchen, and I'll show you to our room."

He felt for Eddy. Widows came to him all the time not believing their husbands had committed suicide. It made sense. After so many years of marriage, being told the love of your life believed their only escape was death would be tremendously hard.

Leslie pushed through the swinging kitchen door and gestured toward a hallway to the back. He followed her down the dark corridor. Old farmhouses never had enough light, and the finished wooden walls accentuated the darkness. Leslie's hands moved continuously, wiping at unseen blemishes on her clothing or the walls. She'd known John since he was a child. Taking him to the bedroom she shared with her husband for forty years had to be awkward.

She showed him every room lining the hall, offering details about each. The first was the spare bedroom friends and family used when staying over. The closet stood open at the back, filled with clothes. The next was the bathroom Doug had just finished. The new olive-green and orange checkered wallpaper looked as if it belonged in the fifties.

Their bedroom stood at the end of the hall. She opened the door and stepped back.

"Here is our bedroom, John. I hope you don't mind, but I haven't been able to go in there for more than a few minutes at a time since Doug left us."

That explained the clothes he'd seen in the spare bedroom closet.

"Don't worry about it. I won't be long."

She nodded and turned toward the dining room.

"I'll be careful, Leslie," he called over his shoulder. She continued walking down the hall until out of sight. Careful wasn't the right word, but he felt as though he were intruding even though she'd invited him.

The bedroom was lit as dimly as the rest of the house. He flipped the switch just inside the door. The room felt cold. Not on his skin, but in its personality. Everything had the stale smell typical of farmhouses. The bed was made and the dark blue drapes pulled shut. Light poured into the room as he opened the curtains. The extra light made him feel more comfortable. A little, anyway.

He thought back to his father's teachings. Ed Reeves had been a police officer and treated John and his brother, Alan, like new recruits, using every chance to impart his knowledge of crime scenes and criminal behavior. Alan used the teaching to become a successful police officer, while John had moved to California to spend a few years on the beach. He'd have to contact Alan soon. John had been in Clarkbridge almost three weeks and hadn't let his brother know he was in town.

The closet still held all of Doug's shirts; most were the flannels he always wore. On one side were Leslie's many shoes lined up against the back wall. On Doug's side, he found a small chest nestled in the corner with a key poking out from the front. John knelt and turned the key. The chest popped open. Inside were three medals attached to red felt and lined up against the back, remnants of his days in the military.

He pulled on the loose brass handle, opening the lower compartment of the chest filled with pictures and old coins. The old black and white Polaroid on top displayed Doug and Leslie sitting in a shiny new Dodge truck, the same one still in their driveway. Most of the pictures were black and white, usually of Leslie. Some were of children, probably nieces and nephews, since the Finchams hadn't been able to have any of their own and never adopted.

Beneath Douglas Fincham's memories, John's own face peered up at him. He moved the other pictures to the side and picked up the scratched photograph. It wasn't really his face, but his father's, younger than John was now. Ed Reeves stood with his arm around Doug. They held up dark bottles, some type of old beer. They had been friends, but John hadn't known they were close enough to share a beer, let alone have their picture taken with arms around each other. He'd have to ask Leslie. Maybe Alan knew something, too.

Thoughts of his brother clenched his stomach. Last time they'd spoken, things hadn't gone so well. John had stopped home for a week on his way to New York. They ended up having the same argument they'd had since high school. Alan would tell John to settle down, do something with his life, and John would argue that he enjoyed his life, something Alan had never done. Alan's wife passed away a few months later, and John had missed the funeral. An unforgivable sin in Alan's eyes.

John returned the picture and locked the chest. The room was bare except for the essentials. Just the bed and two matching dressers. One of the dressers was topped with multiple frames filled with pictures of Leslie, the other of Doug. He stepped to the dresser covered with snapshots of Leslie.

Black socks filled the top drawer to the brim, all perfectly folded. Moving them out of place didn't feel right, but he needed to search everything. *You might as well not do a job if you aren't going to do it right.* One of his father's teachings.

The next two drawers held what most people's dressers did: underwear, old t-shirts, jeans, work pants. The bottom drawer rattled as he pulled it open. He slid his hands beneath more work pants. His fingers caressed something cold. He removed a few pairs of pants and laid them on the floor. Inside was a small wooden box carved with intricate portrayals of deer and other animals, a beautiful piece of handiwork.

John sat cross-legged on the floor with the box across his thighs. He pried the top open with his thumb. A dark orange medicine bottle sat on top of a stack of receipts. He held the bottle up to the light. Hydrocodone. *Vicodin? Were you hiding it from Leslie?* The top receipt had Clarkbridge Medical Center printed across the top. It showed a twenty dollar co-pay for services rendered.

He pulled the rest of the receipts from the box and went through them one by one. Almost all were from the same medical center, usually co-pays, and two were from Holbrook Rehab Services. A few more were for Vicodin, but not enough to be out of the ordinary. Three bottles in a four year period. He slid one from both the medical center and the rehab into his shirt pocket and tossed the rest back in the box.

He closed the dresser and stood. The reciepts weren't much to go on, but they were the only things out of place, a place to start. Hopefully Leslie knew about the Vicodin. He didn't want to ruin the woman's view of her late husband.

Leslie sat at the now clean dining room table with a stack of bills set to one side as she filled out a check.

"All done snooping," John said with a smile. She didn't return the favor. *So much for making light of the situation.* "I have a few questions I'd like to ask."

Leslie nodded and dropped the pen next to her checkbook, clasping her hands in front of her.

"Do you know why Doug took Vicodin?"

"The pain pills?"

John nodded.

"Doc Howard prescribed them when Doug hurt his back falling from the barn. He was too stubborn to go to physical therapy, so Howard said the pills would help if the pain became unbearable. He only took them when we had people over so they wouldn't see him limp."

Doug wasn't taking them as a means to an escape. *Strike one.* "What do you know about these receipts to a

Holbrook Rehab Services?" John pulled the receipt from his pocket and slid it next to her.

"Ah, those." Leslie removed her glasses and rubbed her forehead with both hands. She looked up into John's eyes. "I need you to make me a promise."

"Sure, I mean, I don't know why not. You said you two didn't have anything to hide."

"And we don't," she said. "Having nothing to hide and not wanting the whole world to know are two completely different things."

"Okay." John sat at the other end of the table.

"Did you know Doug was a Vietnam vet?"

"I didn't, but I saw the medals in the chest."

"There was a time after returning that he had sleeping problems. A friend of his suggested he visit Abraham Holbrook, of Holbrook Rehab Services."

That kind of rehab. John thought it had been for physical therapy relating to whatever Doug took the painkillers for.

She went on. "Well, this Abraham fixed him right up in one visit. It was a new psychological technique of some sort. I don't know much, just that it worked. Doug never had another sleepless night until a few years ago, after he hurt his back. Sometimes the pain would have him writhing until he would head to the spare bedroom to let me have some rest. He tried looking up Abraham again, thinking maybe the pain could be in his head, but the doctor was in prison. Before you ask, I have no idea why. Doug didn't want to talk about it, so I didn't press him.

"However, Abraham's son, Russell, was practicing in his place. Doug had high hopes, thinking it would only take one visit with Russell to fix the back pain. Instead, he came home complaining Russell was a quack. Again, I don't know what happened, since Doug never put anything on me he didn't have to. He was so over-protective. So he went to a psychologist two different times. I know things aren't quite as they used to be, but Doug wasn't the type who wanted to share that he'd seen a head doctor. You know how it goes. If you're not strong enough to handle it on your own, then you're weak."

"Nobody will hear about it from my lips." John ran his fingers through his hair. "But remember, you brought us on because you don't believe Doug would have taken his own life as the medical examiner suggested. He also didn't have any known allergies. If I find something that proves you're right, I might have to tell someone about the psychologists. It would be better if people found out from you first."

Leslie rubbed at her head again and slid her glasses back on. "You're right. It wasn't right for me to ask you to promise. Please, just show my Doug some respect while you go about your investigation." Her voice cracked when she said her husband's name.

"Of course, Mrs. Fincham—Leslie. I would never do anything to hurt you or your husband. You two have been friends of the family for years, and I'd like to keep it that way. Besides, who would teach my wife how to cook if you and I were no longer friends?"

A tear slipped from her eye. "Smooth tongue, just like your brother."

John pushed away from the table and stepped close to Leslie, embracing her in a tight hug from behind her chair.

"Apparently a sweetheart like Alan, too," she said, rubbing his arm. "Thank you, John. You will never know how much I needed that."

Bowling Alley

Eddy's words about widows and their partner's suicides ran through John's head on his way to the bowling alley. Leslie might just be looking for closure to Doug's death. Eddy said it happened all the time, and it made sense. The poor lady was with the same man for years, their whole life a routine, one torn away from them the day he died. That big of an adjustment was hard at any point in life, but at her age, it would be devastating.

The blinking neon lights of Clarkbridge Bowling flashed on his right. He pulled into the lot. Eddy and Lena played in a league on Friday nights and needed a sub. Bowling wasn't really John's sport, but it gave him a reason to get out of the apartment. When he'd moved back, Eddy offered to let him stay in their guest room until he found a place of his own, but John preferred his privacy. He didn't want to intrude on his friend's family, either.

The bowling alley looked much larger on the inside than from the parking lot. Green neon lighting ran down the walls of the bowling lanes, and across the ceiling in swirls. There was a bar to his left with five stools, each taken with a long line behind.

Friday night at Clarkbridge Bowling must be a popular hangout.

Eddy and Lena waved him over to their table. They wore their team colors, sky blue bowling shirts with 'Bailey Detective Agency' imprinted on the back.

"Hey, Johnny. Have a seat," Eddy said. An iced glass already sat in front of John. Eddy filled it without asking. "Some good ole pale ale there for you, buddy. I know you prefer the dark stuff, but this is the drink special. Two dollar pitchers."

John lowered himself to the blue plastic chair matching Eddy's hideous bowling shirt. "Pale ale will do just fine, Eddy. Thanks. How are you doing Lena?"

Lena sipped on her own glass of ale. "I'd be doing a lot better if your buddy here would stop staring at my ass."

Eddy shrugged. "What can I say?"

"You can say you're married," Lena said.

The few times John had been around Eddy and Lena at the same time, their banter revolved around Eddy staring at one of her body parts. It always seemed in jest, though. Even now, she smiled while voicing her complaints.

Eddy stood and filled his own mug. "Come on. You know Sandra doesn't care if I take a gander now and then." He plopped back down in his seat. He must have come early for the drink special. His glassy eyes wandered back and forth while looking at John, as if he saw more than one of him.

"Well?" John said to Lena.

"Well, what?"

"Let me see what all the fuss is about. Stand up and let me take a look." John gestured for her to stand.

Eddy sputtered into his beer, blowing foam on the table.

"So that's how it's going to be now, huh?" Lena shook her head. "You two boys get together and you pick on the only girl?"

Eddy and John nodded.

"Fine," Lena said standing. She stepped in front of John and lifted the back of her bowling shirt. She bent over and shook her hind-end back and forth.

It was John's turn to sputter. Lena wore black spandex pants, not leaving much to the imagination. Eddy said she'd been a college athlete, and it was obvious she still worked out.

Lena turned around and sat back in her chair, topping off her glass. She looked to Eddy, and then to John, and let out a hearty laugh. "You boys can pick your tongues up now. The show is over."

John's mouth snapped shut. Maybe there was another reason for him to stay in Clarkbridge. Since breaking up with his fiancée the year before, he hadn't thought much about women other than in passing. Lena's show was a nice counter to the depressing afternoon he'd spent with Leslie.

John brought his thoughts away from his testosterone. "Whose place am I taking anyway if you two are the only ones who work for the PI agency?"

Eddy smiled. "You remember old man Tobias?"

"The guy who tended your yard when you were a kid?" John said.

"That's the one."

"Holy shit. He has to be like two hundred years old."

"He's my neighbor now. It was actually his idea to put the team together. He doesn't mind advertising for us as long as he gets to play. I guess he has the flu."

John's phone rang. He needed to take it outside to hear anything over the too loud eighties music.

"Where are you going?" Eddy said. "We start in fifteen minutes."

"I'll be back before then. I need to get some dollar bills," John said.

"For what?"

"So I'm ready next time Lena gives me a dance."

Lena pulled an ice cube from her water glass and chucked it at him, missing his head by inches. John smiled and walked toward the exit.

The phone display showed the call was from Rachel, who was returning his call from earlier. A childhood friend, she lived in Seattle now and was his go-to girl when he needed any kind of information.

He pressed the talk button and shouted into the phone. "One sec, Rach. I need to get outside." He stepped outside in front of the bowling alley, the music dying down to a whisper. "So you got my message?"

"Sure did," Rachel said. "I had a chance to look up Holbrook Rehab Services, and they're clean as a whistle. They're located in Millstead, about twenty-five minutes from you."

"I remember. I dated a girl from Millstead in high school."

"Of course you did." Rachel laughed.

"Okay, okay. They're clean as a whistle. What about Abraham and Russell? You find anything on them?" John moved farther from the entrance. More people showed up the closer it came to the league's starting time.

"I need to dig a little deeper. Russell's record is just as clean as the Holbrook Center, but Abraham was in prison when he died. The strange thing is I can't find anything that says why he was there. The local newspapers only said it was a shame and that he was under investigation, but they never said for what."

"With a small community like Millstead, you'd think everybody would talk."

"That's what I thought, too. I'm sure I'll find something."

Another call beeped through on John's phone. He held the phone out for a better view. *Eddy.* "Sorry, Rach. Gotta go. I have a bowling league to conquer."

"A bowling league? Really, John? You sound more like your old man every day. Don't let the small town ways get you." Rachel cackled again. "I'll see if I can find anything else on those two."

John said his thanks and headed back inside.

"Johnny!" Eddy waved him over. "Hurry up, man. We're starting."

Lena stood at the edge of the runway, poised to move into her bowling stride. When Eddy yelled, she looked back to John. She wiggled her bottom and winked.

A grin split John's face. *Thank God for spandex.*

5. M. E. and the Cafe

Medical Examiner's Office

"Are you ever going to let me drive?" Rita said, looking in the visor mirror and adjusting out of place strands of hair.

Allie had been a constant hair primper, too. Sometimes their similarities startled him. With his brow raised, he glanced at Rita in the passenger seat of the cruiser. "Are you even old enough to drive yet, young lady?"

She slapped his shoulder. "Not funny. Where's Chief Burleson sending us anyway?"

"He wants us to have a word with Charlie Parrish," Alan said.

"Is he the medical examiner?"

Alan sometimes forgot Rita wasn't from the Clarkbridge area. She didn't know everybody like he did. "That's him. I guess he's done with Lonny Krogman's autopsy."

"I still can't believe that happened." Rita snapped the visor shut. "Clarkbridge is supposed to be a quiet little suburb. I'm tempted to call my dad to tell him about it, but he's freaked out enough about me being a police officer. Speaking of my dad, when do you want to meet him?"

Alan coughed to cover his surprise. "Ah... I'm not sure, Rita. We should probably wait a little longer. Don't you think?"

She crossed her arms and lowered her brows. "Six months isn't long enough, Mr. Reeves? If we wait much longer, Dad will think you're hiding something."

She's cute when she pretends to be mad. "Okay, fine. If you think he'll be freaked out, let's at least wait until things settle down a bit on the Krogman case."

Rita harrumphed. Alan pulled the cruiser into the medical examiner's parking lot and cut the engine. They climbed from the vehicle into the oppressive heat and headed toward the brick building.

"What about John? Are you going to call him back?" Rita said.

John had the strange ability to show up at the most inopportune times. Alan was too busy with work, and with Rita for that matter, to deal with John right now.

"I will, sooner or later. Let's just say he's not at the top of my buddy list right now." The message John left on Alan's work phone had been the first time he'd heard his brother's voice since the day of Allie's funeral.

"It would be good for you to see him. You two should make up; it's been over five years."

"I really don't want to talk about this right now, Rita." The words came out more abrupt than he'd planned.

Rita nodded and opened the door.

Alan put his hand on the door and waved for Rita to go ahead. "Sorry. I'm more stressed about Doug and Lonny than I realized. You're right, getting back with John would be good."

She stopped and turned to him. For a brief moment, he thought she would kiss him right there in the doorway. Instead, she just smiled and said, "You do that, Mr. Reeves."

He followed her into the somber office lit by bright fluorescent lights, the light bluish green adding to the dour office. The stench of formaldehyde wafted from the rooms in the back, reminding Alan of the hospital.

A petite, bald woman tapped away at a keyboard behind the front desk. "One moment, please."

Alan drew up short. The bald head and dark glasses reminded him of the way Allie had looked after two years in and out of chemotherapy.

The woman pulled her gaze away from the computer screen, a pleasant smile on her face. "Captain Reeves and Officer Vasquez I presume?"

They nodded.

"Mr. Parrish is in room four. Around the corner there to your left." She pointed behind her.

Rita showed the woman a big smile. "Thanks, sweetie."

Rita is so perfect, Alan thought. *What does she see in a forty-something broken-down man like me?* He counted his blessings and followed her to room four.

Charlie Parrish stood at the back wall writing on a pad of paper with his back to the entrance.

"Charlie?" Alan said.

Charlie turned, his tanned skin in contrast with his bleach white smock. It kept the fluorescent lighting from making him look as sickly as it did most. "Hey there, Alan. Good to see you again, barring the circumstances, that is. What's it been? Three years?"

"About that long." Charlie's complexion and surfer hairstyle always made him look out of place in wan lighting. "Actually, it was when we found the three missing college kids down in the river by Krogman's."

Charlie lost his smile and nodded. "That was a sad time. Did you ever find who gave them the laced marijuana?"

The tox report showed the three college kids had been high at the time of their drowning, their marijuana laced with a designer drug.

"The case is still open," Alan said.

"Well, that's too bad. Anyway, we're here to talk about Mr. Krogman. Did you receive my preliminary report?"

"I didn't. We were on patrol, so Chief Burleson sent us over right away."

"Well, there's not much in it really." Charlie dropped the pad of paper on the counter and walked to the covered body on the steel table. He pulled back the sheet, uncovering Lonny's stub where his hand had been.

Rita shuddered and crossed her arms.

Alan glanced at his partner. "You okay?"

"Yeah," Rita said, with another shiver. "Just a little cold in here."

"Sorry about that," Charlie said, probably guessing Rita's real reason for shivering. "We need to keep it that cool in here to delay decomposition. I'd much rather be out in the ninety-five degree weather myself," he said, his lips parting to show his gleaming teeth.

Rita returned the smile, if a bit crooked, and took a few steps back.

"Everything seems to be consistent with the wound patterns here," Charlie continued, running his gloved finger over the stub. "The angle of the cut patterns and the tissue damage was probably self-inflicted by the cleaver you found. The bone at the wrist was more crushed than cut, which is consistent with the dulled edge of the cleaver. If the edge had been serrated, the cut would have been smoother."

Rita put a hand over her mouth.

"Hey, Rita. Could you get a hold of Chief Burleson and let him know we're chatting with Charlie?" Alan said.

"Sure. I'll get right on that." Rita bustled from the room in a hurry.

"First autopsy I'm guessing," Charlie said, eyebrows raised.

"How'd you guess?" Alan said with a laugh. "She's a tough little thing and all business when we're out on the street."

"How did you get hooked up with her for a partner? She makes me want to drop the doctor gig and become an officer myself."

Alan's face flushed, not out of jealousy, but because Rita had that effect on most men. "Just lucky I guess."

Charlie looked up from the stub and smiled. "You've got that right." His attention went back to Krogman. He lifted the sheet to show the bottom of Krogman's legs. "The same goes for down here, Alan. Most likely self-inflicted if you look at the angle of the cuts."

"And the tox report?"

Charlie covered the body back up with the sheet. "Everything came back clean. Minus the anti-depressants, Lonny was as clean as they come. How is this possible, Alan? Do you think somebody forced him to do this?"

"I can't see how that's possible. If somebody forced him to do it, he wouldn't have been able to keep going. He'd have passed out from the pain or something. Before I made it far enough to remove limbs, I would have let whoever was doing this kill me."

"I thought the same thing," Charlie added. "His wife didn't see anybody?"

"Kandi was working the front desk the whole time. She was reading a book when she heard him thumping around upstairs. She thought he was just moving stuff around. Didn't hear a scream or anything. The only way in and out of their room is through the front door. The three windows are thirty feet in the air on the back of their house. Somebody would have had to climb a tall ladder to make it up there, and we found no evidence supporting that idea."

"Well, I don't know what to say. That's really all I have. I'll go over everything again; though, I doubt there's anything to find."

"Thanks, Charlie. I appreciate your help. If you find anything, contact me or Chief Burleson." Alan turned to leave.

"Hey, Alan?"

Alan turned back to Charlie.

"You better go take care of Rita. If you don't, someone else will." Charlie smiled and went back to the pad of paper at the back of the room.

Alan left and nodded to the woman behind the front desk. He stepped into the heat and started toward the cruiser. Rita leaned against the hood, arms crossed.

What the hell did he mean by take care of Rita? Did he say that because Krogman's corpse made her sick? He needed to pay more attention to their body language, make sure they didn't let off any noticeable vibes. He enjoyed having her as a partner; he didn't want to mess it up for either of them. Not that they weren't allowed to have a relationship, but it was severely frowned upon, especially for a Captain and a new recruit. If he were forced to leave his job, what would he do? The life of a police officer was all he knew.

Corner Cafe

John sat near the rear wall of the Corner Cafe, the same restaurant his father had visited almost every day of the week to drink coffee with his friends. The once white walls were stained yellow from the years of smoking before legislation made it illegal to do so in a public place. John sipped his coffee. His vibrating phone wobbled across the table in front of him. He picked it up.

"What's up, Eddy?" he said.

"You already at the Corner Cafe?" Eddy said.

"Yeah, Alan's not here yet."

"I wondered if you saw the news this morning. They just said Lonny Krogman is dead."

"The old man at the tubing place?"

"That's the one. Alan is on the case. They showed a sound bite of him telling the people of Clarkbridge to remain calm. I guess they found Lonny all messed up."

The bell over the entrance to The Corner Cafe rang as Alan stepped in. John smiled and waved Alan over. He didn't smile back. *Not good.*

"I gotta go, Eddy. I'll catch you later." John hung up and waved the waitress over. "Could you grab a coffee for my brother too, please?"

She headed toward the coffee machine. He hoped Alan hadn't had breakfast yet. The scent of fresh coffee and greasy bacon made John's mouth water.

Alan sat down across from John. His eyebrows were pulled down, jaw muscles flexing and relaxing. This wasn't going to be easy. John had missed Allie's funeral and Alan was still upset about it.

"Hi, Alan. Good to see you." John put on his best smile.

"What are you doing here, John? I thought you were some big bodyguard in New York."

The waitress sat a coffee in front of Alan. "Did you need creamer, honey?" she said.

"Not today, Denise."

Alan came to The Corner Cafe often enough to know the waitress's name, just like their father.

"I was. Kind of," John said. "I'm back in Clarkbridge for a while, though. Eddy gave me a job. I've been staying at the Highland Apartments."

Alan took a drink of his coffee and pushed the menu on the table to the side. "But what are you doing here?"

"I told you, I'm working for Eddy."

"You always have something up your sleeve, John. You never go somewhere just for the sake of going. Especially someplace like Clarkbridge."

Things weren't going well. He hadn't expected a big hug from his brother, but he had hoped time might have healed part of the rift that had grown between them.

"Look, Alan. I had a close call a year ago. I took a few arrows to the chest and had a hell of a time with the infection. Right around the same time, my fiancée broke up with me. I thought about the things you've told me in the past, about getting my act together, doing something with my life. What better way than to come home to Clarkbridge and work with Eddy?"

Alan's expression didn't change the entire time John spoke. Alan sat his coffee cup down and his shoulders began to shake. A few seconds later, he laughed so loud Denise and a few of the guests at her tables looked in their direction.

"I don't get it," John said. "What's so funny?"

"You...," Alan broke into a laugh again. "You were engaged? What in the hell was she thinking?" Each word was louder than the last. He laughed so hard the table shook.

John had to smile. It was good to see his brother happy, even if it was at John's expense.

"It's good to see you laugh, big brother," John said.

The laughter calmed down.

"Don't call me big brother, John. You know I hate that." Alan sighed. "I hate to say this, but it's good to see your ugly mug too. I doubt you had some life-changing experience, but at least you're trying. That's more than you've done in the past."

Alan had always walked the straight and narrow, honor held in the highest regard like their father.

"I missed you, too." John paused. "Look, Alan, about Allie—"

Alan's face lost a little of the joviality.

"Let's not talk about Allie right now. I just started liking you again. Let's save that conversation for another day."

John nodded. "Agreed. I have to ask, why don't all of you wear those shoulder radios you see in the movies?"

"Mostly because us old-timers don't like the change. Some are afraid to have the cord used against them, and some don't like changing the batteries on the cordless type. Why do you ask?"

"I've found them invaluable as a bodyguard, and all the cops I've met use them. I just wanted to hear what an *old-timer* thought. And I noticed the two gold bars on your collar. When did you make Captain?"

"About a year ago. I didn't really want it, but Chief Burleson wouldn't take no for an answer."

Denise swung by their table and topped off their coffees.

"Well, Denise, it looks as though I'll be staying for breakfast after all," Alan said.

"Sure thing, Alan." She pulled an order pad from her stained apron. "The usual?"

"Why not?"

Denise looked to John. "What can I get for you, honey?"

"I'll take whatever he's having. Minus onions," John said.

Denise finished writing on her order pad and walked back toward the kitchen.

"Still haven't overcome your aversion to onions, huh?" Alan said.

"Just because you suck the things down raw doesn't mean I have to like them."

"They're good for you." Alan laughed.

"Anyway, this isn't a purely social visit. I had some things to chat with you about."

Alan's brow lowered. He spoke in a monotone voice. "What is it, John?" He lifted the coffee cup for a drink.

"It's probably nothing, but I've been looking into Douglas Fincham's death, and—"

"You what?" Alan slammed his cup down, coffee sloshing to the table. "It's an open police investigation, John. You shouldn't be snooping around."

"Wait, it's not what you think. Leslie went to Eddy for help. He passed the case off to me because he thought it was probably a dead-end, and so far, I agree. He said grieving widows come to him all the time when their husbands commit suicide."

Denise rushed over with a towel and wiped up the mess between them. Alan apologized for spilling.

"Even if that is the only reason," Alan said, "you shouldn't use her like that. With Doug gone, she doesn't have the money to pay a PI."

Denise brought another pot of coffee over and refilled Alan's cup.

"I know. Eddy told her she wouldn't have to pay unless we found something. We're doing it pro-bono I guess you could say."

Alan let out a sigh. "What is it you want to know?"

John ran his hand through his hair. "First of all, I'm not trying to step on any toes. If you think I'm stepping over the line, I'll back off."

"You're stepping over the line, now," Alan said.

John's eyes opened wider.

"Look, John. I can't say much, but what I can say is this; something strange did happen. I was there. The thing is, I don't want anybody in Clarkbridge getting worked up if it wasn't a suicide."

John leaned forward in his chair. "You were there?"

Alan nodded.

"I'm sorry, Alan. I know you were close with the Finchams. Let me just ask you a couple things then. The sooner I learn something, the sooner I can go to Leslie with the facts."

"I'll answer what I can, but keep your nose out of people's private business. Okay?" He lifted the fresh coffee to his mouth and took a sip.

John nodded. "Deal. Have you ever heard of Abraham or Russell Holbrook?"

"Abraham..." Alan rubbed at his chin. "Is that the psychiatrist who was killed in prison?"

"That's the one. What do you know about him?" John pulled out a tiny red notebook and pen, placing them on the table next to his coffee.

"Nothing really, other than what I just said. Where'd you come up with his name?"

John paused. "Remember what you said a minute ago about staying out of people's business?" Alan nodded and

John continued. "Let's just keep it at that then. Can you look anything up on him?"

"You want me to use taxpayer money to look for information on a dead psychiatrist because you have a hunch? I don't think so, John. Not that I don't want to help, it just wouldn't be right."

John shrank in his seat a little. "Could you at least keep an eye out for either of those names, and if you hear something, let me know?" The mini red notebook went back into his front pocket next to the pen.

"I can keep an eye out. Depending on how or where I hear the names, though, I can't guarantee I'll be able to contact you. I'm not at liberty to discuss details of an ongoing investigation. You know that."

"Just promise you'll do what you can," John said.

"No promises."

6. Argument

John's New Office

John sat behind the archaic computer desk, the only area in his new office not covered in dust. Boxes filled with old files blocked the one window in the room, leaving the single bulb over John's desk as the only light. Eddy said the room had been used as a storage area for old case files. Computer illiterate, he had never seen any reason to change his ways. Lena and John had talked Eddy into investing in a laptop computer. They used the excuse that his old-fashioned ways wore on the rain forests with all the paper he wasted. Other than the multitude of boxes, the room looked like a stereotypical private investigator's office, dark wood paneling and a door with patterned glass that looked like rain. The only thing missing was John's name stenciled on the door. If he stayed long enough, he'd talk Eddy into letting him do it, even if just for fun.

Eddy's silhouette appeared on the other side of the door's window. He opened the door and poked his head in. "Hey, Johnny. Like your new office?"

"Once I clear the dust bunnies from my sinuses, I'll enjoy it more. Come on in; have a seat." John waved him in.

Eddy sat in the rickety chair in front of John's desk, the torn leather creaking. "You'll never guess who just called me." Eddy leaned forward and rubbed his hands together.

John couldn't keep his smartass response from bursting out. "Mr. Pittenger? Asking if you'd come over and take a shower with him?" Their high school gym teacher once had a thing for Eddy.

"Real funny, John," Eddy droned in monotone. "Where'd you get that amazing sense of humor?" He sat up straight. "If you're done making jokes, you might be interested to hear we have another client, and I'll be sending her your way."

"Who?"

"Kandi Krogman."

"Are you kidding me? The cranky witch from the tubing place? You'd think with a name like that, she'd be sweeter."

Eddy shook his head. "Nice." He stifled a laugh. "Just hear me out. Normally it takes a few weeks before a widow comes looking for answers, but Kandi jumped on the train real fast with this one. She says there's no way Lonny killed himself."

John sighed. "Not even a month and I'm already getting the crazies. Didn't the paper say he wigged out and lopped off his own limbs? I heard something about a jar too."

"That's what the paper said, but Kandi says differently. Look, I know this is a bit much, but I figure there's only so much time you can spend working on the Fincham case. At least check things out? She's staying at her sister's house."

"If she isn't so deep in the bottle she can't breathe," John mumbled.

"That's what I thought too," Eddy said. "She says her drinking is the reason the police won't believe her. She said she's drank for years, and it never affected her before. In a way it's true, I guess. I've never heard of her getting a ticket, drunk driving, disturbing the peace, or anything."

"Yeah, because she stays locked up in that barn-house of hers, pounding the spirits. At least she used to. Can she even afford a PI?"

"She already paid."

"Huh. Maybe they had the right idea living like they did. I should look into converting a barn."

"Johnny, you—"

"Don't worry about it, Eddy. I'll look into it. But I'm charging you double for this one."

Eddy sputtered and his eyebrows shot up.

"I'm kidding." John grinned. "I'll head over to her sister's when I'm done with this stack of files. And, where's Lena? I haven't seen her the past couple days. She was supposed to help with this data-entry."

Eddy stood and opened the door. "I don't know. She doesn't tell me when she's taking time off. It's part of the agreement we have."

Same old Eddy, letting an attractive woman boss him around.

Eddy leaned toward John and whispered. "You be careful with that one, John. She's a good girl. I don't want you spoiling her innocence."

John's laugh filled the room. "Spoil her innocence? From the way she acted at the bowling alley last week, I doubt she knows the meaning of the word."

Meeting With Kandi

The dusty gravel crunched beneath John's tires as he pulled into Alicia Godfrey's driveway. Kandi Krogman's sister was well known for her obsession with plant life. Perennials, annuals, and arborvitae blanketed the yard, every color of the rainbow and then some. Alicia would probably argue each one had its place.

John stepped from the Wrangler. Kandi sat on the porch swing puffing on a cigarette. She jabbed her smoke into an ashtray, stood, and walked through the jungle to where he waited. Drawing near, she tipped her chin toward the backyard and continued. He followed. Greenery filled half of the rear grounds—hydrangeas, a few ferns, and one potted Japanese maple. Children's toys populated the rest. John was sure the rest of the yard would have been filled with plant life had a play area not been required for the daycare Kandi's sister ran.

Kandi collapsed into a hanging wooden swing and lit up another cigarette. Her greasy hair swung perilously close to the cancer stick with each breath of wind. John stood by the fence upwind.

I wonder if there's a law about chain smoking at a day care. "Hello, Kandi. I'm sorry for your loss."

"Let's get to business, John. You're not here for small-talk. Lonny didn't kill himself, and the police don't believe me."

Why do I even try to be nice? "Why do you say that?"

Kandi stopped staring at the ground and turned her bloodshot, dark-ringed eyes in his direction. "Because I said he didn't. Why do you care? You're getting paid. You just need to find out who killed him."

The word around town was that Lonny drank, too. John could see why.

"I'm sorry, Kandi." John took a step closer, and Kandi blew smoke in his direction. He stepped back against the fence. "I'm still a little new to all this. I hoped you could give me something to work with, somewhere to start."

"You can start looking at our house. Chief Burleson said the cleanup crew is done over there. I'm not sure what they left, but I'm not a private investigator." She lowered her eyes. "I can't go back there, anyway. Every time I think about the place, all I can picture is Lonny sitting there smiling like a freak."

"Okay. I can do that." He paused. "What do you mean he was sitting there smiling like a... freak?"

A single tear escaped her eye and ran down her cheek, falling to her baggy blue and green sun-dress. "That's how I found him. He was propped up in his chair with that bloody damn cleaver in his hand, smiling like I gave him a hooker for his birthday."

John at Krogman's

John noted the police tape at Krogman's tubing had been cut at the front door. *I'll have to let Alan know about this one. He'll be pissed if it was one of the Clarkbridge officers.*

The Krogman's home still smelled of the chemicals the cleaning crew had used to remove the body fluids, but the porous wood floors would hold the stains until somebody came in with a sander. Coming back home would be hard for anyone after something so gruesome.

Eddy had suggested he use latex gloves, but he'd grown used to the mechanic's gloves from his work on the Jeep. He tugged the gloves up higher on his arm and pulled the Velcro tight around his wrist. They weren't really needed since forensics had already finished with their collection, but the thought of touching anything at a murder scene sickened him.

He flicked on the antique lamp next to the recliner. The dim lamp and the light seeping in around the shades did little to brighten the drab room. The dreary colors and the sparse furnishings felt as if they sucked the life from him. *No wonder they drank so much.*

Finding the pictures and receipts when he searched Doug Fincham's bedroom had been lucky. He started with the same area at the Krogman's. Their mattress sat on the floor without a frame, the bed unmade. A thick rag of a cover wrapped around the toilet seat. No vanity walls or screen blocked the view. *They must have been comfortable together,* John thought with a small laugh. Lonny had rigged the whole setup himself, according to Eddy. Their place looked more like a loft than a home. John didn't know if he admired or pitied a couple who built their living area and business out of a barn.

A single dusty dresser, painted the same barn-red as the walls outside, sat just inside the door. Twisted curtain hangers replaced a few missing handles. John slid each drawer out one at a time, flipping through the clothing. *No hidden boxes in the Krogman's shared dresser.* John searched the clothing hanging on the bar from the ceiling, a homemade version of a closet. The lone item in their bed stand was an old King James Bible.

No luck in the living room, either. An old chicken bone and a few coins gathered lint in the recliner. The only other place for something to be hidden was in the homemade end table. It appeared to have been put together with used two-by-fours. The drawer stuck until he gave it a hard yank. A TV Guide slid to the front.

He went through the kitchen next. Cleanliness seemed a rarity for the Krogmans. The sinks sparkle suggested blood had been scraped away with a cloth over and again. John shuddered. Kandi hadn't given him many details, but Eddy had brushed a grisly painting. His friend Corporal Cooper Forbes, a cop, often fed him crime scene details over a pint.

The refrigerator contained a case of Schlitz, a bottle of mustard, and a jar of pickles. Grime and crusty food caked each shelf. He searched the other drawers in the kitchen, finding much of the same: dust, antique silverware, hardened crust in the crevices.

He pulled at the drawer next to the sink. A wad of paper fell to the floor, and more threatened to spill over from the top. He picked up the fallen wad and examined the receipts bundled together with a rubber band.

Nice place to store paperwork.

A thump sounded downstairs. John froze.

Alan and Rita Find John

Alan ran his fingers across the cut tape on the Krogman's door.

"Why do you think the tape was cut?" Rita said behind him as they stepped into the home.

"I'm not sure." Alan shook his head. The door to the top floor stood open. He waved for Rita to follow. "Chief Burleson didn't say he was sending somebody else over here. I guess the cleaning crews could have left it that way. Maybe Kandi stopped over for some clothes or something."

Rita grabbed Alan's shoulder. He paused.

"Explain to me again why we're here?" she said. "Why not just wait for forensics to send us their report?"

"I'm not much for patience when somebody is killed in Clarkbridge, even if he did it himself."

Rita removed her hand and nodded. "Now I see why the Chief likes you so much. Were you an overachiever in school, too?"

Alan gave a quick smile and stepped onto the steep stairwell. He took the stairs two at a time. The smell of cleaning chemicals wafted past when he opened the door. The lamp next to the recliner lit the room.

"Well that's—"

"Hey there, Alan. Fancy seeing you here."

Alan palmed his sidearm, lowering himself into a ready stance. Rita drew her weapon and kicked the door shut behind her. John stood in the kitchen, leaning back with gloved hands on the sink.

Rita aimed at John's chest. Alan was tempted to let her continue.

"Stand down, Rita."

She looked to Alan with surprise, but the barrel didn't waver.

"This is John. My brother."

Yelling

"What the hell are you thinking, John? You can't be here. We just talked about this."

John sat on the bench outside Krogman's tubing, his face dark red, looking abashed. *Or maybe upset?* Alan stood in front him, arms crossed, and Rita a few steps behind.

"Let me explain," John said.

John spent most of his life explaining. He'd said the same thing to Alan on the day of Allie's funeral.

So much for John cleaning up his act. "No, John. There is no reason you can give that would make this okay. You're at a crime scene. It's an ongoing investigation, a murder investigation! You need to leave. Now." Alan pointed to John's Jeep. He pictured their mother using the same tone with John so many times as a child.

"Kandi asked me to be here. She said to—"

"I don't care. You can't just come over here and cut your way through the police tape just because someone asked you to. I should take you in."

"I'm working with Eddy Bailey on this. She hired him."

"That's not how it works. If you're working for Eddy, you should have contacted the department before you went traipsing around."

John's shoulders sagged. Guilt flooded through Alan, but his brother needed to grow up. John shook his head and stood, starting toward the jeep. He stopped a few feet past Rita and turned back.

"It wasn't supposed to be this way, Alan. I was trying to help. I'll have Eddy phone Chief Burleson. And the tape was cut before I got here."

Alan nodded toward John's Jeep. John rolled his eyes and walked the rest of the way to his vehicle. He climbed in and pulled away. Alan let out a breath he hadn't realized he held.

Rita stepped close. "I'm sorry, Alan. I can see you two still have some issues. What if Mrs. Krogman did hire Eddy Bailey?"

"Doesn't matter. Like I said, he should have gone to the station first. I don't understand why he refuses to mature. I thought... I had hoped this time was different. I love my brother, Rita, but I can't be around him if he refuses to change."

Rita nodded and rubbed his shoulder.

"I'm sorry you had to see that." His attention focused on the yellow police tape hanging from the door. "John may not act like an adult, or think the rules apply to him, but he's smart enough to not tamper with a scene."

"You don't think he cut it?" Rita said.

"I don't. Let's contact Chief Burleson and see if he knows anything." Alan rolled his shoulders, glancing to Rita. "Thanks for being here. Not just here, at the Krogmans, but for being, you know, my... more than a friend."

Her lips parted into a smile. "Let's go see if we can find anything up there before my tough man shows any more emotion. I don't want him to break."

7. A Third Death

Drinking at Snark's

"Arthur! Another Guinness please." John waved his hand and pointed to his table.

"Coming right up." The white-haired bartender tossed his towel on the bar and reached into the cooler.

Eddy sat across the table from John, shaking his head. "How can you drink so much Guinness?" He sipped at his pale ale.

"What's the matter, Eddy? You can't pound the liquid steak?" John joined Eddy in a hearty laugh.

"So what's the occasion, anyway?" Eddy slid his glass to the side. "You're on your sixth. How am I supposed to celebrate when I don't know what we're celebrating?" Eddy's eyes grew wide. "Wait, did you learn something about the Fincham case? The Krogmans? What's going on, man?"

Arthur set another dark brew on the table. John picked up the glass and studied the milky thick foam as the small nitrogen-filled bubbles drifted toward the brim.

"It's nothing as grand as that." He set the Guinness back on the table. John looked over Eddy's shoulder. "Ah, there she is. Now the party can start."

Lena turned her scintillating eyes in their direction and threw them a quick wave. John admired the way she floated when she walked, always on her toes and a little bounce to her step. *Oh, what I'd do to her if I had more time in Clarkbridge.*

"What's going on, boys?" Her sing-song voice resonated in John's ears. She pulled a chair out.

"I'm not sure." Eddy swept his hand out in a grand gesture toward John. "Apparently, John here is having a party."

"I'm glad you came, Lena." John smiled and patted the seat of Lena's chair.

Lena lifted a single brow before taking her seat. Arthur placed a frosted glass filled with pale ale in front of her.

John lifted his glass, the foam having dissipated, and stood, mug held high. He steadied himself on the table with his free hand. With a quick shake of the head, he straightened himself. "Let's have a drink."

Eddy and Lena each lifted the thick mugs and clinked them together.

"To new beginnings!" John downed half of his in one swallow.

Eddy and Lena glanced at each other and back to John, pausing before bringing their own drinks to their lips.

Eddy wiped the light layer of foam from his upper lip. "I thought we already celebrated your homecoming, John. What's going on?" The drink began another trip toward his open mouth.

John wiped at the condensation on his mug, eyes searching the dark drink. "We did." His lips parted into a wicked smile as he gazed further into the glass. "Now we're celebrating my leaving."

Eddy's drink paused inches from his chin.

"What?" Eddy and Lena said at the same time.

John laughed. "I've spent too much time here already. It's time to leave. I had a little talk with Alan today."

Eddy's glass finished its trip to his mouth for another drink. He gurgled the drink down and wiped at his mouth. "You're leaving because of Alan?"

John nodded.

"Well, that's a bunch of bullshit. I need you, John. I took on those extra cases just for you. You can't leave right in the middle."

"I can. And I will. Our talk took place at Krogman's today. Alan threatened to lock me up for interfering with the investigation."

Lena's eyes flicked back and forth between them.

"I know you said I could go over there," John said. "And Kandi even asked me to, but he's right. I shouldn't have interfered."

"You have rights as a private investigator. If the owner of the home asked you to be there—"

"Regardless, I can't go back. You should have seen the look on Alan's face. I know when he doesn't want me around. This has been his home for years, I won't mess that up. I'm sorry, but I'm leaving at the end of the week."

Eddy nodded slowly. "You have to do what's right for you... I guess. I was just getting used to you being back. Was it really that bad?"

"Worse than the time he caught me with his girlfriend."

"Wow. That *is* bad. I wish you would think things over. Maybe Alan just needs some time to get used to the idea of you being back. At least stop over for dinner with Sandra and the kids before you go. Henry and Maria will miss their Uncle John."

Eddy knew how to tug on his heartstrings. His kids had taken to calling him Uncle John since he came back. Seeing the pain on Eddy's face was bad enough, but it would be ten times worse on the children.

Lena held up her glass. "Well, if you're leaving, then leave the right way. Let's drink!"

John polished off the rest of his stout and waved to Arthur to bring them another.

Alan's Bedroom

"You're going to wear me out, woman." Alan wiped a hand across his forehead. "I need to take up running again just to keep up." He leaned on the television stand and eyed Rita still in his bed.

Rita smiled over the glass of red wine in her hands. She pulled the thick sheet up to her shoulders and smiled. Seeing her in his bed always made him smile. Alan looked forward to their rare nights together more than anything else in his life. What she saw in him, he'd never know. One day he'd have to ask, but for now he said another silent thanks.

She placed her glass on the bed stand, the sheet falling to display her tan flesh. She patted the bed next to her. "Why don't you come back over here and warm me up some more? The wine isn't quite doing the trick."

Alan couldn't help but smile. *Could my life get any better?*

"What are you grinning at?"

"I'm not sure how much warmer it can get in here." He moved to the kitchen doorway and continued studying Rita, working up the ambition to pour himself a drink. Hard to do when he couldn't take his eyes from her arresting smile.

"I'll show you how much warmer it can get." Rita lowered the sheet to her waist and patted the bed next to her again, this time with more force.

Sometimes when they were finished, he'd stand like this, taking in the scene, the smell, the feel, she an exotic painting, and he just an outsider, a surreal moment.

Alan's phone rang in the kitchen. He'd left it in his pants when Rita unzipped them after dinner.

"Don't you dare answer that." She crossed her arms and glared.

"You know I have to."

"You're not on call tonight. That's why I'm here. Remember?" She picked her wine glass back up, rolling her eyes.

"It'll only take a second."

She gave him a dirty look as he left the room. Her stubbornness was the reason they were together now. She was the one that had beaten down the wall he'd built around himself after Allie's death. She was the one who had kissed him while they stood in the police station garage, forcing her tongue deep into his mouth until he'd succumbed.

He picked up his phone. It displayed Chief Burleson's number.

"Hey, Chief. What can I do for you?"

"Sorry for calling so late, Alan. I'm not interrupting anything, am I?"

Alan looked toward the bedroom. Rita stood in front of the bed with the television remote, flipping through the channels wearing nothing but her skin.

"Um... no, not at all," he stuttered.

"Can you come in? Actually, not to the station, but to Tolman Chiropractic?"

"I thought Coop was on call tonight?"

The Chief paused. "He is, Alan. But I need a few more faces over here. Yours in particular. I tried calling Rita, but she isn't answering."

That's because she's standing nude in my bedroom. "Sure, Chief. Give me a half hour."

He snapped his phone shut and stepped back into the bedroom.

Rita turned to him, the light from the television flickering on her body. "Don't even tell me," she said. "I know that look."

"Chief Burleson wants me downtown. You should probably check your messages too."

Rita turned the television off and tossed the remote on the bed. She grabbed the sheet and wrapped it around herself like a towel after a shower.

"Did he say what's happening?"

"He didn't. Look, I'm sorry, I—"

"Don't be. This is our job. There are things more important than carnal pleasures." A devious grin came to her face. "Though not many." She dropped the sheet to the floor and walked toward him, smooth body swaying with each slow step. When she was close enough, she took a firm grip of his manhood in both hands. "Do we have time for a quickie?"

Tolman Chiropractic

By the time Alan reached Tolman Chiropractic in downtown Clarkbridge, two cruisers and an ambulance were parked outside, lights reflecting from the city's businesses. The forensics unit pulled in beside him. Chief Burleson and Cooper Forbes stood outside conferring with Barbara Sheppard, Herbert Tolman's long-time girlfriend.

"Chief. Corporal," Alan said, nodding to his fellow officers. He looked over to Barbara. Eye makeup ran in unsightly streaks down her face and leaked onto her tight, yellow blouse. "Good evening, Barbara."

She gave him a close-lipped smile and covered her eyes. Her shoulders shook as she broke into sobs.

"What's going on, Chief?"

"Coop, give Ms. Sheppard a ride to the station, if you would," Chief Burleson said. Cooper placed his arm around the distraught woman and guided her toward a cruiser. The chief watched a moment before turning to Alan. "This isn't good, Alan. Something goddamned awful is going on here. We need to figure it out, and fast."

"What do you mean?"

"Herbert Tolman is dead."

"Herb?" Alan pictured the man's bushy white mustache and his pink cheeks, an old card playing buddy of his father's. "What happened?"

Chief Burleson turned toward the chiropractic office, fingers rubbing his chin. "Forensics is here now, so just stay out of their way. But get in there and take a look. None of it makes sense." He turned to Alan. "Were you able to get a hold of Rita? She still hasn't returned my calls."

He opened his mouth to respond, not sure what to say, and stopped when Rita stepped around the ambulance.

"Hey, Chief. Captain Reeves." She nodded.

She would have made a good actress.

"Officer Vasquez." Chief Burleson returned the nod. "Could you accompany Captain Reeves into Dr. Tolman's? Tolman was friends with Alan's father." He turned back to Alan. "Normally I wouldn't put him on a case he may be emotionally involved with, but this is a unique situation. None of the other officers are prepared for something like this."

"Let's check it out." Rita started toward the chiropractor's office. Alan hurried to follow.

When Chief Burleson was out of earshot, Alan whispered to Rita's back. "How do you do that?"

"Do what?" She glanced behind and winked.

They'd just stepped inside the front office when Alan let out a laugh. The two officers already inside shook their heads.

"Gibbs, Donald," Alan said.

Sergeant Donald Clark pointed toward the back office. "Howdy, Captain. Head to the back office there. Chuck Parrish is already checking things out."

Alan said his thanks, not sure what to expect. The scene was eerily similar to the one at the medical examiner's a week before. A body lay on the bed in the center of the room covered with a sheet, only this time it was a chiropractic bed instead of the cold stainless steel. Charlie Parrish stood by the back wall writing on a notepad.

Charlie looked up when they walked in. "Hey, Alan. Hello again, Rita."

"I didn't think I'd be seeing you so soon," Alan said.

"What's the matter? No love for your local medical examiner?"

Alan wondered how Charlie came to be a doctor. From his boyish face, and chummy personality, he seemed more fit to be an actor or bartender.

"What have we got?" Rita said.

Charlie shoved the notepad in his pocket and stepped closer to the body, grabbing the edge of the sheet. Rita took a step back and looked toward the door.

"It's okay, Rita. This one's nothing like the Krogman case," Charlie said. "Though just as strange," he added to himself. He pulled the sheet back from Herbert Tolman's face. The man looked as though he were sleeping. "His injuries are all internal."

Alan heard the officers in the welcome area talking. He glanced back through the door behind him. The forensics team was in the office area fiddling with their equipment.

He turned back to the body. "All internal, you say?"

"That's right, Alan. But I'm not sure how it happened. I'll know more when I get him back to the lab."

Alan stepped closer to Tolman. "How do you know he has internal injuries at all? He looks as though he's napping."

Charlie reached under the side of the sheet and pulled out an arm. It bent at an awkward angle, almost rubbery.

"Most of his body is like this," Charlie said. "Many of his bones are broken, yet no external wounds other than the two on his rib cage. And those look self-inflicted."

"Self-inflicted?" Rita asked.

"Yeah. There's no reason to show you, but the bruises on his ribcage are consistent with having punched himself in the ribs hard enough to break a couple on each side. One hand-print on each side."

Neither of them said a word, but just looked at Charlie. Alan didn't know what to say. He half-expected Charlie to finish with his typical punch line, but it never came.

The doctor glanced up from the arm. "I honestly don't know what to say. I don't know how he could have done this himself, but I believe he did. And this is how Ms. Sheppard found him, laying up here on the bed."

"Why were he and Ms. Sheppard meeting at the office this time of night?" Rita said.

"My guess," Charlie said, "is they met for some type of midnight rendezvous. They've dated almost ten years. Why else would she wear that blouse she has on? You know how these doctor types can be: they bring their sex life to work with them."

Rita's already tan skin darkened. "Um... he looks like he's in his late sixties. And she can't be more than forty-five."

Charlie looked at Alan, then back to Rita while he placed Tolman's arm back under the sheet. "As I hear it, women prefer older men."

Her face darkened even more.

"Why don't you see if Gibbs and Clark need help out there, Rita?" Alan said.

She nodded and stepped out of the room.

Alan shook his head and whispered. "You really like stepping over the line, don't you, Charlie?"

Charlie straightened and pulled out his notepad, flipping through the pages. "What can I say? I spend too much time with dead people. I have to get my kicks somehow." He looked up with a large smile.

"I'm going to take a look around," Alan said. "Let me know if you find anything else. Otherwise, I'll see you at your office."

Charlie nodded and went back to his notepad.

Clark and Gibbs worked their way around the front office, searching through the desk drawers. Rita flipped through an appointment calendar.

Alan nodded toward the small booklet in her hands. "Anything interesting in there?"

She grabbed his sleeve and pulled him toward the front window. Under her breath, she said, "Does Charlie know something? Did you tell him?"

"Tell him what?" Alan said with a wink.

Rita punched him in the shoulder. "Hijo de puta."

He winced. "Of course not. Why would I?"

"I don't know. Bragging rights?"

"And what does… whatever you said mean?"

Gibbs squeezed in next to them and rifled through the table by the front window covered in brochures.

Somehow, Rita was already two feet away and looking over the chiropractor's desk.

"I think maybe we should talk about this later, Officer Vasquez," Alan said. "Who did Doc Tolman have appointments with this week? Maybe we'll get lucky." He hadn't meant for the pun, but Rita smiled nonetheless.

Alan pulled out his notepad and wrote down the names as Rita read them off.

"Wait, what was that last one?" he asked.

"Tomlinson?"

"No, the other one."

"Holbrook?" Rita said.

"That's the one. What was the first name?"

"Holbrook, Russell."

"Well, shit," Alan said.

Rita looked at him, eyebrows raised.

"I think maybe I need to call John back."

8. John Joins

John Wakes

The bed shook, just enough to wake John. His dry mouth and the pain rapping at his skull reminded him where he was the night before. He rubbed at his temples.

I'll never drink that much again.

Of course, he'd been telling himself the same thing since the first time he'd woke up with a hangover at age thirteen.

He blinked a few times to clear his eyes. When he opened them the rest of the way, in front of him was the most beautifully shaped bare rear end he'd ever seen. Lena bent down and pulled up her hot-pink thong.

"Thank you, God," he mumbled.

Lena glanced at him over her shoulder and gave her butt a little shake. "Sorry I woke you so early," she said, moving about the room, gathering her clothing as she went. "I'm meeting a friend for tennis in a half-hour."

"How in the hell can you play tennis after drinking that much last night?"

"It's a gift," Lena said. "Never had a hangover. I've been sick to my stomach a few times, but I guess I just have a good metabolism."

Eddy had called a cab not long after Lena showed up at Snark's. Lena almost matched John drink for drink over the next two hours. Before he realized what was happening, she'd sat on his lap and described in detail all the things they eventually came to his apartment and did.

She sat in the recliner in the corner of his room, tying her shoelaces.

I hate this part. "So… should I call you tonight?" He hoped it didn't sound as awkward to her ears as it did his.

Lena looked up and smiled. "Why? Are we boyfriend and girlfriend now?"

"It's… I just—"

She finished with her shoes and jumped onto the bed next to him. She forced her tongue into his mouth, kissing him as passionately as she had the night before. A moment later, she stood and grabbed her purse from the nightstand.

"I'm just kidding, John. I had a great time, but you don't have to call if you don't want to. But I hope you do. Not tonight, though. My favorite show is on and I'm babysitting for Eddy in the morning. But whenever you'd like another romp, give me a call."

She leaned over and gave him a peck on the forehead.

Why can't all women be like Lena?

He fell back asleep and awoke two hours later to his phone ringing. It sounded much like a machine gun going off in his brain. He slid the phone from the nightstand to his bed. The caller ID showed Alan's number. The memory of yesterday's events rolled through his mind. John would leave Clarkbridge, not because his brother told him too, but because it was for the best. Though, after the night with Lena, staying a little longer was tempting.

He flipped open his phone. "I already told you, I'm sorry, Alan. What else do you want me to say?"

"Are you drunk?" Alan said.

"Kind of. I mean a little. I had quite a bit last night. Why are you calling?" There was a pause on the other end of the line. "Alan?"

"Remember Herbert Tolman?" Alan asked.

"Old guy, bushy mustache."

"That's the one. He's dead, John."

"You called to tell me an old buddy of dad's croaked?"

"I think it might be related to Douglas Fincham and Lonny Krogman."

John sat up in bed too quickly. Dizziness overcame him and he fell back, smacking his head on the headboard.

"You still there?" Alan said.

"Yeah," John groaned, rubbing his head. "Why do you think they're related? And why are you telling me this? I thought you didn't want me intruding on your police work."

Alan sighed. "I'm sorry, John. I should know better by now; you always seem to put shit together faster than I do. Anyway, come have a cup of coffee with me down at the Corner Cafe. I'll give you more details then."

Did Alan just apologize? His brother was as bullheaded as they came; sorry wasn't part of his vocabulary.

"Sure. What time?"

"It's eleven now. Noon?"

Eddy would be pissed. John had told him he'd help with another bounty this morning. One last job before he left. It wasn't even noon yet and his day was already getting interesting.

Help

John plopped down in a chair across from Alan. His eyes bloodshot, hair matted on one side, and his clothes wrinkled.

"Jeez, John. Did you drink a whole keg last night?"

"No. Just half," he said with a laugh. "Where's the waitress? I need coffee."

Alan waved Denise over, the same waitress that had served them a few days earlier. He ordered coffee for the both of them. The little bell over the door jingled as Rita came in and sat down with them.

"John, this is Rita. Rita, this is John."

"I remember her from Krogman's. She's a little more attractive than the last partner you had," John said. "Wasn't his name Bill?"

Alan clenched his teeth. "She's my partner, and I'd appreciate it if you'd show her a little respect."

"I thought I was." John looked to Rita and offered his hand. "Hey there, Rita. John Reeves. Better known as Alan's annoying little brother."

"You look chipper," Rita said to John. "Late night?"

"You could say that."

Denise sat three cups down filled with coffee that smelled like it had been on the warming plate too long.

John looked back to Alan. "So, what's this about Herbert Tolman?"

Alan and Rita filled him in on the details. The broken bones and Russell Holbrook's name in the calendar.

"I've never seen anything like it, John. And Charlie Parrish, you remember him?"

John nodded. He winced as his hands shot to his temples. Wrinkles appeared on his forehead from squeezing his eyes shut.

Alan smiled. "Need some aspirin?"

John gestured for Alan to continue and sighed. His eyes opened and he downed half his coffee in one drink.

"Anyway, Charlie said he hasn't either. Said from what he could tell, the wounds were self-inflicted, just like Krogman's."

John's knuckles turned white from his grip on the coffee cup. "Krogman's wounds were self inflicted? I thought he had his feet and one of his arms lopped off. Kandi said the police thought it was a suicide, but holy shit. How is that possible?"

"Before I say more, I need your word you'll not discuss this case with anyone until it is closed."

"Of course, Alan. But what about all that stuff you said yesterday? About how you could take me in? I meant what I said about not stepping on any toes. I have plenty of other places I could be."

"I spoke with Chief Burleson this morning. I told him you were a private investigator working on the Fincham case and you had information pertinent to our investigation. He said to bring you on and share information. I think the respect he had for our dad helped. He may just want outside eyes on the case too."

The Chief's words had shocked Alan at first, but then Burleson had explained that if Alan trusted his brother, so did he. The problem was, he didn't know how much he trusted John, at least not when it came to his work. Alan had spent years on the force, specially trained in the arts of investigation. But John was a brute, trained in the arts of being a bodyguard, and who knows what when he was overseas in the military. John had always been better at the investigation games their father made them play; the same reason it had driven him crazy to see his brother waste his skills.

A serious look came across John's unshaven face.

"I'll do this, Alan. But only until you don't want me here. Intruding on your investigation is the last thing I want. You've worked your butt off to get where you are, and you're good at it. I won't ruin that. I'll help, but the moment you want me gone, say so, and I'll be out of Clarkbridge within the week."

John continued to surprise him. Now he felt even guiltier about yelling at him the day before. "Deal," Alan said.

"So," John said turning to Rita, "are you single?"

9. The Photo

The Photo

Alan sat at his desk filling out the morning paperwork. John would arrive soon. Chief Burleson wanted a chance to meet Alan's brother before officially bringing him in on the case. Ed Reeves had always preached that when you worked with other departments, or other officers, or in this case, private investigators, the key to success was one-hundred percent cooperation. Every person has their own unique outlook.

Alan just hoped he'd made the right decision. His brother had great potential as an investigator, but potential doesn't always equate to success. He hoped John took advantage of the opportunity. Alan had built a solid career and didn't want to endanger that by breaking Chief Burleson's trust.

The desk phone rang. Alan dropped his pen on the desk, thankful for a break. "Captain Reeves."

"Alan, this is Chief Burleson. Come on back to my office."

Alan returned the phone to its cradle and started down the hallway to the Chief's office, uneasiness settling over him. His thoughts wandered. When Burleson called someone back to his office, usually they were reprimanded or received a raise. Alan hadn't done anything to be reprimanded for. The Chief might have some new information on the case, though.

Alan picked up the pace. He paused with his hand poised to knock.

What if he knows about me and Rita?

His hands shook. Sweat beaded on his head. The Chief's door opened. Alan still stood with his hand out in front of him.

"Alan? What are you doing?" Chief Burleson said.

"I, uh..."

"Go in and have a seat. You look like crap." He looked over Alan's shoulder to his personal assistant. "Hey, Lori? Could you get us some coffee?" The woman nodded and pushed her thick glasses up on her nose.

The Chief closed the door, walked around, and sat behind his desk, the wheels on his office chair squealed as he rolled forward. Alan's eyes went to the awards behind the Chief's desk as they always did when in his office. The injury that had won Chief Burleson the Purple Heart still caused him to limp on occasion. Alan's father had hung his military commendations in this same office when he was police chief.

Burleson paused a moment. "You okay?"

"I'm fine. Just a little under the weather."

"You'd better get some extra sleep tonight then. I need you at the top of your game for this one. Calls have come in all morning. The people of Clarkbridge are putting things together about the three deaths, most of them likely untrue. The Clarkbridge Clipper called this morning, as well. They're sending somebody over for a statement." The Chief waved his hand. "But that's not why I called you in here." The man leaned forward placing his elbows on his desk, as he steepled his fingers.

"What is it, Chief?" Sweat dripped down between Alan's shoulder blades. If he ruined his own career, he'd find a way to deal with it. If he ruined Rita's, she might never forgive him, despite her words to the contrary.

"Something has been brought to my attention, and I wanted to come to you with it first, before you heard it from anybody else."

He should just come clean with it now, get it out in the open. The Chief would appreciate him more for it. "Look, Chief, I can explain."

"Explain what?" The Chief leaned back in his chair and opened his desk drawer.

"Wait. I, uh..."

"Maybe you should go home early, Alan. You have sweat rolling down your forehead. I don't want it affecting your ability to do your job."

Alan quickly brushed at his forehead with his sleeve.

The police scanner behind the Chief chirped. "Car twenty-two. We've got the possible 484 down at Fast Mart. Over and out."

The Chief shook his head. "Petty theft? It's probably one of the Larson twins again. It'll do those boys good when their dad gets back from overseas." He reached into his drawer and pulled out a Ziploc evidence bag. "I'm not sure if this means anything, yet, and I hate to put it on you when you're obviously ill, but it can't wait." He tossed the bag to the desk in front of Alan.

Alan leaned closer to inspect. Inside was a picture. He used his fingertips to hold down the sides of the plastic for a better look. His heart hammered. "Where did you get this?" It came out as a whisper.

"The forensics team found it at Dr. Tolman's office taped to the bottom of one of his desk drawers."

The picture showed four men smiling, arms around each other's shoulders, and beers in hand. Dr. Tolman and his bushy mustache, Lonny Krogman with his rotund belly, Douglas Fincham wearing a flannel shirt, and Alan's father, Ed Reeves.

"What does this mean?" Alan whispered.

"I hoped you could tell me." The Chief leaned forward in his chair.

"I really don't know." He couldn't take his eyes from the picture. "My father used to drink on occasion with Krogman, and he served in the Corp with Tolman." He looked to Chief Burleson. "Everybody knows our family has been friends with the Finchams for years, but why are they all together like this? I don't remember having ever seen any more than two of them together at any one time."

"So, you have nothing you can tell me?"

Alan shook his head.

"What about John? Would he know anything?"

"I doubt it." Alan pulled the plastic tight again, eying the photo. "I'm four years older, and I barely remember my dad spending time with these guys. And John always had his mind on other things. You can ask him when he comes in if you want. He should be here soon."

"That won't be necessary." The Chief stood and crossed his arms, stepping to the window. "You can ask him yourself. If you don't think he'd know anything, you're probably right. My question now is whether I should take you off this case."

Alan tossed the picture back on the desk and stood. "No! I mean, please, I would like to stay on. I can't see how any of this fits, but I won't let it affect me." He didn't like sounding so defensive.

The Chief looked over his shoulder. "Can you be sure about that, Alan? I could get hell from Mayor Snively over this. I'm putting myself on the line here." He sighed. "But I really could use you. We're already short a few this month. If I take you off, that means overtime for somebody else, tough with our budget already strapped as it is."

"You can count on me, Chief. If at any point you or I feel I'm a detriment to the case, I'll walk away."

Burleson nodded and looked back through the window. "Get to work on this, Alan. After you get some rest. The sooner we learn what's happening, the sooner we can calm the people of Clarkbridge."

Alan had his head down in thought as he walked back toward his desk. What could it all mean? What's the connection? Or was the picture a random thing?

He looked up. John sat in front of Alan's desk, reading the newspaper.

"Front page news," John said. "Somebody must have connections at the Clarkbridge Clipper to get this out so fast." He turned the paper over and held it up. In large letters across the front, the headline read, 'Serial Killer in Clarkbridge?'

"Are you kidding me?" Alan snatched the paper from John's hands. "Three old people die in Clarkbridge and everybody jumps on the Serial Killer train? I wonder if Chief Burleson has seen this."

"If not, you might want to let him know," John said.

Burleson walked by with a coffee in hand. "I told you the people in Clarkbridge were scared." The Chief pulled the paper from Alan's hands, tossed it in the trashcan, and walked away.

"Was that him?" John asked.

Alan nodded.

"Maybe today isn't the best day to meet him. He looks pissed."

"You're probably right."

Cooper Forbes stood next to the entrance to the department speaking with a man in a dark suit. The man folded his umbrella and shook off the excess water. Cooper pointed to John and Alan. The man nodded and headed in their direction, umbrella tucked under his arm.

He held his hand out toward Alan. "Captain Reeves, I presume?"

"I am. And you are?"

"Dr. Russell Holbrook."

Meeting

John held out his hand to Russell. "Dr. Holbrook. John Reeves. The quiet guy standing here is my brother." He nodded to Alan, normally so sure of himself, standing speechless.

"A pleasure to meet you as well."

Alan gained his composure and held his hand out to the seat next to John. "Please, have a seat." He gave his head an almost imperceptible shake. They both sat.

"What can I do for you today, Dr. Holbrook?" Alan asked.

"I read this morning's Clarkbridge Clipper and saw that another patient of mine had passed away."

"Dr. Tolman was your patient?" John asked.

"He was." Russell nodded. "I'm not sure if you've heard of me or not, but I am a psychiatrist. I have an office over in Millstead, but that is only part of my business. I also work as a consultant on occasion. In this scenario, I thought it best that I present myself to you and offer my services. Though a small department, Clarkbridge Police Department is renowned for their capabilities, so I thought it only a matter of time before I was contacted."

"And why would we contact you?" Alan said.

"Were you not?"

It was like watching a tennis match. John's head swung back and forth, anxious to see what happened next. This guy was the only connection they'd found to multiple deaths. He wanted to jump in, but didn't want to step on Alan's toes after recently regaining his trust.

"We were." Alan crossed his arms. "But how would you know that?"

"Let's be honest, Captain Reeves. I enjoy watching the crime and psychology television shows as much as the next man. My name was found at two of the scenes, and I'm their psychiatrist. Regardless of the reason, any investigation would require you to contact me, if only to inquire on my whereabouts during said murders."

John couldn't hold back anymore. "Who said they were murders?" Alan's eyes bored into him. "And how did you know your name was found at two of the scenes?"

Russell leaned his thin frame forward, pulled the paper from the trash, and tossed it on the desk. "The Clarkbridge Clipper."

A smile came to Alan's face as he leaned back in his chair. "Let's start over, Dr. Holbrook. Sorry about the questions. Our father was a police officer. His teaching worked better than even he realized. I thank you for your offer as a consultant, but I need to run it by Chief Burleson." Alan nodded toward the newspaper on his desk. "And the way things are going, I'm sure he won't mind a little extra help. Before any of that though, we need to get your official statement."

Of course, Burleson will let him help. He's our only possible suspect, John thought.

"Completely understandable, Captain Reeves," Russell said.

"Please, just Alan."

Russell nodded and straightened his Windsor knotted tie. Alan pulled a stack of papers from his desk and set to filling in the information.

John pointed to the paperwork on Alan's desk. "That will only take a moment. Standard procedure and all that. You don't mind if I sit in on this, do you? I'm a private investigator working for Leslie Fincham and Kandi Krogman."

Alan looked up. "John, let's get this statement out of the way before we speak any more of the investigation."

"What I meant to say is that you don't need to worry about saying anything in front of me."

"Nor would I for any reason, John. I have nothing to hide. I am simply here because three of my patients have died in the past month."

Alan looked up again.

Russell went on. "That is not something a psychiatrist likes to hear. It's bad for business as you can imagine."

"Three patients?" Alan asked.

"Yes. You did know all three were my patients didn't you?"

Alan shook his head.

"Oh, dear. Well, let's see—"

"One moment, Doctor Holbrook," Alan said. "With the city this nervous after the serial murder article this morning, it's best if we take a seat in one of the back rooms. Keep from prying ears. You don't mind, do you?"

"Not at all."

The three men stood. Alan gestured toward a door on the far side of room. The sign on the front read 'Interview Room Two.'

They stepped into the windowless room. Doctor Holbrook sat on one side of the long table, John and Alan the other.

"John," Alan said. "Although you're part of this case, you're still under certain restrictions. While you may sit in during the questioning, you will not be a part of it."

John nodded. Alan was good at this whole police officer thing when he wanted to be. The rigidity in his voice made John want to do what he said. He'd have to discuss these restrictions. Taking a backseat wasn't something he was used to.

John glanced to Holbrook. The man sat calm and reserved, glancing back and forth between John and his brother. If he were in the same situation, he wasn't sure he could stay as calm as this guy was.

Alan spoke to Holbrook. "I'll ask a few questions. Please answer to the best of your ability. When we're finished, feel free to add whatever you'd like. Until that point, just answer the questions I ask and no more."

"Yes, Captain Reeves." Russell nodded and placed his elbows on the table.

"I'll start with what you said at my desk. You mentioned three patients?"

"Yes. Douglas Fincham, Lonny Krogman, and Doctor Tolman were all patients of mine at one time."

Alan wrote in the folder he'd brought. Not looking up, he asked, "And where were you last night at ten in the evening?"

Russell leaned back, crossing his arms and looking to the side.

"This is part of the reason I came in when I did." He released a long drawn out sigh and looked back to Alan. "You see, I spent last night with my secretary. When I read the newspaper this morning, I knew it was only a matter of time before you would need my statement. I didn't want my evenings with Mrs. Hodge to wind up in the paper as well."

"Mrs. Hodge?"

"Yes, Mary Hodge. She's been my personal assistant at the Holbrook Center for just over a year."

"Are you married Doctor Holbrook?" Alan said.

"I'm not. But Mary is and has been for ten years. You can see why I didn't want this brought into the public eye. Like the deaths of three of my patients, having an affair with a married woman is bad for business."

Alan nodded. "Are you saying Mrs. Hodge wouldn't be willing to make a statement as to your whereabouts last night?"

"Not at all. I'm sure she would. I hoped you would show me a little professional kindness and speak with her at my office."

Alan paused. "I'll take that into consideration, Doctor Holbrook. As long as you're as up front with the rest of the questions as you have been so far, I may be able to help you out. I just want to find out what happened to these men."

"As do I," Russell said. "Last evening I arrived at Mary's house a little after eight. Her husband is a truck driver, and he left around seven. Mary and I were together until two in the morning. She will confirm everything I've said."

"And you were in her home the entire time?"

Russell cleared his throat. "We were in her bedroom the entire time."

Alan spent another fifteen minutes asking questions about Doctor Holbrook's whereabouts on the nights of the other deaths. Two of the nights, he was with Mary. The night of Fincham's death, he was out of state on a consulting job. John was impressed the man had a girlfriend in her late twenties since he looked to be in his mid-forties. John had been with his share of younger women in the past, but he wondered if the women Russell had been with were enamored with his profession more than the man himself. The man was professional in every way, down to the suit he wore. The rain he'd walked through on his way into the station hadn't even wrinkled it.

When they finished the interview, Alan told Russell he'd recommend to Burleson they let him join the investigation, and that his psychological background would be helpful if indeed there was a connection between the men.

Doctor Holbrook said his goodbyes, opened his black umbrella, and headed out into the rain once more.

"What do you think?" John said.

"Squeaky clean," Alan responded.

John had thought the same thing until he heard the words uttered by his brother. The same words Rachel had used, and she was rarely mistaken. The man sounded sincere, even looked so, yet he was a psychiatrist, and a good one at that. He probably knew more about body language and voice inflections and everything else to do with interrogations than John and Alan put together.

Nobody is squeaky clean. He needed to check in with Rachel again, see if her digging was fruitful.

"There's something I want you to see," Alan said, heading toward the back hallway.

"What is it?" John said following.

"See for yourself. Forensics found it taped to the bottom of a drawer in Dr. Tolman's desk."

10. g Tum-mo

Russell's Abilities

"Hey, Alan. Chuck Parrish's office is still on Saturn, right?" John said into the phone. Alan had called and asked him to meet with Charlie Parrish.

"Same place, John."

"Be there in a minute." He was a half-mile away.

Lena had been dressed and ready to leave for another tennis rendezvous before John finished the morning phone call with Alan. They shared a five-minute make out session, and then she left without saying when they'd see each other again. He'd always wanted a girl like Lena: independent enough to enjoy their time together and no need for updates on his every move. The strange part was he found himself hoping she'd call.

The second night with Lena had been as pleasant as the first. John had to admit, he liked the girl. Besides having an amazing body, she was fun, and not just in bed. Three days had passed since their first midnight encounter. Yesterday, she stopped into his office and asked if he had plans for the evening. He'd grilled steaks while she stayed in the kitchen and mashed red skin potatoes and fried some fresh garden squash. They finished dinner, watched an old horror movie, and spent the next three hours exercising in the bedroom. He hadn't had that much fun since... Kelly, his ex-fiancée.

John pulled into the medical examiner's parking lot. Dr. Holbrook's silver Audi rolled to a stop next to John's Wrangler. Holbrook slid from his sleek car and waited for John by his door.

"Good morning, Dr. Holbrook," John said, closing the Jeep door behind him.

"You can call me Russell, John. We work together now."

John nodded and started toward the office where Alan would already be. He was always early.

"So, Russell, why are you here? If you don't mind me asking."

"No, not at all. Alan called and asked that I be here this morning. I've explained to Mary that Chief Burleson accepted me as a Clarkbridge Police Department consultant, and that any of Alan's or the Chief's calls take priority over everything else."

John held open the glass double-doors for Russell. "Well, Alan has a reason for everything he does, even if he doesn't share."

"Sounds like an intelligent man."

Russell stopped at the reception desk where an attractive, petite woman greeted them with a pleasant smile. John was so drawn to her smile that at first he didn't notice she only had a thin layer of blond peach fuzz on her head.

Her eyes went to a note on her desk. "Dr. Holbrook and Mr. Reeves?"

"That's us," John said. "I'm Mr. Reeves—John, and this is Dr. Holbrook." He gestured to Russell in his perfectly tailored dusky gray suit. John glanced down at his own outfit: khaki shorts and flip-flops. *Hopefully there isn't a dress code.*

Russell held his hand out to the clerk. "Please, call me Russell."

"Okay, Russell," she said, shaking his hand. "I'm Laura. Mr. Parrish is just down the hall, room three." She pointed down the short hallway to her right.

John took a few steps toward the room, but paused when he saw Russell hadn't moved. He'd leaned over the receptionist's desk with a look of... *what? Caring? Genuine concern?* John couldn't tell.

"Laura?" Russell said, his voice quiet, pleasant.

"Yes?" Laura answered, just as hushed.

"How long have you been in remission?"

John almost interrupted. *Why the hell would he ask something so personal? He doesn't even know her.*

A tear formed in the corner of Laura's eye. "It will be two months tomorrow." Her cheeks flushed, but John didn't think it was anger. Russell nodded and brushed away the tear that had fallen to her cheek. This woman he'd never met opened up to him in less than a minute— and about her sickness.

Unbelievable.

Russell's eyes went to the hair just beginning to grow on Laura's head and then back to her eyes. "You are beautiful, Laura. Utterly beautiful. Don't let the sorrow overcome your vitality. You're amazing on the inside as well as out. You will conquer this, but you must believe it."

Tears brimmed in her eyes. She turned away from Russell and lowered her head. He used a finger to lift her chin and gaze back to his.

"I meant every word I said, Laura."

She nodded.

He reached inside his suit coat, pulled out a card, and handed it to her. "If you ever just need to talk, please call. No matter the time. I'll be available. You're worth it."

She nodded again, cradling the card with both hands as if it were her lifeline. "Thank you, Russell."

Holbrook straightened. "You're welcome, Laura. I look forward to your call." He gave her a wink and walked to John's side.

John started toward room three. Russell followed, a smile just touching the corners of his mouth.

Where does he come up with that stuff?

A few feet before the door to room three, John shook his head and turned to the psychiatrist, crossing his arms. "Okay, Russell," he said just above a whisper. "What in hell happened back there?" John nodded toward the front desk.

"What do you mean?"

"What do I mean? How did you do that? How did you know she wouldn't freak out when you asked about her sickness? And what about other women? Or did it only work with her because she used to be sick?"

Russell's lips parted into a grin. "That's a lot of questions, John." He laughed. "It's all a matter of mindfulness. Keeping your mind open to your surroundings."

"Now I'm more confused."

"I'm surprised. You seem to have a knack for body language and the like. You don't have a background in psychology?"

John shook his head. "Not at all. The closest I came to earning a degree was all the crap my dad taught us about being a cop."

Russell squinted, studying John. He nodded. "There's more to you than we see on the outside. Though I doubt it was the Marine Corp that made you this way." He paused again. He gestured over his shoulder to Laura. "It was in her eyes, the slight wrinkles forming at the corners. She's much too young to have wrinkles yet, at least for being a non-smoker."

John's brows shot up. "A non-smoker? And how do you know that?"

"Her fingers would have been stained yellow, the skin on her upper lip thinned. It's not just that. The way she held her shoulders, she holds a tremendous weight. It wouldn't surprise me if she had or has a loved one with cancer as well. The cuffs of her jacket were frayed along the bottom, her finger nails cut short. Both possible signs of stress. The arms of her office chair were torn, too. You can learn a lot about a person by observing."

This guy is great. "That so?"

Russell nodded.

"What can you tell me about me?"

Russell's eyes went to the door. "Should we keep your brother waiting?"

"He won't mind. He's used to me being late. Just give me a little."

Russell nodded, his hand going to his chin as he looked John up and down. "Your military training goes beyond the Marines. Something happened to you when you were a child to make you this way. I'm guessing you spent some time as a mercenary as well."

John realized his mouth hung open. He snapped it shut.

"People look up to you, a natural leader. But you've never felt comfortable in your own skin. Probably moved around a lot. Spent time in multiple short-term relationships. Wait." He paused, leaning closer.

John looked down and wiped at his shirt.

"You can't wipe that away, John," Russell said. "You hold a pain deep inside, deeper even than the pain Laura hides. It hurts. Even now. It's a part of you, driving you in ways even you don't understand."

"Okay," John said. "You're freaking me out. You sound like a fortune-teller. Maybe we should go in now?"

"I apologize. Making you uncomfortable wasn't my intention. I've done this a long time, over twenty years. It's my life's work, and it was the same for my father." He reached into his jacket pulling out another card. "The same goes for you. If you ever want to talk."

"Thanks, Doc. But this head case can handle his own problems." John reached to the knob and opened the door, letting the fluorescent light spill to the floor in the hallway.

From behind him, Russell said, "I have no doubt you can."

g - Tum-mo

Rita drummed her fingers on her belt. "Is John always late?"

Alan smiled. "Most of the time."

John stepped into the room looking decidedly uncomfortable. He kept glancing over his shoulder to Russell Holbrook.

"Thanks for coming, both of you." Alan shook Russell's hand and gestured to Rita. "This is my partner, Officer Vasquez." He turned to Charlie. "This is the medical examiner, Dr. Charlie Parrish. He's responsible for the autopsy reports on all three vics. He's completed Dr. Tolman's report and wanted us to be here in person. And before you ask why, I don't know. He wouldn't say."

"Sorry about that, Alan," Charlie said. "No reason to repeat myself. It's odd enough as it is. Having all of you here to ask questions was the best idea."

"This is all of us," Alan said. "Go ahead and start whenever you're ready." Charlie was an oddball at times and liked to overstep his boundaries, but no doubt, he was good at what he did.

"Where's the body?" John glanced around the room.

Charlie held up a folder. "Everything we need is in here. I've taken plenty of pictures if you feel the need to look. But first, I just ask for you to bear with me. Now, I'm listing Dr. Tolman's cause of death as unknown, but it appears it was a suicide."

"What!" Alan cut in. "No way, Charlie. You can't tell me this guy broke his own bones. It was hard enough to buy Krogman doing himself in, but this is just impossible."

"Tell me about it," Charlie mumbled, shaking his head. He pulled his shoulders back and cleared his throat. "Let me tell you what I know. I'll leave it up to you to figure out how it's possible. Other than the two bruises on his abdomen, the only injuries he has are the fractures and some lacerations caused by the bones penetrating the skin.

cold, they were able to dry the sheets using only their body heat."

"No way," Rita said.

Russell laughed. "Yes way. Multiple other cases have been studied and proved accurate. I think maybe that's what happened here."

"You think Dr. Tolman was a Tibetan monk?" John said.

"Of course not, John. I told you I don't know how, but at least we know it is possible for him to do this on his own."

"I'll definitely have to look into it," Charlie said. "It's a long shot, but at this point, it's the closest thing we have to an explanation."

Alan stepped forward to look closer at the photos. "Dr. Tolman used the power of his mind, to what? Just shatter his bones?"

Russell came to the table as well. "I'm not so sure he could just make them shatter. But I can see him increasing the tensile strength of his muscles to such a degree to make this possible. Similar to the way a mother, weighing not much more than a hundred pounds, can lift a two thousand pound car from her child."

"So," Rita said, "who volunteers to tell Chief Burleson a group of wannabe Tibetan monks are killing themselves all across Clarkbridge?"

Back To Krogman's

"What are we doing here at three in the morning, John?" Eddy held his flashlight aimed toward the entrance to Krogman's Tubing. "And won't Alan be pissed? I thought this was the reason you two had the argument the other day."

"He won't be pissed when I tell him what I find." John used his pocketknife to cut the new tape across the door. *I have to ask Alan for my own roll of police tape.*

Eddy's head swiveled side to side as he searched for would be pursuers. Not that he'd see anything in the pitch-black night.

"How do you know you'll find something?" Eddy said. "You didn't before."

"Sometimes it takes a few days for what you see to sink in." John pulled the door open and turned to face Eddy. "And three in the morning is when it came to me. Hand me my flashlight, and let's go."

Eddy followed John into the building.

"They ah... they cleaned everything up, right?"

"For the most part," John said. The steps creaked as they moved up the stairwell. "They couldn't quite get the blood stains out of the floor, but everything else is spotless."

John opened the door to the Krogman living room, only the flashlights allowing them to see. "Back here, in the bedroom," John said.

"Wait."

John turned back and shined the flashlight at Eddy's chest. His friend wore a burgundy sweater and blue jeans.

"What is it, Eddy? And why do you look like you're dressed for dinner?"

Eddy looked to his sweater and shrugged. "I get cold at night."

"It's like eighty degrees out."

"Who cares what I dress like? At least, eighty percent of my wardrobe doesn't consist of khakis and flip-flops," Eddy said.

"Touché."

"Anyway, I've been meaning to ask you something."

"Right now?"

"Why not right now?"

"I don't know," John said. "Maybe because we're in the middle of some dead guy's living room?"

"Just listen a minute. I don't normally ask you personal questions, but I've been thinking about something."

John waited for him to go on.

"It's just, you're not a quitter. In fact, you tend to always go too far. That's part of the reason I've always got along with you. Even when we were kids, you—"

"Out with it, man," John said.

"Why were you going to leave? Clarkbridge, I mean. You said you were straightening out, calming down. Moving to Clarkbridge and working with me was supposed to help you with that, but one argument with Alan and you were ready to hightail it out of here."

John sighed. "Isn't it enough that I'm still here?" He turned his flashlight back toward the bedroom and began moving again. "Come on, let's talk while we search."

Eddy followed, his light shining back and forth around the living room.

"I meant it when I said I'm glad you're back, John. I think it's good for you. For my kids, too. They love you like family."

John opened the top drawer of the Krogman's dresser. Something was in their bedroom. Something that didn't belong, he just couldn't remember what.

"I love your kids, too. What's that have to do with my leaving?"

Eddy's light stopped moving as he shined it on John. "I want you to stay. Whatever your reasoning was for going, I want to make sure it doesn't happen again."

John turned from the dresser. Eddy's light shined right in his eyes.

"Down." John gestured for Eddy to lower the light. "Not in the eyes, keep it on the torso."

The light went to his stomach.

John let out a sigh. "You want to know why I was going to leave?"

Eddy nodded, his flashlight bobbing up and down.

"Because Alan didn't want me here."

"But—"

"I know that doesn't seem like a big deal, but it is to me. I spent too much of my life competing with Alan when we were kids. I didn't realize he looked at it as a competition to see who the better son was. I think being adopted affected him more than he let on. Anyway, Clarkbridge is his hometown. I know it's mine as well, but not in the same way. He's built a life here, people respect him." John looked to the floor. "He deserves that respect more than I ever will. He's a good man. I didn't want to take any of that away from him."

Eddy stepped close and put his hand on John's shoulder. "You're a good man too, John. I know there are some things you haven't told me about your time overseas, but you don't have to. I've known you practically my whole life. Besides, if the kiddos love you, you can't be all that bad."

"Thanks, Eddy." John raised his flashlight and moved toward the hanging closet. "I'm glad you don't ask about this crap all the time."

Eddy laughed. "You could probably use a little more emotion in your life. That's pretty cool you were willing to leave because of Alan. I guess I only thought of me. Maybe you did grow up. A little anyway."

John shined the light into Eddy's eyes on purpose. "Watch it. This emotional guy can still kick your ass." He lowered the flashlight, shining it on the bed stand. "That's it!"

Eddy jumped. "What?"

John walked to the bed stand and yanked the drawer open. A King James Bible slid to the front. He picked the tome up and held it out for Eddy to see.

"A Bible?" Eddy said. "We came back to the Krogman's for a Bible?"

"Look deeper, Eddy. You think Kandi and Lonny are the Bible thumping type?" He held the book by the front and back cover, the pages fanning out beneath. He gave it a shake. A piece of paper slid from the pages onto the bed.

"What is that?" Eddy shined his light on the small white square sitting on the Krogman's unmade bed.

John kneeled and picked the paper up. It wasn't paper at all, but a Polaroid. The same picture Alan had shown him the day before. He held it up for Eddy to see.

Eddy bent over and squinted. "Is that your dad? Wait, that's Doug, Lonny, and Dr. Tolman with your dad."

John slid the picture into his back pocket. "It sure is, Eddy. Alan's going to want to see this."

11. The Trots

The Trots

Alan stuffed the bundle of overflowing Kleenex into his trashcan, grabbed the straps of the trash bag, and lifted it free. He sneezed before he could tie the bag shut and spilled a few of the phlegm-filled tissues onto the floor by his desk.

Chief Burleson stood behind him. "It's times like these I wish you weren't so damn bullheaded."

Alan lifted his eyes to the Chief. Wetness tickled the insides of his right nostril. He quickly grabbed a tissue and covered his nose to keep snot from pouring out. The Chief blurred through Alan's watery eyes. "Sorry, Chief." He sounded like Kermit the Frog. "With a few of the guys still on vacation, I thought it best if I came in."

The Chief retreated a step, as if the extra distance would keep the germs away. "Cooper called and asked to pick up a shift today. How about we just let him take over for you? It wouldn't hurt Rita to work with somebody else anyway." Chief Burleson paused and turned to the empty desk Rita shared with Sergeant Shaw. "Is she in yet?"

"There she is now." Alan dropped the used tissue into the trash and grabbed a fresh one. He plopped down into his seat.

Boy, I bet you'll really impress Rita today, Alan.

Rita and Cooper walked in from the garage.

"Afternoon, Chief." Cooper nodded to Burleson. His eyes fell to Alan. "Whoa, Captain. You look like shit."

Alan held the tissue over his nose as if suffering a nosebleed. He might as well have.

This damn thing needs an off switch. "Just think, Coop. I only look like this when I'm sick. You have to deal with it all the time."

Rita giggled and Chief Burleson held a grin of his own.

"Enough," the Chief said. "Coop, you're with Rita today. Alan, just go home, get some rest."

"You mind if I stay for a bit and finish up this paperwork?"

"Fine." He pointed to Alan's nose. "Just keep that thing plugged up long enough to get it done."

Alan nodded.

"Alrighty, let's go, Rita." Cooper headed back toward the garage.

"Get better, Alan." Rita spoke loud enough for Cooper to hear. "Not sure how long I can handle being around this goon."

"Real funny, Rita," Cooper called over his shoulder.

She gave Alan and the Chief a smile before following Cooper toward the garage.

Chief Burleson turned to Alan. "What do you think?"

Alan paused. "What do you mean?"

"She's got a great ass, doesn't she?"

Alan's throat constricted to the size of a pencil.

Chief Burleson laughed. "What do you think I mean? How's she doing out there? You think she's going to stay in Clarkbridge awhile?"

Alan coughed uncontrollably. He'd almost blown it again. He and Chief Burleson had been friends for years; he should expect that kind of humor. He cupped his mouth until the coughing fit ended. "Sorry about that, Chief. Rita's still doing great." He coughed again. "I think she'll be here for a good long while."

"Good to hear. I like her. She fits in." He shook his head. "You better hustle up with that paperwork. I don't want you making anybody else sick."

Chief Burleson turned and called to Lori for a cup of coffee on the way to his office. She stood by her desk bent over the fax machine outside the Chief's office. A sheet fell from the machine. She caught it and looked up at Alan. She darted around her desk and scurried up to him. He wished he had half the woman's daily energy. He never saw her take a sip of coffee, but she moved as if fueled by half a dozen shots of espresso.

"Hey there, Alan. This just came in for you." She dropped the paper on his desk and sped back to the break room.

Alan squinted at the photo she left, a copy of the picture the Chief had shared with him from Tolman's Chiropractic, the one with his father and the three dead men. John had scribbled a note at the bottom.

"Holy shit." The words came out before Alan could stop them. He jogged to the Chief's office. He rushed in, not thinking to knock. "Chief, you need to take a look at this."

Burleson turned. He held his hand out. The taste of bile flooded Alan's mouth. His stomach heaved. Barf poured onto the floor. The Chief hopped back, and the vomit just missed his shoes.

"What in the hell, Alan? Really?"

Embarrassed, Alan wiped at the remnants of breakfast dripping from his chin and mouth. "Sorry, Chief. I'm not sure where that came from."

"From your mouth, I'd say. Head to the restroom and get cleaned up. I'll have Lori take care of this." He held the back of his hand to his mouth and paused. He let out a huff, and grabbed the fax. "What is this?"

Alan didn't reply; he bolted for the restroom. His body wasn't finished revolting. The door slammed against the wall as he flew into the bathroom. He slid across the floor and just made it to the trashcan before throwing up again.

What the hell? So much for this being a cold.

His gut gurgling and cramping, he barely made it to the toilet in time. He held on to the trashcan with and pulled it into the stall with him. The seconds stretched into minutes as he sat there, losing it from both ends.

"Alan?" The Chief's voice echoed off the bathroom walls. "How you doing, buddy? Um... never mind, stupid question. Anyway, I have this stuff my wife gave me. I don't remember what it's called. I tore the label off. But it's for times like this you could say."

The Chief's hand appeared under the stall holding a dark blue bottle.

"Just take a swig or two. I know it helps me. When you're finished, come on back to the office. And bring that trashcan with you just in case."

Another half hour passed before Alan could stand. *I don't think my body has anything left to lose.* On wobbly legs, he lurched back to the Chief's office, trashcan in hand. The door stood open. *Probably airing it out.*

"Hey, Chief." The garbled words burned his constricted throat with each syllable.

Chief Burleson looked up from his desk. "I'd tell you to take a seat, but you just do whatever you need. Did that stuff work?"

Alan nodded and moved to put the bottle on the Chief's desk.

Burleson held up a hand. "Why don't you just hold on to that. I'll have the wife pick up more if I need it." He still held the fax Alan had given him. "Is this real? Or is your brother pulling some kind of hoax?"

Alan dropped into the seat in front of the Chief's desk, stomach still rumbling. "John wouldn't joke about something like this. It must be real."

"And he found it at Krogman's? How could we have missed this?"

"It wouldn't have stood out as something too out of the ordinary." Alan belched and quickly pulled the trashcan close.

The Chief turned his head.

"I'm okay. False alarm." Alan let go of the trashcan and hugged his stomach. "Why would anybody attach any significance to a picture of the house's owner? Plus, John's note said he found it tucked inside a Bible in the Krogman's nightstand."

The Chief turned back and nodded. "Why don't you head home now. Don't worry about the paperwork."

The police scanner on the table behind the Chief beeped, and Cooper's voice bellowed from the speakers.

"Shots fired, shots fired! 10-17, shots fired! Need backup at 4296 Pandora Lane."

"Rita!" Alan leaped to his feet and started for the door.

The Chief's hand clamped down on his arm. "You aren't going anywhere, Alan. Either take a seat, or head home. You won't do us any good like this."

Apex

"Thanks for meeting up with me, Russell." John took a swig of Guinness and wiped foam from his lip. "Tell me how you pulled that stunt with the medical examiner's clerk earlier. Seriously, how did you know she wouldn't freak out? I mean, come on. You didn't even know her. Normally, when you talk to somebody about their sickness, especially the big C, they don't want anything to do with you."

Russell Holbrook sipped his own stout. He set the frosted glass on the bar. "It's my pleasure, John. I don't mind the occasional consumption of spirits. As for your question, think about it. You have military training. Were you as capable as you are now just out of boot camp?"

They were only a couple pints in, but John's concentration already lacked. "You're telling me it's instinct? When I'm under fire, I react, and that training comes into play. Talking to a woman isn't exactly like being shot at."

Holbrook lifted his glass and poured salt onto the wet napkin. "To some it is. We're all animals of instinct. You, probably more than most."

John swiveled his stool to peer at the dance floor behind them. Sweaty college kids milled in what might have been construed as dancing but looked a whole lot more like dry-humping. "You come here often? I didn't picture you as the college crowd type."

Holbrook followed John's stare. "This place? Apex isn't normally like this. You picked a bad night to ask me for a drink. It's college night; the only night college kids can afford the drinks here."

A lanky kid dressed in ripped blue jeans and a black hoodie dipped the girl he danced with. The dip went a little too far and they both fell to the floor, giving John a good belly laugh.

"As long as they have Guinness on tap, I'm good." John finished the rest of his beer and called the bartender over.

The clean-cut kid behind the bar wiped his hands on the towel at his waist. "Another Guinness?"

"Sure thing." John squinted at the bartender's nametag. "Thanks, Patrick. And grab another for my friend here."

Holbrook held his hand up. "Thanks, John. But this will be my last. I have work tonight and in the morning as well."

"Me too." John raised his freshly poured brew. Flashing strobe lights from the dance floor reflected from the glass. "Too bad you worked in Detroit today, we could have met closer to home. Snark's has great drink specials. Especially for old friends of the owner."

He perused Holbrook's slate gray suit and buttoned collar. *How can a man enjoy a relaxing brew with his tie still done up tight?*

"I don't believe I've had the pleasure of entertaining guests at Snark's."

John let out a hearty laugh. "I wouldn't plan on entertaining anybody there, unless it involves seeing how many nights in a row you can drink there without getting in a fight." He wondered again about Holbrook's suit. "How do you stay so prim and proper? We're drinking at a bar, and you look like you could walk into a business meeting any minute now."

Holbrook glanced down at his suit and adjusted his tie. "I'm a professional, John. In my line of work, the patients must view me as such. They often share their darkest secrets. If I don't look as I do, they don't trust me. They must know I'm there for them as a psychiatrist doing everything in my power to help them. I must look the part."

He might be on to something. John hadn't really thought about the way he dressed affecting anybody. It's not like he went around in sweat pants and a t-shirt, but his leather jacket and blue jeans or khakis might put some people off. He'd have to pay more attention when he met clients for Eddy.

"Tell me about your patients, Russell." John lowered his glass to the bar.

Holbrook raised an eyebrow.

"I don't mean all your patients. The ones in the case. Not all the crazy stuff, just their personalities. You actually think they could have committed suicide? Or do you believe what the Clarkbridge Clipper said?"

Holbrook lowered his drink to the salt covered napkin and pivoted on his stool to face John. He steepled his fingers and placed his elbows on his lap. "Is it okay that we discuss this in a public place?"

John waved his hand. "Apex? Don't worry about it. The music is loud enough; nobody can hear a thing we say. Besides, they're just college kids. They're thinking about their next lay, not what some old fogies talk about at the bar."

Russell nodded. "That's the tough part about the field of psychology. Very rarely do we actually deal in solid facts. It's more about the increased or decreased likelihood of a specific behavior occurring, and what the possible motives behind those behaviors are."

"You're losing me, Dr. Holbrook. Do you think they killed themselves?"

Holbrook's brow furrowed. He nodded and looked into John's eyes. "I believe they could have, yes. Is it a certainty? Not by any means. I can't discuss the details of our sessions, but I can point out what you already know. All were war veterans. You can draw your own conclusions from your experiences in the military. They were all elderly, and only one was happily married."

"What does elderly have to do with it? The old people I know spend their time chatting about the old days, about their great accomplishments, and about how horrible kids are these days."

"In the United States, around one in ten people over the age of sixty-five are considered to have major depression. The suicide rates are almost thirty percent higher in their age group."

John shook his head. "We need to spend more time together, Russell. Not so I can learn about old people and their depression, but for this wealth of information you can call on at any time. It's like having a walking encyclopedia at my side."

Holbrook laughed and swallowed a belt of his Guinness. He placed the glass on the bar and pulled out his wallet. "I thank you for the compliment, but it's really only about the field of psychology. My father was a strict man. It was his belief we should pursue our dreams with the utmost care and drive."

"Don't worry about the drinks." John grabbed Russell's arm. "Your money isn't any good when you're drinking with me. You're too fun." John waved the bartender over for the bill. "You're not leaving yet, are you? We barely have these pints started."

"No, not yet." Holbrook put his wallet back into his suit coat. "Just planning ahead." He squinted and looked down at the bar. "Looks like you missed a call."

John's eyes followed Holbrook's to his cell phone on the bar. A red light blinked on top.

"Let me get that for you." Holbrook reached for John's phone. His hand bumped his drink and sent the thick black liquid spilling across the bar. It washed over John's phone and onto his lap.

John stood quickly, allowing most of the precious drink to pour on the floor, but much still splashed onto his pants.

"What a mess." Russell grabbed a pile of napkins and wiped at the counter and John's phone. "I'm sorry about that, John. Must be these drinks are affecting me more than I thought. I don't drink much. Why don't you go to the bathroom, get cleaned up. I'll take care of this."

The crotch of John's pants had a growing wet spot. He laughed. "Wow. I haven't seen a spill like that in a long time, Russell. Maybe next time we stick to light beer."

He laughed again and headed toward the bathroom. Russell gave an embarrassed wave and continued wiping at the bar.

The bathroom walls had almost as many mirrors as the rest of the bar. *Like I really want to look at every other guy taking a wiz.*

The paper towels didn't help much, but his pants looked a little better. He tossed the used towel into the trashcan and caught himself on the counter. He'd lost his balance. *Whoa, take her easy, John.* He should have eaten a heavier lunch. Six pints was his usual limit when he had to drive, but he'd best call it a night if he wanted to make it home safe.

He opened the thick oak door, the only color in the bathroom not white, silver, or mirrored. He stepped into the lounge. The table to his right grew in size. His hands caught the edge just before he smashed his head. He'd been falling and not even realized it. Two college girls seated at the table gave him dirty looks and turned away.

"Sorry about that," he mumbled. *Maybe I'm coming down with something.*

He pulled himself upright and looked to the bar. He hoped Holbrook would agree to drive him home. Two kids sat in their seats at the bar. He searched the rest of the stools. Holbrook was gone.

"That's kind of rude," John muttered to himself. His words were garbled, as if he spoke through a long hollow tube. The room spun, the edges of his vision darkened. "Oh shit."

12. Sibling Rivalry

The Tortilla Factory

Alan stared at the rhythmic blinking lights on the police scanner. His .40 Smith and Wesson sat in its holster on the kitchen table in front of him. The roiling in his stomach had calmed, but sweat continued to roll from his brow, dripping onto his clasped hands. His knees wouldn't stop bouncing.

The scanner hadn't made a peep in over an hour. He'd rushed home from the department only to catch the tail end of Chief Burleson's communications. The Chief and four other Clarkbridge squad cars were on the scene. Two County cops showed up soon after.

Alan grabbed the silver mug from the table and took a long pull. He needed the caffeine to stay prepared.

Prepared for what? For them to call me in?

As if Burleson would let him come in after Alan had showed off his bathroom skills earlier; though, he felt better now. He considered contacting the Chief anyway.

The mug almost tipped over when he sat it down. He caught it with his free hand. "Damn it, Alan. Calm down." He wondered what Rita would say if she knew he talked to himself.

Why the hell aren't they calling me?

Burleson would be too busy, but Coop should have at least texted him, let him know how Rita faired.

"Fuck this." Alan grabbed his weapon from the table. The holster caught on his mug and spilled the rest of his coffee.

Chief Burleson couldn't keep him away. Rita was his partner. His lover, even if nobody knew. He left the coffee and locked the door behind him. He ran to his truck and deposited his weapon in the passenger seat.

Alan pulled into the dirt parking lot of an old tortilla chip factory. The normally ten-minute ride took just over five. Blue and red lights flashed across his vision from the cruisers. The factory had been closed earlier in the summer due to bankruptcy. A few lights still shined from the two-story building.

Alan parked away from the cruisers and approached on foot, strapping his holster in place. Burleson stood by his squad car speaking with one of the county cops.

The Chief turned to Alan and shook his head. He started toward Alan, hands held palms out in front of him. "No. You need to leave, Alan. Right now."

"I can't, Chief. Rita's my partner. I—" Alan let the Chief stop him in place.

"Listen to me, Alan." The Chief moved his head in front of Alan's vision every time he tried to catch a glimpse of the other officers at the factory. "You shouldn't be here. You're not on duty. How'd you get past the road block?"

"It's me. You really think Clark would stop me? Come on, Paul. I won't get in anybody's way." He didn't actually expect Chief Burleson to let him on the scene, but he had to try. The Chief would be held responsible if anybody found out an off-duty cop entered an area under investigation.

"You call me Chief when we're in public. You know that." Burleson sighed and shook his head. "I know about you and Rita."

Alan stopped trying to look around his friend and instead concentrated on his face. "What do you mean?"

The Chief smiled. "You're letting your love for her cloud your mind. How couldn't I know? We've been friends for years, Alan. The only other woman you've looked at like that is Allie."

Alan's gaze dropped to his feet. "Just tell me what happened. Is Rita okay?"

Burleson removed his hands from Alan's shoulders and turned to face the factory. "We don't know. We can't find her."

"What do you mean you can't find her?" Alan took a step toward the building.

Burleson caught his arm. "Just wait. We have a perimeter set up with the help of the county officers. Four cops are inside looking, but I doubt they'll find anything. You saw Clark on 5th with the road block; Gibbs is up on Kline Avenue. One of the county boys is already canvasing the homes nearby." The county cop still by the Chief's squad car crossed his arms, looking impatient. "Listen, Cooper is in his cruiser. He's pretty shaken up. Go have a word with him; he could use a friend right now. He wasn't made for this. Go see what you can find out. If any of the county cops ask, you're a friend and Coop's psychologist."

Alan nodded.

Burleson stepped over to the county cop and put his hand on the rotund man's shoulder, leading him in the direction of the factory and away from his car. Alan anxiously walked to the Chief's car, a black Chevy Impala, the rotating beacon sent blue and red over the scene. He fought the urge to run. Cooper sat in the passenger seat, head held in his hands.

Alan opened the door and sat in the driver's seat. Cooper shot a quick glance at Alan and quickly returned his face to his hands.

"You okay, Coop?"

He nodded.

"Can you tell me what happened? Where Rita is?" He tried to sound soothing. Cooper had always been sensitive and was almost always assigned with another cop. The life of a traffic cop fit him better, but they weren't used in Clarkbridge.

Cooper leaned back and turned to Alan, his eyes puffy and bloodshot. "I'm so sorry, Alan. There wasn't anything I could do." He took a sudden breath, and another, shoulders heaving.

Alan placed a hand on Cooper's shoulder and faked a disarming smile. "Just calm down, Coop. I'm here now. Everything will turn out fine. Just tell me what happened."

Cooper's hands went back to his temples. He closed his eyes and rocked in his seat. "We...we..."

Alan patted him on the shoulder again. "Breathe, Coop. Take your time." *Damn it, Coop. Give me something!*

The distraught cop heaved in a deep breath and let it out slowly. "We had a call for domestic violence. We knew it had to be some kind of joke. Why would there be domestic violence at a tortilla factory?"

Alan patted him again. "What happened after you responded to the call?"

Cooper took another deep breath and let it out in a sigh, still rocking. "We started toward the factory—" He paused and cleared his throat. "We were almost there when I realized I forgot to radio in about responding to the call. Rita told me to go do it. So I went... to the car. I had the CB mic in my hand when I heard gunshots. I couldn't tell where they came from at first. I looked at Rita through the windshield. She glanced at me once and unholstered her weapon. She ran inside without me." Cooper whimpered.

Alan forced himself to keep from running into the factory. "Why did she go in without you? Did she enter through the front door? How many gunshots were there? How many more after she entered?" The questions rolled from his mouth.

Cooper rocked faster. "I don't know, Alan. I just don't know. It all happened so fast."

Alan held in a growl. "So she went in without you. What happened then?"

It took a moment for Cooper to respond. He whimpered again before going on. "That's when I radioed in the 10-17. I didn't wait for a response, though. I went in after her. Through the front door right there." He pointed. "Into the main office. The lights were all on, but I couldn't hear anything." He sat back and looked Alan in the eyes. "I searched for her, Alan. I looked everywhere in that damn building, but she was gone."

"She couldn't have just disappeared."

"I know. But she did. I couldn't find any sign of her. That's when everybody else showed up. We set up the perimeter as soon as we could, and they've been searching ever since."

Alan shook his head. "It doesn't make any sense. Where could she have gone?"

Coopers words came out as a wail. "I don't know, Alan. I told you, I couldn't find her anywhere."

"I know, Coop. I was talking to myself. Trying to figure this all out." *Why would Rita go in without Cooper?* It was probably the domestic violence call. She must have thought there was some truth to it. *Damn it, Rita. Why'd you have to be the hero?* Dumb question. He knew the answer. Because that's who she is. "You gonna be alright in here by yourself, Coop?"

He nodded and continued rocking.

Alan climbed from the Chief's car and dialed Rita's cell. A ring chimed from the direction of the factory. He took a step toward the building but thought better of it. Tillman, the cop closest to the factory entrance, tilted his head to the side. He bent over behind a small spruce. When he straightened, he held a glowing cell phone in his hand.

"Hey, Chief." Tillman held the phone out toward Burleson.

They quickly bagged the phone as evidence. Alan didn't know what he'd expected, but he couldn't think of anything else to do. At least the adrenaline seemed to have calmed his earlier sickness.

He waved to Burleson and headed back to his truck. Staying at the scene wasn't helping. Emotions rolled through his mind unchecked. They needed to be calmed, his mind cleared. Rita needed his help. He sat in his truck, debating whether he should leave. The soft rumble soothed him somewhat.

What am I supposed to do, Rita? Where did you go? John! His hands weren't tied like Alan's. He and Eddy might be able to help; though, he didn't see how.

He dialed John's cell. It rang twice and went to voicemail. "John, it's Alan. Call me when you get this. Something's happened to Rita. I... need your help. I don't know what to do. Please, just call me when you get this."

Morning After

Alan had barely slept when he came home from the factory. What little sleep he got, terrorized him. Rita ran off with another man. Rita was kidnapped and tortured. The Tortilla factory blew up with her inside.

He leaned on the edge of his bed, cell phone in hand. He'd hoped he'd come home to Rita in his room, or sipping a drink at the kitchen table. Maybe a note on the refrigerator's dry erase board explaining where she'd gone. Nothing. Not even a phone call.

The phone in his hands vibrated. He leapt up and grabbed his gun from the bed stand.

"Calm down, you fool," he mumbled to himself. The caller ID showed Cooper's number. "What is it, Coop? Did they find Rita?"

"Hey, Alan. Um... no. But I have something I need to tell you. Don't get mad. It probably doesn't mean anything, but I thought I should let you know." Cooper sighed into the phone and paused.

"Out with it."

"It's just... I saw John with Rita two nights ago. I didn't really think anything about it until now."

"What?" *He must be mistaken.* Rita and John had only spoken the few times when Alan had been there. "What do you mean you saw him with her? Where?"

Cooper cleared his throat. "Him and Rita, along with some other girl were drinking together at Chester's."

"Chester's? That little pub over in Millstead?" Alan and a few of the guys had shared drinks at the Hawaiian themed hole-in-the-wall pub years ago. He remembered thinking the theme an odd one for Michigan.

"Yeah. Me and Gibbs stopped over there to watch the game. They were all over each other. I assumed she would have said something since she was your partner."

Alan's heart tried to beat out of his chest. "All over each other? There's no way, Coop. I know Rita. She would have told me."

"So she didn't?" Cooper sighed. "I'm sorry, Alan. I'm sure them being together has nothing to do with last night. I just thought you should know before I said anything to the Chief. I don't want to, but you know, he wants to know anything we know."

"Wait, you think my brother had something to do with this?"

"No, no, Alan. That's not what I'm saying. It's just," Cooper sighed again. "Rita and that other girl were all over him. Hugging on him, doing shots together. It just seemed weird to see her that way. Rita's always so uptight, er... professional."

It was Alan's turn to sigh. "Tell Burleson whatever you know. I'll look into it. I'm sure it's nothing, but at least then I can feel like I'm doing something." He walked to the kitchen, the coffee calling his name. "Thanks for giving me the heads up, Cooper. Better to hear it from you than the alternative. Let the Chief know I'll talk to him."

"Will do. We're all still on top of this, Alan. We'll get Rita back; you can count on it."

Alan poured the filtered water into the coffee maker. John hadn't returned his call from the previous night. So much for him being more responsible.

The only time I need him and he can't even call back.

Hangover

Cartoons? I don't remember turning on any cartoons.

John's eyes squinted open. His television played a rerun of some cat and mouse cartoon from twenty years ago. He blinked.

He leapt from bed and pulled his Glock from the bed stand. His eyes shot from side to side, taking in his bedroom. He dropped to the floor. Nobody under his bed or behind the recliner in the corner. Glad to have the cartoons blaring on his television, he tip-toed to the kitchen doorway and peaked around the corner. Empty. Staying as silent as possible, easy to do when barefoot, he checked the rest of his apartment.

Nobody.

John walked back to his bedroom and sat the Glock on the bed stand. "What in hell happened last night?" Sitting on the edge of his bed, he scrubbed his eyes with his palms.

Where the hell did I go last night? And why am I so groggy?

He hissed. "I drank at the Apex." As if only the thought could bring it on, a pounding began in his temples and worked its way back to his neck.

Holbrook!

He'd been drinking with Russell. The last thing he remembered was cleaning the spilled beer from his pants in the horribly decorated bathroom.

A beep came from the kitchen. *Voicemail.* He flipped the switch on the television and began a pot of coffee before checking his messages. He'd need a pot or two to make it through the day.

John laughed as he measured the scoops of coffee. "What the hell, John? You can't handle your alcohol anymore?" He couldn't remember the last time he'd blacked out. Even more embarrassing was that he did it in front of his new co-worker. He sighed and set the coffee to brewing.

The chair at his kitchen table groaned as he flopped down and picked up his phone. "At least your new friend was nice enough to make sure you didn't lose your phone." He dialed his voicemail. The first message came from Eddy. He asked John if he'd heard from Lena. "I'm not her baby sitter, Eddy." He pressed the nine to delete and waited for the next message. Alan's voice came on the line. A burst of adrenaline flew through John's body, almost obliterating the hangover. *Rita's gone?*

A knock came at his door. He pressed the quick dial button to call Alan. The linoleum floor drew the warmth from his bare feet as he stepped to the door. He pulled it open to see Alan standing in the hall.

"Oh." John removed the phone from his ear and hung up. "I was just calling you. Something happened to Rita?"

"Can I come in, John?"

"C'mon in. Man, you look like shit. Just started a pot of coffee and you look like you could use some."

Alan nodded and sat at the table.

John noticed the bulge under his brother's jacket. "When did you start wearing your piece when you're off-duty?"

Alan dismissed his comment with a wave. He rubbed at his bloodshot eyes with his palms, much the way John had moments before. "So you got my message then?" he mumbled.

"I did." John closed the door and walked to the cupboard. "You guys know anything yet?"

Alan took his hands from his face but kept his eyes on the table in front of him. "They tried triangulating her mobile phone signal at first, but her cell was left at the scene. The 911 call they responded to couldn't be traced of course. In other words, nothing."

John pulled two cups from the cupboard and sat one in front of Alan. "Creamer?"

Alan nodded.

"How'd it happen? Aren't you usually on patrol with her?" Alan's jaw muscles tightened and his brows lowered. *Wrong question.* "I mean... look, Alan, I know you two had something going on. I'm just surprised you wouldn't know what happened."

Alan's face relaxed and he turned his body to face John by the fridge. "What do you mean we had something going on?"

John pulled the creamer from the fridge door and sat it on the table between them. "Come on, Alan. You've never been a good liar. I knew you had the hots for her the first time I met her at Krogman's."

"If so many damn people knew, why the hell were we hiding it?"

"Because that's who you are, Alan. Although I don't see anything wrong with it, it's probably that whole interoffice romance bullshit that kept you from telling me. I figured it wasn't any of my business."

Alan's muscles tensed as he pushed from the chair, one hand flying toward John's neck. John could stop him, but this was his brother. Alan caught his throat and pushed him against the wall, knocking the old plastic clock to the floor.

"If you knew we were a couple, why in hell did you go out with her behind my back?" The words came out through clenched teeth.

You're lucky you're my brother, John thought. Even with his head still pounding, it would be easy to drop his brother where he stood; a knee to the groin, an open palm to the pressure point by his jugular. Instead, he slowly brought his hand up and tapped it on Alan's wrist.

Alan's eyes went to his hand at John's throat. He relaxed the grip and turned away. "I'm sorry, John. I... I'm just so angry. Just tell me you didn't go out with Rita." His shoulders slumped.

John rubbed his throat, tamping down his anger. "I don't know what you're talking about. The only woman I've been with since coming home is Lena."

"Lena?" Alan's shoulders still slouched, but he turned around and took his seat at the table again. "The girl working with Eddy Bailey?"

John inhaled a deep breath, savoring the smell of the freshly brewed coffee, and let it out slowly. "That's the one."

A small smile grew on Alan's face. "Isn't she only like eighteen?"

John brought the coffee pot to the table and filled their cups. "She's twenty-four. And why does that matter? Isn't Rita half your age?"

"Good point." Alan's smile disappeared. "Why would Coop make something like that up?"

"Cooper Forbes? That dweeb is still on the police force?"

"It's Corporal Forbes now. He's a good cop, John. He helps in his own way."

John thought he saw the hint of a smile. "Whatever you say. But why would he make the story up about me and Rita?" John poured cream into his cup and slid the container to Alan.

Alan picked it up and added his own. "I don't know, John. I can't put any of this together. Who would take her?"

"How do you know somebody took her? That she didn't just leave on her own?"

Alan shook his head. "Somebody had to have taken her. She wouldn't have left without telling me."

"You sure?"

Alan lowered his brows again.

John held his hands up. "Sorry, I said I knew you two were an item. I didn't say I knew how close."

"Trust me; she wouldn't have left." Alan's brow furrowed. He leaned his elbows on the table. "Look, John. I wouldn't ask if I didn't need you. Can you and Eddy help out on this one? I don't know if it will help, but there's only so much I can do."

John sat speechless. He gave his head a slight shake and sat back, crossing his arms. "Well damn, Alan. You love her."

Alan sputtered.

"That's great. I mean, it's horrible she's disappeared, but you really do love her. I wasn't sure if I'd ever say that about you again."

Alan gained his composure and let his shoulders fall loose. "That's beside the point. Will you help me?"

John couldn't help but smile. Allie's death had killed Alan's spirit, or so John thought. It felt like a horse kicked him in the gut. Here he was, smiling like an idiot, while his brother's love had disappeared, possibly been kidnapped.

"Of course I'll help you, Alan. Anything you need."

A quizzical look happened across Alan's face. He tilted his head to the side. "Where were you last night? Why didn't you return my call?"

"Oh man, I had a few drinks with Russell Holbrook on the north side of Detroit."

"You didn't call me back because you were drinking?"

"No, I actually blacked out for a bit. Russell and I were having this great conversation. Next thing I know the room does a loop-de-loop, and I spill my beer." John's eyes went to the stained kitchen table. "Or maybe he spilled? I don't remember." He looked back up to Alan. "Either way, I blacked out and he brought me home on his way back to Millstead. That or he called me a cab. I should give him a call."

"Why were you drinking with Holbrook?"

"Why not?" John polished off the rest of his coffee and poured more.

"You barely know the guy."

"Since when have I needed an excuse to pound a few Guinness?"

13. Through the Darkness

Back to the Factory

"Thanks for coming. Both of you. Let's get in out of the rain." Rings circled Alan's bloodshot eyes, shades darker than the day before.

You look like a zombie, John thought. He pulled his jacket tighter. "Burleson's okay with us being here?"

Alan paused at the entrance to the tortilla factory. "Yeah. He's the one who suggested you and Eddy come with me." Heavy rain splashed around them. "Officially, I'm on a leave of absence this week." Alan's words misted the air; it was chilly for July in Michigan. He lifted the police tape for John and Eddy to step under.

John pulled the door open and let Eddy through. The scent of baked corn wafted from inside. John pointed at the tape. "That reminds me. I don't suppose I could get a roll of that tape for myself?"

Alan rolled his eyes and stepped past.

"That's what I figured." John followed.

Dust littered the desks and paper was strewn across the floor. Ceiling lights flickered. A stack of computer monitors sat just inside the door.

"What's with the monitors?" Eddy used a finger to draw a line in the thick dust on one of the desks.

Alan squatted just inside, squinting at the floor. "They're being liquidated. There's supposed to be an auction next week for the office supplies and machinery." His lips curved into a tight smile. "The owner is pissed Chief Burleson made him delay it until next month." Alan crawled to the nearest desk, turned on his back, and slid beneath like a mechanic working on a car.

Eddy glanced at Alan. His eyebrows furrowed as he turned to John and mouthed, "Is he okay?" John smiled and nodded. Eddy shrugged and walked toward the rear of the office.

John squatted next to his brother. "Is there something in particular we should look for, Alan?"

"Anything, really."

"Hasn't forensics already combed the whole building?"

Alan slid from beneath the desk and held out his hand. John pulled him up. "They have, John. But if you remember, they missed the picture at the Krogman's." Alan dusted off his hands on his jacket and stepped to the next desk.

"You think this is related to the Krogman's?"

Alan shook his head before dropping to the floor and sliding under the second desk. "Not necessarily. The forensics team finds clues for us; finger prints, fibers, you know. But they aren't so good at catching something out of place, out of context. That's the real reason we're here. Burleson thinks they may have missed something we won't."

"Makes sense, I guess."

John walked to the rear of the office where Eddy flipped through a stack of papers on an office chair. "And what are you looking for?"

"Me?" Eddy paused.

"No. The other private investigator with us, the invisible one."

Eddy rolled his eyes and continued flipping through the papers. "I have no idea what I'm looking for. The way Alan searched beneath that desk tells me he's looking for anything. Something out of place."

They spent hours searching the office area. Alan crawled beneath every desk, pulled out every drawer, and looked in every stack of papers.

They moved on to the machines in back. With the goods removed, there wasn't much to search. One desk sat against the back wall, but was empty. Alan even took to looking inside some of the machinery.

John searched as well, but left most of it to Eddy and Alan. Detail work wasn't his style. Instead, he let his mind wander, running over the facts of the case. Not just Rita's disappearance, but the mysterious deaths as well. He sat at the single desk and pretended to look through the drawers while he ruminated.

The ring of a cell phone brought him out of his pondering. Alan pulled his head out of the machine he'd been searching and slid the cell from his pants pocket.

"Captain Reeves," he answered. His shoulders tightened. "But—" He closed his eyes tight and sighed. They opened and his shoulders slouched. "Okay, Chief. I'll be right in."

John left the desk and approached Alan as he climbed down from the tall machine. "What's up?"

Alan let out a low growl. "Chief Burleson wants me to come in for a consultation with Holbrook."

"We can stay. If there's anything to find, I'm sure Eddy will be the one to find it." His brother leapt the last few feet down to the floor and started toward the entrance. "Oh, and tell Russell thanks for the ride last night."

Alan waved over his shoulder and left.

Eddy leaned over the bright red railing surrounding the storage area on the upper level and called down to John. "Where's he going?"

John yelled up. "Police business."

His friend nodded and went back to studying the floor. John climbed the stairs to the storage area. Eddy lifted pieces of cardboard from the floor one by one.

"Anything?"

Eddy shook his head. "Nope. I'm not sure there would be anything up here anyway. If what Cooper said was true, there wouldn't have been enough time for Rita to get up here really. Unless whoever took her somehow hid in the factory while the police searched. Though I don't see how that would be possible with so few places to hide."

"If Alan thinks they missed something, they probably did. Just keep looking."

Eddy paused and looked back at John over his shoulder. A moment later, he continued his search of the cardboard on the floor. "So what's up with Lena anyway?"

John leaned on the railing with both hands, looking out over the open factory. "What do you mean?"

"First you two are banging like a couple of college kids, and then I don't hear from her for a week." Eddy's eyes never left the floor.

John's eyes widened, and he turned from the railing. "She told you about that?"

His friend's hand paused with a flattened cardboard box half lifted. "No. You just did."

"Well you sneaky shit."

Eddy stood and wiped his hands on his pants. "What can I say? You taught me well."

With a laugh, John clapped his friend's shoulder. "That I have. I need to take a piss." He took a few steps toward the stairs leading to the lower level and paused. He turned back around. "Wait. You haven't heard from Lena in a week?"

"No. Why?"

"I haven't either." John rubbed the stubble on his chin.

"Don't worry about it. She's a lot like you. Probably just pulling a disappearing act for a few days."

"She do that often?"

"On occasion."

John sighed. His eyes went to a stack of boxes in the corner. "You check those yet?" He pointed.

"Not yet. You want to help?"

"Maybe when I'm done in the bathroom."

John descended the steps and walked to the bathroom by the entrance to the office area. Eddy had already searched the room earlier and come out a little pale. The rest of the factory was fairly clean considering it had been closed for months, but the bathroom smelled of stale urine. John didn't want to guess what the stains on the toilet seat were from. He used a bundle of toilet paper to lift the seat.

His left hand went to the wall over the toilet. He closed his eyes and began to relieve himself. He imagined what it must be like for Alan right now. John pictured his ex-fiancée, Kelly, kidnapped and gagged. The one time she'd been in the hospital, he'd barely slept for days. He and Alan were alike in that regard. His stomach turned over. Killing anybody who took Kelly was the only answer. The law didn't matter in situations like this. To have somebody take a piece of you is unforgivable.

His father wouldn't like this train of thought. Ed Reeves would say something like, "Let justice serve its purpose, even if that justice is you." But there were no clues about Rita. Nothing. No note, no footprints, nowhere to lay the blame. Alan must be ready to explode. Chief Burleson probably sensed it when he suggested John and Eddy help out.

He's using us to keep an eye on him.

John opened his eyes and gave himself a shake. No reason to close the seat, he'd just waste more toilet paper touching it again. He stepped to the sink and turned on the tap. He paused as the cold water poured over his hands into the filthy sink. He spun back to the toilet. *Something out of place.* Alan's words echoed in his mind.

He turned the water off and squatted in front of the toilet, seat still up. Located in the midst of the stains on the very top of the toilet seat was a single large fingerprint, like a thumbprint. John held his hand in front of the print, positioning his thumb as if it was on the exact spot as the print. Somebody might have used their thumb to open or close the seat, but it didn't look quite right. The angle was off.

Maybe if I were putting the top back on the toilet tank and the seat was open?

Blood coursed through his veins as his heart beat doubled in pace. The top of the toilet tank had no smudges, no dust. He'd left his mechanic's gloves in his jeep so he grabbed more toilet paper and wrapped it around his fingers. He lifted the top of the tank and sat it on the floor, peering into the murky water. Nothing but rust and sediment. He depressed the toilet lever and kept his eye on the tank. Just as the flapper fell back into place to allow the water to refill, the ceiling light reflected from something moving beneath the sediment.

John yelled back through the door. "Eddy! Get your ass down here."

He turned back to the bathroom and searched for anything else out of place. A plastic trashcan sat pushed into the corner, empty except for the paper John had just tossed in. He tipped it over with his shoe to look at the bottom but saw nothing.

He heard Eddy's footfalls approaching. "Give me a pair of the latex gloves."

"You haven't worn them this whole time?"

"I didn't really touch anything important. Just give me a pair and quit your yapping."

Eddy gave John a dirty look and pulled a pair of the gloves from his jacket pocket. John snatched them from Eddy's hands, snapping them into place.

"Stand right here." John pointed to the side of the toilet closest to the handle.

Eddy's brows furrowed. His mouth hung open for a moment. "Wait. What are we doing? This bathroom is kind of small, John." His eyes went to the brown and black goo on the seat. He covered his mouth with his forearm. John barely heard his muffled words. "What is that?"

"Not now, Eddy. Just listen to me."

Eddy nodded and pulled his arm from his mouth. He held his breath and shuffled his way into the corner, keeping away from the seat.

"When I tell you, flush it and hold the handle down."

Eddy nodded.

John moved to the other side of the toilet closest to the sink. "Okay, now."

Eddy stretched his arm out as far as it would go and pushed the handle down with his pinky. The water in the bowl swirled as the tank water lowered. When the water was almost gone, John reached into the sediment where he saw the reflection moments before. He slid his fingers back and forth across the ceramic. Something slippery passed under his glove. He grasped the edge and lifted it from the tank. A thin plastic baggy.

"You can let go now."

Eddy quickly let go but stepped up next to John, apparently no longer worried about the grotesque toilet seat. "What is that?"

"I'm not sure. Turn on the sink."

Eddy turned on the water. John placed the baggy under the water and lightly scrubbed the reddish brown sediment. Slowly, a white piece of paper showed itself within the baggy. John pulled it from the sink and held it up between him and Eddy for a closer look.

He studied the baggy under the light. "It looks like a piece of paper." When Eddy didn't respond, he moved the baggy to the side. Eddy stared, his face white as the paper. "What is it, Eddy? Are you okay?"

His friend bent over. His shoulders heaved as he retched into the small pink trashcan.

John turned the baggy over. It wasn't a piece of paper, but a Polaroid. His father and the three dead men, beers in hand.

Three Man Consult

Alan knocked on Chief Burleson's closed office door. "Come on in, Captain Reeves."

The three men sitting before Chief Burleson's desk made the small office more cramped than usual. One of the men was so large he could have counted as three men.

"What's going on, Chief? I thought this was a consultation with Mr. Holbrook." Alan glanced to Holbrook in the middle seat and nodded.

Chief Burleson's slightly bloodshot eyes watched him. He didn't look as bad as Alan did himself, but it was obvious he hadn't slept much the night before either.

"I'd tell you to take a seat, but we're a little short at the moment."

Holbrook stood and gestured toward his chair. "Please, take a seat, Alan. You look like you could use it more than me."

Alan began to protest, but Chief Burleson cut in. "Just take the seat, Alan."

He stepped around the giant of a man to sit between him and Cooper Forbes. Holbrook leaned against the bookshelf, arms crossed.

Burleson let out a heavy sigh. "You know Doctor Holbrook and Corporal Forbes." He nodded to each in turn. His eyes settled on the man to Alan's right. "And this is Manny Rodriguez. They've brought something to my attention you should be aware of."

The giant man, Manny, crossed his arms and let out a harrumph. Cooper leaned forward with elbows on his knees, feet bouncing.

"All three of them? Does this have something to do with Coop supposedly seeing John and Rita at Chester's?"

"Manny and Doctor Holbrook saw them as well."

Alan leaned back in the folding chair. "I'm not so sure about that, Chief." He shook his head. "I spoke with John about it yesterday. He said he's never been anywhere with Rita."

"Then how do you explain three separate witnesses?"

Why is he calling them witnesses?

Chief Burleson continued. "I see by the look on your face you're not convinced. Doctor Holbrook, could you fill him in?"

Holbrook pulled away from the bookshelf and folded his hands together in front. "Well, the evening Corporal Forbes speaks of, I also visited Chester's for a drink. Mrs. Mary Hodge joined me as well. You remember her?"

Alan nodded. *He must not want Manny or Cooper to know about the affair. Maybe you shouldn't sleep with a married woman if you don't want people to know about it.*

"Mrs. Hodge and I occasionally stop at Chester's after a particularly long day of work. That night was no different. John sat in a corner booth with both Rita and another young woman. And you understand my situation with Mrs. Hodge. I didn't approach. Officer Forbes was there as well, at the bar. I recognized him from when I met you and John here at the station. When Mrs. Hodge left, Corporal Forbes and I struck up a short conversation. We both commented on how out of character Rita and John seemed to act."

Like you know anything about John or Rita. Holbrook had done nothing to question Alan's trust, but he must be making the story up. "And you just happened to hear Rita disappeared so you came to Burleson to tattle on my brother?" Alan knew he overstepped his bounds. His shoulders tightened with each word.

Chief Burleson raised his hands. "Now just calm down, Alan."

Holbrook looked to the Chief. "It's okay, Chief Burleson. Captain Reeves' logic is valid. May I continue?"

Burleson nodded.

Holbrook's eyes went back to Alan. "It does sound like an extraordinary set of circumstances, but you are reading too much into the details. Chief Burleson asked me to come in today for the consultation you mentioned. While we spoke, Corporal Forbes entered and asked for any news concerning Rita. I asked if the information pertained to our current investigation. They both said no, but out of curiosity, I asked how John handled things since they were an item."

Alan gritted his teeth. "They weren't an item."

"Chief Burleson asked why I said as much. That's when I told him about the evening at Chester's. Corporal Forbes confirmed my story."

"And what about you, Mr. Rodriguez?" Alan turned to Manny.

The giant man jumped at being addressed. The chair beneath him creaked. "Me. I, ah, I was there that night too. I didn't know nothin' was wrong until he asked me to come to the station." He pointed at Cooper.

Alan turned to Coop.

The buggy-eyed officer's feet quit bouncing. "If John said he wasn't there with Rita, I knew you wouldn't believe me, Alan. Manny is kind of... hard to miss." He shot an uneasy smile in Manny's direction. Manny rolled his eyes and looked away. "So I called Chester to see if he knew Manny's name. He did, so I looked up his number and asked if he'd come in to talk with Chief Burleson."

Alan stood, his chair slamming to the floor behind him. "Just hold on a minute." He rubbed at his brow and stepped behind Manny and Cooper. He turned to face the rest of the men in the office. "It just doesn't make any sense. Besides John being with Rita, I don't understand why you'd need a witness to prove you were right. Even if they were there, it's not like anything happened to make you think John had anything to do with Rita's disappearance."

Manny chimed in. "Actually, man, there kinda was."

Alan rolled his eyes. "Okay, Mr. Rodriguez, what is it you *think* you saw?"

Sweat broke out on Manny's forehead. "Not much, really. The two women got in a fight, yelling back and forth. Like a catfight, you know? The bartender said take it outside. I needed to get home. When I left, they all sat in a Jeep, still yelling like they was crazy."

"Horseshit!" Alan couldn't take it anymore. "If this is such a big deal, why in hell didn't you bring John in here too? We're doing all this talk behind his back. Let him at least defend himself."

Burleson stood and held his hands out in front again. "This is why I wanted you to take a seat, Alan. As you said, this doesn't mean anything. We need to find out who the other woman was and contact her."

"Oh." Cooper half raised his hand and quickly lowered it to his side. "I know who the other woman was, Chief. Manny recognized her."

Chief Burleson shook his head and looked to Manny. "Well?"

Manny let out a girlish giggle, strange to hear from such a large man. "Yeah. I remember her from when I was sent to jail for child support. I didn't know her name, but she was with the investigators, with the Eddy Bailey guy."

Cooper stood and stepped to the side of Burleson's desk, opposite of Holbrook. "I called Eddy a couple hours ago but he wasn't home. His wife, Sandra, recognized the description I gave her. She said it sounds like Helena Chandler. They call her Lena. I tried to contact her this morning too but she hasn't responded."

Lena? Alan shook his head. "Look, Chief. John is seeing this Lena girl, he told me as much yesterday, but there's no way he'd lie to me about this." He glanced back and forth between Holbrook and Cooper. "I don't want to cause any trouble with either of you, but I'd take John's word over anybody. He doesn't lie; he doesn't need to. Even when we were kids, he didn't lie. Drove us all crazy."

Holbrook leaned back against the bookshelf, the corners of his mouth turning up. "Everybody lies, Captain Reeves."

Chief Burleson's phone rang. "I need to take this. Everybody just be quiet a minute." He picked up the phone and put it to his ear. "Chief Burleson." His eyes went to Alan.

Adrenaline burst through Alan's body. What little energy he had in him grew ten-fold. *It has to be information about Rita, or he wouldn't have looked at me like that.*

"Thanks, Gibbs. I'll take care of it." Chief Burleson sat his phone back in its cradle. He paused and took a deep breath.

"What is it, Chief? Did they find Rita?" Alan hated the man for making him voice his concerns. *Why the hell doesn't he just say it?*

"They have a match for the print found at the tortilla factory. John Reeves."

Tunnel

Eddy finished puking in the trashcan and rolled over to sit on the cement bathroom floor. "That sucked."

"Tell me about it." John couldn't help but laugh at his tender friend. "If I have to see you throw up one more time I'm gonna be pissed."

"Sorry about that." Eddy ran his sleeve across his mouth and climbed to his feet. "What do you think it means?"

"It means you're a wuss."

"Real funny. I mean the photo."

John peered around the bathroom again. Closer this time. If there was a print and the picture, there had to be something more. The walls were solid, no cracks in the greenish blue eggshell paint. The solid cement floor left out any chance of a trapdoor. He looked to the ceiling. A drop ceiling like in the office area.

"Eddy, grab me a chair from the office."

Eddy's eyes followed John's to the ceiling. "You think there's something up there?"

"No. I want to sit down and relax awhile."

His friend's face flushed in the dim light of the bathroom.

"Sorry. You know how I get when somebody asks too many questions. Just grab me the chair and we can find out."

Eddy rushed from the bathroom.

Drop ceilings are typically only so many inches from the real ceiling above, meant to cover any pipes or electrical cables considered to be unsightly. He didn't know what to expect, but it was the only place they hadn't searched.

Eddy rolled a padded desk chair into the center of the bathroom.

"Hold on tight." John placed one foot on the chair and a hand on Eddy's shoulder. He pushed himself up on the chair until his head was inches from the yellowish ceiling.

The first panel lifted easily. He removed the piece and handed it down to Eddy. Dust coated John's shoulders. The chair wobbled. John caught his hand on the metal grid above him. "Take it easy, Eddy. This grid won't hold me."

"What am I supposed to do? Use my mind powers to lower the panel down?"

John laughed again and caught a piece of dust in his throat. He hacked a few times until it dislodged. "Just be careful." He moved his feet to the arms of the chair to lift him high enough to see above the panels. He pulled his flashlight from his jacket pocket and shined it through the dust and cobwebs.

"Nothing that way. Spin me around to face the other direction."

Eddy did as John said. When the chair came to a rest, he shined the light in the direction of the toilet over the drop ceiling.

"Well, no shit."

"What is it?" Eddy sounded like a little kid guessing what was in his Christmas present.

"I'm not sure, but it's no ordinary ceiling. There's a tunnel leading in the direction of the office area. Looks like it's a vent of some type."

"Why?"

John shined the light in Eddy's eyes. "How the hell am I supposed to know?"

Eddy waved his hands. "Get that light out of my eyes, you weirdo. I just figured you might know. You're the one that used to work construction."

John turned the light back toward the tunnel. His words came out as a whisper, his mind running in circles. "Residential construction, Eddy. A little different." He paused and looked down to his friend. "Push me over toward the toilet. I'll remove a couple more panels and check it out."

Eddy stared a moment. "Maybe we should call Alan first." His hands slapped around at his jacket, looking for his phone.

"That won't be necessary, Eddy. And get moving."

He rolled his eyes and put his hands on the chair, rolling it slowly toward the toilet.

"We're a part of this case too. Chief Burleson asked us here to help Alan out. If he didn't want us looking for evidence, he wouldn't have called us."

They came to the last panel directly above the toilet. John pulled it from the metal grid and handed it down to Eddy.

"Hold tight." John put the flashlight in his mouth and reached both hands up into the tunnel. He pulled himself into the tight crawl space. He called down to Eddy. "Somebody has definitely been through here recently. No cobwebs and there are scuff marks through the dust. I'm going to see where it goes."

Eddy sputtered from below. "But, wait a sec. What if… wait. Should I go with you?"

John pulled the flashlight from his mouth and shined it into the tunnel; it came to a corner ten feet ahead. "Nah, I'll be fine. Stay down below and see if you can follow me from down there. I'll call out." *As long as I'm the only one up here.*

The tunnel was just big enough to allow him to reach back to his ankle and remove the Glock from its holster. With the gun in one hand and the flashlight in the other, he crawled toward the corner ahead, stopping every time his cargo pant pockets caught on the seams holding the tunnel together.

He reached the corner and called out. "Eddy. Can you hear me?"

Though muffled, he heard his friend's voice coming from below. "Yeah, I can hear you. You sound like you're above the wall between the office and the work area."

Almost to the office area then.

He turned to the left, the only way the vent elbow allowed him to go. Up ahead, was another corner, only a few feet from the first. This one turned to the right. "Okay, I'm turning right now."

"We're in the office area now." Eddy sounded nervous.

Probably about to puke again.

It took him a few minutes to reach the next corner. The tunnel looked like a heavy-duty ventilation shaft. But if it was, it should have opened up over the bathroom and connected to a cooling or ventilation unit, not had the drop ceiling covering the entrance. The joints holding the shaft together jabbed him in the knees as he crawled. The next corner turned to the right. He shined his light ahead. The tunnel ended, but that didn't make any sense. He should still be over the office area.

"Where are we now, Eddy?"

"Um, right dead center in the middle of the office area. Are you turning again?"

"Yeah. Right."

"That takes you toward the entrance."

"Let's keep going." John shuffled, scooted, and crawled deeper into the tunnel. The knuckles on his left hand ached from the Glock pressing on them while he crawled. Sweat fell from the tip of his nose, leaving dark circles in the dust.

He finally reached the end of the tunnel. *No more turns, no latches, nothing.* "Where am I now?"

John barely heard Eddy's answer. "Hang on." He waited, about to call out when he heard Eddy again. His voice came from in front of him, the other side of where the vent looked to end. "Give it a push, John."

He crawled the final few feet and braced himself to give the end of the tunnel a mighty shove. He pushed with the hand holding his weapon. The end gave way too fast and he almost fell out, dropping the Glock in the process. He held the metal door open to see Eddy standing a ways below him outside, blocking his eyes from the rain.

Eddy bent over and picked up the gun. "Thanks. You're lucky this didn't go off and shoot me. Imagine explaining that to Sandra."

John laughed. "Why do you think I use a Glock, Eddy? They're safe. They don't fire when dropped."

His friend stepped away from the building, his head turned side to side. "No wonder they never found that tunnel."

John poked his head out from the building but didn't have a good view. "Why do you say that?"

"It looks just like any of the other exhaust fans on this side of the building." He pointed farther down the wall than John could see.

"I need to turn around so I can get out of here. Back up. I'm coming down."

It wasn't a long drop, but it was far enough he could break an ankle if he landed wrong. He turned the flashlight off and put it back in his pocket. The ventilation shaft went black. When situated with his feet facing the end of the tunnel, he pushed out with both feet. Flashing lights reflected off the metal walls around him.

What the hell?

His knees slipped on the rain water blowing in. He lost his balance and slid backward. His hands caught the very edge of the tunnel as the door slammed shut on his fingers. Eyes closed, he let go and hoped for the best. The ground met his back and slammed the air from his lungs.

It took him a moment to understand what had happened. He couldn't force in a breath. Rain pelted his face. He opened his eyes, blinking quickly to keep out the rain.

"Alan?"

Alan squatted next to him with his hand held out. "Get up, John. You okay?"

"I think so," John mumbled. With Alan's help, he pulled himself up and began wiping at the mud on his pants. Lights still flickered about him, red and blue. He paused and looked up. Two Clarkbridge police cars faced him, their headlights piercing his eyes, their beacons flashing. John turned to look behind him, up at the tunnel he fell from, and back to Alan. "What did I miss?"

He waited for Alan to smile, to tell him this was all a joke.

"I'm here to take you in, John."

John's laugh echoed off the factory wall behind him. Alan still didn't smile.

"Really?"

"Yes, really. You're under arrest in connection with the disappearance of Rita Vasquez." He held out a set of cuffs.

"You gotta be fucking kidding me."

14. The Station

Back to the Station

Through the mesh metal divider of the squad car, John watched Cooper rub his knees with the palms of his hands. The country music on the radio whispered just loud enough to hear over the rain pounding the roof and windshield.

John wondered what could have happened in the little time since Alan had left them to finish looking over the tortilla factory. He left for a consultation with Holbrook and Chief Burleson.

And why the hell are they bringing in Holbrook for Rita's case?

John looked to Alan in the driver's seat. "Are you going to tell me what's up? Or do I have to keep guessing?" He struggled against the cuffs already chafing his skin. Alan hadn't been gentle putting them on.

Alan glanced in the rearview mirror and back to the road. "I'm not at liberty to discuss the case with you, John." He let out a deep sigh. "Just be quiet until we get you to the station. You know the drill."

"Yeah. Cooper did a wonderful job reciting the Miranda rights."

Cooper's face flushed.

"Sorry, Coop. That wasn't very nice of me. I'm sure you only forgot your lines because you were arresting somebody you've known half your life. I can see how that would make you nervous."

Cooper remained silent, continuing his hand movements.

Alan growled. "Shut up, John. Wait until you have your lawyer."

John rolled his eyes and leaned back in the seat. "Sure. You know me. I'm great at keeping my mouth shut. Especially when I don't know what the hell is going on." John smiled and leaned forward again. "Did Eddy tell you what we found?"

Alan's brow lifted. "Other than the ventilation shaft? Not much. Why?"

Cooper cut in." Chief Burleson said not to talk to him, Alan."

"Shut up, Coop," Alan and John said at the same time.

John thought he saw the hint of a smile at the corner of Alan's mouth. Cooper crossed his arms and stared out the window.

"We'll be at the station in less than two minutes, John." Alan's voice took on a cop-like tone, all business. "Talk."

"Why don't you guess?"

"Don't give me that shit. Either you found something or you didn't. This isn't a game."

John began to lift his hands in apology but only succeeded at digging the cuffs into his wrists. "Okay, okay. Let's just say this time it wasn't hidden in a Bible."

Breaks screamed. John flew forward until his face pressed against the metal grate between the front and backseats. The squad car swerved to the side of the road and slid to a stop.

Alan's belt was off and he had turned in his seat before John slumped back into his own. "You found another photo? Tell me. Now!"

"We did. Eddy should still have it in his back pocket. You're taking him to the station too, right?"

His brother mumbled to himself as he pulled his seatbelt back on and veered the vehicle onto the road.

"Yes," Cooper spoke up. "We're taking Eddy to the station too, but for different reasons. Chief thought we should ask him a few questions." He slapped himself in the forehead. "Damn it, John. We're not supposed to talk about this. Please, just sit back and let us get back to the station."

Alan's face took on a determined set. From what John could see of his brother in the mirror, his jaw muscles flexed repeatedly and his brows caved inward. Alan stomped on the accelerator, throwing John and Coop back into their seats.

That a boy, John thought. *Remember what dad taught us. Concentrate on what you know. The other pieces will fall into place.*

Taking John In

Alan's mind swirled with possible scenarios. Why had they found the photo in the factory? Did it have something to do with Rita? Every time they found one of these photos in the past, a body had been found as well, mutilated or broken in some way. Why wasn't there a body at the factory? Had someone done the same to Rita?

He needed to get to the station, and fast. The sooner they analyzed the photo, the better. If Rita was in trouble... or worse. He couldn't think like this.

Focus on the facts.

Chief Burleson had told him to bring John in. His prints were at the factory, but it didn't make any sense. Nothing made sense. The photo. It meant something, and he'd find out what.

They came to a stop behind the station, the parking lot half-flooded from the downpour. Alan stared ahead through the pounding rain. Ideas flitted around at the edge of his thoughts, hinting at giving answers but never coming close enough. Everything weighed on him at once. His physical exhaustion, the emotional pain. All of it made concentrating nearly impossible.

"What are we waiting for, Alan?"

He ignored Cooper's question and glanced in the rearview mirror. John stared back. They held each other's gaze. "Get out."

Cooper spun in his seat to look at John. He turned back to Alan. "Me?"

"Just get out, Coop. We'll be in right behind you."

Cooper looked as though he were about to argue, but instead, he groaned and climbed out into the deluge. He jogged into the station, holding his jacket pulled up over his head.

Alan opened his door and climbed from the cruiser. He stepped to the rear door and opened it for John. His brother slid from the center seat and out of the car, hands cuffed tightly behind his back.

Alan closed the door and stepped behind him. "This is probably the only chance I'll have to say this. I know you didn't take Rita. I don't know what the hell you were doing in the factory, or why you'd be stupid enough to leave a fingerprint, but there has to be a reason." He grabbed John by the cuffs and gave him a shove toward the department door. "There are cameras inside and out. Be careful what you say. We'll get you out of this."

John nodded. Alan expected more from his brother. Questions maybe, or at least a sarcastic comment.

How can he stay so calm?

They paused at the back entrance by the garage where Alan typed in the security code. When it unlatched, he pulled it open and led John to the holding area where he used a second code to open the cell. Alan unlatched the cuffs and closed the door behind John.

John rubbed at his wrists and sat on the concrete bench.

Now, to find Eddy and that damn picture. Turning, he bumped into Cooper.

"Uh, Alan? Chief Burleson wants to see you." Cooper jabbed a thumb over his shoulder. They started toward the Chief's office when Cooper mumbled, "Mayor Snively is in there with him. They both look pissed."

Alan paused and ran a hand through his rain-soaked hair. "Just what I need."

Lori Browning, the Chief's assistant, bustled around the corner ahead of him. "Hey, Alan. Chief Burleson—"

"I know, Lori." Alan waved. "Coop already told me."

The mousy woman loitered for a moment before disappearing back around the corner.

Alan took the final few steps to Chief Burleson's door and heaved a heavy sigh, savoring the few quiet moments he had to himself. Mayor Snively didn't show up to the station for social reasons.

He opened the office door. Mayor Anna Snively faced him from Chief Burleson's chair where she sat with her hands steepled.

Not a good sign.

The chief stood to the side with arms crossed, leaning against the bookshelf, much as Holbrook had hours before. With eyebrows drawn down and mouth pinched, he held back whatever he wanted to say.

"Captain Alan Reeves," Mayor Snively intoned. "Please, take a seat." She gestured to the chairs in front of the Chief's desk.

He chose the chair in the middle and sat down slowly. *Snively.* The name, and the Mayor herself, reminded him of a snake. No doubt, she worked harder than any other mayor Clarkbridge had seen, but Alan questioned her motives. She often played up her role as the first female mayor-elect in Clarkbridge. That was all fine and well, but she felt the need to prove her effectiveness on a regular basis.

If she'd heard about his foray into the Tortilla factory crime scene, he and Burleson were in for a lashing. "To what do I owe the privilege, Mayor Snively?" He'd kill her with kindness.

She leaned forward on the desk, fingers separated and spread wide. "Enough with the bullshit, already. Tell me your side of the story."

"My side of the story?" He put on his most innocent look and wiped at a stray drop of rainwater dribbling down his forehead.

Snively pounded the desk and stood. An obvious attempt to tower over Alan despite her barely five-foot tall frame. "I said enough! I don't know what you two think it means to be a police officer in Clarkbridge, but the game ends now." She slammed her hands on the desk again for emphasis.

Chief Burleson's face reddened with each word. "Anna, just calm down a minute."

The Mayor pointed at Burleson. She shook her head and continued her stare at Alan. She brought her hand back down to the desk and inhaled a deep breath. "Tell me what you thought you could accomplish by portraying a psychologist at Beal Tortilla. Did you think you could just waltz onto a crime scene while off-duty and not have me hear about it?"

Alan's gaze wilted to the floor a moment before again meeting the Mayor's glare. "It was strictly my fault. I allowed my emotions to get in the way of my job. Chief Burleson had nothing to do with it."

She sat back down, resuming the steepled hand look. "That's funny. County Officer Mair said the Chief physically stopped you before letting you pass. Do you mean to tell me Officer Mair lied?"

"No, I mean yes." *Kindness, Alan. Kindness.* "No, Officer Mair didn't lie, but Chief Burleson didn't really physically stop me either."

"So Paul didn't... let's see here..." Mayor Snively lifted a paper from the desk and held it between them."... approach and hold you back with both hands on your shoulders?" She let the paper fall back to the desk.

"He did, but he wasn't really holding me back. We've worked together a long time. He knew I'd be distraught, and it was his way of calming me."

Her lips curled into a sneer. "He knew you were distraught, but didn't have the wherewithal to keep an emotionally unstable officer from a crime scene? A scene the officer had connections with?" She shook her head. "I don't know, Captain Reeves. Sounds as though Chief Burleson had a lot to do with it."

"Look, I admit, he probably shouldn't have allowed me in there."

Mayor Snively sniffed and crossed her arms.

"But he was busy with the other officers. He couldn't have known the case would take these turns. Clarkbridge is a small town. Things like this don't happen. We were short-staffed, and he knew Cooper and I had a past together. He was right to let me in. I was the only one Cooper would open up to."

She leaned forward and picked up another stack of papers. "Yes, Corporal Cooper Forbes. It says here he completely fell apart." She threw the stack down in front of Alan. "I think the city of Clarkbridge needs to take a look at the hiring practices of our local police department."

Chief Burleson cut in. "Now, you just wait a minute. I told you we made some mistakes, and I take complete responsibility, but you don't come in here questioning the reliability of my officers. They're my team and they're good at what they do. You have no right."

Mayor Snively gave Burleson a dismissive wave. "Don't get your panties in a bunch, Paul. I'm not here to question your authority." Her face became more stern, all edges and tight angles. "What I am here to do is see that this fraternal attitude ends now. I shouldn't have to hear from the county sheriff that a Clarkbridge officer visited a scene while off duty. The repercussions go way beyond what happened with Cooper. Don't you both realize we could lose a prosecution on a technicality because of this?" She shook her head and turned to Alan. "You are off the Rita Vasquez case."

"Wait, I—"

She cut him off. "I don't want to hear it. You're lucky I don't have you removed from the force. As of now, you are on administrative leave. You will take one week to consider your actions. Before you leave, I expect a full report about what was said and done at the Beal Tortilla factory. And I expect the same for today's debacle with your brother. You both treated these situations as though they were your own personal game to play. If I hear one more word about anything like this happening again, you can kiss your careers goodbye. Understood?"

"Understood," Alan mumbled.

"Understood," Chief Burleson chimed in. "But I hope you realize the restrictions you're putting on us. Alan is my strongest asset. Not only does he have the most experience, he's the only one who has *any* experience with kidnapping cases. Removing him will not only hurt the department, but it severely depreciates the likelihood of finding Officer Vasquez."

Mayor Snively closed her eyes a moment. When she looked up, her eyes held the most passion Alan had seen from her in the three years she'd been mayor. "Getting Officer Vasquez back to us unharmed is of our utmost concern." The passion disappeared as she looked at Alan. "Fine. You can stay on the case, but only as a consultant. I want you nowhere near the tortilla factory again, or any other scenes that may come into play."

Alan quickly nodded. He hoped his shock at hearing her admit defeat, if even in this small way, didn't show. *She'd do anything to keep up the tough-girl persona.*

She gathered the papers from Burleson's desk and stormed from the office without another word.

The Chief worked his way behind the desk and into his chair. "Man, I hate that woman. But she's right you know."

"I'm sorry I got you into this, Chief."

"You know as well as I that you didn't get me into this. I could have made different decisions, but what's done is done. Let's concentrate on getting Rita back. At Mayor Snively's request, I've contacted the FBI field office in Detroit to make them aware of our current situation.

They've offered any help we need, but I'd rather keep this within our department. For now, at least."

Alan stood. "Did we keep Eddy Bailey here for questioning?"

"We did. Cooper should be with him now."

"He and John found another photo, Chief. The same as all the others."

Burleson's mouth fell open. "You've gotta be shitting me."

The Savior

The Savior untied the strings behind his back and pulled the apron over his head, tossing it on the cement floor next to him. "So it's done then?"

"It is. They took John Reeves in for questioning yesterday. He won't be released for a few days at least, if at all. They'll likely keep him longer with Alan off the case."

"Good. Are you prepared for the work I've assigned you for tomorrow?"

"About that. I'm not sure it's the best idea."

The Savior raised an eyebrow.

"I mean it's a great idea, but I don't know if I should be the one doing it. Isn't there somebody else? I don't feel comfortable since I know them, you know?"

The muscles in the Savior's cheek twitched. "You dare question me? Think of all I've done for you, for your family. Do you really want to go back to the way things were before? I can do that you know. Remove the changes we've made."

"No! Please, I mean. I'll do it. I just thought I should let you know how I feel."

"I don't care how you feel. Your emotions mean nothing." The Savior's shoulders relaxed. He smiled. "Come with me. And bring that apron."

The skinny man picked up the apron and quickly followed.

"I don't like having to explain myself to the likes of you, but if it will make tomorrow go by easier, then so be it." They walked down the hallway toward the red door, the red room, the Savior leading the way. "When you question my commands, I question your loyalty."

"Forgive me, Savior. It won't happen again. I know... I appreciate everything you've done for me and my family."

The Savior removed the steel latch from the red room's door and entered. "Tell me again, how many children do you have?"

"Two, my Savior."

"A boy and a girl?" He grabbed the apron from the skinny man's hands and threw it back over his head. He tied the strings in back.

"Yes. My boy, Ben, is seven, and Olivia is four."

"Wonderful ages. They learn so much during their formative years. Are they happy?"

"I'd like to think so. I mean, yes. They're happy. We're all happy."

The Savior pointed to the stainless-steel desk holding his tools. "Grab me a scalpel please."

The skinny man hurried to the desk and carefully lifted the scalpel by its handle. "Shouldn't I be wearing gloves?"

"No need. Infection isn't a possibility." The savior leaned over the woman on the table in front of him and ran his fingers in a tight circle over her belly.

The skinny man handed over the scalpel and stepped back.

The Savior glanced up from the woman. "What's the matter? You seem more skittish than usual."

"Just nervous about tomorrow is all."

"To be expected, I suppose."

The Savior leaned forward and sliced into the skin of the woman's belly, cutting a precise circle, following the line he'd traced with his fingers. Blood pooled in her belly button. The woman's chest moved up and down faster as her breathing increased, but she stayed unconscious.

The Savior continued. "If you're all so happy, then why would it even cross your mind to take it away from them? Because that is precisely what would happen if you disobeyed me."

The skinny man held his arm over his mouth to keep from vomiting as he watched the Savior delight in his work. "I would never disobey."

"See that you don't." The Savior wiped the bloody blade on his apron and slid his free hand into the woman's stomach cavity. "Come over here and feel this. Absolutely amazing."

15. Release and Death

Getting Out

John removed the last peeling from his orange and tossed it in the paper baggy next to him on the concrete bench. The same breakfast three days in a row. One orange, two kiddy-sized Cheerio boxes, and a twelve-ounce carton of milk. The Clarkbridge holding cell wasn't exactly a five-star hotel, but would it kill them to throw in an apple once in a while?

He stood and walked to the cell door. Through the small glass window, he saw Lori pounding away at her keyboard. Every few minutes, an officer walked by, and once an hour, one checked in to see if their only prisoner needed anything. He'd read the three golf magazines they gave him from front to back at least five times already. Since he'd been shot in the chest on a par-three course a year ago, golf wasn't exactly his favorite sport.

The only time they'd interrogated him was the first day. The questions revolved around how he'd found the photo with Eddy and where he'd been every night for the past week. He still didn't know how the hell one of his prints had ended up at the tortilla factory. The building hadn't been there last time he lived in Clarkbridge. He hadn't known it existed until Alan told him about Rita's disappearance.

And where was Alan? Chief Burleson had been lenient from the beginning with his brother's participation in the investigations. Alan could have at least stopped in to let him know what was happening with the cases.

John went over the facts in his mind. Why was the old photo of their father and the three dead men found at the factory? The three other occasions they were found involved some old guy who'd found a creative way to take his own life. Yet Rita was nowhere to be found.

Corporal Gibbs stepped to the window. John moved back and sat next to the golf magazines and his peel-filled paper baggy.

The door opened and Gibbs poked his head around the corner. "You need anything, John?"

John wadded the paper baggy into a tight ball and tossed it to the officer. "A bigger breakfast?"

Gibbs covered his laugh with a fake cough. "Ahem. Nothing then?"

"Just wondering when they're going to question me again so I can get out of here."

"I think they're preparing now." Gibbs glanced behind. He brought his head back inside the door. "Yeah, Chief Burleson just gave me the nod. You ready?"

"Hang on, let me grab all my belongings." John made a show of searching the small cell. "Oh wait, I don't have any."

Gibbs rolled his eyes and walked the rest of the way into the cell. His voice took on the professional tone every officer had when speaking with a suspect. "Okay, Mr. Reeves. Please turn around and place your hands behind your back.

John did as told. "Really? Cuffs again? Maybe I should have taken your advice and contacted my lawyer after all."

"I, um... I can ask the Chief if..."

John glanced over his shoulder at the clearly uncomfortable cop. "Don't worry about it, Gibbs. I was just kidding. Throw those babies on me." He wiggled his hands.

Chief Burleson's form appeared in the doorway. "No need for those, Gibbs."

John turned to face the chief. "You trust me now, Chief?"

Burleson's face held the same grumpy look it had sported since Alan brought John in. "I wouldn't go so far as that. Your lawyer called and suggested we let you go."

Gibbs latched the cuffs to his belt and squeezed past Burleson and back into the station.

John smiled. "So a single thumbprint isn't enough to hold somebody for kidnapping? Wow, I'm surprised." *Shit, John. Shut your mouth.* His anger seethed at having been held in the first place. Staying a few more days for police harassment didn't sound like much fun.

The Chief's brow drew down further. "Don't make me regret this, John. The only reason I give a shit what your lawyer says is because of Alan. Just be sure to stay close to Clarkbridge. Alan says you couldn't have done it, but that trust only goes so far." Burleson turned from the door. "Gibbs, get back here. Grab John's belongings and get him out of here." He turned back to John. "And in case you haven't guessed, you're off the Krogman case."

John stifled a laugh. "Yeah, I guessed as much. Though you really don't have a say in the matter. I'm still a PI, and I still have my license."

The Chief's face grew red. "We'll just see how long that lasts."

The Taxi

Almost an hour later, John opened the front doors of the Clarkbridge Police Station and stepped out into a sunny, humid summer day. He squinted against the bright sun, thankful to feel the sunlight on his skin and not the fluorescent crap they always had in holding cells.

His front pocket vibrated. He pulled the cell phone out and flipped it open. "Hey there, beautiful. Since when are you a lawyer?"

Rachel, his friend from Seattle, laughed on the other end. "What makes you think it was me?"

"Oh, I don't know. Maybe because you're the only person I know who could pull it off? Besides, Alan and Eddy wouldn't be stupid enough to get involved and hire a real lawyer."

"Actually, Eddy is the one who called me when Alan took you in. What's up with that anyway? What a jerk. But I really did hire a lawyer. A friend of mine out there in Michigan. She owed me a favor. Plus, telling her money wasn't an issue seemed to sway her."

Butterflies danced in John's stomach. "A real lawyer? Jeez. Just how bad does she think my situation is?"

"She doesn't think they have a case, but she suggested you give her a call anyway. Just to touch base. Why don't you remember going to the factory? Eddy says they found your print the day Rita disappeared."

The Clarkbridge Taxi Service pulled up to the curb in front of him. "Just a sec, Rach." He climbed in the back of the cab and gave the driver his address. "Okay, back. That's just the thing, Rachel. I was never there. I'd never heard of the place until Alan told me about it."

Rachel whispered, "How is that possible?"

"What's that?"

"I asked how that's possible. Unless you've come down with an acute case of Alzheimer's, I don't see how you could have forgotten something like that."

John let out a loud laugh. The driver glanced in the rearview mirror. John called up to him, "Sorry about that." He returned his attention to Rachel. "I don't know, but if you find out, be sure to let me know. Hey, Rachel, I hate to cut this short but I have a few other phone calls I need to make. Thanks again. I'll be sure to toss a bonus on top of your salary this month."

"Oh, shut up. You know that's not why I do this."

"I love you too." John hung up before she had a chance to yell at him. She hated when he said that.

He cycled through his contacts and found Alan's number. Two rings later, Alan answered. "You know I'm not supposed to talk to you. I'm going to hang up now."

"That's fine. Just wanted to let you know I'll be at your house in a few minutes."

Finding Rita

The cab dropped John off at his apartment. He ran in and grabbed the keys to his Jeep, not bothering to change his clothes. To be safe, he'd kept an eye out for a tail, taking side streets and backtracking until he pulled into Alan's driveway. He parked next to the old Ford truck that had been a birthday gift from their father when Alan was only sixteen. It looked the same as it had the day they brought it home.

Alan sat in a rocking chair on his porch with a Clarkbridge Clipper in his hands. He stood and met John at the base of the steps.

"You shouldn't be here, John. If anybody found out, I could be fired."

John exaggerated turning his head side to side. "Who's going to see me out here? Dad's old farmhouse is the only thing within viewing distance."

Alan glanced toward the dilapidated house a quarter-mile away. He closed his eyes and shook his head. When he opened them, he said, "That's not the point. I was told, not by the Chief but by the Mayor, that we'd all be canned if I talked with you."

"So I'll park the Jeep out back. You're not planning to have any guests over tonight, are you?"

His brother growled and waved his hand before marching into the house. John ran back to his Jeep and pulled it around behind Alan's garage. He came in through the back door to see Alan standing by the pristine kitchen table, pouring two cups of coffee.

"Creamer's in the fridge." He picked up his cup and walked from the kitchen to the living room.

John quickly topped his cup off with creamer and joined his brother. Alan sat on the edge of the couch and leaned forward, the steaming mug held between his hands.

John sat down in the faded blue recliner across from him. "We need to talk."

Alan just looked at him.

"Okay, I'll go first then. The first time I went to that tortilla factory was when I went with you and Eddy."

Alan still said nothing.

"Something is going on in Clarkbridge, and I don't know what it is. Somebody set me up."

Finally, his brother moved. He sipped his coffee and leaned back against the orange and brown corduroy sofa. "And who do you think is setting you up?"

John peered at the horrid design on the couch. "Why do you still have that old thing anyway? Mom and Dad didn't even like it."

Alan glanced over his shoulder and back to John. "Why do you still care? I needed a couch after they passed. They weren't using it, so I am."

John shook his head. "Anyway, I have no clue who would set me up. Or why. But can you think of any other explanation? You know I didn't have anything to do with Rita's disappearance. You said as much outside the station."

"I really don't know what's going on, John. I've gone over every detail in my head dozens of times." He gestured to a stack of folders on the couch next to him. "I don't know what the next step should be. Maybe Chief Burleson should bring in the FBI like he mentioned. We're certainly not getting anywhere. It's been days, and we haven't learned anything new about Rita." Alan placed his cup on the handmade wooden table in front of him and leaned forward, placing his head between his hands. "I just don't know what to think anymore."

John hated seeing his brother like this. He'd responded much the same way when Allie had passed away.

"I'm so sorry, Alan. I wish I could do more, but I can't help but think somebody planted that fingerprint just to throw you guys off. To make the department question the direction the case was going."

Alan crossed his arms. "That's just the thing. It wasn't, and isn't, going anywhere. We know just as much now as we did when Doug died at the station. Zilch."

"We have to be missing something, Alan. There are connections here; we're just not seeing them. We're too close."

Alan slumped back onto the couch and ran a hand through his hair. "Now you sound like Dad." He paused and a small smile appeared on his face. "Which isn't necessarily a bad thing in this case. What do you suggest?" His brow rose expectantly.

"What do I suggest? What did Dad always say when he was stumped on a case?"

They said the words at the same time. "We need a new pair of eyes."

"Exactly," John said. "And I think I know who. Let's get Eddy over here."

"Now? I'm not supposed to talk to him either."

"Does that really matter? We need to find Rita, end of story."

Alan nodded and stood. He walked to the kitchen and came back holding his cell to his ear. "Hello, Eddy? This is Alan Reeves. Could you stop over to the house for a bit?" He paused. "That's right. John was let out today, and he's here now. We need to have a word with you." He said his goodbyes and tossed the phone onto the couch. "Said he'll be here in ten. You really think he's the best person to have look at this?"

"I do, Alan. He's kind of fruity like Cooper when the game is on the line, but he has a good head on him. As long as he's not under any pressure, he might see something we've missed."

Alan's phone vibrated on the couch and buzzed the theme song to Criminal Minds. He leaned over and picked it up. John raised an eyebrow and smiled.

"Don't ask. Rita's idea." His brow furrowed. "Oh, it's the station. I have to take this, I'll be right back." He stepped into the kitchen.

John sipped at his lukewarm coffee. With enough creamer, it tasted just fine cold. He rose and walked to the kitchen doorway, standing close enough to hear the conversation.

"No. I haven't talked to him. You and Mayor Snively both said I shouldn't be in contact with him after his release." Alan turned and looked to John peeking around the doorframe. He rolled his eyes. "If that's what you really want, Chief. I can do that." John heard Chief Burleson's voice on the other end of the line. Alan pulled the phone back a few inches until the yelling stopped. "Will do. That's why you called?"

Alan turned shades paler and plopped down into a kitchen chair in the span of a heartbeat. John's skin went cold, and he almost dropped his coffee mug.

"So who is it? Is it Rita?" A pause. "What do you mean you don't know for sure? Is it, or isn't it?" Tears formed at the corners of his eyes. "Okay, I got it. I'll be there as soon as I can." He slammed the phone shut and stood, knocking the chair over behind him. He didn't bother to pick it up. The phone went into his pocket as he shot into his room. He came out belting on his holster.

"Whoa, what's going on, Alan?"

"They found two women," Alan said, his voice flat. "Both beaten to a pulp, not recognizable. They think one is Rita."

John set his coffee on the table and began searching for his keys. "Oh, God. Are they okay?"

"No. One is dead and the other is on her way to North Detroit General Hospital. I'm going there now." Alan opened the front door.

"Wait, I'll come with you."

He paused and looked back. "That would be a bad idea. Stay here and meet with Eddy. We still need to learn what's happening."

John nodded. "Alright. But if you need me, call. None of that, 'I'll get fired' bullshit."

His brother stood in the doorway a moment longer. "If Rita's dead, I'll... I'll kill whoever did it."

16. New Set of Eyes

Eddy's Eyes

John lounged in the rocking chair on Alan's porch and flipped through the Clarkbridge Clipper. The front page showed a close-up of Mayor Snively with the headline, "Mayor Vows to Find Missing Officer." *Like you'll have anything to do with it.* He flipped to the weather on the next page and smiled. *Hot and humid, just the way I like it.*

Eddy's Nissan hatchback shot swirls of dust into the air from the gravel road before pulling into Alan's driveway. He climbed out and waved at the clouds of powdery dirt floating about his head. He wore the same thick burgundy sweater he'd worn at the Krogmans' place when they'd found photo in the Bible. Sweat dampened his forehead.

"Really? It's hot as hell and you're still wearing a sweater?" John nodded to the thick garment.

"What?" Eddy paused halfway to the porch and glanced down. "It's not that hot."

John chuckled. "If you say so. C'mon in." He stood and opened the screen door.

Eddy followed, flapping the bottom of his sweater.

"You wouldn't have to do that if you invested in a few t-shirts."

Eddy rolled his eyes and slipped past John into the farmhouse, stifling a yawn.

"Don't worry. I'll brew some coffee for your caffeine-junkie ways." John started another pot of coffee and gathered the stack of case files from the living room. He tossed them on the table in front of Eddy.

"What's all this?" He slid the photos and folders around, slipping the Krogman's grisly photos to the bottom.

"That, my friend, is your new case. At least we hope it's your new case because we can't figure out what the hell's going on." He patted his friend on the shoulder. John poured them both steaming cups of coffee, placed them on the table, and sat across from Eddy. The chair groaned as he leaned back on the hind legs.

"You're serious?"

John nodded. "Alan and I have some ideas, but nothing concrete. We need something solid to go on." His grin faded. "Before we get into this, I need to tell you where Alan is. Chief Burleson called him from Detroit. They found two women, beaten beyond recognition, and believe one is Rita."

Hot coffee dribbled down Eddy's chin as he sputtered. "What do you mean they found two women? Were they..."

"One alive, one dead."

"How can you say it all calm like that?" He lifted a napkin and wiped the wetness from around his mouth. "Your brother's partner might be dead and you say it like your telling me the score to the Tigers' game last night."

"Seven to two."

Eddy's head tilted to the side like a confused puppy. "What?"

"Tigers beat the Royals last night on the road. Seven to two."

They stared at each other a moment, one in disbelief, the other beaming.

"You are so weird, John." Eddy shrugged. "I mean it though, how do you say it so calm like that? I feel guilty even thinking about laughing at your corny jokes."

"Look, I don't know what your deal is with all the questions tonight. I'll cave, but let me ask you a few

questions first. Do we know for sure if either of the two
women they found is Rita?"

Eddy shook his head.

"If one of them was Rita, would we know which one
was dead?"

"No," Eddy admitted, his voice nothing more than a
whisper.

"Regardless of the answer to either question, would
me sitting here stressing out and acting all emotional
affect the likelihood that one of those women is or isn't
her?"

Eddy remained quiet, his silence a mirror of the
confusion that lowered the man's eyebrows and thinned
his lips. "You were never this cold growing up, not in
school that I recall. Did the military teach you to have the
emotions of a dead fish?"

John stood and drank the rest of his coffee. He
slammed the cup on the kitchen table. "My God, man.
I've been in jail for the past three days. The first thing you
do is drill me with more questions than the chief of
police? Give me a break." He paced the floor between the
kitchen and living room, the linoleum worn through in
places where Alan had spent hours doing the same after
his wife passed.

Eddy held his arms up. "No need to get all cranky.
I'll stop with the questions. I'm glad you're out. Speaking
of that, how did your thumb print show up in the factory
anyway?"

John leaned forward and placed both hands on the
table. He carefully enunciated each word. "That's what
you're here for, Eddy." He resumed pacing. "Alan and I
both feel there's something going on, but we don't know
what. I don't want to give you anything else, or it could
color your opinion of the case. We want you to look it
over without any outside disturbance. Maybe find
something we missed."

Eddy shuffled and straightened the files. The paperwork held his gaze. "And you both just thought I would go along with this?"

"Well...yeah. Why? Don't you want to?"

"Of course I do. Just wanted to make sure it was of my own volition."

"You ass." John cuffed him on the back of the head. "You're lucky you're my friend, or I wouldn't be so nice."

Eddy didn't respond; instead, his eyes focused on the paper like a shark to blood.

He'll be at this for hours. "I'm going back out front. You want me to call Sandra and tell her you'll be a while?"

Giving a non-committal wave, Eddy mumbled just loud enough for John to hear, "Yeah, yeah, sure."

John laughed and headed to the front porch. *Just like he was in high school.* He'd depended on Eddy back then, not for studying, testing was easy, but with the homework. Playing three sports and dating Rachel McCall didn't leave much time for busy-work. Eddy always obliged without complaint. He enjoyed, 'stimulating his brain,' as he'd called it. Even when John's parents were out of town and he invited Eddy over for a party, he brought his schoolbooks.

"What would I do without you, Eddy?" he said to the empty porch. John planted himself on the rocking chair and pulled out his cell to dial Eddy's wife. He glanced at the time. *Alan should have called by now.*

Hospital

Alan pulled his truck into the hospital parking ramp. The old Ford F150 barely fit between two over-sized SUVs. He tossed the hospital parking ticket on the dash.

Rampant emotions and the case details addled his brain. Just when he brought his terror under control, anger forced its way in, only to switch back to fear. Disturbing visions of Rita flashed through his mind. With how gruesome the other scenes had been, he couldn't help but wonder what horrific atrocities she'd been forced to endure. His eyelids slammed shut as he fought back the tears. Breathing deeply, he went over his phone call with the Chief again.

They couldn't tell if either woman was Rita. *Because they were beaten so badly? Why does Paul even think one of them is Rita to begin with?* Gibbs and Coop were on patrol together when the call came in. A housekeeper found the two women in a motel room south of Clarkbridge. She'd thought they were dead because of the blood spattered about the room. Gibbs determined one still had a pulse, though faint, and called EMS.

A car alarm brought Alan out of his thoughts. He opened the door and lowered his weary feet to the pavement. Inside the hospital entrance, he dialed the Chief back.

"Where are you, Alan?"

"On the crosswalk, level three."

"Come down to one. I'll meet you in the ER waiting area."

Alan pressed the down button on the elevator repeatedly. "So is she okay? Rita, I mean? Or... or was she the one who...."

"We still don't know. Just come down; we need to talk."

The Chief hung up. Alan wrestled back another round of tears. *Why doesn't he just tell me?* The questions fought to burst from his mouth. Deep breaths barely managed to quiet them.

He pressed the elevator's down button again, but it still didn't open. A glowing 'Stairway' sign hung from the ceiling next to him. The slanted arrow pointed to the hallway to his left. He sprinted to the stairway entrance and yanked the door open. Taking three steps at a time, he reached the first floor in a few rapid heartbeats.

The doorway to floor one opened directly into the emergency room waiting area. His glare flitted back and forth.

Chief Burleson stalked around the corner, a dark expression on his face. He moved past Alan and called over his shoulder. "This way."

Alan followed into a private waiting area with a volunteer officer posted outside the entrance. Two steaming Styrofoam cups sat on the wooden coffee table in the middle of the room. Paul dropped into one of the padded chairs and picked up a cup. He gestured to the chair across from him.

Alan sat. "Tell me the whole story, Chief. What's going on? I don't like this."

The Chief gestured to the other cup. "Take a drink, Alan. Relax."

Alan slid forward in his chair, lifted the cup to his lips, and drank; the liquid burned all the way to his stomach. Paul had slipped in a generous shot of Jack Daniels. Alan coughed and wiped at his mouth. "Thanks. Now, can we get on with this?"

The Chief's shoulders slumped; he twisted his cup back and forth against his palms. His gaze went to the floor. "We don't think Rita made it, Alan. I'm sorry."

The cup slid from Alan's hands, coffee splashed across the floor. The empty cup rocked back and forth before coming to rest. His eyes went to his shaking hands. Tears fell to the saturated carpet.

"Look, ah, if you need a minute ...."

"No." Alan's hands balled into fists, but they continued to shake. He ground his teeth to keep from screaming. Prying his gaze from the puddle at his feet, he glared into the Chief's eyes. "Who did it?"

"We don't know. There is a team at the scene now. We should know more by morning."

"Why did you have me come here?"

The Chief cleared his throat and repositioned himself in the chair. "It was my call. We still aren't one hundred percent positive on the identification yet."

Alan forced himself to remain seated. Sadness had overcome him when Allie passed away, but he'd expected it. She'd been sick for months. With Rita ... it was so unexpected. Pressure built in his temples and behind his eyes. A flicker of hope burned in his chest. "Then why did you say Rita didn't make it! How do you know?" A small part of him felt bad yelling at his longtime friend, but the anger quickly washed it away.

"I didn't know all the details when I spoke to you earlier." The Chief's stare flitted away. "And I don't know all the details now." His eyes came back up. "Just listen for a minute. And sit back a bit, would ya?"

Alan hadn't realized he'd moved to the edge of his seat, hovering over the desk as if he'd pounce. With a growl, he sat back and crossed his arms.

The Chief nodded. "When Gibbs and Coop found the two women, they were clothed. Found them side by side on the bed, arms crossed on their chest, like they would be if they were in a, um, if they were prepared for burial."

Alan closed his eyes for a moment and quickly brought them back open. "What makes you think either of them is Rita?"

"The deceased vic wore Rita's uniform."

A knock sounded at the door. The volunteer cop, Gallagher, Alan remembered, leaned in and nodded to Alan. He turned to the Chief. "Chief, we might have an ID on the victim."

"Which one?"

The officer cleared his throat. "The one in the ER. They found her driver's license. It was ... inside her."

"Inside? How?"

"It was sewn onto the inner wall of her abdomen."

Alan grabbed a small trashcan from the corner and vomited. When he looked up, both the Chief and

Gallagher watched. "Go on. Who is it?" The muscles in his stomach and shoulders twitched and tightened into knots. He fought to contain himself. Waiting the few agonizing seconds for the tall cop to continue almost drove him insane.

"Her name is Helena Chandler. A student living up in Clarkbridge."

Alan fell to the floor, the coffee soaking through his jean pants.

Rita's gone.

The one person since Allie he could open up to. The woman who had saved him. The same woman who now destroyed him. Pain seared his very being. He'd thought for so long there was nothing left of his heart. Then Rita came into his life.

The room went black.

17. Alan Wakes

Alan Wakes

Brilliant fluorescent lights beamed down into Alan's eyes. He licked his dry lips. Officer Gallagher's words echoed in his mind, "Her name is Helena Chandler." Why couldn't Rita be alive in the ER right now?

Lena's just some student, a nobody...

He forced the negative thoughts from his head. He pushed up from the hospital gurney and slid his feet to the floor. Down the hallway stood Chief Burleson chatting with a nurse. They both rushed to his side when he stood.

Burleson reached Alan first and put a hand on his back. "Whoa, calm down a second, Alan."

"You should listen to your friend, Mr. Reeves." The nurse nudged him back toward the bed. "That fall gave you a nasty goose-egg."

Alan's hand went to the ache in his temple. The lump didn't hurt as bad as the dull throbbing in his brain. "Shouldn't this hurt more? And why am I in the hallway?" He let the nurse guide him back and down onto the hard mattress.

"Let's prop you up a bit." She scurried into the room next to them and came back with two bleach-white pillows. "It's completely normal. There isn't much blood flow up there because of the swelling. And you're in the hallway because we don't have enough rooms in the ER right now." He winced when she piled the pillows beneath his shoulders and neck. "I'm guessing you have a headache?"

His vision swam when he nodded. He pressed a hand to his temple again.

"I put in an order for an MRI. We need to take a look at that brain of yours." The nurse patted him on the shoulder.

"That's not necessary. I have places I need to be." He leaned forward.

Chief Burleson's hand rushed to Alan's chest. "I don't think so, buddy. What you need is to have this checked out. I don't want one of my officers out there with a brain injury."

Alan moaned. "What did I hit it on anyway?"

"You, ah ..." the Chief sighed, "you hit it on the corner of the coffee table." He turned to the nurse. "Nurse Jalen, could we have a moment please?"

The nurse's short ponytail bobbed as she nodded. "That's fine. Just make sure he doesn't go anywhere."

"Scout's honor."

Nurse Jalen rounded the corner.

Fingers venturing over the new lump, Alan said, "I can't believe you still use that line."

Chief Burleson stifled a small laugh. "As long as it works." His face took on a serious cast. "How's that head of yours feeling?"

"Not as bad as it probably looks. It's dull, with some sharp twinges. I've had worse."

"Listen to Nurse Jalen. If she says you stay, you stay."

Alan growled and propped himself up on his elbows. "How long have I been out?"

"A little over an hour. Look, Alan. I'm sorry about Rita, I really am. I won't pretend to know what you're going through. If it's any consolation, I promise you, I'll get whoever did this."

Alan rubbed his eyes. "*We* will get whoever did this." No way in hell would he let whoever did this get away without significant punishment.

Chief Burleson stepped back and leaned against the wall, crossing his arms. "I'm not so sure that's a good idea. You heard what Mayor Snively said; you're off the case."

"She said I wasn't to be at any of the crime scenes. If I get there first, then I didn't know it was a crime scene yet."

"Don't push her. I want whoever did this as bad as you, but don't let your emotions guide you."

Alan laughed. "Did my dad teach you that one?"

Paul's face flushed. "Not so much teach it as he shoved it down our throats. It doesn't matter where I learned it; it's good advice."

Using the bed for support, Alan sat up and placed his feet on the floor. The hallway continued to twirl. He clenched his eyes shut until the spinning stopped. "I need to call John."

"What the hell did I just say?" Burleson looked away from Alan and mumbled under his breath. "Why do I even try? Bull-headed bastard won't listen anyway."

"Look, Chief. I get that you're trying to help, but I can't stay here. I had John give Eddy Bailey the case files from the Krogman case."

"You did what?"

Alan held his hand up. "John came straight over after leaving the station earlier. We talked about it. We needed a new set of eyes on the case."

The Chief pulled his badge off and held it out toward Alan. "Here. You might as well have this. What the hell do you need me for? It's not like I'm the Chief of Police."

"Do you trust me?"

The Chief sputtered a moment while clipping his badge back in place. "You know I trust you. But you're making it a little hard to do right now."

"I know, and I'm sorry. Just give us a few days to look things over. Eddy is our best bet right now. We have nothing, you said so yourself. Let me get back home. Just don't tell Snively about John's help. I'll let you know if I learn something." He turned toward the exit.

"I don't know anything about this."

Alan waved. He almost bumped into Nurse Jalen as she plowed around the corner.

"Get back to that bed, Mr. Reeves." She pointed one hand behind him and put the other on his chest. "Dr. Terrell didn't clear you to go yet. If you leave before that time, we'll tag you as not fit for duty."

He glanced back to see if the Chief was listening. He was. Burleson rolled his eyes and nodded. "She's telling the truth. Same thing they told me last year when I came in with those migraines."

Alan huffed and plodded back to the uncomfortable hospital bed, wincing at the smell, a combination of bleach and cheap air freshener. He pointed to Chief Burleson. "I'm still leaving when this is done. You just better keep me company here so I don't go stir-crazy."

Chief Calls

The rocking chair vibrated. John's eyes flicked open, and he glanced at his cell on the chair's arm. *Alan.* "About time. What's going on?"

"John, this is Chief Burleson."

"Oh, fuck."

Burleson chuckled. "Don't worry, Alan and I had a little talk. He told me about you and Eddy."

The chair rocked behind John. He'd stood without realizing it. "You don't sound pissed. What do you think about bringing Eddy in?"

"Honestly? I think you two are piled waist high in shit. But if there's anything I've learned about the Reeves family over the years, it's that they're good waders."

"Thanks for the vote of confidence."

Burleson's annoying laugh burbled through the phone again. "I meant that as a compliment. Look, I'm actually calling to give you an update on Alan. I'm sure you noticed on the caller ID, but I'm on Alan's phone. I figure you two are in deep enough already, no need to join you."

"Get on with it, Chief. You're worse than a talk show host. Just tell me what's behind the curtain."

He sighed. "It's about Rita. We're fairly certain she didn't make it."

The screen door slapped shut behind John as he stepped into the kitchen to check on Eddy's progress. His friend stared at the wall with a blank look on his face, a stack of files held in front of him.

John smiled and continued into the living room. "What do you mean by 'fairly certain?' And how's Alan holding up? I can't imagine he took it real well."

"Not well at all. He blacked out and hit his head on a coffee table. You should see the goose egg. He's in for an MRI right now—"

"An MRI? Is it that bad?"

"No, nothing like that. They just need to make sure he's well enough to return to duty. Standard procedure for a police officer with a head injury. And I say fairly certain about Rita because we don't know for sure. The facial swelling and multiple lacerations makes recognizing either one nearly impossible. Here's the strange part, and I'm only telling you this because you're on this case whether I like it or not, but we can't get a fingerprint from either woman. They were burned off. Both women had multiple chemical burns."

Burned off? "What about dental records?"

"We're working on it, but they take a while. We have to check on possible missing persons just in case it's not Rita. We gotta find out who her dentist is too. Not as easy as it sounds."

"Got an ETA for Alan?"

"Nurse said he'd be home by midnight. Look, I need to go. The guys will be wondering where I got off to. I probably won't be able to talk to you again until we find out what happened. Take care, John. Help us get whoever did this. Your dad was a cop. You know how much this means to us."

John glanced through the farmhouse window to the sun beginning its descent. "We'll figure it out, Chief. You just be sure to keep that psycho, Snively, off our backs."

"Snively," Chief Burleson growled. "I'll do my best, but that witch has a way of forcing her nose into other people's business."

"Hey, John?" Eddy called from the kitchen. "Can you come here?"

"Gotta go, Chief. Take it easy." John hung up and followed Eddy's voice into the next room. "You figure something out?"

"I'm not sure." He held his reading glasses up off his nose and squinted at the photo of Ed Reeves they'd found at the Krogman's. "Isn't that your dad's tractor back there? Behind them a bit on the right?"

Leaning in for a closer look, John saw the 1953 Ford Jubilee. "It looks like it, but plenty of other farmers had the Jubilee back then."

"True, but look right there. You can see the 'H' next to Tolman's head."

"How the hell did you see that?" John leaned in further. The 'H' was the last letter in the name Sarah, the name his father had painted on the front end of his tractor. He'd said the Jubilee reminded him of his Sunday school teacher when he was a kid; beautiful and built like a machine.

Eddy didn't respond. He sat the picture to the side and picked up another file.

"So they were at my dad's farm. What's the big deal?"

Eddy squinted as he concentrated on the paper in his hands. The tip of his tongue flicked back and forth like a snake.

"Hey!"

Eddy dropped the paper. "What are you yelling for?"

"I asked you what the big deal was about them being at my dad's farm."

"Oh, I'm not sure. It just seems weird."

John groaned. "Eddy, you fruitcake. I thought you had something." He pulled out a Budweiser from the fridge. "You want one?" He held a beer up.

"No thanks. I'm good."

John put the extra back.

"Wait!"

"Wait what?"

Eddy closed his eyes. John couldn't tell if he was concentrating or constipated. "Oh never mind. I can't remember."

John laughed and popped open his brew. "Yup. Definitely a fruitcake."

18. Killer

Holding Lena's Hand

Alan gazed from the third floor window into the hospital courtyard, focusing on the sway of the orange day lilies in the late afternoon breeze. His thoughts wandered elsewhere. Eddy hadn't found anything new after combing the details of the case. He said he needed to 'ruminate' for a few days, let the information soak in. Alan had heard of cops doing the same, and they'd been successful, but Rita's killer still roamed free.

He clenched his free hand into a fist. A deep breath calmed him. Lena moaned in the hospital bed beside him.

"Hey there, Lena. Just me, Alan, again." He squeezed her hand. "How are you feeling? The doctors said the swelling on your brain has gone down some and that you might even wake up soon." He ran a finger across the blue rose tattooed on the inside of her wrist.

Nurse Kaitlinn strolled into the room. "Here so early, Alan? I don't usually see you until eight or nine."

"Early? It's almost dinner time." The nurse's golden curls fell about her shoulders. With her hair pulled back into a ponytail the past three days, he hadn't realized how vibrant it was. "Got off work early today. Thought I'd drop in for a bit."

Kaitlinn smiled and tossed a pile of pillows into the closet. "You're a sweet man; I hope you know that."

"You say the same thing every time I see you. Much more and I'll start to believe it. Why no ponytail today? Big date?"

Her cheeks reddened. She giggled and glanced in the mirror a moment before facing Alan again. "What a mess. The big date is with my little guy. He's sick. I'm picking him up from the babysitter. Apparently the shrimp we ate last night is now in the kitchen trashcan."

He wrinkled his nose. "That's not good. How old is he?"

"He turned six last month. His names Jaydon. Want to see a picture?"

Alan laid Lena's hand next to her on the bed and came to the nurse's side. "Absolutely."

Kaitlinn flipped over her name badge and removed two photos. "This is an older one, when he was three. His first T-ball game." She held the second picture up. "And this one is from his birthday party. He's such a ham."

"He's beautiful, Kaitlinn. He really is." He noticed how close Kaitlinn stood and quickly stepped back.

"Thanks, Alan." She slid the photos back into her badge. "What about you? Any little cops running around at your house?"

Alan sighed. "Unfortunately, no. My wife and I never got around to it before she passed away."

"Oh, I'm sorry. I didn't know."

Alan smiled. "Don't worry about it; it was a long time ago. You go pick up your little guy. Sounds like he needs his mom."

"You're right; I better get going." Kaitlinn turned, but paused in the doorway. "Hey, Alan? Take care of yourself. You look like you could use some sleep."

The Criminal Minds ringtone belted its melody from his phone on the desk next to Lena's bed. Thankful for the interruption, Alan waved to Kaitlinn and hurried to his phone.

"Hey, John. Anything new?"

"No. Just heading over to Eddy's house. Sandra cooked up some of her famous grilled tacos. You coming?"

"Not tonight."

"At the hospital again?"

After the MRI scan on his head days before, he'd calmed down and visited Lena to show his support. The day after, Chief Burleson had explained that Lena's only family lived in Arizona and didn't plan to visit for reasons unknown to him.

Alan turned away from Lena, not sure if she could hear what he said. "I'm here now. You really should stop in again. She doesn't have anybody, John."

John sighed into the phone. "You know I'm not good with hospitals. And I stopped in there yesterday."

"You said hi to her and then we left for lunch. I'd hardly constitute that as a visit."

"I know, I know. I'll try to get in there soon. It's just weird. We weren't even that close. I don't want it to be weird if she wakes up and I'm there. Never mind me, why are you even there?"

"I told you yesterday." He exaggerated the enunciation of each word. "She has nobody." Alan pushed at his temple with the palm of his free hand. "And right now, I don't either. It helps just to speak to her." When Allie had been sick, he'd spent much of her final month doing the same.

"You do what you have to do, but it sounds like you're there for you more than her."

Alan's anger heightened. "Maybe I am. Does it matter when it's good for her?"

"I guess not. Anyway, the invitation's still open. Sandra always makes extra. And look, I'll try to get in there tomorrow some time."

Alan hung up and sat back down next to Lena. He twined his fingers with hers. "Don't worry. I'm not going anywhere. I may not be the best company, but I'll do my best." He slid the drawer open on the bedside cabinet and pulled out a Home and Gardening magazine. "Let's see here. Where did we leave off yesterday? Ah yes, the benefits of arborvitae. Great reading."

Lena moaned again, quiet, comforting. At least it sounded comforting.

Killer Found

"Excuse me, Mr. Reeves?"

In Alan's dream, the nurse spoke through his mother's mouth.

"Officer Reeves?"

"Why do you keep calling me that? I'm your son. Don't you remember?"

The nurse swatted him on the arm with a pillow. He wiped his shoulder across his mouth, an old habit from childhood when he'd fall asleep in his mother's arms and slobber profusely.

A ruddy-faced woman stood over him, gloved hands on her hips. "Mr. Reeves? Are you awake? You were talking to yourself. Quite loud, I might add."

"What? No. I mean yes. I'm awake. What time is it?"

"It's almost seven. I'm Nurse Dowlen. Kaitlinn said you might still be here. She didn't say you were staying the night."

Alan's face flushed. "Was I snoring too loud?"

"Couldn't be any louder than these cheap scrubs." Nurse Dowlen tossed the pillow from her hands into the cupboard and swished her way to the other side of Lena's bed to check on her vitals. "That's what I get for trying to save a few bucks. And no, you weren't snoring. Dr. Frabotta plans to run a few more tests tonight and wanted to give you a chance to say goodnight."

Alan nodded and pulled his jacket from the back of the recliner. He took Lena's hand in his own. "Looks like they're kicking me out for the night. If they give you any trouble, you just tell them—"

His cell phone blared the Criminal Minds theme song through his jacket pocket. His already red face flushed further. Nurse Dowlen raised an eyebrow.

"Don't ask." Alan glanced down at Lena. "I won't leave without a proper goodbye. Let me grab this real quick." He flipped the cell open. "Captain Reeves."

"Hey, Alan. This is Charlie Parrish. Ah ... the medical examiner."

"I know who you are, Charlie. Did you find something?"

Lena murmured the quiet moan Alan had become used to. He gave her hand a gentle squeeze.

Charlie cleared his throat. "Are you sitting down?"

Alan's heart skipped a beat. "What? What is it?"

"Well, you said to call you first if me or the forensic team came up with anything. I figured that would be fine since we—"

"Out with it!" Alan gave an apologetic smile to Nurse Dowlen. She'd jumped and almost upended the water cup Alan kept with him while visiting.

The cell's speakers distorted Charlie's loud sigh. "The women they found in the motel, well, we put the order in as a rush. The semen from both victims matched the same person."

"So you found a match in the database? Who is it?" Blood pulsed through his temples; the phone shook in his hand. This was it. Whoever this attacker was, whoever had killed Rita, was about to find out how far a Reeves would go to avenge those they love.

"Yes, he was in the database. The military database. It was your brother. It's John."

Grilled Tacos

"Seriously. When are you going to tell me your secret?" John bit into his fourth taco, reveling in the light summer breeze that cooled the damp layer of sweat coating his forehead.

"She won't tell you." Eddy laughed from the other side of the picnic table. "I told you before, it's a family recipe."

John swallowed and wiped the grease from his chin with a napkin. "I've tried making these at least ten times. The meat ends up falling into the coals and starts a grease fire. Come on, Sandra. This is a safety concern."

Sandra guided another bite of taco into their youngest child's waiting mouth. "I'll tell you when I'm done feeding Henry."

"No she won't," Eddy said under his breath.

"No she won't," Eddy's other three children chimed in. The oldest at age twelve, Edwin Junior, played king of the mountain while the two girls, Maria and Holly, fought their way down the twisty slide Eddy built into their backyard swing set the summer before

John took his eyes away from the children and looked to Sandra. "Verbal contract," he said around a mouthful.

"Way to be a good example," Sandra said. "At least wait until you've chewed once or twice before talking."

He hurriedly chewed and swallowed. "Sorry. Don't spend much time around kids these days." He concentrated on the spiced meat in his shell. "They're just so... I don't know. Awesome."

Henry chirped, "Awesome! Awesome!" Chunks of meat and corn shell tumbled from his mouth.

"You see what you did?" Sandra faked a huff and spooned another heap into Henry's mouth. "You hear that Eddy?"

"What's that, hon?

"Your cell's ringing."

"Ooh, thanks. Be right back." Eddy hustled into the house.

Sandra cast a sideways glance at John. "You really start fires when you grill tacos?"

John made a show of chomping. With a prim and proper tap of the napkin on his lips, he spoke with a

British accent. "Why yes, my dear. Now, do be a good lass and fill my hand with another ale." Sandra and Henry both stared. He lost the accent. "What? Not proper enough?"

Henry squealed; Sandra followed with a laugh. "Oh, John. It's so good to have you back. I've missed you."

"It's good to be back. I wish things were a little smoother, but you know me. Can't seem to keep my ... buns? That okay to say?"

She rolled her eyes. "It's okay this time."

"Can't seem to keep my buns out of trouble."

The back door slammed shut. John's attention went to Eddy standing on the back patio.

Eddy's pale face matched the white deck chairs. "Kids, inside. Now."

Their three children on the swing-set paused in unison.

"I said now!"

Sandra removed Henry's bib and pulled him to her chest; tears formed at the edge of his eyes. She started for the back door. "What's happening, Eddy? Is everything alright?"

Eddy's eyes never left John. "It'll be okay, honey. Just go inside. I'll be in shortly."

The chunk of taco in John's mouth didn't taste so good anymore. He spit it into his napkin and stood, grabbing his beer on the way up. "What happened? Is Alan okay?"

"I'm sorry, John."

"Sorry for what, man? Spit it out."

"You have to go. Right now. That was Chief Burleson on the phone. I don't have long to explain, but they found evidence. I don't know how, but they did. He thinks we may be in danger. They're sending officers over now. You need to go."

John brought the ice-cold Budweiser to his lips and chugged the last few gulps down. He placed the empty bottle on the picnic table and glanced at his watch. "Well, shit," he glanced back to Eddy, "looks like it's time for me to leave." He paused on his way to the backyard gate and put his hand on Eddy's shoulder. "I'm guessing you didn't hear the squad cars pull into your neighbor's driveways a few seconds ago?"

"How did you—"

"How often do your neighbors come home at exactly the same time and stop fast enough to slide on the pavement?"

Eddy shook his head.

"It's okay, man. I'll be fine. Just take care of your family. And thanks for sending them inside."

Splinters flew from the gate, the lock landing at their feet. Three Clarkbridge officers hurried in, weapons held ready. Three more stepped to the patio from the back door.

John held his arms up and went to his knees. He nodded. "Hey there, Gibbs. How's the wife? And Coop, nice to see you can hold that thing without dropping it."

"You have the right to remain silent—" Cooper began.

"Come on, Coop. You read these to me last week. I think I can remember." John smiled at the woman about to place cuffs on him. "Sergeant Shaw, I like the new hair color. Really brings out your eyes."

Savior

'Partita for Lute in E Major,' the Savior's favorite, crackled through rusted speakers. "I just love how light-hearted this piece is. I could listen to it over and again, for days."

"Yes, my Savior. It is a very beautiful song."

The Savior shot him a glare over the protective rim of his glasses. "And what do you know of Bach?"

The skinny man quickly looked away. "Nothing of course. I only know it's beautiful because you said so."

Behind the clear plastic mask, a smile crept onto the Savior's face. "I apologize. I truly should appreciate you more. The work gets to me sometimes." He bent back down to his task. "But I didn't ask you here to discuss music. It's been done then?"

"It has."

The smile grew larger as a sonorous laugh came from the Savior, fogging the mask. He tossed the scalpel over his shoulder and yanked off the bloody gloves. "This is great. You installed the devices, correct?"

"I did, my Savior. I just hope I did it right. I've never worked with camera equipment before."

The Savior slapped him on the shoulder. "Come with me. We'll see how everything looks. I can't wait to see the look on Alan's face when he confronts John at the station."

19. Killer Taken

Report

Alan's truck whined as he hurled down the freeway faster than he'd driven in years. He glanced at his phone on the seat next to him. Still no signal. "God damned phone." He pictured pounding the phone through the truck and into the pavement.

How could they find John's semen at the scene? It made some sense with Lena, but with Rita?

The cell phone beeped. He had a signal. "About time." Forcing himself to keep from throwing it out the window, he dialed Charlie again.

"Charlie Parrish."

"This is Alan. Explain to me how this is possible. You know for sure John's DNA was found on both bodies?"

"I'd rather not discuss the details over the phone. I sent a copy of the report to Chief Burleson. I'm sure he'll let you look it over."

"C'mon, Charlie, I'm going crazy here. I'm fifteen minutes from Clarkbridge, and all I can do is stare at the freeway, wondering how my brother raped and killed my girlfriend."

A soft sigh breathed through the phone. "Girlfriend? I uh… hang on a second. I'll go grab the report from my desk."

"Thanks. I just can't… Just can't…"

"Take a deep breath, Alan. I don't want to see you in here on my table. Calm down. I'll tell you what you want to know in a moment."

The phone bounced on the passenger seat where Alan tossed it. He took Charlie's advice and huffed multiple deep breathes, digging the fingers of his free hand into the lizard design seat cover Rita had given him on his birthday. Each breath calmed him more than the last. He imagined his hair turning grayer by the second.

The sign flying by his window read, 'East Groveford.' Keeping one hand on the wheel, Alan picked up his phone from the seat. "I'm back, Charlie."

"Good. I have the report right here. I'll only ask this one more time. Are you sure you want to hear this?"

The muscles in Alan's mouth squeezed tight. His teeth creaked. With another deep breath, he relaxed. "Yes. Tell me what you can."

Charlie cleared his throat. "Okay, I'll give you the basics. You don't need to know all the medical mumbo jumbo. I'll start with the DNA testing. Semen was found on both bodies. I found the evidence on Rita. The other was found on Lena via the SOEC kit used by hospital personnel."

"And... the sex wasn't consensual?"

"The partial skin tearing in specific areas combined with bruising leaves little room for misinterpretation."

Alan forced himself to unclench his teeth. "Other physical evidence?"

"Let's see." Alan heard Charlie rifle through papers. "We also found debris and blood under Rita's nails. Blood type is o-positive, but we haven't confirmed any matched DNA yet. Do you know John's blood type?"

"It's o-positive. Keep going."

"Sure, um... let's see. Also found on both were coarse hairs and a few dark fibers. The fibers haven't been identified yet either, but we're confident they come from blue jeans. That looks like the important stuff. If you want any more you'll have to check with Chief Burleson.'"

"It doesn't make any sense, Charlie. No motive, no reason to do this, and it's not like him. Women always fawn over John. Why would he do this? Something isn't right."

"I'm not sure what you want me to say. I just look at the facts."

Alan looked at the phone in his hand for a moment; he hadn't realized he'd spoken aloud. "Of course you do. Look, I need to go. Thanks for the information. Contact me right away if you find anything else."

He hung up. Before he could set the phone down, it rang again.

"Hello, Chief."

"Alan, I know what you're thinking. You get it out of your head right now. How far are you from the station?"

The Taylor Teetotalers softball stadium lit up the already bright sky next to the freeway. "Just passed the Teetotalers. Probably five minutes away."

"When you get off the exit, you take a left and head to your farmhouse. If you come within a mile of this station, I'll slap the cuffs on you myself. Mayor Snively is already on her way down here; though I don't know what the hell for." Burleson growled. A solid ka-thunk hitting metal sounded through the phone, an old habit from the Chief's chewing tobacco days. Nobody dared look into the depths of the Chief's trashcan.

"I can't. Go home, I mean. What will I do there? Freak out until I drive to the station anyway? Come on, Chief."

Burleson sighed. "I can't come close to imagining what you're going through right now, but you'll have to trust us. We all know something isn't right about this. Whether that something is your brother or not, we'll have to wait to find out. Charlie is good at what he does. Give him some time, and maybe we'll learn something else." The Chief's voice muffled for a moment, like his hand was held over the phone. "You still there?"

"I'm here, Chief, but just barely. You have to give me something to do, some way to help. I can't just go home."

"We have enough going on at the station right now. When they get back here with John, I'm sending Sergeant Shaw over to your house. You better be there. If things calm down enough, maybe you can contact the guy with the glasses we spoke about the other day. The one you and John went to school with."

Why should I see Eddy? Is he just trying to get my mind off John? Not likely. "Fine. I'm heading home. Shaw better not pull that grandmotherly shit she does down at the station."

"Just do what she says, Alan. Don't give her a reason to take you in too."

"One more question, Chief." Alan felt his shoulders sag a little in the seat. "Did John come quietly? He didn't make a scene, did he?"

"John? Quiet as a kitten." Chief Burleson paused. "Hell no, he didn't come quietly; he yapped all the way to the station. If we'd had a human-sized muzzle, I'd have thrown it on John myself."

Uppercut

They placed John in the same cell he'd been in before; the same three magazines graced the cement bench. "Well, hi there, ladies. Fancy meeting you here."

The caveman-like cop gave John a not so gentle shove toward the back of the tiny room.

John shot him a glare. "You're pretty tough when I got these cuffs on, Sergeant Clark. Why don't you take them off and try that again?"

The huge cop looked John up and down like a piece of meat. "Okay."

Shit. "Look, no need to get all macho cop on me. I know you all have this small-town cop thing going on right now, but I didn't do it." John was certain he could take out the officer, but the guy had at least fifty pounds on him. It would hurt. The name Donald didn't fit the guy. "Where'd you get that first name anyway? Your mama a Disney fan?"

Clark threw an uppercut into John's stomach.

Stupid. "Okay," John squeezed out through constricted vocal cords. "I guess I deserve that. Just don't do it again."

The meaty fist came at John again. This time, he was ready for it. Bent over from the previous hit, he had a good view. He stepped to the side and squatted slightly. The man's fist brushed his shoulder. He leapt forward driving his shoulder into Caveman's stomach. Air whooshed from the cop, and he stumbled into the edge of the cell door. Before he gained his footing, John turned to the side and threw a roundhouse kick to the side of his knee, bringing him to the floor, just hard enough to let him know John meant business, but not enough to maim him for life.

"I told you not to do that again." John stepped back against the cell wall and leaned back as if enjoying the view. "You'd best listen to me if we're gonna be friends." He glanced up. Chief Burleson and Corporal Gibbs watched from the doorway.

Gibbs bent down and helped Clark to his feet. "You son-of-a-bitch," Clark said through clenched teeth. He pulled his arm away from Gibbs.

"Enough!" Chief Burleson called. "Get cleaned up, you idiot. You had your fun."

Clark pointed at John.

"Ooh. Are you going to point me to death now?" John laughed.

"That goes for you too, John," the chief said. "Leave him be. You humiliated him enough."

John nodded. "Not to sound like a kid, but he started it."

"And you finished it. I get it. You're a big tough guy." Chief Burleson stepped in as Gibbs helped Clark out of the cell. "Now turn around so I can get those cuffs off you. You start anything with me and I'll shoot your ass."

"I hear it's better if you aim for the mid-section. Not many arteries in the ass."

"Just turn around." John faced the wall. Chief Burleson slid his key into the cuffs and leaned close. He whispered, "Alan says you didn't do it. Either way, you're in deep shit. Quit with the act or you'll only make it worse." He slid the manacles off and backed away.

John turned around and faced the cell door. Gibbs had come back, his skinny frame leaning against the doorway. "So what's the next step then, Chief? Should I just call my lawyer right now?"

The Chief nudged Gibbs out of the way and faced John again. "You can call your lawyer when we say you can."

"It's going to be like that?"

Gibbs' normally calm demeanor disappeared as he took a step toward John. "Yeah it's going to be like that, you scum. You don't kill a cop in Clarkbridge and get away with it."

Burleson patted the scrawny cop on the shoulder. "Take it easy, Gibbs. This isn't the Wild West. Get back to work." He turned back to John. "You take it easy too, John. Like I said, you can call your lawyer when we say you can. It shouldn't be long."

John held his hands out to his sides. "In the meantime, I'll just hang out here until you need me. Take your time. I have a heap of great reading material anyway."

Emotions

Minutes after Alan arrived home, Sergeant Shaw pulled into his driveway. He brewed a pot of coffee, the only way he knew to calm himself down.

"Alan? You in here?" Shaw's slight Southern drawl irritated him. She'd lived in Michigan for years; she should be rid of it by now.

"In the kitchen."

Shaw sauntered through the kitchen doorway. He hated how she always sauntered. It wasn't a stroll or a walk or even the stiff stride officers have because of the tight bullet-resistant vest. It was a saunter. He wasn't ready for her grandmotherly and sage advice either. She'd been around the block a time or two, and she let you know. She wasn't much older than he was, just experienced in the ways of the world.

Alan's eyes went to her hair. "Your hair. It's different."

"You Reeves boys have always had good eyes. John noticed right away that I'd changed the color."

Blood rushed to Alan's face. He wasn't mad at Shaw, and he didn't really hate her, just the situation. He'd focused his anger on her until she mentioned John's name.

"Oh. I'm sorry, Alan"

A smile crept to the corner of Alan's mouth. Genuine concern showed on her face, and he'd been ready to jump down her throat. "I'm the one that should be sorry, Ruth. My anger got the best of me."

Shaw's shoulders relaxed as she let out a sigh. "I can tell. It's not often you call me by my first name. The last time you called me Ruth was at the station's Halloween party. If I remember correctly, you drank too much beer while on that cold medicine." Her voice deepened in imitation of Alan's. "Hey, Ruth, grab me a beer. Hey, Ruth, why're you always so laid back? Hey, Ruth, how come you're such a sweetheart?"

Anger and pain rolled out of Alan. Ruth Shaw had that effect on him. "You are a sweetheart. Chief was right to send you. Anybody else and I might have punched them."

Shaw brought her arms up and made fists. She bounced from toe to toe. "You feeling tough, big boy? You wanna see if this old lady can fight? Bring it."

Alan laughed, and it was deep. From the belly. His shoulders shook with the effort and his chest heaved until he hiccupped. The laughs turned to sobs. Shaw circled him in her arms. Though she was tall for a woman, Alan still towered over her, wetting the shoulder of her uniform with his tears.

She patted him with one hand and the other cradled his head. "It's okay, honey. You let it all out. That's what I'm here for. All that stress, all that pain, you let it come out through your tears. Don't hold nothin back."

And he didn't. Emotions he'd suppressed since his wife's death poured forth, mixing with the loss of Rita and John's supposed involvement. The Chief pretended he didn't know anything about people, but he read Alan like a book. There wasn't another person alive that could have this effect on him.

"Thanks, Ruth. You're heaven-sent."

Walk

Alan wasn't sure how long they stood in the kitchen with Shaw holding him while he cried like a baby. Eventually, they separated and sat at the kitchen table, gossiping about the station, not something he did often, but it relaxed him.

"Did you hear about Gibbs last week?" Shaw giggled. She sipped what must have been her tenth cup of coffee. "Andrea caught him at the computer chatting with some stripper."

"Again?" Alan laughed. "I don't understand how he can afford it on our salary."

"I know! I thought the same thing. They have five kids. Andrea obviously puts out."

Coffee poured out of Alan's mouth and down the front of his t-shirt. "My God, woman. Warn me before you say something like that."

"Like what? That Gibbs and his wife bang like rabbits? That they have five kids and they've barely been married five years? You'd think with all that testosterone, he wouldn't be so skinny."

Alan stood. "I'll be right back. I need to grab another shirt." He started toward his bedroom.

"Alan?" Shaw called from behind. "You're not using your shirt as an excuse to skedaddle are you?"

He smiled. She'd lulled him into a false sense of security with her easy manner and kept her head in the game the whole time. "No, Ruth. You have my word. Just grabbing a shirt." An idea came to him. "You know, you and I haven't had a chance to discuss any of the recent cases yet. You want to go for a short walk? Just around the property for a bit? I'd like to get your input and the fresh air would do me some good."

The grandmotherly smile appeared on her face again, deceiving since she wasn't much older than him. "I'd love to, but it'll be dark soon. Might want to hurry."

He quickly changed into a long sleeve shirt. If they made it as far as the swamp on the back of his property, the longer sleeves would protect some against the mosquitoes.

They walked down an old two-track and along the fence-line separating his field from the neighbor's.

Ruth nodded to the weed-filled field topped with small white flowers. "Is that clover?"

Alan glanced at the layer of green beneath the tall weeds. "Dutch white clover. My dad used to plant it for the deer in whatever field needed rotation that year. I don't know if it helps, but he said it did. Since I don't farm, I plant it every year. At least I used to. It's been a while since I've taken care of it though. Life always seems to get in the way."

Shaw nodded, her constant smile tugging at the corner of her mouth. "I miss old Ed sometimes. He was a good cop. I was a rookie the year he passed away."

It was a story she'd told him before. How she'd given up her career as a nurse in Detroit to protect others from ending up like the patients she tended. He nodded and waited for her to go on.

"We didn't come out here to talk about old times though. Tell me about the cases. Or the case rather, since from the sound of things, they're all related."

Alan paused. "You think they're related too?"

She took a few steps then turned to face him. "Just from the tidbits I've heard. Let's talk about what we know. That was one of your dad's favorite sayings." She laughed and waved him forward.

He followed. "It *was* one of his favorites. I'm surprised you remember."

"Of course I remember. I was the rookie. Ed was the big man on campus. His training never stopped, even when he wasn't in uniform."

"Tell me about it." It was nice thinking about his father, and he'd done so more than usual lately. The picture with his father and the three dead men had seen to that. "Let's see, what do we know? Douglas Fincham, Lonnie Krogman, and Herbert Tolman; all dead from abnormal wounds in abnormal circumstances. Each one different, but same in the strangeness department. We found that picture at every scene. You heard about the picture, right?"

Shaw hopped over the small tree lying across their path. "How couldn't I? That's all Chief Burleson and Coop have talked about the past couple weeks."

Alan hopped over the tree too. "I figured as much. I'm not sure what to think about the picture. It's the three of them and my dad. As I told Burleson, they knew each other, but I don't remember my dad ever mentioning them more than once or twice while growing up. Yet they have their arms around each other like best friends. And they're drinking alcohol. My dad never had a problem, but my mother frowned on it. That Southern Baptist upbringing made her frown upon a lot of things. Actually, I didn't think of that before. I need to take another look at the picture."

"Why is that?" She slapped at her hand. "Damn. Mosquitoes have been horrible this year."

He pointed to the swamp. "That certainly doesn't help. You want to head back or work our way over to the other side of the property?"

"Let's keep going. I'm in no hurry. Will we have time?" She glanced to the sky.

"Sure we do. It doesn't take that long. About the picture, I just realized I never paid attention to where the picture was taken. Sure it was a farm, but whose? My mom wouldn't have let them drink out in the open like that on our property."

They wended their way through a small briar patch and out onto another two-track.

Through the partial darkness, Alan saw Shaw's brow lift. "Really? She was that strict?"

"It wasn't as much strict as it was her belief. I can't believe I didn't think of it before now." Ice shot through Alan's veins. He paused again, staring at the ground in thought. "My God. How couldn't I have thought of it before?"

Shaw came to stand beside him, wrapping her around his shoulder as she nudged him down the path. "Whatever you just thought of, keep walking while you tell me. It's getting dark."

He lifted his eyes. A light glowed through the thin woods to their side. "You're right; we should keep moving. Think about it, Ruth. Who took the picture? Who's standing behind the camera?"

"Oh. I hadn't thought about it either. I'm surprised you didn't."

Alan hefted a thick branch and broke it over his leg. "Damn it."

She patted him on the back. "It's okay. These things happen. Besides, does that really matter since—?"

"Since what? My brother did it?"

"Look, I don't know if he did or not, but the evidence is pretty well stacked against him."

Anger shot through Alan. He fought down the urge to yell. "Don't you see? He's not like that. He gives half his money to local orphanages for God's sake. Even if he did those things to Rita and Lena, how could he have done the other things? It's impossible. Doug died in my arms at the station. You were there. How could John have had anything to do with that?"

They walked in silence. "I was there," Shaw whispered. "And I've never seen anything like it. When something out of the ordinary happens, it's easier to point a finger and have it over with."

"Even when the finger points at my brother?" Alan growled. "I'm sorry I got on you, but how could it have been him? And how are these fucking cases related!" He hadn't meant to yell. The frustration he felt earlier boiled to the top. "I need to talk to Eddy Bailey again."

"As in Eddy Bailey the PI? What's he have to do with anything?"

"He's the one who got John mixed up in all this. I'm not saying it's his fault; it's just circumstance. But he has a good head on his shoulders. John and I went to him with the case hoping he'd see something we couldn't."

"And?"

"And I don't know. I haven't spoken to him since. I've spent all my time at the hospital with Lena." He pulled his cell from his jean pocket. "I'll call him right now."

They paused when they reached his backyard. The phone rang five times and went to voicemail. "Eddy, this is Alan. We need to talk. Give me a call as soon as you get this." Alan took a deep breath. "I heard John was at your house when this all went down earlier. I'm sorry your family had to go through that. Look, ah, just give me a call."

"Not home?" Shaw stepped onto the back porch and opened the door.

Alan followed her into his house. "If he is, he isn't answering. I can't imagine them going anywhere this late on a school night. Especially after what they went through earlier."

When they reached the kitchen, Shaw picked up her coffee cup and shook it at him. "Hey, you have any to-go cups? It's late and I should get home. Early shift in the morning. Burleson said to just hang out until you calmed down. I think you've done that as much as you're going to, considering."

Alan let out a deep sigh. "Thank you so much for coming over tonight, Ruth. I don't know if I'd have been able to keep myself here without you. I really appreciate it."

She placed her cup on the table and stepped in front of Alan. Her hands cupped his face and pulled him close. She kissed him right on the lips. He thought it should surprise him, but it felt natural from her.

"Alan, you're a good man. I know this is hard right now, but you stay strong. I've known you for a long time, and you're made of tough stuff. Be strong. Things will work out the way they're supposed to. You remember that."

Words wouldn't form. Her manner, so like a loving mother, caught him off guard. He stepped away from her and pulled a Styrofoam cup from the cupboard. "Here you go."

She poured her drink into the cup he'd given her and walked to the front door. She turned back. "Why don't you meet me for breakfast tomorrow at the Corner Café? You know, just two cops sipping on some java. It'll be early, of course."

Alan nodded and showed her a half wave. He didn't watch her leave.

Rita's funeral was set to take place within the week and he just kissed another woman. Technically she kissed him, but he hadn't stopped her. Guilt flooded his emotions.

Why should I feel guilty? Rita's gone.

He slammed his fist on the counter. Warmth grew across his hand. Blood oozed from the small gash on his knuckle and dripped on the slate counter-top.

20. The Drop

Eddy

Two days had passed since the cops busted down Eddy's backyard gate in the effort to arrest John. As though he were stupid enough to fight them. Even with his car blasting air-conditioned air at him, sweat pasted Eddy's clothes to his body, and it wasn't only because of the sweater this time.

"Are you sure this will work? I mean, what if someone finds out? Can't I get in big trouble for this, Rachel?"

Rachel McCall sighed into the other end of the phone. "Not if you do it as I said. How would you get in trouble? You're visiting a friend, and you'll do it on accident. It's not like they'll know what happened."

"But what if they do?" He hated that Rachel made him so nervous. *Of course she thinks it's easy. She's on her butt out in Washington. I'm the one putting my ass on the line.* "Never mind, okay? I'll do it. Let's just go over it one more time."

"You know John would do it for you, Eddy."

"I do know, but that doesn't make it any easier. John always does crazy shit."

Eddy spent the last few minutes of his drive to the police station listening to Rachel's plan. And it *was* Rachel's plan. He'd never think to do something so foolish. John said he didn't have anything to do with the death of Rita, so that meant he didn't, no matter what the evidence suggested. Eddy had never dealt with a situation like this before. He hoped he never had to again.

"Gotta go, Rachel. I'm heading in."

"Call me the minute you get home. If you mess this up, we'll have to think of something else, and fast. I'm not sure when the FBI agent will arrive."

Jail Again

John's eyes fluttered open. A fluorescent light flickered from the ceiling directly over his face. He sat up and stretched his neck. The cement bench wasn't so bad, but a softer pillow than magazines would be nice.

Keys clinked on the heavy steel as Sergeant Clark peered through the cell door window. He pulled the door open and stepped in.

John put on his best smile. "Well, hi there, sweetheart. You stop in for another tumble?"

Clark's face reddened. "Get up. You have a visitor."

"My lawyer? Good." He gestured to the ceiling. "That damn flashing light was about to give me a seizure."

"Stand up and turn around."

"Yes, ma'am." On a normal day, John pelted the world with snide remarks. After a few days in jail, they poured from him like rounds from a semi-automatic. His ex-girlfriend had called it a defense mechanism.

He faced the wall and the officer roughly placed the cuffs on his wrists. Clark thumped him in the back as he passed by. John caught himself on the doorway. "Really?" he said over his shoulder. "That the best you can do?"

The large cop smiled. "Shut up and get moving. We're going to interview room three."

"My visitor is interviewing me?" He took a turn at Alan's desk and headed down the short hallway, remembering the way from when they spoke with Russell Holbrook. *Where's he been anyway? He nosed right in on the other case.*

"You say something?" Clark grabbed the cuffs and lifted.

John's shoulders creaked. "Just commenting on the five-star treatment I'm getting."

The huge cop giggled. It sounded odd coming from someone so large. Clark opened interview room three and ushered John in. Eddy sat on one side of the table, face solemn. The sweaty locks of hair sticking to his forehead made his austere look almost comedic.

"Hey, buddy." John nodded to his friend. "You catch the game last night? Yeah. Me neither."

Eddy started to wave then must have thought better. His his arm dropped back to his side, and he lost the partial smile that had shown up with John's arrival. "Hello, John."

Clark sat John down across from Eddy. He checked the cuffs again. "I'll be right outside, Mr. Bailey. If you need anything, ring the buzzer or just call out. There's another officer posted on the other side of the two-way mirror, so don't worry about Reeves trying anything."

Eddy gave him a polite nod.

John heard the latch slide home behind him. "You shouldn't be here, Eddy. Don't get mixed up in this any more than you already are."

Eddy tapped his fingers on the table. He brought them to his face and smoothed his eyebrows. He sighed and tucked his hands under his legs. His toes rapped against the floor. "Trust me. I know I shouldn't be here. But... I wanted to talk to you. You know. Just say hello."

John let out a huff. "Sure. That sounds like the most natural thing in the world. Hey," he said in a sing-song voice, "Let's all go down to the police station and hang out with the guy everybody thinks killed his brother's partner."

Eddy's face burned bright red.

"Sorry. Jail gets old fast."

Eddy pulled his hands from beneath his legs and clasped them together on the table. John thought he heard something smack the floor. His eyes glanced to the camera, then back to Eddy.

What the hell was that?

His friend blinked one eye. "There were more than just a few of us who wanted to speak with you, John."

The sweat on his friend's face doubled within seconds. "Are you okay?"

"Yes. I'm completely fine." Eddy paused a moment. "Okay, not really. I'll just tell you. Nobody else is allowed to see you because of the investigation. Chief Burleson only allowed me in because he knows I went over the details of the case with you. There isn't anything you can tell me that I wouldn't already know. And in case you did, he's on the other side of the two-way mirror." Eddy's shoulders slumped as he leaned forward in his seat. "I don't know if he wanted me to tell you that or not, but I'm not very good at lying."

"That's the truth." The laugh he let out felt good. "Thanks, Eddy. I haven't had much of a reason to smile the past few days."

"There you go again." Eddy's partial smile slid back into place. "You're in jail on a suspected murder charge, and you make jokes. You're so weird."

"Why shouldn't I joke? This whole damn case is a joke. Why am I the only one who can see I'm being set up?" John slowed down and enunciated each word. "Why are you here, Eddy?"

A heavy sigh escaped his friend's mouth. "I'm here to ask if you did it. I don't think you did, but Chief Burleson says the evidence is air-tight. He hoped that I'd pull a confession from you."

"A confession to what?"

Eddy slammed his fists on the table. "This isn't a game, John!"

The door opened. Sergeant Clark poked his head in. "Everything okay, Mr. Bailey?"

Eddy's face flashed red yet again. "Sorry about that. I just got a little worked up." Eddy faced John again when Clark closed the door. "I'm serious, John. Things could get out of hand at any moment. You need to keep your head in the game."

The outburst had surprised John as much as the brute outside the door. "You just said it wasn't a game, but now you want me to keep my head in the game? Make up your mind, Eddy."

His friend closed his eyes and tilted his head toward the floor.

"Okay," John said. "I get the point, but until my lawyer calls back, I'm not sure what you want me to do. I've read the damn magazines in there so many times I could almost rehash Tiger Woods' entire career without missing a beat. I'm going crazy and nobody will tell me what's going on. They let me have another call this morning so I tried Rachel. She won't even call me back, and she's the one who gave me the lawyer's name in the first place."

The anger left Eddy's face. He sat back in his chair. "Um... I talked to your lawyer. She says she'll contact you shortly."

"You talked to my lawyer? How do you even know who my lawyer is?"

Eddy's eye twitched again. At least it looked like a twitch. One eye blinked and the other didn't. It looked more like a nervous tick than a wink.

"Why do you keep doing that?"

"Doing what?"

If a light bulb hung over his head, it would have just blinked on. *I'm such an idiot. No wonder he's acting like a freak.*

John leaned forward and made a show of stretching his neck. It wasn't much of a show since it was still tight from the night before. *Two cameras, both on Eddy's side of the table at the ceiling, one two-sided mirror to my right.*

"That's right." John shook his head and over-exaggerated another stretch. "I remember Rachel saying she'd have the lawyer contact you if she couldn't reach me." *C'mon, Eddy. You're smart. Just go along with it. You're not lying; you're just agreeing.*

Eddy's head tilted slightly to the side before he caught himself. If the cameras were on John's side of the table they might have seen how large his friend's eyes just were. "Of course. Yes, she, um, she contacted me and said she's having trouble with her car. That she'll contact you when she's in town."

John let out a monstrous groan. He leaned forward until his chest pressed against the table.

"Are you okay?" Eddy's breathing picked up pace. He reached forward and patted John's back.

"Yeah. I think so." He moaned again. "It's those tuna sandwiches they gave us last night. My gut hasn't felt right since." John screeched at the top of his lungs, a sound similar to a rooster crowing.

Eddy popped up from his seat. "Oh, my God, what's going on, John?"

John fell from the plastic chair into a heap under the table, rolling and writhing in pain. Through the tears, he saw the door open. Sergeant Clark was at his side in moments.

Clark grabbed John's jaw and spun his head around. Dark brown, almost black, eyes glared at him. "What's going on, Mr. Bailey? Do you know what's wrong?"

"I have no idea. He was just fine and then he started with that wretched noise." Eddy came around the table to stand over Clark's shoulder. Chief Burleson burst around the corner.

A horrendous belch poured from John's mouth, lasting several seconds. All three of the other men in the room leaned away.

John smacked his lips a few times. "Wow. That was a good one. Thought my stomach was going to burst. How old was that tuna?"

Eddy stifled a laugh. Clark rolled John over and pulled on the cuffs to stand him up.

The Chief stood inches from John's nose. "What the hell was that all about, Reeves?"

John displayed a sickly grin. "About two or three liters I'd say." When the chief didn't respond, he went on. "What can I say? I'm sorry. I haven't burped like that in years. I thought maybe my spleen had burst from the pounding it took at Clark's hands the other day."

Burleson shook his head. "Are you okay or do we need to bring a nurse in?"

"I'm feeling much better now. Thanks for asking."

"You want me to take him back to his cell?" Clark said.

The Chief looked to Eddy. "Is that okay with you, Eddy? Or was there something else you needed to speak with him about?"

"I'm sorry, Chief Burleson. I tried what you suggested. I don't think he's going to talk. I may as well go."

The Chief nodded. "Get him out of here, Clark. And, John?"

John looked back over his shoulder.

"Don't be pulling that shit again. If you plan to have some other random bodily function happen, tell us about it first."

John let himself be pulled away by Clark. The cop looked grumpier than usual behind him. "What's your problem, Clark? You should be happy. I saved you another ten minutes of standing around outside my door."

"I'll take another ten minutes of guard duty any day over smelling your stinky tuna burps."

A deep laugh came from John, and from Clark as well. It must have surprised the cop as much as it did John, because he flushed and didn't say another word until he was about to close the cell door.

"I suppose I could grab you another magazine if you want. I have a couple on my desk I was about to toss."

Their scuffle a few days before must have earned Clark's respect. Either that or the cop was a great actor. John didn't want to lose that respect now. "That would be great, Clark. And ah... sorry about the whole tackling you into the door thing."

Clark nodded and closed the cell door.

John hurried to the toilet at the back of his temporary living quarters and dropped his pants. He sat down and bent low as if his stomach hurt. Deep inside his pocket was the cell phone Eddy had dropped in the interview room.

I don't know how the hell you expect me to use this, Eddy, but thanks.

The phone vibrated. He almost pulled it out to see who the call was from but he didn't know how close of an eye Burleson had on him. It vibrated two more times in quick succession.

What the hell?

It vibrated three times in a row again, this time much slower, then followed with three fast vibrations.

Well, holy shit.

A memory flashed into John's mind. He sat in a chair across from his father in their basement. Another training session.

"Okay, Johnny. This one will take a bit to learn, but it's needed. I'll explain why later. For now, concentrate on the length of each flash." Ed Reeves held a small flashlight pointed at the wall between them. Three quick flashes. Three second flash, three second flash, three second flash. Three quick flashes. "Did you get that?"

"I did, but what does it mean?"

"That was an S.O.S. Kind of like when you hear ship captains yell mayday. The letters don't necessarily stand for anything, but they mean you need help."

"But why would I need help?" John was only seven or eight at the time, still much to learn about the world.

"You never know, and you never know when you won't have a phone or a radio that works right. It's called Morse code. You must learn it. It could save your life one day."

John opened his eyes. The phone continued to vibrate. He closed his eyes to concentrate again. "S.O.S... This... Rachel... Respond... With... Side... Button..."

You sneaky woman. What are you up to now? John couldn't imagine what would possess Rachel to try something so idiotic, or how she talked Eddy into going along with it.

He slid his thumb along the side of the phone and felt a raised button. Happy at his dad's odd parenting habits, he responded. "Here."

"Snively called FBI. You need out before arrival."

John faked a yawn and leaned back to glance over the cement partition. He expected to see Clark or Gibbs peering through the small glass window on the door. Nobody showed their face.

Leaning forward again, he took hold of the phone in his pocket. "How know?"

"Hacked mayor email."

What did I ever do to deserve a friend like you, Rachel? With a smile, he coded his response. "Plan?"

"Message midnight. Be ready."

"What to do?"

"Patience. Cocky mouth shut lay low."

He stifled a laugh when he translated her words. He shot a quick glance over the partition again. "Explains no lawyer. Talk soon, babycakes." She hated the nickname he'd given her when they were an item.

Rachel responded once more before the phone went silent. "Asshole."

21. Escape

Donuts

"Hey, Ruth. It's Alan Reeves. I'm sorry for calling so late, but could you stop over?"

"You better be careful, Alan. A woman might think you're inviting her over for a less than proper evening."

"No, it's not that, I just—"

"I'm kidding. I was watching reruns of Blue Ice. You ever seen it?"

Ruth's casual attitude released the tension in Alan's neck. He hadn't realized the extent of his anxiety. "I've heard of it, but never watched it. I get enough of the police at work."

"That's what everybody in the department says. Is there something you needed or are we having another heart to heart?"

"I don't know if I'd call it a heart to heart, but yeah, a talk is exactly what I'm looking for." Lately, most of his talking happened with Lena at the hospital, but he hadn't visited much.

"One personal counselor, coming right up. I'll be over in fifteen minutes. Just don't expect me to be my usual chipper self."

Alan hung up and settled into the rocking chair on his porch. Sleep wouldn't come. He'd hoped a break from work would ease the terror-filled nights. Instead, they'd increased.

The oak rocking chair his father had built tilted back and forth on thick runners, creaking against the floorboards. The evening's muggy heat grew worse as the night wore on. He remembered sitting on his parents' front porch, their father in the same chair spinning tales late into the evening for John and him. As a child, he'd assumed the forays into cop-land adventures were a secret from their mother since it was always just the boys. Now older, he realized she probably left them to it and considered the storytelling a bonding experience between father and sons.

Tears threatened to fall. He wiped his eyes and forced the thoughts of his childhood away. With Ruth Shaw arriving in a few minutes, he focused on where their conversations might turn. Alan imagined what Rita would say. 'Wow, old man. You reached out this time. No more holding your emotions back?'

Truth was, he wasn't sure why he had called Ruth, except she was the only one he'd opened up to about the case. Eddy wouldn't return his calls. They'd never been that close anyway. Eddy and John had been a few years behind him in school.

Thinking back, Alan felt guilty he'd considered himself too cool to hang out with the likes of Eddy, a geek in every sense of the word including the glasses. Alan had been a football player, and the quarterback as well, though John almost pilfered that role. The coaches had wanted to see how the athletic fourteen-year-old fared in the pit with seniors.

Alan's cell vibrated his front pocket. The Caller ID showed Ruth's name. "Ruth? If you can't stop over that's fine."

"Are you kidding me? When a handsome young man like you calls me to his house this late at night, I wouldn't miss it for the world. I'm actually calling to see if you still prefer the custard donuts. I stopped at the all-night place to fill up on gas and thought sugar would do us good."

That's Ruth, always thinking of everybody else. "Custard sounds great. Ask my vest. I'm about to move up a size."

"I noticed. Last time I saw you in uniform, your buttons looked like they were about to jump ship."

"Just get over here with those donuts before I change my mind, you brat."

The grin on his face felt strange, as if he'd spent so long frowning that his facial muscles had forgotten how to do anything else. His thoughts wandered to the tight smile Rita had saved for him when in the presence of other officers. They'd talk about it later when alone, how they fooled whoever they were with. They should have known better than trying to fool other cops.

Minutes later, Ruth's LeSabre convertible pulled into the driveway. Alan met her at the car.

"Have to enjoy these warm nights in Michigan while you can," she said. "Tomorrow may bring snow." The driver-side door creaked when she opened it.

He hefted the bag of donuts from her hand. "Let me get those for you." He started toward the house and opened the bag to check out the goods.

She caught his sleeve, spinning him around to face her before he could get more than a step away. Her arms flew around his midsection in a tight embrace. She whispered into his chest. "With you being a tough guy, I didn't figure you'd let me do this if I asked."

After a moment's hesitation, he returned the squeeze. They held each other close until she finally pushed him away.

She smacked him on the shoulder. "That's for calling me a brat. Now let's break out that coffee I know you're brewing." She yanked the bag from his hands. "And let's eat these on the porch. It's too nice to be inside, even if it's late."

Alan followed, smiling at how lucky he was to have a friend in Ruth. "The weather's nice now, but my gut tells me it's going to rain."

Leaving

John glanced through the window on his cell door once in a while to check the time. The hours ticked by. He'd tucked the cell phone behind the toilet and covered it with sanitary paper.

He still couldn't believe he was going along with Rachel's idea. Being wrongfully arrested was one thing, escaping from jail was a different story. Besides breaking the law, if they caught him again, the prosecutor would press the jury about how his escape showed his guilt.

Push-ups, crunches, and stretching left him limber while in his cell. Since his chat with Rachel, he'd doubled his everyday routine to relieve stress. Exercise helped a little, yet he still jumped at every little noise. Fighting for his life, or another's, came naturally. Breaking the law; not so much. He'd done so in the past but for good reason. Like the time he'd pressed his Glock to a cop's head while the oaf sat on a public toilet. Then, he'd needed answers from the dirty cop to protect his friend. Protecting his own hide from the police wasn't as easy.

Spending years in prison wasn't a pleasant thought but the anxiety and fear he felt now stemmed from how Alan might treat him if he believed the evidence over John's word. John didn't lie without justification, he never had and Alan knew this, but this situation was different. Somehow, his semen had been found at the scene of Rita's death. How, he had no clue.

Thanks, Clark, for sharing that piece of news with me.

The burly cop had treated him with a measure of respect since their bonding moment earlier in the day. He'd stopped in a few times at Chief Burleson's behest, mentioning the new evidence off hand. Either Clark shared the information to be nice, or the Chief had him do it to measure John's response.

When Clark had delivered dinner, he mentioned it wasn't a tuna sandwich. He'd winked and left. John had a laugh when he found a salmon patty instead. He'd finished the meal in record time, addling his anxiety-ridden stomach with more acid. Though he'd faked the cramps when chatting with Eddy, they weren't far from the truth.

John sat with both feet up on the bench and pretended to read one of the golf magazines, his toes tapping to the rhythm of his rapidly increasing heartbeat. He rolled the magazine into a tube and held it to his eye like a telescope. The clock read five minutes to midnight.

Time for a long trip to the John.

He snickered at his own joke and stepped behind the cement partition. With a quick glance through the window, he dropped his pants and sat, pushing his feet forward enough that anybody peering in would assume he used the toilet. He removed the heap of toilet paper and left it in case he needed to hide the phone again.

At first, he tapped his feet in anticipation. He imagined how wiggling feet might look to a passerby and stopped. To pass the last bit of time, he counted the seconds. He reached to the floor and used the pile of toilet paper to form a circle. A square. An idea formed. He set the paper just how he wanted.

The phone vibrated across the floor.

Rachel's message came through. "Ready?"

"4 what?" he coded back.

"Last code I send. Communicating slow. Call. Phone vibrate. No ringer."

The phone vibrated. He flipped it open. "You realize this is crazy, right?"

"Definitely. I accessed the cameras and computer systems. Everything is operated by computer, and I mean everything. Also, I'm receiving two separate feeds from the cameras."

"What's that mean?"

"Someone else may have tapped the system. Doesn't matter right now. I can see your every move. Pull up your drawers and stand up."

He hurriedly covered himself. "How in hell do you know I have my pants down? They're not supposed to have a camera in here."

"I can't. Your feet stick out."

He rolled his eyes and pulled up his jeans. At least his trick had worked. He paced the short length of the cell. "What's next?"

"Close the phone and hide it right now!"

John had learned not to question Rachel. He slid the phone into his back pocket and fell onto the stone bench with a crunch. He cringed.

Keys jingled against the outside of the door as Sergeant Clark's face appeared through the window. He opened the door and leaned in. "Hey. I'm leaving for the night. You need another magazine, or are you good?"

John pretended to be distraught. Not hard to do at the moment. "Oh, I suppose I'll be alright."

"Alrighty, how are you feeling? You want me to grab something for your stomach?"

Just leave already. "Much better, thanks. Must be that salmon did the trick."

Clark laughed and closed the door, locking it behind him.

He counted to one-hundred before the phone vibrated beneath him. He turned away from the window and slid the phone out. He flipped it open, noting the loose hinge. "Jeez, woman. I almost pushed the phone through the cement with my ass. Warn me next time."

A giggle whispered from the phone. "I'll send in a smoke signal next time. Turn around and get ready."

John did as told.

"The big guy is about to leave. I was going to wait until the girl cop at the front desk left for a bathroom break, but this will work just as well."

He waited for her to go on. A few seconds passed, and he couldn't wait anymore. "What are we waiting for?"

"Calm down, toughy. The big guy and the girl are chatting. Wait. Okay, she followed him to the front. You don't have much time. When I open the door, step out and close it behind you. Go right until you come to a short hallway with light blue walls."

"When you open the door?"

A quiet buzzing came from the door. With a low click, the latch slid free. He nudged the door and it swung open a few inches. *Well, son-of-a-bitch.* John held the phone to his ear and glided from the cell on silent feet. The door closed as quietly as it opened.

"Go, now! She's coming back. And stay low."

Crouching, John hurried to the light blue hallway past desks and office chairs, the same hallway that lead to the interrogation rooms. "I'm there," he whispered.

"I know. I can see you, remember? Now shush. Two more officers are in the break-room. You'll need to pass them on your way out. There's no door, so we'll have to time it."

John caught himself before he cussed. *I'm so going to bitch you out if I make it out of here. You know I hate being shushed.*

"Hold for a second and stay low in case the girl cop goes to the bathroom. She's back at the front desk now. There's one cop at the pop machine in the break room. He'd see you if you tried now. Stay close to the wall on your right. The break room is about thirty feet ahead, also on the right. Once you pass it, you'll continue another ten feet and take a right."

John glanced in the direction of the break room. More desks were on his left, the wall on his right held signs and pictures of missing children. Directly ahead was a wood-paneled wall showing America's Most Wanted. Squatted low, John's knees pressed against his stomach, reminding him that he hadn't actually used the toilet in his cell before leaving.

Great time to forget to take a piss, John.

In the military, they were taught to go where they were when in the field. They might not move for hours or days. The police station isn't like some sandy side street in the Middle East. A puddle in the middle of the waxed glossy floor would stand out. He certainly wouldn't get caught with wet pants either.

"Okay, go," Rachel chirped. "Stay low. The desks between you and the woman at the front should keep you hidden."

"Should?"

"Shut up, John. It'll work. Now be quiet."

He stayed in a crouch and waddled down the hall, each movement reminding him of his need to urinate.

Savior

"Whatever you're doing, stop, and come to me. Now!"

The skinny man's voice whispered through the phone. "What is it? I was just about to tuck my kids in."

"Don't question me! I am your savior. Do as I say."

"I apologize. I'll grab the keys and be right over."

"Stay on the phone. We need to talk." The Savior tapped his foot while he waited. Muffled voices came through the phone for a moment, followed by the sound of a car door opening and then slamming shut.

"I'm in my car now. What is it, my Savior?"

The Savior fought to keep his anger under control. "John Reeves is up to something. He has a phone in his cell."

"That's not possible. I took his phone myself."

"Not *his* phone, you idiot. *A* phone. He's talking on it right now. He sat bent over on that toilet for so long, I thought he was sick. He had to have been signaling someone this whole time!"

The skinny man's voice cracked. "Sh- should I go to the station then?"

"Yes, ignore what I said first. Go to the station and find out what's happening. Wait a moment." On the screen, John hustled to the cement bench in his cell and sat down. "Something is happening. Get on your way, but keep me on the line."

A muscular cop looked in on John. They exchanged a few words before he left.

"There! He has the phone out. He's speaking to someone right now."

The skinny man's engine roared in the background. "I'll be at the station in less than two minutes."

"No. Don't wait. Call the station now. Tell them John has left his cell."

"I don't see how that's possible."

"Question me no more! Do as I say. You will pay for your insubordination later."

"What do I tell them? How would I know he escaped?"

The fear in the skinny man's voice only stoked the Savior's emotions. "It does not matter. Figure it out later. For now, do as I say."

"Yes, my Savior."

22. Hump and Donuts

Hound

John sidled up to the break room doorway and peeked in.

"Stop!" Rachel yelled in his ear.

He lurched back, his already pounding heart doubled in speed. John held up his middle finger hoping Rachel watched from the camera tucked above an office door a few feet away.

"Well, that's not very nice. Tell me again why I'm getting you out of jail?"

He showed the camera an exaggerated smile.

"Better. Now wait a moment. The guy just grabbed his soda from the machine. He's back at the table again. Go."

John resisted the urge to look into the break room as he shuffled past, focusing on each quiet step. The hallway to his right came fast. He rounded the corner.

"What's that face, John? Looks like you're in pain. Never mind, just get down that hallway. The last door on your right leads to the garage. You should be able to stand up now. The evidence room partition should block you from the cop up front."

If muscles could talk, or a bladder, they'd thank John for standing. He shook both legs out, easing the tightness. Bending at the waist, but not as low as before, he started down the hallway. He crept past a few offices; the city clerk, the treasurer. The Chief's door at the end of the hall he remembered all too well. *I wonder what Burleson will think of me escaping his department.* A smile formed on John's face. He reached to open the garage door.

From the front of the station, a phone rang as loud as a freight train. At least it sounded like a train to John's ears. He slid through the doorway and spun around to peer around the edge toward where the female cop answered the phone.

"Clarkbridge Police Department. Can I help you?"

Whatever the person on the other end of the line said, it wasn't good. The cop leapt to her feet, head snapping to the side so fast John wondered how it didn't break. Her glare focused directly on his cell.

"John," Rachel cried from the phone still held tightly to his ear. "Go now. Don't hide; don't wait. Go!"

He had just enough time to see the cop dart from her desk.

"Oh shit." He closed the door as quietly as he could manage with adrenaline bursting through his system. He slid the phone in his pocket and surveyed the dark garage. The single bulb high on the vaulted ceiling flickered when thunder rumbled outside. Tight legs carried him toward the only visible door in the back. John slammed down the metal handle and rushed into a deluge. The parking lot's flood lamp combined with flashing lightning lit his way across the parking lot and through the houses behind the station. He hopped a mesh fence into the second yard he came to, slipping on the grass when he landed. He caught his balance and ran deeper into the yard.

Another lightning flash imprinted a gray doghouse into his vision. He dropped to his knees and slid behind the house. He peered around the edge toward the station garage. Through the misty darkness and torrential rain, light pierced the night from the flood light over the garage. The doorway framed at least two cops. One took off to his right, the female he guessed by the shades of hair blowing about her head, the other tilted its head to the side, probably speaking into a shoulder radio.

If he couldn't see them, they definitely couldn't see him. Warmth slid across the hand John held to the side of the doghouse. He almost screamed. Long ears and a smile greeted him in the form of a hound dog.

"Well hey there, buddy. You get back inside your house. It's much too rainy for you to be out here." The dog let out a low growl when John glided his hand across its furry head, a playful growl. "Trust me. I'd much rather stay here and play. But I've got places to be." He patted the hound on the head one more time and turned toward the next fence to climb.

The hound dog's deep howl soon joined the shrill scream of sirens belting out behind him.

The Hump

John leaned on a fallen white pine to catch his breath, Beech Road only yards behind him. A heavy fog had formed soon after the downpour. Sirens continued to howl throughout the city. Rachel guided him according to where the officers reported they were or weren't searching. At one point, he'd climbed into another doghouse, this one much larger than the first. He'd been thankful the animal wasn't there. Any doghouse he could fit into had to be home to a giant.

The damp, earthy air filled his lungs. Headlights crested the hill on Beech Road. He crouched. Probably not necessary, but he wouldn't take any chances. He'd headed straight for the nearest wooded section on the outskirts of the city, two miles from the station. It felt like ten. The unnatural stress frayed at his nerves. The break was more about calming himself than catching his breath. On a normal day, two miles was an easy jog.

The tail lights disappeared. He stood and took stock of his wooded surroundings. Unfortunately, the thickest woodland area was in the opposite direction he needed to go. Even if he stuck close to the city, which he didn't plan to do with all the Clarkbridge officers sure to be following, his destination hung at least another ten miles away.

Closer to fifteen. He growled. *Suck it up, John. Just like a fifteen mile hump.* Even if he wasn't carrying a hundred pounds of gear as he had as a Marine, a ten to fifteen mile trek was no easy task.

He grinned in resignation and hurried north through the thick forest.

Phone Call

Alan dug his teeth into another custard donut. Ruth smiled and slid the last bit of a mini-kruller into her mouth. Rain pelted the now closed roof of her convertible. The downpour began moments after Alan pressed the brew button on his coffee maker. Watching Ruth hustle through the rain and then wait while the automatic roof closed had lightened Alan's mood. He gave her a flannel shirt to wear while hers tumbled in the dryer.

He squinted in the direction of her car. "You have fog lamps on that thing?"

Ruth wiped the stray crumbs from her mouth with a napkin. "I do, and it looks like I'll need them. I can't believe the fog grew so thick so fast."

They sat in a comfortable silence. Alan finished his snack and sucked the sugar from his fingertips. Ruth shot him a look that reminded him to use his napkin. He finished and tossed it into the empty donut bag. "You know, Ruth. I invited you over to help me relax. Not stuff me full of sugar and caffeine. The point is to get more sleep, not less."

"Whatever, you booger. This is the thanks I get for bringing over your favorite food?" She paused and tilted her head to the side. "You hear that?"

"Hear what?" Alan laughed when he realized he tilted his head to the side as she had.

"Sounds like sirens."

"I don't hear anyth—oh. There it is. I'll turn on the scanner." He stood from the rocking chair.

Ruth huffed. "You sit your butt back down. Neither of us are on call. Whatever it is, they can handle it."

Alan paused with his hand on the screen door handle. "Really? You can turn it off like that?"

"I don't know what you mean by 'like that,' but yes, I can ignore sirens."

He shrugged and sat back down. "I guess I can if you can."

Ruth gave a satisfied nod and cradled her hands on her lap, peering at the falling rain. She hopped a couple inches in her seat. "Oh."

Alan stood again. "What is it?"

"My cell phone. I'll never get used to these darned things." She slid her hand into the purse tucked into the corner of her seat and pulled out her phone. "Sergeant Shaw," she answered. Her eyes shot to Alan. "Are you sure? Dumb question. Of course you're sure."

He couldn't sit back down. The look she'd given him chilled him to the bone. He held his hands up in question.

She waved for him to sit back down. "I'm actually there now. I'll let him know. Thanks, Chief." She hung up and tossed her phone back into the open purse.

"So?"

"Don't get snippy with me." Ruth stood. She pulled open the screen door and gestured for him to go in first.

He stepped into his house and sat at the kitchen table; though, he wanted to pace. *Why do women always feel they need to control a man?* "Will you tell me what's going on already?"

Ruth stood in the doorway between the kitchen and the short breezeway to the front door, her jovial attitude gone. "Promise you won't do anything stupid."

Alan fought to stay in his chair. "Who starts a conversation like that? How can I promise when I don't know what's going on?"

She sighed. "Fine. At least promise you'll *try* not to."

He waved for her to go on.

"John escaped from the Clarkbridge jail."

Alan shot to his feet. "What? How?"

"The chief didn't say much, but he did say they weren't sure how. May have been a computer glitch."

Rachel. He didn't voice his opinion out loud, but Alan would bet his favorite mounted deer head that she had something to do with it.

"Why'd you make that face, Alan?"

"What face?"

Ruth moved into the kitchen. "The one you're making right now. I grew up with three brothers; I know when a man is hiding something."

Alan slumped into his chair and ran a hand through his hair. "It's probably nothing. I don't want to say anything unless I have more proof."

She crossed her arms. "Don't ignore this. If you know something, tell me. Don't protect John, it will only make things worse in the end. Think about what you said the other day, about how you let your emotions get in the way."

He placed his elbows on the table and looked her in the eye. "If I knew something about the case, I would tell you." *Just let it go, Ruth. If there's even the slightest chance John is innocent...* He sighed and let his face fall into his hands. *Don't be a fool, Alan. Look at all the proof they have.* The facts and what Alan felt in his heart fought a silent argument in his mind.

Ruth's gentle touch settled on his shoulder. "I know this can't be easy, but stay with me. I may be a fellow cop, but I'm also your friend. If you need to talk, I'm here."

Alan reached back and rested his hand on Ruth's. "I know, Ruth. And I appreciate that more than you know." He stood, keeping her hand held in his own. "I should go to the station. Learn what I can. I might be able to share some insight into what John was thinking. At least try."

She must have sensed his determination. "Fine. I'll tell Chief Burleson you're coming in. But I'm driving. And we leave when I say."

"Let me grab my firearm and we'll be on our way." *And please, God, don't let John give me a reason to use it.*

23. Tree House

The Station

Alan sat in the passenger side of Ruth's LeSabre, a moist towel beneath him. They had doubled back to his house when they realized she still wore his shirt. The station had enough problems without the two of them starting another rumor.

She ran from his house holding the donut bag over her head. She tossed the wet bag to the backseat and sat on a towel of her own. "Thanks for letting me borrow your shirt. And this towel too. Who knew car seats could absorb water so fast?"

Alan smiled but didn't say anything. He continued to picture John escaping from his cell. He didn't see how it was possible, but he wouldn't put anything past his brother. Or Rachel.

Ruth phoned Chief Burleson when they left for the station again. "I told Alan the same thing. He might see something we don't. Be there in a couple minutes." She paused. "You want me to ask him what? That's what I thought you said. Just a sec."

"What?" Butterflies danced in his stomach.

"He wants to know if the word 'bump' means anything to you."

"Bump? Like bump on a log?"

"They found toilet paper on the floor of John's cell shaped into the word 'bump'."

Alan gazed at Ruth as she drove, but his mind traveled to another time. His father, Ed Reeves, stood before him, hammering a nail into a two-by-four. The piece of lumber would become the first rung of a ladder leading to the tree house he built that summer.

John, only two or three years old at the time, yanked on a low hanging branch attached to the tree they planned to work on.

"You be careful, Johnny," their father had said. "That branch doesn't look very sturdy. You could fall and get a bump."

No sooner than the words were out of his mouth, with a crack, the branch snapped from the tree. John lost his balance and stumbled backward until he fell. The back of his head slammed on the pile of lumber meant for the tree house.

Alan had stifled a giggle, but their father rushed to his brother's side. Ed Reeves slid his hands under John's arms and hefted him high into the air. "What did I tell you, kiddo?"

"Bump!" he had yelled through the sobs while rubbing the back of his head.

Ed kissed John's head and placed him on the ground, hands still held on his shoulders. "You'll be okay but listen carefully. There will be times when you want to do things your daddy says not to. Remember, every word I say is to keep you safe. To protect you."

John had nodded and whispered, "Bump."

For years, John called the tree house 'bump.' Alan didn't know if it was because he remembered falling down, or if he'd associated the word with the place.

"Alan."

He shook his head.

Ruth glanced at him from the driver's seat. "You still with me? Chief wants to know if it means anything."

Alan shook his head. "No. Nothing."

Ruth squinted in his direction a moment before responding to Chief Burleson. "Doesn't mean anything to him either, Chief." When she hung up she pulled to the side of the road. "I don't know what's going on in that brain of yours, but let me remind you again. If you know something, you'd best tell me now. It will make things easier in the long run. You know this."

The logical side of Alan won the battle. "Fine. I'll tell you what I think 'bump' means, but now you have to make me a promise." The glare she shot him almost changed his mind but he held strong. She slowly nodded. "Promise you'll let me check it out alone. If John's where I think he is, he has something to tell me. If you knew John like I do, you'd know he wouldn't do something like break out of jail without good reason."

"There aren't many good reasons to break out of jail. If he's there and we don't tell the Chief, you know the consequences. Fines, jail time, even accomplice to murder if he's found guilty."

Alan continued to wait for her answer.

"Fine. I promise. Where is he?"

"Head back to my house."

Ruth shook her head. "If I get in trouble for this, Captain Reeves, you'll learn the real definition of punishment."

Flashlight

Alan dug under a pile of boots and hunting gear stashed in the closet.

"Why not just use your tactical flashlight?" Ruth called from behind.

He called to Ruth over his shoulder. "I could, but they don't have a very wide beam. My hunting flashlight uses an LED bulb. It's almost as bright as a tactical flashlight, and the beam is much wider. I don't think John will cause any problems, but in case there really is something wrong with him, I'd like to see him before he sees me. Regardless of what is or isn't going on with his brain, John is a dangerous man."

The words must have satisfied her because her questions stopped. Moments later, he crawled backward out of the pile with the lantern flashlight held in his fist. "Here we go." He pushed the screen door open to leave. Ruth began to follow. "Wait," he said. "You need to stay here."

"Here? You're not taking my car."

"I'm not. I'm going to the woods behind my parents' old house."

"What?"

Alan let the door close and led Ruth toward the kitchen. "John may be headed toward an old tree house we played in as children. You said you'd let me go alone."

For a moment, he thought she'd changed her mind. Her features softened. "Take your firearm with you. I don't want you getting hurt. And if you're not back here in fifteen minutes, I'm calling for backup."

"I'll need longer than that. It'll take me at least that long just to get back there. It's heavily wooded, nighttime, foggy, and rainy."

"All reasons you shouldn't be going out there alone."

"Trust me, Ruth. You know I'm not stupid. Would Ed Reeves have raised a stupid son?"

Ruth turned away and stood on the tips of her toes, digging around in the cupboard for another coffee cup. "I'm brewing another pot then. It's already well after midnight. I was kidding earlier when I said I'd spend the night with you." The hint of a smile appeared at the corner of her mouth.

Alan found himself admiring the tight fit of her jeans. He shook his head. "Actually, I think I'll join you. If John has to travel this whole way on foot—and I don't think he's stupid enough to steal a vehicle—then he'll probably need at least another hour to get here."

Ruth turned to him, eyebrows raised. "You're just going to sit here and have a cup of coffee while your brother skedaddles his way through the woods to your old play house?"

"It's a tree house. And yes, I'd much rather spend it here with you than out in that crap." He gestured over his shoulder to the kitchen window.

She nodded, pink coloring her cheeks. "Well good. However, I do have to mention that your brother was stupid enough to break out of jail. Why would stealing a car be any different?"

Alan pulled a kitchen chair from the table and sat. "Good point. If he gets there before me, then he can just wait. Hopefully the roof blew from the tree house years ago. That's the least he deserves for putting me through this."

Ruth spooned ground coffee into the machine. "Now you're thinking clearly."

"What reason did you give the Chief for us not coming down to the station?"

She glanced at him and smiled. She went back to preparing the coffee. "I didn't realize you couldn't hear me when you were in that closet. I told him we were headed back to your house so I could warm you up."

Slogging

An hour and a pot of coffee later, Alan slogged down the muddy path toward the back of his property. The rain hadn't slowed and the mist grew thicker. He'd told Ruth to call the chief if he didn't return within two hours. Working his way to the old tree house would take a half hour minimum. He wanted the extra time to himself since John would likely take longer to arrive through the rain and dense fog.

The tree line at the edge of his property came sooner than expected. He followed it left to his parents' property. Technically, it was his property since they left it to him in their will. He never thought of it that way though. The way he still viewed the living room couch as theirs. They were no longer with him, but their memories lived too strong in his mind to view it in any other way.

Water trickled down between his shoulder blades. The old Carhart jacket held the rain out longer than expected. His hat was another story. Rain water poured from the brim in rivulets.

He spotted the break in the tree line on his right, surprised the path was still well worn. The flashlight's beam shook. He lowered his eyes to his hand. It shook as well. Pausing, he inhaled the musty air and let it out slowly. The facts in his mind continued to battle with what he felt in his gut. The accusations against John couldn't be true. Yet, all the facts said they were. Unless his brother had suffered some sort of psychotic break, the facts had to be falsified.

Who could do that?

Alan recounted every element of the murders he could remember. He didn't know what good it would do. He'd done the same every day since Rita's disappearance, since before. Something was missing, some cohesive element that should bring everything together. He faced every brother's nightmare; he had to choose between his sibling's word and the damning facts.

He began moving again.

The one person his mind returned to over and again was Russell Holbrook. He'd offered his services to the department based on his belief they would come looking for him anyway. It made sense, but his squeaky clean record didn't sit right. He knew more about the victims than anybody else, especially if his credentials as a renowned psychiatrist were true.

Where were you when Rita disappeared?

The easy explanation was that the department hadn't called him in. Why would they contact him on a seemingly unrelated case?

Light reflected from water running down the bark on the looming, wet oak tree before him. He moved the flashlight beam slowly up the glistening trunk. Still intact, the tree house listed slightly to the side, the huge branches having grown over the years. He aimed the light at the glassless window. A pair of eyes glowed back.

Muddy Knees

John leaned against the inside of the tree house wall. The trip hadn't taken as long as expected, but his lungs and muscles burned from the effort. Now it was up to Alan to understand the message he left with the toilet paper. He chortled. Thinking about it now, it seemed such a crazy thing.

Not any more crazy than escaping from jail.

The phone lit the tree house as he flipped it open to check the signal. Nothing. He'd had three full bars until soon after entering his father's old clover field. He'd spoken with Rachel a few times in the city to help with his escape but chose to save the phone's power since he didn't know when or if he'd have a chance to charge it.

He closed his eyes. Heavy rain pounded the shingled roof, beating out a steady cadence. Other than the rain and fog, the weather was pleasant enough. For as late as it was, the heat pressed against him like a blanket, his sweat mixing with his rain-soaked clothes. Tomorrow's humidity would slow even the most prolific runner.

The light crack of a branch brought John's eyes open.

Please, let it just be Alan.

He rolled on to his hands and knees. Below him, only yards away, stood a dark figure in the night, a flashlight in hand. The beam moved slowly up the tree until it focused in his eyes.

"Hey there, Alan. Kind of late and rainy to be out playing at our childhood haunts, don't ya' think?"

"Get down here, John. You better tell me if you have any weapons too."

Shit. He doesn't trust me. "Coming down. Just don't get trigger happy. I don't have any weapons." The ladder built from two-by-fours held strong as he lowered himself down step by step. When he reached the bottom, he raised his hands and took his time turning around. "See? No weapons."

"Down on your knees."

"Really? Come on. I told you where I was so—"

"I said get down. Now!" The flashlight shook in Alan's hands.

John nodded and fell to his knees on the mucky forest floor. "Take it easy. Am I allowed to talk yet?" Alan rushed forward and put the barrel of his gun to John's forehead. *Definitely doesn't trust me.* "Look, I don't know what you heard, or what they told you, but I had nothing to do with it."

Alan's words pushed through gritted teeth. "Then why did you escape? Why would you do that if you weren't crazy enough to kill Rita? No more bullshit!"

The gun's nozzle pushed John back to sit on his feet. The flashlight shined in his eyes from inches away. "An FBI agent will be at the station tomorrow. I'm being set up, and nobody can see it. If I waited until the agent showed up, they'd haul me off to another location and I'd never have another chance to figure this out." The pressure from Alan's gun eased on John's head.

"How do you know? The Chief didn't even tell me that."

"That's because he doesn't know. That bitch, Mayor Snively, brought them in."

"I asked how you know."

John sighed. "Promise me you won't tell anybody." The weapon pressed harder into his skin.

"I'm not promising you anything. If somebody is really setting you up, they're doing a hell of a job. But the semen, John, how do you fake that?"

"How the hell would I know?"

"Just tell me where you heard about the agent."

A tear may have run down Alan's face, but John couldn't tell with all the rain. *If this goes bad, I'm sorry Rachel.* "Rachel McCall hacked Snively's computer."

Alan stepped back, finally removing the weapon. "Rachel? She can do that?"

John rubbed at the indentation on his forehead. "She can, and more. I told you she was good."

"What else did she tell you?"

"We'll have time for that later. Right now I need you to listen to me. I may know who's in on this."

Alan lowered but didn't holster the weapon. He stepped back and lowered the light to the ground between them. "How could you possibly know?"

"Can I put my arms down now? Maybe sit? The long-ass run wiped me out."

Alan gestured to the ground with his flashlight.

John slumped deeper into the mud and fought with weary legs until he sat cross-legged. Not the most comfortable place to have a conversation, but better than on his knees. "Russell Holbrook. It seems obvious now that I look back, but I still don't see any motive. He's the only one who knows details of the case and isn't a longtime friend of either you or me. He stuck his nose into the investigation. Both you and I know it seemed an odd thing at the time."

"Proof?"

"None. Just a gut feeling. Think about it. The night I went out with him for drinks, I just happened to black out? I assumed it was the alcohol, but now I'm not so sure. I wish I'd remembered to call and ask him about it."

Alan nodded and holstered his gun. "I keep coming back to Holbrook too. He just seems like the only piece that doesn't fit. That's not much to go on. If Snively is truly bringing in the FBI, we don't have much time."

His brother's words surprised John. "So you feel it too? I've had Rachel on it this whole time. So far she hasn't come up with anything. I don't have a signal out here, but when I get closer to town, I'll tell her to get on it."

"When are you planning to go to town?"

"Soon, I can't help but think Eddy might be in trouble. I'm the obvious target, but why? Since we don't know, I think it's best you keep your backside covered until we learn. Whoever is doing this has specific targets, and they all have some connection to you or me."

"Easy to do since Clarkbridge is so small." Alan shook his head. "What do we do now then? What will you do with Eddy?"

John rolled to his side and pulled himself up, wiping the mud from his hands on his pants. "I just want to check on him. Make sure he's okay. Like I said though, my phone doesn't have a signal."

"How'd you get your phone back?"

"It's a long story."

"Just tell me later." Alan reached into his pocket and brought out his cell phone. "Want to try him on mine? There's a signal. Not strong, but it's there."

John's roiling stomach settled. He had his brother's trust again. At least partially. "Yeah, let me give him a try." The phone rang until Eddy's voicemail picked up. John handed the phone back. "Not answering, though it is pretty early in the morning."

Alan glanced at his phone before placing it back in his pocket. "It is late. I need to get back to the house before Ruth calls the chief."

"As in Ruth Shaw?"

"Yeah."

"Shit." *Hopefully she has a short memory.*

"What is it, John?"

"I may have made fun of her hair color when they picked me up at Eddy's house."

"May have?"

"Okay. I did make fun of her. I didn't mean anything by it. I was under a lot of stress. Look, I need to get going to Eddy's. What will you tell Ruth?"

Alan waved for John to follow. "Come on. I'll at least see you out of the thick stuff. I'll tell her the truth. When I didn't find you here, I sat and waited awhile."

Minutes later, they worked their way through the last bit of brush. They paused at the edge of their parents' clover field. The flashlight beam disappeared in the heavy mist after only a few feet.

John placed his hand on Alan's shoulder. His muscles tensed so John let go. "I don't know what's going to happen, but either way, thank you, Alan. I'll head to Eddy's now. I'll have him contact you when I get there."

Alan shook his head. "Not a good idea. I wouldn't be surprised if that bitch Snively already has our calls monitored. I shouldn't have even let you call Eddy a minute ago but I didn't think about it. From here on out, we should limit communication unless we find something solid. And we better find it fast. You have one hour before I report to the Chief I found your tracks out by the tree house. If I don't tell them, you know they'll question me."

John nodded and heaved a breath thinking about the five-mile trek ahead of him. Much shorter than the last, but no more pleasant. He turned to leave.

Alan called from behind him. "John?"

He paused.

"Be careful. Remember the weird factor from the other cases. If Holbrook is truly in on this, expect him to have friends."

24. Note

Savior's Warning

"Kneel."

"But, my Savior, it wasn't my fault." The skinny man whimpered, falling to his knees. The uneven cement floor dug into his skin. "I wasn't even there."

The Savior slid a scalpel to the sobbing man's scrawny neck. "You say you love your children, yet your actions prove otherwise. Your instructions were simple. Keep John Reeves in jail."

"Please," the skinny man mewled. "I do love my children. Give me another chance. I'll get him back. He couldn't have gone far."

The Savior leaned forward, his face even with his sniveling disciple. "You will not fail me again," he whispered. "Or I'll speak the single word to send you back to the hell you came from." He straightened and absently wiped the scalpel on his pant leg. "Or would you rather I speak it now?"

Sweat flew from the skinny man's face as he shook his head.

"One simple word. That's all it takes. Do you miss watching your daughter bathe? Or maybe it's the disgusting thoughts about your son you miss."

The skinny man pulled at his Savior's side. "Please! God, no. Don't say it. I'll do whatever you want. Those thoughts weren't me. I'll die if I go back to the way I was before."

The Savior glanced down at the shell of a man. "You'd do well to remember this moment. There will not be a next time. If you fail me again, the word will be spoken. Now stand and quit your begging. It's pathetic."

The skinny man wiped at his tears. "What is the one word? How will I know when you say it?"

The Savior slammed his fists down on his work station. The tall jar filled with alcohol and used scalpels smashed to the floor. "You won't know, you fool! If I say it, you'll be who you were before."

The skinny man crawled back and dry-washed his hands.

"Just leave." The Savior waved to the red door. "I don't wish to see your face any more. Just bring Reeves back to the department. Or better yet, bring him to me. In the meantime, I have these new toys to play with." He gestured to the new bodies covered to the neck with pristine white sheets. "I'll enjoy making them scream."

The Note

John dialed Eddy's number again. No answer. *Where the hell are you, man?*

Traveling to Eddy's house took longer than expected. Shortly after John left Alan, the rain slowed to a mist. He had fallen asleep the last time he stopped for a rest. The fog made it hard to tell for how long. He stood in a small supply shed less than a mile from Eddy's home. He had no idea who the shed belonged to, but they wouldn't be happy to find a random guy on their property chatting on a cell phone.

A deep breath and he trotted off, his stomach growling. *I hope you have some food ready for me, Eddy.*

Now he had to figure out what to do once he reached his friend's house. He couldn't knock. If Sandra found him, she'd call the police. He wouldn't blame her; she had four kids to protect.

At the rear of Eddy's backyard, he crouched and crawled between two arborvitae hedges. Lights filled almost every window. *What's with the lights? And why aren't you answering your damn phone?*

A whimper came from somewhere ahead. John held his breath. He heard it again. *Oh, God. Don't let me be too late.*

He stayed low and hurried into the yard, eyes focused on the house. He paused, waiting to hear the groan again. Nothing. John moved from bush, to shed, to swing set, hoping the dense fog hid him from anyone lurking in Eddy's house.

Urging himself on, he came within feet of the back porch when he heard the whimper again, lightly echoing against the neighbor's house. *Outside. Somewhere in front.*

He slid his back against the pale siding and worked his way toward the front with no obstacles to hide behind. He peeked around the corner. Eddy sat alone on the front steps, face in his hands, sobbing.

John stepped around the corner, eyes flitting from side to side. When only a few feet away, he whispered, "Eddy." No response. He whispered louder. "Eddy."

The sobs paused. His friend looked up, dark circles ringing his wet and bloodshot eyes. "John? Where have you been? I looked for you all morning."

John nodded toward the rear of the house. "You mind if we hold the questions until we're someplace a little more private?"

Eddy followed. He kept glancing at a piece of paper in his hands. When they reached the back porch, Eddy collapsed into one of the cheap lawn chairs. John continued to stand. After the night's long run, cramps would assault his muscles if he sat.

"What is it, Eddy? Why are you crying?" John gestured to the paper. "And what's that in your hand?"

Eddy covered his face again and continued to sob. "We messed up, John."

"What? I can't hear you with your face covered like that." John leaned back against a porch support beam and crossed his arms.

The paper fell to the floor as Eddy dropped his hands. "I said we messed up. I don't know how, but we did."

"What do you mean?"

His friend pointed. "Just read the note."

John picked up the damp paper. Tears streaked ink down the page but left the words discernible.

"Your family is now mine to do with as I please. You stuck your nose where it didn't belong. Your wife and children may yet live if you return what is mine. Bring me John Reeves, or their lives will be forfeit. Since I know John all too well, this part is for him. Your father once shared spirits with Sarah while your mother was away. Join me there."

"What the hell is that supposed to mean?" John held the note out to Eddy.

Eddy took the paper and slumped back into his seat. "I don't know, John. I'd hoped you would have some idea."

"Shared spirits? This can't be literal, unless whoever wrote it is completely insane. Which I'd say is a pretty good argument at this point."

"Did your dad ever cheat on your mom?" Eddy wiped at his tears and stood. "None of this matters anyway. I need to call the police." He turned to go into the house.

"Wait. Let's think about this a minute. What happens if you call the police? They take me back in and who knows what would happen to your family?"

His friend spun around, a trembling finger raised at John. "This is your fault! Whatever you did, you got us into this. Why shouldn't I call the police?"

John sighed. "Come on, Eddy. You know me; I love your family as my own. You know I'd never do anything to endanger them. I'm as confused about this as you are. Think about it. This whole thing stinks. Somebody set me up, and now they're pissed I got out. I'd like to know how the hell they found out so fast."

Eddy lowered his finger. "It wouldn't be hard. I saw your picture pasted all over the news and that was hours ago. I left to find you and came back to find... to find..."

"I'm sorry, Eddy. Let's figure this out and get your family back."

The lawn chair squawked when Eddy fell back into it. "I don't know. This involves my family, John. I can't lose them."

John fought to control the edge in his voice. "If I go back to jail, what will that accomplish? Not only will whoever wrote this note have won, but also I won't be able to help you. Let's take ten minutes to figure this out, and if we can't by then, I'll call the police myself."

Silence stretched between them, their eyes held on each other. Eddy nodded and his shoulders pulled out of the slump. "Then we best hurry." He sat forward and held the note out between them. "What about the part when he says your mother was away? Why would she have been away? Can you remember her ever leaving your dad? Maybe temporarily?"

"No. She didn't work. Most of what she did was right there at the farmhouse, usually taking care of me and Alan."

"Did she go on any vacations? Family trips?"

John rubbed the stubble on his chin. "Not that I remember. Wait. She did spend a couple nights at her sister's when I was a teenager. My aunt had pneumonia, and her husband was on the road, a truck driver."

"What about the spirits? Would your dad have gone out drinking with... holy shit!" Eddy's face paled. "The picture."

John pushed away from the support. "What picture? What do you mean?"

Eddy stood, his hands fidgeting. "The picture! The one we found at the Krogman's. Remember when we were at Alan's house, and I told you something seemed odd about it?"

"What about it?"

"The beer. They were at your parents' house. Your mom didn't let your dad drink when she was there. I remember when you told me that in high school. I thought it was weird he wasn't allowed to drink on his own property, but your mother didn't care if he went someplace else to do it. The bar, or a wedding."

"Spirits," John whispered.

"That's right. The beer. He drank the beer with Sarah, the name he painted on his tractor, when your mom was gone. I remember her telling the story at dinner one time. She'd tease about how much he needed her and said the one time she was gone for a week he'd nearly drank himself stupid."

John's heart thudded in his chest. "Not with her sister then. Her mother, my grandma, had passed away. She stayed with my grandpa for a full week. I remember the story." He ran a hand through his wet hair. "Whoever wrote this is at my dad's place? Why?"

Eddy folded the paper and slid it into his front pocket. "*Why* doesn't matter right now. Let's get the vests and gear from my office and go out there." He sprinted into his house and came back moments later with car keys in hand. "Let's go."

"I should call Alan and tell him where we're going."

"Alan?" Eddy's eyes grew wide. "Does he know you broke out of jail?"

"Yep."

"And he didn't throw you back in?"

"Nope. Crazy, right? He saw things my way though. The only way we can catch whoever did this is if we work together."

Eddy waved for John to follow. "You can call him on the way if you'd like. But I doubt he'll let us go out there alone. His emotions about Rita may have given you a break once, but this is Alan we're talking about. Sooner or later, his cop side will kick in."

"Right. I'll text him when we get there."

25. Evidence

Coffee Spitting

Alan watched the sun's rays slowly spread across his bedroom ceiling. He'd barely slept after returning from his conversation with John at the tree house. Ruth had listened to his conversation with Chief Burleson. She'd covered her mouth to stifle her laughter when the chief chewed Alan out loud enough for her to hear while he held the phone a foot from his ear. He'd told Burleson the same lie he'd told Ruth. That he'd searched for John at the tree house and found footprints, but not his brother.

He groaned and sat up. The muscles in his neck and shoulders ached from the tension. "What law are you going to break today, Alan?" he said to himself.

Strong coffee and a cold shower took the edge off. He cleaned up, shaved, and drank another pot of coffee. Once he'd worked up the nerve, he dialed Chief Burleson's number.

"Hey, Chief. Any news on John?" Alan plopped himself onto his couch.

"Nothing yet. We sent a K-9 unit out to the tree house but didn't find much more than you. They lost his track over by Kline's pig farm. Not sure how he pulled that one off."

"You sent a K-9 unit out here and didn't tell me about it?"

"I figured you could use the sleep. Besides, we technically didn't cross onto your property. Speaking of your parents' old property, did you know there was a light left on at the farmhouse? We noticed when we ran the K-9 around the property in case he holed up there."

"Really? Did you find anything?" Alan sipped coffee from his mug.

"Nothing except the light."

"I probably just left it on when I went over there last week. Thanks for letting me know. Hey, you think I could come into the station today? I'd like to check over some of the evidence from the Fincham case."

"I don't see a problem with that. Are you up to it? Mayor Snively shouldn't care too much as long as you shut yourself into the evidence room. Speaking of that wench, did I tell you what she did?"

The conversation with John came to mind. "What's that?"

"She called in a favor from one of her friends over at the Detroit FBI field office. They're sending an agent to look over the case. Her exact words to me were, 'Since you shits can't tell the difference between your head and someone's ass, I'm sending in the FBI.'"

Alan spit coffee down his chin, holding the phone away from the mess. He placed his mug on the end table and used a sleeve to wipe the dribble from his chin.

"You there?" the Chief said.

"I'm here, Chief. Just had a little accident with my drink."

"Spit your coffee out, did ya'? I did the same when she said it to me. Anyway, might want to head in here soon. Not sure how much freedom we'll have once that agent gets here."

"Sounds good. I'll be there shortly."

Evidence

A half hour later, Alan stood at the evidence room entrance, filling out the paperwork explaining exactly which evidence he'd look over. He signed his name and handed the form to Lori. "Thanks, Lori. You care if I just head in? Chief says he wants me hidden away."

Without looking, the restive woman tossed the paper on her desk and continued typing. "That's fine."

Alan waited a moment in case she said more. She continued to pound away at the keyboard. "Thanks, Lori," he said under his breath. He stepped into the evidence room and closed the door behind him.

Mostly empty racks filled the room. On the final rack against the back wall, three boxes stood out, each with the case name written in black marker across the front; Fincham, Krogman, Vasquez. He closed his eyes and took a deep breath. He released it and looked to the wall on his right where they kept prisoner goods. Prisoner items and evidence filled the same room since Clarkbridge wasn't much more than a village according to state standards. Their cells rarely held more than a few people at any given time anyway. The large plastic baggy that should have held John's belongings wasn't there.

Damn it.

He needed to look busy in case anybody came in. He hefted the Krogman box down to the empty desk and sat down. He spread the contents out in front of him, mostly pictures of the horrific crime scene. Checking John's evidence was his first priority but looking over the Krogman information would do for now. Patience wasn't his strong suit lately, but he'd continue to look over anything he could until John's items were returned.

No sooner had he lifted the first photo, the evidence room door opened. Cooper pushed through the doorway backward and turned with the only other box belonging on the shelves. Written on the front in permanent marker, the name Tolman stood out.

"Oh. Hey, Alan. Lori didn't tell me you were in here." He sat the box on the edge of the desk next to the Krogman files.

"Lori doesn't say much these days."

Cooper let out his honk of a laugh. "Now that's a fact. You'd think being as wired as she always is that you wouldn't be able to shut her up." He glanced at the contents spread out on the desk. "Ah, going over the Krogman case again, huh?"

"Not much more I can do with Snively looking over the Chief's shoulder all the damn time." He shuffled together the pile of photos. The top photo showed a close-up of Krogman's hand in the Mason jar.

Cooper spun away and held his forearm over his mouth.

Alan covered the photo with a folder. "Sorry about that, Coop. I covered it up."

He peeked one of his buggy eyes over his shoulder at the desk. "Sheesh. That's just gross. Thanks for covering it up." He gestured to the Tolman box. "I can barely stand that one. I don't understand how you guys can look at that stuff and not get sick."

"I'm not sure how others do it, but I worked plenty of gory cases while in Detroit. That's why I came to Clarkbridge, to get away from this crap." He shook his head. "Anyway. What's up with the Tolman case? Find anything new?"

Cooper sat in the only other chair at the desk. "No. It's weird. Chief thinks John... oh, I'm sorry Alan."

"Don't worry about it, Coop. I know what the Chief thinks about my brother. What were you going to say?"

"Just that he thinks John played a role in all these cases. Besides being way out there and weird, I don't see a connection between any of them."

"What about the photo?" Alan removed the photo of his father and the three dead men from the stack and tossed it in front of Cooper.

The fidgety cop began to turn his head away; probably afraid Alan would show him another unpleasant photo. He paused a moment before leaning in. "I just don't know what to think about those. Don't make any sense to me." He hopped straight up, feet almost coming off the floor.

"You okay?"

Cooper sighed and straightened the rest of the way, pulling his cell phone from his back pocket in the process. "I'm okay. This darn thing vibrated and scared me.

Alan's hearty laugh filled the small room. "Oh, Coop. I love having you around. You might want to think about laying off the coffee though."

The cell phone vibrated again. Cooper slid the front open and concentrated on the screen. "You're one to talk. How many pots have you drank today?"

"The difference between you and me is that I can handle my caffeine."

"Oh. I gotta go. You mind putting the Tolman box back?" He shot toward the exit and yelled back over his shoulder, "Thanks, Alan!"

Poor guy. Alan picked up the box and moved it to the back shelf. One of the flaps popped open. He pushed the flap out of the way and peered inside. *John Reeves?* One of the stickers used to organize evidence had John's name written on the front.

He pulled out the baggy. It wasn't evidence, but the bag filled with John's belongings.

What the hell were you looking at this for, Coop?

He figured the Chief had every officer looking everything over. Clarkbridge had never lost a prisoner before. According to Shaw, the whole station was on edge.

Alan tossed the bag on the desk. He glanced over his shoulder at the closed door. *Just a quick look.* The baggy was still open. Alan shook it until John's wallet and keys landed in his hand. He opened the wallet. *Only a twenty? Not normal for John.* He pulled out a couple business cards: a coffee and donut shop, a kennel. *A kennel? Where are your pets now?*

A buzzing sound came from the desk. Alan sat John's wallet down and shuffled through the papers and plastic baggies. It buzzed again. He pulled his phone from his pocket to make sure it wasn't a phone call. Nothing. The phone went back to his pocket. He heard the buzz again, this time a blinking light caught his attention. The cell phone inside John's baggy vibrated.

He dumped the phone into his hand. The screen blinked. He looked closer. His breath caught. The screen read, "Pick up the phone, Alan!" After the momentary shock wore off, he glanced to the door again.

Stop, you idiot. As if looking at the door will keep it closed.

He flipped the phone open. "Hello?"

"Alan, this is Rachel McCall. From high school."

"I know who you are, but how in hell did you—"

"I have the station tapped but this isn't time for discussion. Agent Milanesi just called Chief Burleson and said she doesn't want you looking at any more evidence, or even coming in to the station. Who knows how long it will take him to remember you're at the station now? John asked me to look up information on a guy a while back. I couldn't find anything right away, but one of my feelers just did."

"Your what?"

"Never mind that, just listen. He wanted to know about a man named Russell Holbrook, some psychologist or something. But he's clean. What I did find is disturbing. His father, Abraham, was arrested years ago by none other than Mr. Ed Reeves."

"What does that have to do with anything?"

"Take a guess, who else was in on the case."

Alan ran a hand through his hair. "No way."

"That's right. Fincham, Tolman, and Krogman. Fincham was a key witness, Krogman a guard at the prison where Abraham worked, and Tolman a detective like Ed. This is all probably confusing right now, but I faxed you the paperwork. I labeled it as private. That Lori gal dropped it on your desk."

"Krogman worked at a prison where Abraham worked? What did Russell's dad do there?" Sweat trickled down Alan's back. He didn't have a clue what Rachel was talking about, but if it fit, it was the first piece of evidence that brought the victims together.

"I have to go. Chief Burleson just left his office. Wipe your prints from the phone and put everything back. I'll call you soon." The phone went dead.

He quickly wiped the phone on his shirt and tossed it into the baggy along with John's wallet and keys. He slid the bag closed and tossed it back on the shelf where it belonged. He hurried back to the desk and fell into his seat as Chief Burleson stepped into the room.

"Hey, Alan. Sorry to bother you but you better pack it up. Snively's hound dog just called. Apparently we're no longer allowed, yes, I said allowed, to look over the evidence. Not until she gives us permission."

"No problem, Chief." Alan gathered the photos and paperwork and tossed them into the box labeled Krogman.

"Really?" Alan heard the Chief say from behind him. "You've questioned everything about this case. Now I tell you that you can't look it over any more, and you just say, 'no problem?'

Alan's face flushed. He tucked the box flaps down and sat it on the shelf. "Well, I admitted that I went too far as it is. Snively's already breathing down your neck. No need to muss things any further." He smiled at the Chief and gestured for them to leave.

The Chief squinted his eyes for a moment. He pushed the door open to let Alan through and smiled. He patted Alan on the back as he left the evidence room. "Well, good. Glad to hear you're seeing things my way. You do realize this means you're on leave completely then?"

"I do." Alan walked to his desk. "I just have a few things I need." He rolled Rachel's fax into a tight spiral and tucked it into his back pocket. "How long will I be on leave?"

The Chief followed him to the desk. "As long as it takes, I guess. We'll just have to play it by ear. I'm sure Snively will want you gone until these cases are complete. At least until it's out of our hands, which it basically is already. Who knows, maybe we can get you on patrol over in Leverton until this is over. They're always short staffed."

"Sounds good, Chief. Just let me know. You need anything else?"

Chief Burleson tilted his head to the side. "Are you okay, Alan?"

"Do I look sick or something?" He laughed. "I'm fine, considering my partner was murdered and my escapee brother is the primary suspect."

The Chief looked away. "Yeah, I mean, I know things are rough right now, but you seem to be handling it awfully well."

"Honestly, with everything that's happened, I'm just trying to stay focused, keep my head in the game." Alan patted Burleson on the shoulder on his way by. "I'm fine, Chief. I really am. You always said a turtle showed more emotions than me. If I need anything, I know I can count on you. It goes both ways too. You know my number."

Alan said a quick goodbye and left. He hoped he hadn't overplayed his nonchalance with the Chief, but he didn't know what else to do. If he'd said every minute without Rita was hell and that the one person he trusted more than all others in this world supposedly killed her, what would his reaction have been?

Not opening the fax from Rachel on his way home took every ounce of his will power. When he made it to his house, he rushed to the kitchen table and flattened the roll of papers. He stared at the front page. If the fax truly held everything Rachel said it did, who did he contact first? The Chief? Ruth Shaw? Should he tell the FBI agent? He changed his thoughts from should to would. Of course he *should* contact someone, but would he? Who could he trust?

26. Blue

Talk

Alan spread the multiple page fax across the table. Ruth was the only other cop he trusted right then. He phoned her and asked if she would check over some new evidence he had. She'd gone to the station early to help with the search for John. After a short argument about whether he should bring the evidence in, she agreed to look it over first. He'd said if she felt the same way afterward, she could bring the evidence in herself.

He picked up the stack containing information about Douglas Fincham, the man whose death had started everything. Next to the stack, the color copy of the photo laid before him. Rachel had been nice enough to add in all the case files she found on the department's system. Every few minutes, his eyes went to the photo. He didn't know why. A clue, something, worked at the edge of his consciousness. The photo held a truth he couldn't figure out.

The doorbell rang. "Hello?" Ruth called from the front door.

"C'mon in, Ruth."

She stepped into the kitchen, still in uniform. "When you said evidence, you meant it. What is all this stuff?" Her eyes worked back and forth across the documents.

"Before you sit, my coffee pot said it missed you."

"You lazy ass." She turned to the coffee machine on the counter and began filling it. "A pleasant host would have hot coffee on hand. Most people know a cop can't function unless filled with a steady stream of caffeine."

Alan smiled and looked back to the Fincham papers. "You ever heard the name Abraham Holbrook?"

"Nope," she called over her shoulder. "He related to the shrink that came in on the Tolman case?"

"He is, actually. It's Russell's father."

Ruth finished and pressed the brew button. She turned to face Alan and leaned against the counter. "Okay. What's this have to do with the evidence?"

Alan absently tapped a pencil against his lip. He spun the copy of the photo so Ruth could see it right side up. He pointed the pencil at Tolman. "It started with this guy. Dr. Tolman. His wife worked at the Detroit Penitentiary as a nurse."

"The one that closed down a few years back?"

"The same. Well, Herbert, that's Dr. Tolman's first name, worked for the downtown Detroit police department as a detective. His wife came to him and said she wanted to tell him something but that she couldn't because of patient confidentiality."

Ruth held her hand up to pause him. "How do you know this? That's not something typically found in a police report."

Alan smiled. "You're right. This is from Dr. Tolman's personal files."

"I don't even want to know how you have those."

"Just hear me out, and grab me a cup of that coffee before I slobber all over the table from the smell." While she held a mug under the coffee maker, he continued. "So Dr. Tolman wants to help his wife out. The only thing she'll tell him is that she heard rumors about this guy Abraham. At one point, Holbrook had been hired by the government, at least this is what Tolman wrote in his report. He was hired to run experiments on the prisoners at some penitentiary in southern Alabama."

Steam danced from the coffee Ruth placed in front of him. She sat down with her own mug and held it tight in front of her. "Keep going. You've piqued my interest."

"Tolman found most of this out later. Once he had a name to work with, he told his wife to forget ever saying anything to him and go back to work like nothing had happened. Anyway, he finds out the rumors were true about Abraham. The government allowed him to run his psychological experiments in the hopes they'd find a way to control the prisoners, or at least control their urges, maybe find a way for them to work their way back into society."

Ruth laughed. "Let me guess. It didn't work so they canned him."

"Exactly." Alan flipped through the stack. "It says here that a prison in Southern Alabama, no name given, was shut down for unknown reasons. Soon after, our dear Abraham is hired as the head psychologist to work with prisoners at the Detroit Penitentiary. After he'd been there a few years, Tolman's wife, who'd worked there for around ten years at that point, noted an influx of patients coming to her about migraines. She'd heard the rumors about Abraham from other colleagues and put the two together. She never found any reason for their severe headaches, but they all had one thing in common. They were drug users. Every one had track marks."

"They don't check for that in prison?"

Alan stood, carrying a few of the papers with him. He paced back and forth across the kitchen. "The same thought occurred to me. Tolman doesn't mention anything about it in his report, but with the cover up, I'm surprised even this information was left."

The kitchen table creaked as Ruth leaned forward. "A cover up? This sounds like one big conspiracy theory."

"Tell me about it." Alan grinned. "I'm not finished. I'll get to the point. Well, come to find out, Abraham had indeed begun his experiments on the prisoners again, this time without permission. Tolman needed a witness but knew prisoners didn't work well in that respect. He learned that Abraham ran a practice outside of the prison as well. I don't know if I believe the coincidence, but supposedly, one night over a beer with an old friend, our very own Douglas Fincham," Alan stopped by the table and tapped his pencil on Douglas in the photo, "he discovered that Doug had gone to Abraham for sleep problems. Long story short, Abraham gave Doug a shot in the arm he said would cure everything. He had a raging headache for a week and never went back, though his sleepless nights ended."

Ruth motioned for him to keep going. "Get to the point."

"The point is, Tolman now had a reason to investigate. Lonnie Krogman, the guy who used his body as a human cutting board, was a security guard at the time who Abraham incorrectly judged as uncaring. Krogman jumped at the chance to put away the 'arrogant bastard' as Tolman says here. My dad served in the military together with Tolman and apparently they were close friends at the station. Ed Reeves already had a reputation on the force. They joined together and used that reputation to further their investigation. Eventually, they all put Abraham away."

"Where is Abraham now? And I'm still not seeing the connection. Not completely anyway."

Alan slumped into a kitchen chair. He'd practically been bursting at the seams to tell somebody about the new evidence. Now that he had, weight fell from his shoulders. "I feel like I could fall asleep right here at the table."

Ruth ambled to his side and rubbed his shoulder with a gentle touch. "Are you okay?"

He waved her away. "Yeah. I'm fine. I didn't realize how worked up I was over this new information. It's nothing conclusive, but at least it gives us another direction to go."

She poured them both another cup of coffee and took a seat. "A direction that's not your brother."

"Exactly."

"You never answered my question. Where is Abraham now?"

"Oh." Alan sifted the papers a moment. "Here it is. After his funeral right here in town at Hindel's Funeral Home, he was buried over in the Taylor cemetery."

"The one by the big softball field?"

"That's the one. I say we give it a visit." Alan dropped the papers to the table and stood.

Ruth's brow lifted. "Right now?" She rubbed her temple with her free hand. "I don't know if that's such a good idea. Chief Burleson was pretty clear when he said you needn't go traipsing around this case any more than is completely necessary."

Halfway to the front door, Alan paused. "Did he really say that? Or was it the FBI agent?"

She froze. "Who told you about that?"

Alan smiled. "Chief Burleson did."

A smile crept onto Ruth's face. "You booger. You Reeves boys, I tell ya." She stood and walked to the cupboard containing the Styrofoam cups. Over her shoulder, she said, "If we're going for a ride, I'm taking this with me." She pointed to her mug on the kitchen table.

Alan's eyes went to the photo again. He hustled back to the kitchen table and stuffed the picture into this back pocket.

"What was that?"

He watched Ruth pour the steaming liquid from mug to Styrofoam cup. "I need to bring the photo with me. It's driving me crazy. We still don't know who the person behind the camera was, but that's not it. Something keeps pulling me back to it. I want to have it along in case it comes to me." He started for the door.

"Wait for me, you turd," Ruth called after him. She took slow, measured steps, balancing the too-full cup between her small hands.

"Time's a wastin', Ruth," he yelled back. "The longer we take, the more likely John gets hurt."

Petals

Less than a half hour later, they pulled into the Taylor City Cemetery with the top down on Ruth's LeSabre. Gravel crunched beneath the tires as they idled off the road and further into the stark shadows thrown by the tall pines.

"This place is creepy," Ruth whispered.

"What are you whispering for? It's just a cemetery." Alan ran a hand through his hair for what seemed like the twentieth time since they left his home. He'd never enjoyed the wind whipping his hair around in John's jeeps either. His stomach clenched at the thought of his brother.

She slapped his arm. "I know it's just a cemetery, but it's still creepy. Look how old everything looks. Don't they take care of this place?"

"I'll ask Martin Hindel when he calls back."

"You actually think the funeral home director will know where Abraham was buried?"

Alan shrugged. "No. But do you have a better idea?"

"We could try calling Russell."

The Criminal Minds theme song sounded from Alan's front pocket.

Ruth shook her head. "You really need to change that."

Alan smiled and answered the phone. "Hey, Mr. Hindel. Thanks for calling back." He paused. "Okay. Thank you very much." He hung up the phone and pushed it back into his pocket.

"Well?" Ruth said.

"Well, what?"

She slapped him again. "What did he say, you jerk?"

"You're pretty slap happy today." Ruth shot him a glare. "He said it's right up here; to the back and on the right."

"How the heck did he remember that?"

"No clue, but I'm happy we don't have to trudge through this whole cemetery and check out each plot one at a time."

The Buick rolled to a stop at a curve in the dirt trail leading through the cemetery. They stepped into the thick weeds and grass. Vines covered everything; the headstones, the trees, the fence. A light breeze pushed through the tall pines, their shadows dancing across the ground before them.

Alan and Ruth began in opposite directions. The name on the second headstone Alan checked, dark brown laced with darker veins of black, read 'Abraham Holbrook.' "I found it." He waved Ruth over and squatted down.

She came to his side. "What the hell is that?"

Before the headstone, placed within a bramble of thick weeds and grass, lay a single rose with azure blue petals.

Alan glanced up at Ruth. "I don't suppose you have any evidence bags in your car?"

"Yeah, let me go get those for you." She rolled her eyes.

His eyes went back to the rose. "I didn't think so." He separated the weeds and reached in. A thorn pierced his thumb. His hand shot back and he shook it before putting the tip of his thumb into his mouth. "Mmm."

"Saw that one coming." Ruth grabbed his shoulder and pulled him back. "Out of the way. A flower needs a woman's touch."

"Be my guest." Alan stood. He glanced at his thumb. Blood dimpled from the tiny wound.

"Got it." Ruth began to stand but paused and squatted back down. "Now what the hell is this?"

"What?" Alan leaned over her to get a better view.

"Step back, Mr. Impatient." She pulled herself standing. In one hand, she held the object of his thumb pain, a perfectly shaped blue rose with the stem snipped at an angle. In the other, she held a dirt covered plastic baggy. She shook it a few times. Beneath the black soil was a picture.

"The same as all the others." Alan's words were barely audible.

"What does this mean?" Ruth's voice took on a higher pitch than normal, fear tinging each word.

"I'm not sure, but I know one thing. You and I are going to pay a little visit to our local psychiatrist."

Bug Bite

"Pull off here a second." John waved toward the tree line.

Eddy pulled his Nissan to the side of the dirt road, close to the Kline pig farm and only a mile from where John lived as a child.

"What's the plan, John?"

"With the mist gone, we need to approach from the northeast corner of the house. The trees are thickest on that side. We'll spend less time out in the open from that direction. Remember where we used to park our bikes and fish that pond off the Branstead River?"

"The two-track? Yeah. Up here a ways." He gestured down the road in front of them.

"That's the one. If we take a left on that two-track, we should make it far enough in where the Nissan can't be seen from the road."

"What do you mean, 'should'?"

"Have you seen your car lately? It sits four inches off the ground." The wide compacted ruts from years of tractor usage weren't as clear as they used to be. Weeds and the heavy rains might leave the two-track impassable by anything less than a four-wheel drive.

Eddy shook his head. "We don't have time for this. What's the plan once we get there?"

John lost his smile. "Your family may be there. We go in quiet and stay together. I got the lead on this one. I know the property better than you. Keep in mind, this could be a trap, and you know the old saying about the best way to find out if it's a trap?"

Eddy nodded. "You spring it."

"Good. We'll approach from the northeast and enter through the side door. You remember it? The one that opens into the dining room."

Eddy nodded again. "Let's go." Parking just around the first corner on the two-track, they pulled Eddy's bullet-resistant vests from the hatchback, the same ones they wore when picking up Manny Rodriquez. John pulled a vest over his head and tightened the straps. Eddy spun in a circle and scuttled into the car's bumper, his voice muffled from the vest stuck on his head.

John unlatched Eddy's straps. The vest fell into place. "Take a deep breath, buddy. Calm down."

Eddy nodded. "Sorry about that." He reached into the hatchback, hefted a shotgun into his shaking hands, and held the weapon butt first to John.

"No thanks." John showed him his Glock. "This will do just fine. I have three more stashed about my body too. In case our plans don't work out."

"I'll stick with a shotgun. Not everybody is a sharpshooter."

They went over the plans again and set off in the direction of the old farmhouse.

Just outside a small copse of trees, John gestured for Eddy to squat down beside him. "From here on in, no chatter. If you need to say something, find a way to do it with your hands. Too bad you're not military, this would be easier."

Sweat dripped from Eddy's flushed face. He wasn't used to the exercise. The hot and humid Michigan weather didn't help. His eyes darted around them in a continuous motion.

"I forgot to text Alan. Just a sec. Shit. No signal. You have one?"

Eddy dug his phone from his jean pocket. "Nothing."

"I'll at least text him so it goes out automatically when I get a signal." He tapped away at the miniature keyboard. "Done."

"What did you say to him?"

"I said you and I were having a barbecue at my dad's house." John closed his eyes. Thick air flowed in and out of his lungs.

"You okay, John?"

He looked into Eddy's eyes. "Just relaxing a little. We might only have one shot at this. You alright?"

Tears formed at the corners of Eddy's eyes. "I won't lie. I can't help but feel we're endangering Sandra and the kids. I trust you, John; you're like family. But are you sure we shouldn't call the police?"

"Go back and call them if you need to, but I'm not waiting. If your family is here, there's no telling what might happen."

Eddy wiped the dampness from beneath his eyes and shook his head. "No, you're right. If anybody can get them out, it's you."

The vote of confidence was generous of Eddy, but John didn't feel any better about their situation. Entering a house with no more than a two-man team didn't leave him optimistic, but they couldn't wait. Not when Eddy's family might be in danger. "They'll be fine, Eddy. Let's go get your family."

With the sun beating down, the mist had completely dissipated. John led the way through the copse of trees, crouched low, careful to break as few twigs or branches as possible, cringing each time he heard Eddy behind him. Eddy tromped through the brush like a clumsy rhino. They stood fewer than thirty yards from the farmhouse.

A hand caught John's shoulder and pulled him back just as he began his first step into the yard. He spun around. Eddy jabbed his finger toward the front of the house.

"You scared the shit out of me," John hissed. "What are you pointing at?"

Eddy kept his voice low. "I thought you said no talking?"

"I did, but how am I supposed to know what you're jabbing your finger at?

"Isn't that Cooper's car?"

John followed Eddy's stare. The rear bumper of a dark blue car poked around the corner of the house. "I'm not sure. What makes you think it's his?"

"The dent there on the bumper, with the rust around it. He got that one night when we were bowling. Some drunk guy."

"Why the hell would he be here? Oh, no shit. He's probably looking for me."

"That could be." Eddy nodded. "But if he was, why drive his car and not a cruiser?"

Good ole Eddy and his big brain. "Maybe all the others are taken? I'm sure every Clarkbridge cop is searching for me."

"Could be. Still feels fishy."

John's hand covered his mouth in time to restrain the laugh.

"What?"

"Fishy? Who are we? The Hardy Boys?" Eddy didn't smile. *Why the hell would he? His family could be stuck in the house with a psycho and you're cracking jokes.* "Let's check the car out first then. Remember: silence. We've spoken too much already."

John hustled toward the house, Glock held steady at his side, eyes flicking back and forth to the curtain-covered windows. The siding crunched when John spun and slid his back against the wall. Eddy followed suit, stumbling into the house. John paused every few steps, listening for any sounds coming from inside. He reached the corner leading to the front. He poked his head just far enough around the edge to see the porch and car empty.

The shooters stance came naturally as he rounded the house. A blue Corsica ticked and pinged in the driveway.

He turned to Eddy and mouthed Coop's name while pointing at the car.

Eddy showed him an exaggerated nod.

Stay calm. Something weird is going on.

As if his thoughts could summon the actual person, Cooper Forbes stepped from the front door of the farmhouse onto the porch. John held his weapon steady. The skinny man didn't notice him and Eddy standing feet away.

Cooper shook the knob on the front door as if to make sure it was locked. He turned and hurried down the porch, the third step making the 'whump' sound John remembered so well. The car keys jingled when he pulled them from his pocket. He stood by the driver's side door of the Corsica sorting through his keys.

"Psst," John hissed.

The skinny cop hopped a good foot in the air and bumbled with his keys until they flipped from his hands. When he landed, he squatted close to the ground and spun his head from side to side until he noticed John. He straightened. His hands shot straight up in the air.

"What are you doing here, Coop?" Eddy's words came out louder than John preferred.

Cooper dropped his hands and squinted in their direction, as if they stood farther than a few yards away. "Oh, it's just you two. What am I doing here? What are you doing here?" He picked up his keys.

Eddy lowered the shotgun and walked closer. "Have you seen Sandra? My kids?"

Cooper stepped to the rear of his car, head tilted to the side, and opened the back door. He leaned in to the vehicle and called over his shoulder. "Sandra and the kids? No. Why would I?"

John continued to hold his Glock on the cop's back. He moved close to the car, to Cooper's back. Something wasn't right.

Eddy ran a hand through his hair and leaned the shotgun against the car. "I'm not sure. I got this note and it said... never mind what it said. You never told me what you were doing here."

Whatever Cooper fumbled with in the back of the car clinked a couple times before he closed the door, his hands empty. "Chief Burleson sent me out here." He looked to John. "Says he thinks you may hole up here or something, you know? Has me checking every hour on the hour."

"Why the civilian car?" John said. "Seems to me if you were searching for an escaped prisoner who happens to be an ex-marine, you'd want fast access to a radio and more weapons."

"Nah, Chief doesn't really think you did it, John. I'm only out here because it looks good to that bitch of an FBI agent they sent in."

John shook his head. "You're telling me the Chief doesn't want you to bring me in?"

"Oh, he does. Just not like before." Cooper wiped his hands on his dark t-shirt. "He wants it done peacefully, of your own free will."

Cooper dropped his keys again. He bent to pick them up and tripped. A bug bit John in the thigh. He slapped at the pain. His hand hit something hard and cold. His eyes fixed on a syringe sticking from his leg. "What the, frrl..." The words froze in his mouth. John dropped to his knees. Mud squished into his ear. Eddy looked much taller. The whole world lay sideways.

A tangle of feet slid about in front of him. Eddy's face slapped the muck inches in front of John. It held a blank stare and his mouth hung open. Blood rushed from his nose. Blackness forced its way around his friend's head, clouded everything.

Is someone crying?

27. Search

Cemetery

"So you two just happened to be hanging out at the Taylor City cemetery? Quite the scenic view for lunch." Chief Burleson crossed his arms. Behind him, Sergeant Clark dusted Abraham Holbrook's headstone for prints. Corporal Gibbs wandered around searching for other evidence; footprints, tire prints, trash. The Chief decided not to call the forensics team in. Besides placing a strain on the department's already waning funds, a full team wouldn't gather much evidence from an outside source after the heavy rainfall.

Alan opened his mouth to speak. Ruth put her hand on his chest. "I got this, Alan."

He nodded and took a place by the rear of Ruth's convertible.

"Look, Chief," Ruth continued. "You said from the beginning I was to keep an eye on Captain Reeves, that he's to be used for no more than someone to bounce ideas off of. That's what I did. He did some research of his own and found out Abraham here," she gestured toward the headstone, "had connections to the deaths."

Chief Burleson waved to Alan. "Get back over here."

Alan stepped next to Ruth. "What is it, Chief?"

"Just how did you suddenly gather this evidence?"

"It was Eddy." He hated to lie, but he didn't want to bring Rachel McCall, and her questionable methods, into the investigation. "He learned that my father had worked with Herbert Tolman at the same precinct. One thing led to another and we found some of Tolman's old files.

Everything kind of came together." Alan summed up the connection between the deaths and Abraham Holbrook, including his belief that Russell Holbrook may have played a role.

The Chief hadn't unfolded his arms. "That doesn't explain why you came out here."

"To be honest, I'm not even sure. I guess I wanted to get out of the house, maybe feel like I was still part of the case. We didn't have much on Abraham, except that he was dead and buried here."

Chief Burleson glanced back and forth between Alan and Ruth. "I expect a full report from you two yesterday. Get out of here and get it done."

"Wait," Alan said. "What will you do about Russell Holbrook?"

Ruth started toward the driver's side of her car but paused at Alan's question.

One of the Chief's eyebrows rose. "You honestly think this is motive enough to kill?"

Alan shrugged. "I don't know if it is or not, but don't you think we should at least question him? Looking back, it seems awfully convenient that he offered his services to us."

"I agree." The Chief started toward Gibbs and Clark. He called over his shoulder. "I'll have Lori give him a call. He's been up front with us so far. Let's hope it stays that way."

"But—"

Chief Burleson spun toward Alan. "But nothing. You know your place on this. Get out of here before Agent Milanesi shows up." He pointed toward the exit.

"Let's go, Alan," Ruth called from the car.

They climbed into the LeSabre and rolled slowly toward the cemetery exit.

Alan slapped his hand on the seat. "Dammit, I hate this. Holbrook has something to do with this, if not everything."

"How do you know? The evidence doesn't even point in his direction. Maybe motive, but even that's a pretty weak argument."

A jet-black SUV pulled in at the same time they left. A woman with hair as dark as the vehicle she drove, glanced from behind the wheel as they passed, Ruth's LeSabre reflecting in the agent's sunglasses.

"That was good timing." A nervous giggle escaped Ruth's tight lips. "FBI agents scare me. And if this one is friends with Mayor Snively, well, nothing else needs to be said."

"About time something went my way." Alan sat silent, deep in thought. What could Holbrook's motive be? Would he really kill those men simply because they put his father away? And why frame John in the process?

The Buick rolled to a stop at the last light before the on-ramp to the freeway. "Turn right."

"Right? The freeway is to the left?"

"We're not getting on the freeway. Holbrook's office is this way." Alan gestured to his right. "Let's pay him a visit."

The light turned green. The vehicle didn't budge.

"Chief Burleson sounded pretty adamant about this. We need to get that report to him. We don't have a warrant either."

Alan continued to look in the direction of Holbrook's office. The light turned yellow. Ruth pressed the accelerator and turned right before the light flipped back to red.

"Thanks, Ruth. We don't need a warrant just to ask the guy a few questions."

"Don't thank me yet. Burleson's on his last nerve. I'm not sure how many more times he'll forgive you. And if the glimpse we caught of that agent is any clue, I wouldn't be surprised if she found a way to get you canned. If she doesn't eat you first."

Alan laughed. "She did look like a predator, didn't she?"

Great Memory

Rachel McCall's voice answered in her chipper tone telling the caller to leave a message after the beep.

"Hey, Rachel. This is Alan Reeves. I have a favor to ask. I'm on the road right now or I'd do it myself. Could you look up the meaning behind a blue rose? We have one in evidence. I'm not sure it means anything, as it was found by a headstone, but it may be related to the case you sent me information on earlier, so I'd like to hear from you as soon as you get a chance."

Alan hung up and sat his phone on Ruth's dashboard.

"You really think the blue rose has something to do with all this?" Ruth glanced in his direction then back to the road. "It's a cemetery. There were flowers all over the place."

"I'm not sure, but I'm not taking any chances." Alan gestured to his right. "Take a right at the next light." He waited for her to turn the corner before continuing. "Whoever is doing this thinks it's a game. I mean, come on, leaving the exact same picture at the scene of every crime and then at Abraham Holbrook's headstone? I've read about this before, heck, I've seen this before. This is personal. Every little aspect of this case is personal."

Ruth shook her head. "Maybe, but I don't see it. You don't think you're reading too much into it?"

"I don't. Either way, it can't hurt to find out." Alan paused, the cogs in his mind chugging away. *This is personal. I haven't said that before, but it has to be. What else could the photo mean?* He pulled the copy of the picture from his back pocket and studied it.

"You've been staring at that picture on and off all day, Alan. You think you'll find something you haven't already?"

Alan lifted his chin toward Ruth. "You certainly have the questioning part down, but what happened to the supportive side of my personal counselor?"

Red colored Ruth's cheeks. "I'm being supportive. We're driving to Holbrook's, are we not?"

"True enough. Take a left up there on Pine Avenue. His office is in the middle of the business district on the right hand side." His eyes went back to the photo. *Why was my dad drinking? And why was he drinking with these guys? What are they celebrating?* "I'm telling you, Ruth. There's something not right here. I can't quite put my finger on it, but I feel that if I just keep looking I'll figure out what it is."

Ruth turned the convertible onto Pine Avenue. "Sometimes I wonder if you ever listened to your dad. What did he always say when you were looking for an answer that was right in front of you?"

"Work on something else, give your brain a nudge, and wait for it to work things out in its own time." He hadn't realized Ruth looked up to his father this much. She repeated his sayings almost by rote, and she'd only worked with him a year. "How do you do that, Ruth? Remember so much of what my father said."

The brakes squealed as they glided to a stop in front of Russell Holbrook's office. Ruth slid the gear into park and climbed out without looking at Alan. "I've always had a good memory. And like I said, I looked up to Ed. He was a hotshot."

Alan watched her with an intent glare as he left the vehicle. "Ruth?"

She either ignored him or didn't hear. "This is Holbrook's office then?" She gestured to the yellow vinyl siding. "Typical psychologist using a color to brighten the mood of his patients before they even enter."

"Ruth?" Alan said again.

"What?" she snapped.

"Do you have a photographic memory?"

"It's called eidetic, and yes. What does that have to do with anything?" Her face darkened.

"Nothing really, but why didn't you tell me?"

"Can we talk about this later?" Ruth huffed and stepped up to the office door.

The response was comedic coming from her. He'd only seen her lose her temper once in their years together on the force and that was because a convicted sex offender slapped her on the hind-end during his booking.

"I apologize if I've upset you, Ruth. It just seems like an odd thing to hide."

She faced him. "I'm only going to explain this once. I don't tell anybody about it because when I do, they treat me like a freak. On top of that, I still worked my ass off to get the grades I did at nursing school and at the academy. People think it's not fair that I have the memory I do, like I'm somehow cheating them. I sometimes wish I could get rid of it, but it helps me too much on the job to even think about it. There. Are those good enough reasons for you?" Ruth crossed her arms and looked away.

He stepped close and placed his hand on her back. "Come on, Dr. Shaw. I need my counselor back, even if she's not that good."

The corner of her mouth pulled up in a smile. She turned partially toward him. "So you don't think I'm some weirdo then?"

"There's no doubt you're a weirdo, but I knew that before this conversation."

She slapped him on the arm, the small grin taking away from the dirty look the rest of her face held, much the same as Rita used to look at him when he was particularly bull-headed.

The image of Rita sobered Alan. "If this is a secret you'd like me to keep, I'm fine with that. Just know that I think it's great. Not because I wish I had the ability; though, it would be nice, but because of what you said. Your ability to recall memories at will to help a person in need is just about one of the coolest things I've ever heard."

Ruth's arms shot around his shoulders and drew him into a tight hug. She pulled back after a few seconds. "That's probably not real proper out here in the middle of the street. If Holbrook is watching, you know his shrink alarms are going off." She gestured toward the door. "Let's go see what this wacko is up to."

Voices

Voices whispered on the wind, echoing through the cold depths of John's mind. Nonsensical. Nothing more than garbled words tossed together into incoherent gibberish. He spun. First one way and then another. A familiar evil laugh pierced the darkness, familiar only because he'd heard it in his recent nightmares.

Where am I, he tried to say, but his mouth wouldn't move. The words repeated over and over in his thoughts, unable to escape his dry lips. *So thirsty. Where am I?*

The voices grew louder. The laugh again. Something touched his chest, his toes, and his eyes. Something yanked his eyelids open, held them in place by powerful beams of steel. Not steel. *Fingers?*

Searing white light blinded him. Another laugh.

Heat blew gently on his ear. A whisper. "Johnny boy? Wake up, Johnny. Time to play."

Pain throbbed in his thigh, each heartbeat sending another jolt through his tight muscle. *The bug bite? Not a bug bite, a syringe!* His heart jumped in his chest. The pain in his leg increased with each quick thump. *Eddy! Where's Eddy?* Still no words came, unlike the flashes of memory. The syringe, a short scuffle, Eddy's bloodied face slamming to the mud before him.

Where am I! Instead of a yell, a wet moan filled his ears. *Was that me?*

"Calm down, Johnny. Your heart rate is through the roof. I don't want you having a heart attack now."

The familiar voice, similar to the laugh, slid through his ears like a snake. Wriggling, forcing its way into his mind.

"Take a deep breath. Wait, maybe this will help."

Something cold and metallic pried his lips and jaws open. A tube slid into place. He fought until he noticed he breathed easier. He wiggled his toes. Something smooth held them in place, not uncomfortably, much like a sheet. *A sheet!* The adrenaline rushing through his body awakened his senses, his thoughts.

He tried opening his eyes again. Slits of the blinding light pierced his retina.

"As I said, take deep breaths. They will calm you. You've been drugged, but it will wear off soon. Your toes moved a moment ago. I suggest starting there and working your way upward, at least that's what the others said worked for them. Your eyes may take longer. Be patient. We don't want your sight harmed by the lighting."

"Who?" John managed to say around whatever held his mouth open.

"Ah yes, I'm sure you're thirsty. Hold on one moment. I'll get something for you."

If the voice belonged to the same person with the evil laugh, why did they now help him? Maybe he'd imagined the wickedness. Was he in the hospital? *Not the hospital. They would have pumped me full of epinephrine by now.* If not the hospital, then where?

"Here you go, Johnny Boy. This should quench your thirst."

Liquid poured through whatever held his mouth open, too much liquid. Warmth filled his mouth. He gagged and choked. It continued until he thought he'd drown, splashing down onto his neck and chest.

"Oh, I'm sorry about that. Too much? Well, better too much than not enough. Right?"

The metallic taste came back. He'd probably bitten his tongue in the battle for more air.

"This is taking longer than expected, John. Maybe you're not quite the physical specimen I had anticipated."

Whoever spoke to him sighed.

"I'll give you a little more time. Don't take too long though; I wouldn't want you to miss the party."

28. Discovery

Warrant

Ruth tried the doorknob to Russell Holbrook's office. "Locked." She rapped on the door with her knuckles.

"Look here." Alan pointed to a piece of paper hanging on the inside of the office window. "Apparently Dr. Holbrook is on vacation. Awfully convenient, don't you think?"

"I'm sorry, Alan. I don't see it. You and John spent time with this guy. Could he have pulled the wool over the Reeves' boys eyes so easily?"

Alan huffed. He placed his hands over his brow as if holding binoculars and peered through the window into the darkness. "I can't see anything."

"Remember what I just said about not appearing professional?"

He stepped away from the glass. "I don't care how this looks, Ruth. He had something to do with it. I know he did."

Ruth started toward her car. "That's great. I'm sure the judge will agree with you. Who needs evidence anyway?" She pulled open the door and climbed in, waving for him to follow.

Alan held up a finger. "Just a sec; I need to make a phone call." He dialed the station. Chief Burleson's assistant answered. "Hey, Lori. This is Captain Reeves. Can you look up the witness names for the Tolman case? I need to know who it was that worked with Russell Holbrook. Her name was Missy, or Maddy maybe.

"One moment."

Ruth turned on the radio and flipped it to her favorite channel, Detroit's Golden Oldies. The Everly Brothers told them to dream, dream, dream.

Lori's crisp voice came back on the line. "Got it right here, Alan. Mary Hodge."

"Could you give me her home number please?"

She rattled off the digits.

"Thanks, Lori." He hung up and stepped close to the convertible. "I have Mary Hodge's phone number. She worked with Russell. She's married, but they have a thing. I'll bet you ten dollars she's gone too."

Ruth turned down the music. "What does that prove? If they were an item, why wouldn't he take her on vacation with him?"

"Russell was adamant their relationship was only about sex. They've been at it for years, but the husband has no idea. You don't think her hubby would find it strange they both went on a vacation at the same time?"

She pointed to the phone still in his hand. "Give her a call then."

Alan dialed the number Lori had given him. It rang five times before someone answered.

"Hello, this is Captain Reeves from the Clarkbridge Police Department. To whom am I speaking?"

"This is Joshua Hodge. What's this in regards to?"

"I'm sorry to bother you, Mr. Hodge, but is Mary home?"

"She left for Florida a couple days ago on a business trip. Is there something I can help you with?"

Ruth watched Alan from the car. He pointed at the phone and nodded. She rolled her eyes.

"Who did she go on this business trip with?"

"Nobody. Why?"

"It's nothing urgent, but we're going over an investigation and Mary's name appeared on a possible list of witnesses. If she's out of town though, it's not a big deal. Just have her contact us as soon as she's home."

"Oh. Well I wish I could help you more, Captain Reeves. Should I call her? I haven't been able to get a hold of her yet, but she's never been one to answer the phone anyway."

"That won't be necessary, Mr. Hodge. That's all I need for now. I'm not at liberty to discuss the details of the case at this time. If you have any other questions, feel free to dial the police department and ask for Chief Burleson."

Alan hung up and leaned on the passenger door. "Well?"

"Well, what?" Ruth said. "So this couple who've been cheating for years took a vacation together. It's not unheard of."

"But the timing, Ruth. Don't you see it? I just thought of something. Chief Burleson specifically told Holbrook to stay in the area since he's a possible suspect. We didn't pursue it further since he joined in on the case. He answered all of our questions, but we never ruled him out. I'm calling the Chief. If Holbrook really went on vacation, we can at least get a bench warrant issued."

"Sure, I'll just sit here like a good little cop and listen to my favorite songs. I would like lunch sometime soon though. All your questions are making me hungry." Though her comment was flip, she smiled. "I'm fine, Alan. Just make your phone calls. I know better than to question a Reeves when they're on a roll."

Alan's phone vibrated before he could make the next call. "It's Rachel," he said. He flipped the phone open. "This is Alan."

"I have to admit, Alan, I had a pretty good laugh when you asked me to Google a blue rose for you. Doesn't everybody have Internet access on their phones these days? Anyways, I dug a little deeper."

"What did you find?"

"Blue rose. As with all flower colors, they can mean a bunch of different things depending on where you look.

How deep was the blue? Was it lighter, almost like a light purple? Or was it darker?"

"Very dark. That makes a difference?"

"Maybe. The only blue roses in existence are either genetically modified, such as with the light colored ones, or dark blue which are dyed. There were a few meanings that popped up more than the others. It could symbolize a mystery or something unattainable. Or maybe the something is a mystery, which makes it unattainable. I saw a few things about prosperity as well, but not near as much as the other two meanings."

Ruth's phone rang while Alan spoke with Rachel. She answered it and turned down the music again.

"You said you dug deeper?"

"This is the creepy part, Alan. Did you go over all the information I faxed you?"

"I did."

"I don't have any idea what this means, but I hope you figure it out soon. I haven't heard from John in over two hours. He said he'd call by now."

"That is strange. He hasn't called me either." Alan fought to remember John's exact words back at the tree house. Did John say he'd call, or was Alan supposed to call him? *This would be a great time to have Ruth's memory.*

"Well, this blue rose, it's the symbol Abraham Holbrook used for his research. It's in the corner of almost every document he submitted to psychology journals. Something unattainable? Like his research?"

"Rachel, I need you to fax the information you found about the rose to Chief Burleson. The stuff about Abraham Holbrook's research as well. As long as it's legal. Can you make it look like it came from Eddy's computer?"

"I can, on both accounts. I'll have the info to Burleson in a few minutes. And nothing illegal on my end, just lots of digging."

Alan glanced to Ruth. She still spoke on her phone but stared at him with worry in her eyes.

"Thanks, Rachel. You're a life saver."

"I try. If you hear from John, have him call me right away. I'll do the same."

He hung up and slid into the passenger seat. "What's going on?"

Ruth put her hand over the receiver. "Two more people are missing, one an elderly man, the approximate age of the three deaths. They haven't made any connections yet, but Special Agent Predator believes John will go on a murder spree. She told Chief Burleson it was the next logical step according to John's profile, like he's having flashbacks from the military or something."

"Who's on the phone? And who's the other missing person?"

"It's Burleson on the other end. He's getting chewed out by the agent now. She heard him telling me over the phone. And the other missing person is Cooper Forbes. His wife says he disappeared sometime last night, and she hasn't seen him since."

"Coop? I don't get it. He'd never leave without saying something."

"That's what Chief said. Hold on one second; he's back on the phone."

A seed of doubt planted itself in Alan. Had he made a mistake letting John go? His phone rang again. Rachel. "Did you hear from John?"

"No," she said. "But I did forget to tell you something. I don't know if it will help, but out of curiosity I looked up the beer your dad was drinking in that photo. It's from a local brewery in southern Detroit. They went bankrupt two years after opening. So unless your dad has a habit of aging his beer like wine, that means the picture was taken before any of the Abraham Holbrook stuff went down."

"They knew each other before Abraham?"

"That's your job, Alan. I just find the facts. You put them together. Talk soon."

Ruth tapped him on the shoulder. "Hey, the Chief wants to talk to you."

Alan sat his phone on the dashboard and grabbed Ruth's. "This is Alan."

"Where did Eddy get that information about the blue rose on Abraham Holbrook's business stationery?"

"I'm not sure, Chief. He is a private investigator. I just mentioned to him that he should send it to you. Wait, you got it already?"

"I haven't had a chance to read over everything yet, but Eddy says right here at the top what the fax entails. Great work. Listen, I spoke with Judge Wyrick a few weeks ago about this case and told him I might need warrants at any time. He lost a partner, Dave Parker, in the line of duty years ago, so when I told him about Rita, he jumped all over it. Agent Milanesi advised me not to do this, but I have a bench warrant out for Russell Holbrook. He never returned my call last week, and he isn't answering now. It just so happens that the lady he worked with, Mary Hodge, is out of town. Quite a coincidence."

"That's what I said. I called her husband a bit ago."

Ruth tapped her fingers on the steering wheel and watched him, worry still creasing the corner of her eyes.

"Mr. Hodge said you called. He phoned me at the station, said you were real polite and professional. That's about the same time I got Eddy's fax about the blue rose, which is why I'm calling now. I don't just have a bench warrant; we have one to search his work and dwelling as well."

Alan pumped his fist up and down. Ruth tried to hide a smile with her hand. "How did you get another warrant so fast?"

"Agent Milanese showed up at the cemetery right as you were leaving. I needed a reason to get out of there, so I said I had to get paperwork started on a warrant. Ruth said you're at his office now. Is that true?"

"It's true, but I just came here to—"

"It doesn't matter. Get your ass out of there and over to Judge Wyrick's place. He's at home right now over on 12th Street. I'll text you the address. You and Ruth have your gear?"

"Most of it."

"Good. Get it done, Alan. One more thing. If you blatantly disregard my orders one more time, I'll personally kick your ass."

"Got it, Chief."

Patience

Patience wasn't a virtue John Reeves possessed. Thoughts and questions bounded rampant through his mind. Where was he? Who was he with? Why was he so cold? And what was that stench? The foul smell reminded him of a rotting carcass, but the chemical odors wafting about the room made it hard to recognize.

Whoever spoke to him before had turned off the lights. He drifted between the waking world and dreams, the two barely discernible. His jaw ached, his thigh, his head. The hard tube holding his mouth open grew sticky. Saliva built in his throat until he gagged and swallowed.

Lights buzzed on overhead. The light, not as bright as before, still pained him. This time he had more control. John blinked through the tears, held his eyes open in slits until the pain became unbearable. He closed them until the burning dissipated. He repeated the process until his vision returned. Above him hung long fluorescent lights, the kind found in schools or hospitals. Blurry darkness shrouded the rest of the ceiling.

A beeping sound worked through the haziness. *A heart monitor?* He rolled his head to the side. Excruciating pain exploded in his brain. He clenched his eyes shut until it eased. Not completely, but enough that he could open his eyes again. Beside him stood a heart monitor and an IV. Cords and wires cascaded from the medical equipment to his body. He followed the IV line down to his arm where thick leather cuffs held him in place. Pain shot through his clenched fists as he forced them open. A tear slid from his eye and into his ear.

John continued to move and wiggle his extremities, flexing each muscle until the majority of the pain subsided. Sweat covered his brow and drenched his hair.

"Johnny boy! You've decided to join us."

His immediate reaction was to take a defensive stance. The straps holding his arms, legs, and torso in place creaked with pressure. When he tried to speak, his tongue pushed against cold thickness in his mouth. It took him a moment, but he moved his mouth and tongue until he spit out whatever it was that had been shoved in his throat.

He worked the saliva and muscles in his mouth. "Wurr ... Weh..."

The blurry form moved closer. He wore white and his face glowed. "Don't worry. You're close to coming around if your tongue is strong enough to spit out that funnel. The concoction my apprentice gave you is quite strong. Mr. Bailey is only just now wiggling his toes."

Eddy! Where the fuck am I? "Hoos... Hospital?"

"There you go!" The man in white clapped. "Sadly no, this is not the hospital, but trust me when I say it's exactly where you belong."

A second voice joined the man in white, but only a whisper.

"Oh, Cooper, quit whining. His straps are secure. You checked them at least ten times."

Cooper? Cooper Forbes? "Coop?"

The man in white patted him on the chest. "That's right, Johnny. Cooper Forbes is with us."

Cooper's desperate voice sounded tinny. "Why did you tell him I was here? Why would you do that?"

"Shut up!" the man in white snapped. "You know as well as I that he won't leave this place. At least not in any condition to tell somebody you were here."

Adrenaline soared through John's body again. The heart monitor beat faster.

"I don't... I don't..." John's muddled thoughts wouldn't allow words to form.

The man in white bent low, within inches of John's face. His face didn't glow. Light had reflected from a plastic surgeon's mask. Beneath the mask was Russell Holbrook, madness glowed in his eyes.

"I see the recognition, John. That's right. Dr. Russell Holbrook, at your service." Holbrook leaned back and spread his arms. He bowed deeply. "Your life, and I suppose you could say your death, are now in my hands."

"Why?" The word barely gurgled from John's lips.

"Why you ask? Oh, that is a story you must be awake for. In another thirty minutes or so you'll be ready to hear the why. Until then, relax and take deep breaths. You'll be here awhile so please, get comfortable."

John fought against the straps. Fought to force words from his mouth. Fought to understand. "Fff... Fff..."

Holbrook leaned close again. "What was that, Johnny Boy? I can't hear you?" He made a show of cupping his hand behind his ear.

"Fff... Fuck you."

29. Police Work

Vice

Alan stood on Judge Wyrick's veranda. What seemed like hundreds of potted begonias hung from the ceiling, as if they were in a begonia jungle.

"Thanks for this, Judge Wyrick."

The judge caught Alan by the arm before he left. His mostly gray eyebrows settled just above his rimmed glasses. "You find whoever took your partner, Alan. And you do whatever it takes to bring them to justice. I never had the chance. You do this for Rita. And for Dave."

Dave Parker was Wyrick's partner who'd been shot in the line of duty when they worked for the Clarkbridge Police Deparment twenty years earlier. Alan wasn't sure what to say, so he nodded. He leapt down the steps and ran to Ruth standing by the trunk of her car. "Got the warrant. Let's go."

Ruth handed Alan a bullet-resistant vest from her car. "We'll need these."

"You carry them in your trunk?"

She shrugged. "I like to be prepared. Besides, the department can't afford everything we might need." Ruth flipped a latch and pulled open the compartment usually used for spare tires. Inside was police tape, stun guns, a shotgun, handcuffs, ankle cuffs, and twenty other items typically found in police cruisers.

They checked their weapons while Alan slid his vest on. Ruth still wore hers beneath her uniform. They were on their way toward Russell Holbrook's office within minutes.

"You're lucky you let me stop for a to-go burger from Sally's on the way to the judge's place." Ruth patted her belly. "You don't want to see me when I haven't been fed." They came to a stop at a red light. Ruth pressed the button on her dash to raise the roof. "It feels funny wearing this vest and my badge with the top down. Like we're Miami Vice or something." She giggled.

"Damn. I knew I was forgetting something."

The light turned green. Ruth's foot hung suspended over the accelerator. "What did you forget? Do we need to go back?"

Alan grinned. "I forgot my pink pastel Armani jacket and leather loafers."

Ruth squealed with laughter. "You ass!" Her LeSabre shot down the road. "You don't watch Blue Ice, but you know what they wore on Miami Vice?"

"What can I say? It was popular when I was at the academy."

Breaking Doors

Ruth parked her car a block behind Holbrook's office. They climbed from the vehicle and readied their weapons.

The woman's determination surprised Alan. "Have you done this before, Ruth? I know you and I haven't done this together, but with anybody else?"

"A couple times. Why?"

"The look you have on your face. If I didn't know you, I'd say you were about to eat rocks."

She looked away. "This is why I'm a cop, Alan. This is what it's all about. Catching the bad guys so they can't hurt anybody else. I just hate it when we don't know for sure."

"Assurances are hard to come by in this field."

Ruth turned her stony stare in his direction. "Are you sure we shouldn't get back up on this one?"

Alan nodded. "Chief Burleson doesn't think Holbrook will put up a fight, even if he is responsible for the deaths. Plus, there isn't anybody else. He sent Gibbs and Clark over to Holbrook's house and they're both on overtime."

"Good. At least we won't have to do this twice today. What's the plan?" Ruth said.

"Simple. I'll go in the back. You cover the front."

Ruth took off at a jog. Alan waited until she had enough time to reach the front. He scanned the surroundings as he worked his way to the back door. Behind the business district were a few cars and large trash bins. He raised his fist to knock when movement caught his eye. A few doors down, a man wearing a white butcher's vest with trash bags in hand glanced toward Alan and nodded. Alan nodded back and waited for the man to toss the bags in the bin.

He pounded three times and tried the knob. *Locked.* "Russell Holbrook. This is the police. We have a warrant to search the premises." Alan counted to five. When nobody answered, he kicked the door close to the knob. The door flew open and slammed into the wall. Wood splinters littered the carpeted hallway. He moved forward as trained, pistol held before him aimed at the floor, his finger on the trigger guard.

"Russell Holbrook? This is the police." No answer. The office was much smaller than Alan had expected. Ruth peeked in the front window. The short hallway had two doors, both on the left side and closed. The front office was wide open. The only place someone could hide was behind the front desk and Alan had a clear shot. Nobody there.

He waved for Ruth to enter. The front door crashed open.

Impressive, Alan thought. *Those stubby legs are stronger than they look.*

Ruth looked all business with her brow drawn down, her chest raising and lowering beneath her vest. Alan nodded to the door on the left. Ruth backed up a few steps and held her weapon ready. Alan tried the knob. The door creaked open. A small bathroom that smelled of lavender. "Clear," he whispered. He nodded to the next door. The door opened as the bathroom had. Holbrook's office. Alan entered. Ruth stayed in the hallway.

"Russell?" No answer. He scanned the room. "Empty. Come on in, Ruth. Be on the ready in case he comes back."

Ruth stepped into the office and stationed herself near the back wall facing the entrance. "What's next?"

"Now," Alan sighed, "we search. Turn your cell back on in case Chief Burleson calls."

She pulled the phone from her pocket. "He's calling right now." She pressed the talk button and put the phone to her ear. "Sergeant Shaw." She paused. "Sure, one sec." Ruth held the phone toward Alan. "He wants to talk to you."

"Hey, Chief. Why didn't you call my cell?"

"I did. You never answer the damn thing. How things look on your end?"

"All clear. No sign of Holbrook."

"Same thing at his home. I got Gibbs and Clark searching now. I have a couple volunteers on their way to you. The same for Gibbs and Clark. You and Shaw are to do all the searching. If you find anything substantial, we may be able to call in forensics. Otherwise, it's just you two for now."

"Understood, Chief. We're on it."

The Chief whispered into the phone.

"What's that?" Alan clicked the volume button.

"Do you still have my wife's number?"

"I do."

Ruth tilted her head to the side. Alan realized he'd whispered back to the Chief.

Chief Burleson continued. "Call me at her number with Shaw's phone in exactly one minute. If I don't answer, don't leave a message."

"What's this about?"

Rustling came through the phone. Alan heard a woman's voice in the background. "Who are you speaking to, Chief Burleson?"

"Just one moment, Agent Milanesi." The Chief's voice grew louder as he spoke into the phone again. "Hey there, Sergeant Shaw, sorry about that. Keep me updated." The signal went dead.

Alan flipped the phone closed.

Ruth held her hand out to take the phone. "Why did he call my phone instead of using the radio? And why were you whispering?"

"He probably knew we might still be on radio silence and figured you wouldn't answer if you weren't ready. He said to call him back in a minute, and there are a couple volunteer officers on the way to back us up. Looks like we're searching the premises. Can I hold on to your phone a sec?"

"That's fine. What about Gibbs and Clark?"

Alan pulled open the top drawer on Holbrook's desk. "Same thing goes for them." He pulled out a stack of papers and tossed them on the desk. "According to the warrant, we can only search for paperwork containing information about the three victims, but only if it's not their official patient records. Patient confidentiality and all that crap. Judge Wyrick wasn't willing to sign that warrant until we had something stronger." Alan holstered his weapon and looked at his watch. "How long has it been?"

"Almost a minute."

He dialed Ethel Burleson's number. The Chief answered.

"What's going on, Chief?"

"I only have a minute. I'm in the restroom at the department. Knowing Mayor Snively, she may have had Agent Milanesi tap our phones so I brought Ethel's phone to work in case I needed a secure line. Snively has that bitch breathing down my neck, yapping at me about small town departments and their incestuous police work."

"Incestuous?"

"Her words, not mine. Says we spend so much time looking out for each other that we don't do our jobs. Have you heard anything from John?"

Alan stuttered. "No, no, I mean, why would I have —"

"Cut the shit, Alan. I know his buddy left him a phone at the station. I'm not a rookie. This smelled bad from the beginning, but we're almost out of time. You or John need to find something fast. Agent Mila-bitchy is about to call in her friends. She keeps saying we screwed everything up. The sad thing is, she's right. No more taking chances. By the book or nothing at all. I want to find Rita's killer as bad as you, but if we all get canned then the only thing we'll be searching for is another career."

"Point taken." Alan sighed. "I heard from John last night, but not since. We were supposed to contact each other some time today." He pulled the phone back and looked at the time. "It's after six already. I think something may have happened. Maybe he stumbled onto the real killer. Maybe he found Holbrook."

"I wondered the same thing. Damn, gotta go. Be careful, Alan. Keep me apprised of the situation. Make sure Shaw is the one to call though, in case psycho is still following me around barking orders."

Sophie

Ruth flopped down next to Alan on Holbrook's office couch. "Either Holbrook has an amazing maid or he's the most anal-retentive person in history."

"Barely a speck of dust in three hours," Alan mumbled. "Nothing. That's what we found. Nothing!" He slammed his fist on the armrest. He stood and paced the hardwood floor. "The same damn thing Gibbs and Clark found. Maybe we do have the wrong guy."

Ruth's features softened. "I told you from the beginning what we had was barely circumstantial."

Alan shook his head and ground his teeth together. "No. He had something to do with it. I know it."

"You keep saying that, but where's the evidence? We need something solid. At least we have the flimsy motive because of his father's death. Explaining this mess to Holbrook when he gets back won't be as bad as it could have been. I'm glad Chief's finally on his way over. Doubtful, but maybe he'll do the paperwork for this one."

Alan paused. "Where's the picture?"

"The picture of your dad and those guys? Should still be in your back pocket."

He slid his hand into his pocket and pulled the photo free.

Ruth ran her finger in circles on the seat next to her. "We should really tell the other guys to head on home. It's getting late."

"There's something I should see, and I just can't get it." Alan spoke to himself while he stared at the photo. He shuffled to the couch and sat back down. "I keep thinking it's the beer. So what if it was from a local brewery? My dad barely drank. He barely had friends to drink with, and most of them were on the force."

Ruth slid closer and peered at the photo. "Let's take it one step at a time. What about their clothing? Anything strange about the colors? What they're wearing?"

"Not really. They're all wearing flannel shirts, popular at that time. You can tell it's mid-summer by how thick the clover is in the field behind them."

"What about the shadows around them? Are any out of place? Are there any... Wait, that's clover in the background?"

"Yeah. Why?"

"Didn't your dad grow clover? For the deer you said?"

Alan laughed. "Of course you'd remember that." He squinted at Ruth. "Hey, if you have this great memory, why'd you ask me the other night if the custard donuts were my favorite?"

Her cheeks brightened. "Technically, I asked if you still preferred custard donuts. People change their mind all the time."

"Good excuse." He glanced to the photo again and let out a growl. "Look, I need to go. This is driving me crazy. I'm going to head home and check the answering machine, see if John called."

Ruth stood. "That's great, Mr. Reeves. And just how do you plan to get home? I'm the one with a car."

"Can I borrow it? I know that's asking a lot But as you said, Chief Burleson's on the way. You'll have to go over things with him, and he's at least a half-hour away. He can drop you at my place on the way home, or I can just drop your car off tomorrow."

"You're right. That is asking a lot. Sophie doesn't like it when other people drive her."

"Sophie?"

She crossed her arms. "Yeah. Sophie."

Alan stood and put his arm around Ruth. "Remember what I said earlier about you being a weirdo? Naming your car confirms it."

"Oh, shut up." Ruth shoved his arm off. "For someone about to borrow a woman's car, you're not acting very nice."

"I apologize." Alan stepped in front of her and put his hands together, pleading. "May I please borrow Sophie for the evening? And I promise, I'll take good care of her. I'm always gentle with a woman."

Ruth slapped his hands from in front of her. "You turd." She pulled the car keys from her pocket. "You better take care of her. She's had a rough day running around so much."

"Thank you so much, Ruth." Alan grabbed the keys and gave her a peck on the cheek. "I'll get her back to you soon. You want me to leave the keys in the visor in case you stop by tonight?"

"That's fine. I'll come over tonight. Sophie's not the type of girl to stay over on the first date."

Beer and Clover

Alan left Holbrook's office on foot and headed toward Sophie. The joviality he'd just felt wore off as he thought about their day. He'd enjoyed spending time with Ruth, but wished it could have been under different circumstances. He wanted to rush home. John could be in trouble, especially if he hadn't called Rachel yet. She was his go-to girl.

He dropped the top before leaving for home. The warm summer wind blowing through his hair didn't seem so bad now that he had time to think. It was a nice change from his rumbling Ford.

"Where are you, John?" he said. "I could really use your help on this. At the least, we could bounce ideas off each other over a beer."

The mention of beer brought his thoughts back to the photo.

"The clover."

His father had been the only farmer in town to grow clover. The others made fun of him saying he wasted money on something that didn't even work. Yet these same farmers always begged to hunt his property during deer season.

But their mother never let Ed drink at their farm. Sure, he'd sneak a few drinks down in their basement, or sometimes in the work shed, but he'd never have friends over drinking like that.

"What does this mean, Alan?" He continued, glad Ruth wasn't there to tease him about talking to himself. "Why does it matter if the picture was taken at Dad's old farmhouse?"

It had to have been a time when their mother was gone, which didn't happen often. He pulled to the side of the road and used his cell phone to light the photo. He peered at the tractor.

"There it is. It is your property, Dad. But why?" He remembered seeing the "H" on the tractor before but hadn't thought twice about it. It was the last letter in the name Sarah that their father had painted on his tractor. He'd named it after some woman he knew. The phone beeped three times and shut off. "Damn battery."

He pulled back onto the road and drove home, all the while pondering why Ed Reeves had held a bachelor party of sorts with these guys. And what if Abraham Holbrook was the one behind the camera? What did that mean?

The familiar crunching of gravel beneath the tires welcomed Alan home. He put the top up in case it rained again. He threw the keys on top of the visor and headed toward his house.

Adrenaline burst through his system. His feet and fingers tingled. "It's personal," he remembered saying to Ruth. *Why else leave all those photos if it's not personal?*

"You slimy son-of-a-bitch." Alan hurried into his house and grabbed the lantern flashlight from the foyer closet. He locked the front door behind him and checked his weapon once again. He still wore the vest from earlier. It was a long shot, a really long shot, but he wouldn't sleep until he checked. "Holbrook, you better hope I'm wrong about my dad's farmhouse."

30. Children

Not the Children

Holbrook had switched off the lights, leaving John in the dark. "Your punishment for cursing," he'd said.

The tingling ceased, replaced by the feeling returning to his body. John could move every muscle now and form words. A cloud still settled over his mind as if he had a hangover. He no longer felt as if his head had passed through a blender.

Straining against the leather straps proved futile. They held strong. Moving his limbs merely kept them from going numb.

"John?" Eddy's voice rasped much as his own had hours before.

Through the darkness, the heart monitor's blinking lights hinted at Eddy's body lying next to him on another stainless steel table. "I'm here," John said. "Stay quiet and stay calm."

"Where—"

"Save your words, Eddy. Talking will make it worse." Eddy's heart monitor danced a faster cadence. "Calm down. We may be in trouble. You're hooked to a heart monitor. If you get worked up, Holbrook might come back."

Eddy moaned.

"Holbrook has us somewhere. We're on hospital gurneys, I think. He drugged us. Well, Cooper Forbes did."

"Coop?" Eddy sputtered.

"I think so, but I'm not sure. It all feels like a dream now, but I'm fairly certain he was here."

The florescent lighting burst on overhead, searing John's eyes. "Damn it!" he cried. "A little warning next time."

Holbrook's voice came close. "Oh, dear Johnny, does that hurt? How about this?"

A blade slid through the flesh on John's chest from shoulder to sternum. He clenched his teeth and clamped his eyes shut, holding back the scream.

"What's...?" Eddy cleared his throat. "What's going on?"

"Eddy, my boy. So good of you to join us. I have a special surprise waiting for you. You may want to heed John's advice though. Don't speak too much, not just yet, not until you can form more saliva. We don't want you damaging your vocal cords before I've had a chance to test them out."

A stinging warmth spread across John's chest. He forced his eyes open against the brightness to assess his wound.

Holbrook laughed the evil cackle from John's dreams. "I wouldn't do that if I were you, even if you were a marine. Unless you wish your friend here to see you cry."

John flexed his neck to lift his head. A wide strap, similar to a leather belt, ran across his forehead attached to the sides of the gurney, allowing him only to turn his head side to side.

"If you wish to see it that bad, I can remove the strap." Holbrook stepped close and unhooked the buckle.

John snapped at Holbrook with his teeth, missing the psychiatrist's hand by millimeters. He'd felt the warmth of flesh on his lips.

Holbrook smacked John across the face with an open palm. "How dare you? I do you a favor, show you a civilized nicety, and this is how you repay me? Strike one for you, Johnny Boy."

"Kiss my ass, you psycho." John leaned his head forward. Tears almost came. Not from fear, but anger. A precise incision ran from the front deltoid, through his pectoral, down to the lower tip of his sternum. Deep enough that the dark red inner meat of his chest muscles bulged from beneath the skin. Holbrook poured iodine on the wound and pressed into the gash with gloved fingers. John clenched his teeth again. Uncontrollable tremors wracked his hands and feet.

"We need to make sure the iodine gets in there nice and deep. We don't want you dying prematurely. Infection can be a nasty thing." Holbrook leaned back and tapped his fingers against his clear plastic mask, as if deep in thought. "Actually, I happen to have a prime example of infection if you care to take a look." He gestured behind him. "Cooper, please open the curtain."

A dark red curtain hung inches from his feet. John twisted his head, searching for Cooper. He stood in the corner, hands fidgeting at his sides.

"Cooper!"

"Yes, my Savior." Cooper lurched forward and grabbed the curtain.

My Savior?

The skinny cop yanked at the curtain. It slid open to reveal more beds and fluorescent lighting. The room grew bright enough that John could take in his surroundings. Situated on the other side of Eddy were two more beds, and six that had been hidden by the blood red curtain. All but one had the same set up with the heart monitors and IV poles, each held a body.

Moisture seeped through the cement walls and puddled on the uneven concrete. John had no idea what time of day it was. It wouldn't have mattered. Dark paint blacked out the two windows set high on the wall.

Holbrook pointed with bloodied fingers toward the bed on the end, directly across from John. "Go ahead. Remove the sheet on bed six." He rolled John's gurney to the side. "There you go. A better angle for you to observe the effects of infection."

Cooper glanced in his direction but wouldn't make eye contact. He reached toward the sheet and paused.

"Good thinking, Cooper." Holbrook clasped his hands in front and smiled, as if watching a small child play with their toys. "You definitely should wear gloves in this situation. It's not a pretty sight."

The skinny cop scurried to the back wall. He yanked a pair of latex gloves from a box on one of the stainless steel counters, slid them on, and returned to the bed in the corner. He heaved a few deep breaths and held the last one. Grasping the top of the sheet, he slowly pulled it down. He turned and closed his eyes.

Layers of black and green goo stuck to the sheet where it had laid across the corpse. John didn't know much about forensics, but whoever was on the table must have been dead for months. The stench of rotting flesh wafted about the room.

That explains the smell.

Holbrook's demeanor didn't change as it would with a normal person when they saw a rotting body. The slight smile at the corners of his mouth didn't budge. John turned his head away, bile burning his throat.

"You see, John," Holbrook said. "We wouldn't want that to happen to you. I wish you'd been here sooner though; the effects before she passed were quite amazing." He left John in place and spun Eddy's gurney to face the corpse. "Now for the surprise I promised you, Eddy." He waved his hands in another grand gesture. "If you would, Cooper. Lower the rest of the sheets. Let's introduce John and Eddy to our other guests."

"Yes, my—" Cooper threw the sheet back over the decaying corpse and turned to the corner of the room. Vomit poured from his mouth and splashed across the floor. He wiped the remnants from his chin with his shirt sleeve. "Forgive me, my Savior."

Holbrook twirled his fingers. "You can clean that up later, just do as I said."

Cooper nodded and trudged to the next table in line. He pulled the sheet down to the woman's neck.

"Sandra!" Eddy fought against the restraints with more strength than John thought possible.

Ice grew in John's veins, numbing the incision on his chest. He hadn't noticed the size of the bodies beneath the other sheets.

"Don't worry, Eddy." Holbrook laid his hand on Eddy's shoulder. "Your wife is completely fine. She's probably awake at this point. I've given her enough anesthesia that she can hear, see, and feel, but not move. We don't want her hurting herself. She's not even restrained." He waved for Cooper to continue. "Show him, Cooper. Remove the sheet."

"My Savior, she isn't wearing any clothes."

Holbrook's hands clenched into fists. "I know that, you fool. I'm the one who removed them. Do as I say!"

Veins bulged on Eddy's forehead as he continued to fight against the straps holding him in place. Cooper slid the sheet from Sandra's nude body.

"Ah yes, much better." Holbrook steepled his hands in front of his chest. His eyes never strayed from Eddy's wife. "See, Eddy? No restraints. She's quite comfortable. Move on to the next surprise, Cooper."

Holbrook took Cooper's place by Sandra's side. He tossed his gloves to the floor and placed his palm on her belly, paying no attention to anybody else in the room. Moving in a circular motion, he caressed his fingers down her torso and paused above her pubic bone. "You're a lucky man, Mr. Bailey. To have had four children and retain such a beautiful body is most impressive."

"Let her go!" Eddy's pale face grew shades darker.

John's eyes went to Cooper hovering close to the small forms beneath the sheets.

Please, God, don't let it be them.

Cooper slid the sheet down to the child's shoulders. Eddy's oldest son, Edwin Junior, appeared to be sleeping. Tears coursed down Eddy's face. Cooper wiped at tears of his own as he lowered the rest of the sheets. All four of Eddy's children lay unconscious, even little Henry who was so fond of copying John's bad words.

John cried too. "Holbrook, if you hurt one of those kids, I swear, I'll kill you if I have to come back from Hell to do it."

Dusty Footprints

Alan remembered the gear in Ruth's trunk and switched his lantern flashlight for the smaller, high-strength tactical flashlight. He slid it into his back pocket when he reached the last copse of poplars, hoping the full moon and cloudless night provided enough light. He needed the element of surprise if someone hid in his parents' farmhouse.

He hurried to the house and pressed his back against the northern wall, the side facing his property. Now that he was actually there, he questioned whether he should have called for backup. *Quit wasting time. There probably isn't anybody here anyway.*

As if to prove him wrong, moonlight reflected from Cooper's car as Alan stepped around the corner to the front of the farmhouse. He ran through possible explanations. None made sense. Until he remembered Ruth telling him Cooper had gone missing the night before. *Shit, Coop. Does he have you too?*

Alan kept his weapon in hand and inched his way to Cooper's car. The moonlight wasn't enough to see inside the vehicle. He removed the flashlight from his pocket and shined it through the windows. Multi-colored stains and crumbs littered the seats, but no more than what is expected with children. Beside the booster seat sat a dirty napkin partially covering a half-eaten hot dog. The dirty

John Deere cap Cooper wore bowling lay on the passenger seat. A few empty soda cans littered the floor in the backseat. Nothing to suggest foul play.

He moved on to the farmhouse. On his way up the front porch, Alan skipped the third wooden step. He'd always meant to fix the popping sound it made when a boot laid pressure on the planks. He silently padded the last few steps and paused with his hand on the door handle. He glanced back to Cooper's car and around the front yard one more time before turning the knob. It was unlocked. The oak door crept open on silent hinges. It was possible Chief Burleson had left it that way after turning off the hallway light a few days before.

Dust covered the sparse living room furniture, the antique lamps from his grandma, the corner hutch, even the floor where he'd removed the couch for his own use years ago. He ran the flashlight along the rest of the hardwood floor. The Chief's footprints led through the dust toward the hallway at the back. He followed them across the room, his own prints making Burleson's size nines look like a child's.

Alan's breath caught. In the hallway, Burleson's tracks led into a cluster of footprints, dirt tracks, and scuff marks.

Clear Tape

"You have such a way with words, John." Holbrook softly patted Sandra's exposed belly.

Eddy no longer fought. Tears still flowed; moans and whimpers whispered his mournful defeat.

Holbrook stepped between them. "That's too bad. It appears Eddy doesn't appreciate my gift."

"Why don't you let the kids go, Russell," John said. "You have us. Isn't that what you wanted? To get us off your tail?"

"You really think this is about you, John?" Holbrook leaned forward until he was just out of biting range. "You haven't figured it all out yet? It seems the tales my father told about the Reeves family are just that. Tales." He rolled their gurneys so they were parallel with each other again. "I have work to do, and I don't wish to crouch over every time I speak. Let's sit you up. Cooper, you get the Bailey family." He crouched next to John and reached under the gurney.

Cooper set to strapping restraints around Sandra.

"What was all that about leaving them unrestrained?" John said.

"These straps are for their safety," Holbrook said from beneath the table. "You see, tonight I'm putting on a show. And who wants to miss a good show?"

John's bed began to rise. Sandra's did the same. Cooper cranked on a lever beneath, raising the gurney to a forty-five degree angle, high enough to see the whole room if her eyes were open. Holbrook cranked on John's bed until he was the same; each click bounced his head, reigniting the torturous pain in his chest.

Holbrook moved to work on Eddy next. "I suppose since you weren't bright enough to figure it out on your own, I should explain. I'd hate for you to die and not even know why. Don't plan on dying any time soon, though. Now that I have you here, we'll play some games first."

John swallowed the vomit he'd felt rise with Eddy's family held up before him. Their heads lolled to the side, slobber dribbling down their chins. "Just spit it out then. What the hell do you want with us? What's this big mysterious reason your psychotic mind came up with?"

Holbrook cranked once more on Eddy's bed and locked it into place. "What do you think, Eddy? You're a private investigator. Do you have it figured out yet?"

Eddy's eyes shot from one child to the next. John doubted he listened to a word Holbrook said.

"That's too bad." Holbrook sighed. "It looks as if we've lost Eddy for the moment. That's okay. We'll just wake him when the time is ripe." He stood. "Cooper, use the tape on the Baileys as we did with Rita and Lena." A grin split Holbrook's face as he turned to face John. "That's right. We had a wonderful time with the Reeves' girlfriends, didn't we, Cooper?"

Cooper didn't respond. He continued to work on the final bed.

"She wasn't my girlfriend, you idiot," John said.

"That may be, but she was the closest I could find on short notice. You see, you weren't even in my plans until you showed up in Clarkbridge. A nice little present that was. I thought I'd have to chase you and your unsettled mind across the country. Speaking of that, why is it you never settle anywhere, John? Are you not capable of love? Did something happen to you in the military to confuse your delicate sensibilities?" Holbrook's eyes widened. "Were you raped? Please share. I'd like to get to know you better."

John growled. "I'm not your fucking patient. Tell us why we're here."

"Just one moment please." Holbrook held up a well-manicured finger. "Just a bit higher, Cooper. Make sure they can see." He turned back to John. "Now. Where was I?"

Cooper leaned over Sandra with a roll of clear tape in his hand. When he reached for another piece, John saw what Holbrook meant by, 'Make sure they can see.' The tape pulled Sandra's eyelids open.

John suddenly wished he hadn't been so rude to Cooper the past few times they spoke. "What are you doing, Coop? I know you. You're not like this."

Holbrook pulled a stool from the corner and sat next to John. He shot a thumb over his shoulder. "Cooper? You don't know him as well as you think." He spoke up. "What do you think, Cooper? Should we tell Mr. Reeves just what you're like, or should we wait until his brother shows up?"

Again, Cooper didn't respond. He moved on to the children.

"You're right about one thing, Holbrook. Alan *will* show up. And he'll have friends."

"I wouldn't be so sure about that." Holbrook prodded at the wound on John's chest. "Didn't I tell you I can see the department's every move?"

Shit. He's the one Rachel mentioned tapping the police feed.

"Cooper," Holbrook said. "One more thing, bring in my computer when you finish. The one connected to the Clarkbridge Police Department."

"Yes, my Savior." Cooper shuffled from the room.

"What's with 'my Savior' anyway?" John said. "You get off on that?"

"Although it does have a nice ring, Cooper created the endearing term himself. In a way, I guess, I am his savior." He glanced over his shoulder at the entrance to the basement, a thick red door with multiple locks and deadbolts. "Since he's in the other room, I guess I can tell you."

"Don't tell me you're worried what he thinks."

The stool tipped backward as Holbrook howled a laugh. "No. No, of course not. You have to understand Cooper. He's as touchy as a hormonally imbalanced teenager. He's much more efficient when his emotions are in check. Cooper's real problem stems from his childhood."

"Oh, God, here comes the 'let's blame it on his childhood' crap you quacks are always peddling. I don't want to hear this shit."

Holbrook's hand slapped against the incision on John's chest. John bit his tongue to keep from screaming.

"Oh, but you do!" Holbrook said. "Such a sad story. You see, Cooper was molested by two grown men for years, one of them his father. For reasons not yet explained by modern science, Cooper himself is now attracted to young children. He visited my practice when he began having sexual fantasies about his own children.

He'd never acted on those feelings, but simply wished for them to stop." Holbrook leaned close, as if sharing a secret. "The problem with child molesters, John, is that those feelings never stop. Even with drug therapy and the greatest therapists in the world, not one has lost the temptation." He tipped back onto the stool. "Oh sure, some have controlled themselves for a period of years, but given the chance, every single one would do it again. Until now that is."

John huffed. "You're telling me you discovered a way to cure him when nobody else in the world could?"

"That's precisely what I said, John."

John remembered one of his father's favorite sayings about people with ego problems. 'If someone puts themselves up on a pedestal, you kick it out from under them. Just be prepared to fight for your life because there's nothing they hate more.'

"I knew you were full of yourself," John said, "but this one takes the cake. You think you're some great savior because a sick man says you cured him? Give me a break. You can't see past your delusions of grandeur because you're filled to the eyeballs with shit."

Fury burned behind Holbrook's eyes. He hopped from his stool and rushed to a counter against the back wall covered with another white sheet. He threw the linen back. Something clinked against the counter. Holbrook shot back to John's side, his arms held overhead with a scalpel set to impale.

John grinned.

Holbrook's chest heaved, his eyes wild. Spittle showered the inside of the plastic mask he still wore, steaming with each huff of air. His eyes closed. A deep breath and his shoulders relaxed. He tossed the scalpel into a pocket on his surgical apron. The stool squealed across the floor as he pulled it closer to John and sat back down. He lifted his mask and ran a single finger down each eyebrow, flattening the tiny hairs. The mask went back in place before he finally opened his eyes again.

The smile that never touched his eyes returned. "You see, John? It's all about control. Now, where was I?"

Death had never scared John. Not being able to say goodbye was his only fear. He'd burned so many bridges in his life that there weren't many he'd say goodbye to, but his brother was at the top of the list. For a moment, he'd wondered whether Holbrook would really plunge the scalpel into his heart. He'd wondered more whether the scalpel would hit a rib and slice Holbrook's hand.

"You were going to share some big secret about how you're the world's most deranged psychiatrist."

"You know, John," Holbrook said, hunching over with the scalpel somehow back in his hand, "let's take the next step. I won't go too far yet, but you need a reminder of who's in charge here." He punctured the skin at John's right shoulder and slid the blade through his flesh until it met the bottom of the other incision. John couldn't hold back anymore. He screamed for Holbrook to stop. "There, now that we have this nice V shape, your autopsy will go much smoother."

The red door swung open and clanged against the cement wall. Cooper yanked at a heavy-duty desk topped with multiple computer screens rocking back and forth as they rolled across the uneven floor.

"Ah yes," Holbrook purred. He stood and moved close to the desk, settling the swaying monitors. "Use the second outlet when you plug everything in. We've blown enough damn fuses in this shit-hole. I don't want it running off the batteries for long."

Like an arrow to the chest, John knew where he was. The seeping cement brick walls, the uneven floor, the aged wood overhead. "Why in hell are we at my dad's farmhouse? You're supposedly this amazing psychiatrist and you couldn't even afford your own kill room?"

Holbrook's eyes flashed, his hands clasped in front. "You'll understand it all in a moment, but first things first." He clasped Cooper's shoulder. "Remember what we spoke of earlier?"

Cooper somehow nodded and cringed at the same time. "I do, my Savior."

"Get to it then. We'll wait here."

The skinny cop plugged the last cord in and trundled from the room.

Holbrook approached John with his hands behind his back. "You'll definitely want to see this with your own eyes, John. I know you're a voyeur at heart."

John hadn't realized his mouth was open until Holbrook shoved something between his lips, dry and thick. He shook his head back and forth, pushed at it with his tongue. Nothing helped.

"Sorry about that. It's just a wash cloth. Don't worry, it's clean. You might feel woozy for a moment. I didn't want to give you anymore meds than necessary, but I added a tinge to the cloth. You see, I need you to be quiet a moment." The strap Holbrook had used to hold John's head down came across his face and held the wash cloth in his mouth. "There we go, Johnny Boy. Now, just stay here. We'll be back in a moment. Just keep an eye on monitor three. You'll enjoy this."

31. Hell

Crushed Cartilage

Alan tightened his grip on the Smith and Wesson and ran his finger along the cold edge of the trigger guard. The weight felt good in his hand, felt right. With the tactical flashlight still held in his left hand, he scanned the kitchen with deliberate motions, the living room, and the hallway.

A creaking noise echoed down the hallway. He aimed the barrel of his weapon and the flashlight beam toward the sound. Nothing. Just the old farmhouse settling around the support wall.

Damn it all. I hated that when I was a kid too. His sigh sounded like an avalanche compared to the pressing quiet.

A *thwump* sounded behind him. *The porch step!* Alan dropped to one knee and spun, weapon raised. In the doorway stood Cooper Forbes, hands raised, blocking the light from his eyes.

"Coop?"

"Captain Reeves? Put that light down, man. It's hard enough to see as it is."

"Damn it, Coop." Alan slid his gun into the holster at his hip. "I almost shot you." His flashlight picked out glints of metal on Cooper's uniform. "Why are you sneaking around out here?"

"I could ask you the same." Cooper leaned against the doorjamb.

"I remembered some things about the case. Thought I'd check them out."

"With no back up?"

Alan groaned. "I didn't want to waste anybody else's time chasing ghosts." Alan stepped into the living room and settled into his father's paisley recliner close to the front door. Dust puffed into the air. "Hey, when you were out here the other day with the K-9 Unit, Chief Burleson said he came in to shut a light off. Did anybody come in with him?"

"Yeah, a couple of us. We checked the other rooms, made sure nothing else was left on." Cooper moved the rest of the way into the house and closed the door behind him. "What did you expect to find over here?" He leaned back against the door and crossed his arms.

"Before I answer that, what happened to you? Shaw said you were reported missing."

Cooper gurgled his strange laugh. "Me? Missing? She must be mistaken. I told her and Chief I was coming to check on the farmhouse. I thought maybe John would come out here to hide after all. Like maybe he'd seen us check everything and thought it was all clear now."

"Not a bad idea. I thought the same thing actually, but why drive your car and not a cruiser?"

"Oh, yeah, I thought of it after I'd returned home. Hadn't even changed out of my uniform." He gestured to his gear. "I didn't want Burleson on my ass about using department resources."

Alan sniffed. "True. He complains about a lot of shit lately. So?"

Cooper unfolded his arms. "So, what?"

"Did you find anything?" Alan laughed. "Why so jumpy? You still scared of the dark?"

"Not the dark. John."

Alan stood. "John? Come on, Coop, you really think John did that stuff? You've known each other for years. You know he's not like that."

"I'm just going by what the evidence says. Besides, who knows what happens to soldiers when they're at war? He could be having one of them fast backs."

"Flashbacks?"

"Yeah, flashbacks. Who knows what he's capable of now?" Cooper slipped the flashlight from his belt but didn't turn it on. He rolled it back and forth through his fingers.

Alan eyed the flashlight. "Wait, you told Chief Burleson and Ruth that you were coming out here? When?"

Cooper looked to the floor. "This morning, right after she came back in after searching for John. Me and Ruth stood right there in Burleson's office when I told them both. I'm not surprised Ruth forgot; she's never seemed that smart to me anyway, but the Chief? He must be under more stress than I thought."

Saying somebody wasn't smart sounded strange coming from Cooper. He wasn't stupid, but he wasn't the sharpest tool in the shed either. "Let me get this straight. You told both Sergeant Shaw and Chief Burleson—this morning—that you were coming out here to check on my parents' farmhouse?"

Cooper's hands ceased rolling the flashlight. "That's what I said, isn't it? It's not my fault if they both forgot."

Alan's heart skipped a beat. As if he were a child again, he pictured how fast he could draw his cap gun to kill the bad guys. His hand shot to his waist and snatched the gun from his holster, centering the sights on Cooper's chest.

The flashlight fell from Cooper's hands and thumped to the floor. His arms popped up. "What the fuck, Alan? What are you doing?"

Through clenched teeth, Alan said, "Ruth doesn't forget."

Cooper's head tilted to the side.

Rita's smile bloomed in his mind's eye, the dimple she had only on one side. The memory of how it felt to run his calloused fingers through her silken hair. How she giggled when he tickled the tops of her feet. He pictured Lena in the hospital, beaten within a hand's breadth of her life, her stomach sewn back together after the surgeons removed the ID from her abdominal wall.

"What did you do, Coop? If you had anything to do with Rita's death, you're a dead man."

Something stung him in the right shoulder. He spun around. Inches away stood Russell Holbrook, holding a syringe. Alan's gun tumbled from his hand; his arm flopped to his side. Holbrook grinned. Alan's fist from his good hand slammed into Holbrook's nose. The psychiatrist's head snapped back, and he crashed to the floor, blood spurting from the crushed bone and cartilage. Cooper's howl from behind Alan became a muffled whisper.

Alan crumpled, the dusty hardwood slamming against his temple. A flashlight beam shined on Holbrook's limp body. The muscles in Alan's face tugged at his lips just enough to form a smile before the light blackened.

Apex Girl

John watched the computer screen in horror. Holbrook edged closer to Alan, the syringe held out before him. He plunged it deep into Alan's shoulder. Even on the small screen, the crazy psychiatrist's smug grin sickened him.

The leather restraints chafed John's skin. He tugged, yanked, pushed, and pulled. They wouldn't loosen. The strap holding the wash cloth in his mouth muffled the scream he belted out. To his side, Eddy lay silent, eyes closed, chest slowly rising and lowering.

John focused on the screen again. Alan had dropped his weapon and stared dumbly at his limp arm. His brother's fist shot out and into Holbrook's face. The doctor's feet came off the ground as he flew backward and crashed to the kitchen floor.

Great shot, Alan!

The short-lived moment of glory ebbed as Alan slumped to his knees and eventually, the rest of the way to the floor. This time, John's tears flowed freely. The last triumph of the Reeves brothers. Unless Alan had killed Holbrook. John knew the strength behind Alan's left cross all too well, and his big brother had held back when they were kids. There wasn't any holding back when he'd clobbered Holbrook.

Cooper sidled in next to Alan from beyond the edge of the camera's view. His hands wiped at his eyes. *He's crying.* There was something human left in Coop. Maybe they had a chance if Holbrook was injured. As if on cue, the doctor struggled to sit up, hands flying to his face to stem the flow of blood. He shouted something to Cooper and pointed to Alan's unmoving body. The heavy wood forming the basement ceiling muffled the words. The skinny cop helped Holbrook to unsteady feet. They grabbed opposite ends of Alan and hefted him out of sight.

Moments later, the red door leading to John's own personal hell crashed open. Cooper struggled with Alan's broad shoulders, Holbrook with his size thirteen feet. They dropped him on the cement floor, their chests heaving.

Between deep breaths, Holbrook pointed to John. "Remove the cloth from John's mouth. I believe I'm in the mood to hear his snide remarks."

Cooper stepped to his side, removed the strap and yanked the cloth free, careful to keep his fingers away from John's teeth.

John worked his jaw and tongue, stimulating saliva to wet his mouth. Alan's chest rose and fell. Relief overwhelmed John. *Glad you're still alive, brother, I think.*

Holbrook went to his workstation, opening and closing multiple containers; though, John couldn't see which. "What's the matter, John? Nothing to say? Not very often you're speechless."

"I'm still waiting for you to tell me why we're here, what you want."

Holbrook turned, sliding another pair of latex gloves onto his long fingers. "I know you're tired of waiting, but the final piece of the puzzle has just arrived. However, we should wait until he wakes. I wouldn't want to appear rude."

"You'd rather appear psychotic?"

"That's all you can come up with? And here I thought you more creative. I truly hope your brother can formulate better responses." He paused, and with a chortle, clapped his hands together. "This is so wonderful. It truly is. You and Alan are supposedly part of this incredible police family, yet here you both are in my parlor. How does it feel to be played like a fiddle? To be powerless? To know your fate lies in my hands?"

John growled. "The night's not over yet, screwball."

Holbrook reached into a refrigerated unit next to the computer and removed a small vial. Cooper, who'd stood next to the wall quietly with his arms crossed since returning, came forward, his eyebrows climbing his forehead. Holbrook slipped a syringe from his pocket and filled it with the clear liquid. "This is a little present for our friend next to Eddy. What's her name again, Cooper?"

"Beth, my Savior."

"Yes, Elizabeth who preferred to be called Beth. That's right." He gently placed the vial back into its rack in the fridge.

Cooper's shoulders sagged when the unit's door closed.

Holbrook approached the sheet-covered body next to Eddy. "Beth here attended the University of Detroit Mercy. A civil engineering student I believe she said. She joined us the night you and I shared drinks at the Apex. I've no use for her anymore though." He flung the sheet back to uncover a pale-skinned girl, blond hair strewn about her head. The needle slid into the side of her sagging breast. Her breaths quickened.

Cooper reached her side before the plunger pressed the rest of the poison into the girl's body. He held out a thick plastic baggy. When finished, Holbrook dropped the syringe into the baggy and turned to her heart monitor.

John warred with his restraints. Blood flared at his temples, but he was helpless. *Keep talking.* "About the Apex. Just how did I get home that night?"

Holbrook held up a finger. "One moment, John. I enjoy this part."

The girl's heart monitor beeped faster, drowning the sound of her rapid breaths. The beeps sped up to 200 per minute, maxed out and slowly dropped; 120, 80, 40, until it flat-lined. The buzz persisted. A death knell portending inevitable demise.

Holbrook unceremoniously reached one hand beneath the girl and rolled her from the table. Her limp body flopped to the cement floor. "She's yours if you want her, Cooper. Not quite as young as you used to prefer, but beautiful nonetheless. For now, remove her so Alan may take his place."

Wake Up

Alan dreamed of the old farmhouse, times spent there with family, the holidays. His father, Ed Reeves, sat him and Johnny on a knee out on the front porch. Told them about the bad guy he'd caught that day at work. His face turned serious. "John, and you too, Alan, you boys are meant for this. You'll both catch bad guys one day, but be smart. Use your brains. Emotions can get in the way. They can drive you, focus you, but don't let them control your mind." Every word, every story, every waking moment a lesson.

They tracked a deer their father shot, Alan age twelve, having just passed his hunter's safety course.

"Look at these spatters of blood, Alan. What can you tell me?"

He'd peered at the droplets in the thick brush, eager to impress his father, show him he was as good as John. "They're shaped like a teardrop. That means he was going this way," he pointed, "the same direction as the point on the drop of blood."

Little John cuffed him on the arm. "You always get that wrong. He's going the opposite way of the points."

"Don't hit your brother, Johnny." Ed placed his hand on Alan's shoulder. "It's okay, son, but Johnny is right."

Alan's face flushed. "Sorry, Dad."

"Don't be. Your little brother picks up on this stuff fast. You'll learn it when you're ready."

"Alan? Wake up, Alan."

"Wha..."

Cold fingers fumbled at his eyelids, seized hold and pried them open. Blinding white light scorched his eyes. "I said wake up. We're tired of waiting."

"Dr. Holbrook?"

"You're fine. I gave you a little something to jar you awake. You may be dizzy a moment, but it was needed."

Alan remembered his fist crushing Holbrook's nose. He gasped.

"Holbrook, you son-of-a-bitch!" He fought to reach the man. Tight leather straps across his arms, waist, and ankles tethered him to a stainless steel gurney.

"Calm down, Alan." Holbrook slid a hand beneath the clear plastic surgeon's mask and gently tapped the bandage over his nose. "I prefer you not all worked up. You have a powerful left punch. You'll pay for that, but later."

The words Alan's father had spoken in the dream flitted across his mind. *Emotions only get in the way.* Next to the bed, a heart monitor and IV pole was connected to his arm with tubes and tape. He grabbed control of his runaway emotions, heartbeat slowing. The beeping to Alan's side slowed. "What the hell is all this, Holbrook?"

"Oh bother, ask your sibling. I sicken of sharing the same story over and again." Laughter tinged his words.

"Yeah," John said. "Ask your sibling. He'll tell you our home grown cop, one Corporal Cooper Forbes, wants to molest his own children, and this sociopath thinks he's found a cure."

Alan fought against the strap holding his head down.

"If you promise to be good," Holbrook said, "I'll remove that one belt from your head. Johnny Boy already had his removed. Can you be calm?"

Alan nodded against the strap but only succeeded in moving his chin up and down. Holbrook opened the hasp and pulled the leather belt free, keeping his fingers away from Alan's mouth. Alan craned his neck to the side. Eddy Bailey lay next to him on another gurney and on the other side of the private investigator was John, glaring at Holbrook.

"This will help." Holbrook crouched next to the gurney and cranked on something. He stopped when the bed was almost at a forty-five degree angle. "Welcome to the party, Alan. You've missed the fun. I've already begun your brother's autopsy as you can see by the nice V shape carved into his chest."

Blood oozed from John's chest, yet he wore a look of defiance, his brow drawn down into a scowl for Holbrook. Across the room, Eddy's family hung from their restraints, eyes taped open, his wife completely nude.

Holbrook positioned his stool at Eddy's feet and sat, glancing between the three men in front of him; Alan to his left, Eddy in the middle, and John to the right. "I'm sure you have plenty of questions, Captain Reeves, so let's begin. Where should I start first?" He made a show of bringing his fingers to his chin as if deep in thought. "Let's go with John since he was here first. What did you think of the blue rose?"

"What the hell does a blue rose have to do with us being here?" John spat.

The psychiatrist howled a laugh. "Are you telling me you never found it? What else have you two missed?"

"I found it." Alan shifted against his restraints. "It's the symbol your father attributed to his research. But I agree with John. What's it have to do with anything?"

Holbrook's brow lifted. "So you found it and determined it was my father's so called crest. You still don't see the significance?"

Moans drifted from Eddy. "Home."

"Oh, looky here. Eddy's back. This definitely isn't your home, Eddy. Open your eyes so that you may remember." Holbrook turned to the back of the room. "Cooper, tape up our friend Eddy. We don't want him to miss any more than he already has."

Coop! The gurney shook as Alan twisted and pulled, fighting to get free. He'd forgotten about Cooper. "Cooper! What the hell are you doing here? Why are you doing this?"

"Enough." Holbrook held up his hand. "We've already gone through this with John. Cooper helps me because I helped him. End of story. Back to the questions."

Helped him?

Eddy's gurney creaked as he pulled against the straps. "No more questions," Eddy croaked. "Let my family go or I'll kill you!"

"He's definitely back." Holbrook gestured to his helper. "Cooper? Bring me another scalpel."

Cooper hastened to his side with a roll of clear tape in one hand and a scalpel in the other. He handed the scalpel to the psychiatrist and fought Eddy's head into place.

Holbrook wandered over to Sandra's side and placed the scalpel blade on her belly. Tears poured from Eddy's taped eyes. "Is this what you want, Eddy? No? I have a better idea." He spun to face Eddy's oldest child, Edwin Junior, and placed the blade at his throat.

"No! God, no!" Eddy screamed.

"No?" A smile curled into place on Holbrook's face. He removed the blade from the child's throat and stalked back to Eddy. "Calm yourself. I promised your children to Cooper anyway, even if I have to remove his cure momentarily. I'm here for you three." He lifted his mask and used the handle of the scalpel to smooth his eye brows. "However, you must know just how serious I am. Your children mean nothing to me. I'd gladly kill them. Let's not hear any screeching from you again." With a flick of the wrist, the scalpel glided through Eddy's Achilles tendon.

A shrill cry burst from Eddy. Holbrook held a finger to his lips. Eddy quickly clamped his mouth shut and held the screams in, his eyes bulging and chest heaving.

"Now you're learning. I'm sorry, Cooper, but could you wrap this up? I don't want Mr. Bailey passing out before we're done."

"We get the point, Holbrook!" Alan roared. "Let Eddy's family go so we can deal with this, just the four of us."

"You and John, so much alike even though you're adopted." The psychiatrist stepped to the foot of Alan's bed and raised his scalpel in the air. The heart monitor beeped faster. "You know, it's not really fair that John and Eddy have felt the pain of my blade and you have not. Do you have a preference? Your trigger finger maybe? Your member? With Rita out of the picture, I can't imagine you'd need that any time soon."

"Cut me anywhere you want, as long as you let the woman and children go."

"No," Holbrook said curtly. "We'll keep it simple. I've heard this is quite painful." He played the scalpel across the skin on Alan's thighs, his knees, down to his feet, never breaking the skin. He paused. "Now would be a good time to clench your teeth, Captain Reeves." Pain blossomed between two of Alan's toes and slid down his foot, inch by inch, ending at the heel. Alan howled. "Cooper, when you're done with Eddy." He gestured to Alan's bleeding foot.

Tears streamed from Eddy's eyes. John's body was taught against his bindings. Cooper finished taping Eddy's ankle and turned to Alan, unwinding the gauze roll.

Taking his place on the stool, Holbrook pulled his mask back into place. "I have a grand idea. Cooper, when you're finished with Alan, grab my camera. I'd like to savor this moment for years to come."

"As you wish, my Savior," Cooper murmured.

"Let's get this show on the road," Holbrook began. "The real fun won't start until we get this out of the way." His shoulders rose as he breathed deeply a moment. "The blue rose symbolizes the unattainable as the blue rose itself is unattainable. The deep azure can only be achieved with the use of dye. A fun little experiment that was. But that is what my father's colleagues said of his research, that he chased the unattainable. You see, for years, since the beginning of man really, we've searched for ways to stop bad men and women from... well... being bad." He glanced off to the side a moment, a grin splitting his face.

My God. He's enjoying this.

The bandage staunched the flow of blood from Alan's foot, but didn't stop the pain. Salty tears showered down his face. Cooper tied off and taped the last bit of gauze. He hurried from the room.

Holbrook continued. "Some slimy do-gooder of a senator heard about my father's research at the Alabama prison and shut the whole thing down. The government actually paid my father to continue his work here in Detroit. I see from the look on your face, Alan, you didn't know the government had anything to do with it."

"I didn't know, but that doesn't make it any less sick."

The stool squealed across the floor as Holbrook slid it behind him. He paced, demeanor darkening, waving his hands while he spoke, tension radiating from every movement.

"There my father was, Mr. Abraham Holbrook, doing what he did best, searching for a way to help all of mankind. And he was so close." He held his thumb and forefinger and inch apart. "So close to discovering how to fix those men. Murderers, bank robbers, rapists. Society could have been saved from these vile beings." The pacing stopped and he crossed his arms. "This is when your father and his friends came along to destroy everything he worked for."

"My father and his friends?" John asked.

"You didn't know, John? Ed Reeves, Herbert Tolman, Rusty Krogman, Douglas Fincham. Each the lowest scum of the earth." His glare focused on Alan. "Did you? I left you hint after hint. The greenest rookie on your so-called police force should have figured it out."

"Lowest scum of the earth?" John said. "Have you looked in the mirror lately? If your father was half as deranged as yourself, my father and his friends did this world a service."

Holbrook's hand slid into his surgical apron and came out with his bloody scalpel. "Speak of my father in such a manner again, John Reeves, and you won't be around to hear the rest of the story."

The door to the kill room swung open. Cooper stepped in with a digital camera and a tripod. "Where would you like this set up, my Savior?"

Alan sighed in relief. He'd expected Holbrook to teach them another *lesson*. Any more pain and he'd be lucky not to pass out.

"Over there, next to the wall." Holbrook gestured with the blade to the back of the room. "We'll set it to swivel when the fun begins. That way we can see their reactions as well as our work." He resumed his pacing. "That's not even the worst of what your father had in store for Abraham. Of course the government denied any affiliation with my father." The spittle from his brusque words gathered on the inside of his clear plastic mask. "So he was sentenced to a federal prison, taking the blame for something he should have been glorified for." Holbrook raised the blade over his head and slammed it into John's thigh. John didn't make a sound. His face simply darkened. "Then your father had him killed in prison!"

An involuntary yelp had escaped Alan's mouth at the sudden display of fury. The psychiatrist yanked the blade free and wiped it absently on his apron, adding to the slew of brownish red streaks.

"Investigators never found any evidence of the murder, of course, but why else would he be killed within a week? In those few days, he'd sent me a letter while I attended Brown University. He explained everything, said he knew Ed Reeves and the others were after him." Holbrook turned to face them and lifted the plastic mask, a pained expression on his face. "What I truly don't understand, is why they would do this to him when they were so close." He rested both hands at the foot of Eddy's bed.

"So close?" Alan said. "You're saying they knew each other before all this?" The photo of the men drinking together at the farmhouse flashed into Alan's memory. "The military?"

"Bingo, Captain Reeves."

Alan shuddered. Picturing his father as friends with anything related to Holbrook disgusted him.

"Military friends. Like family, they say. Brothers. Yet they had him skewered like some wild animal." Holbrook strode to Alan's side. "Would you enjoy that, John?" he called over his shoulder. "How would it feel to stab your own brother in the back? No? How would it feel to have someone else stab your brother in the back?"

Fear reflected in John's eyes. "Of course I wouldn't enjoy it. I'm not a sick fuck like you." He winced and glanced at his chest.

Eddy whispered something unintelligible.

"What was that, Eddy?" Holbrook asked.

John's friend cleared his throat. "If I stabbed him in the back, would you let my family go?" Eddy's words came out no more than a whisper.

Holbrook tittered. "Now the fun has begun." He turned from Alan and ran his hand through Eddy's hair like a loving parent. "Oh, Eddy. You're just in the wrong place at the right time. You see, the only reason you and your family are here is because of John and Alan. I know they won't break, not as you just have. Only by your family's pain will they talk."

A moan came from across the room and a splash. Cooper vomited in the corner, adding to a pile of what looked like puke already.

"Again?" Holbrook said. "How is it you became a cop? This explains the horrid police work I've come to expect from the Clarkbridge Department." Holbrook went to his stool yet again. "Now that our friend Eddy has crossed the line, it's time to finish up. Morning will come soon, and I'm due back at the office."

"Yeah, about your office," Alan said. "Sorry about the mess."

Holbrook shrugged. "So you managed a search warrant for my office? No matter. No evidence will be found there, or at my home. Or here for that matter. When they discover John's burned remains, they'll find he has a hole in the side of his head and the weapon still in his hand. Poor John finally went off the deep end, capturing his friend's family and his own brother. Killing and mutilating them all and setting his parents' house on fire before shooting himself. Such a tragic, tragic, story."

"You actually think people will believe that?" Alan said.

"Of course they will. The psychiatrist working the case will create an intriguing court document stating exactly why and how it can happen to a soldier of his caliber." A grin grew on Holbrook's face. "You know, Alan, we haven't spoken of Rita yet." He paused and waved to Cooper. "Remove the camera from the tri-pod and bring it here. I want a close-up."

Cooper hefted the camera onto his shoulder and brought it to Alan's side. A tiny red dot lit up on the front. "It's ready, my Savior."

Holbrook approached Alan's side with a lurid gait. He waved the scalpel back and forth a few times before settling it on Alan's stomach. Alan recoiled, his stomach muscles tightening. "Rita was tied to this very bed."

All thought left Alan. Fury burned through his body, anger so mighty he thought he'd explode.

"I see this upsets you, Alan. Then you'll truly enjoy this part. Cooper and I both had our way with her. Multiple times. Sometimes she was awake, sometimes she wasn't. But I made sure she felt every moment."

Alan shook from head to toe.

"You want to know the best part? She's not even dead."

"What?" Alan's body went limp.

John called from behind the doctor. "Don't listen to him, Alan. He's toying with you. These sick bastards killed her. You know they did."

"Does he?" Holbrook said. "I could show you both the videos but they wouldn't do much good. We actually thought both she and Lena were dead, but somehow that little wetback survived."

Alan's restraints pulled tight. "Call her that again and you're dead!"

"That's enough for now, Cooper. Return the camera to the tri-pod." He sat by Eddy's feet again. "What about you, Eddy? Do you think Rita is dead?"

Eyes red from being taped open so long, Eddy said, "How can she not be? We're in hell."

"Such a flare for the dramatic. Maybe you should have made a career in theater instead of accounting and this private investigation nonsense." Holbrook crossed his arms.

Alan feared the answer, but he had to ask. "If she's not dead, then where is she?" He wasn't surprised

Holbrook and Cooper thought she was dead. She'd been beaten worse than Lena, barely recognizable.

"Poor, poor, Alan. Don't you know? You've held her hand every time you visited the hospital the past few weeks."

"But..."

"But what? Confused?"

"The tattoo on her wrist... a blue rose. You put it there."

"Not me, but a talented artist. And the rest was quite easy. A little acid to remove the fingerprints, some bleach and a scalpel to remove Lena's abdominal tattoo, lots of fun pretending they were punching bags."

I'll never have the chance to say goodbye...

"I have a question, Dr. Psycho," John said. "If you and Mr. Molester had your way with them, how is it my semen was found?"

"There we go, Johnny Boy. It's about time you came up with a good question. Again, quite simple actually. The night we drank at the Apex together, I gathered a sample of your DNA on the ride home. Just a small pin prick on the mole on your left foot and I had everything I needed. I don't suppose you ever read forensic journals? No? You see, a group of doctors from Israel published their research on developing artificial DNA evidence. It wasn't hard to determine their techniques from the article."

"What about Douglas Fincham?" Alan added.

"I suppose he could be considered my first official drug trial. You see, I only just developed my serum. Douglas Fincham spent ten days with me, in therapy you could say. The first test was to see if I could remove that damnable back pain he always whined about. It was all too easy. I ordered him to stop feeling the pain, and he did. The cuts and abrasions he suffered while at the police station were an added bonus. I instilled in him the belief that I'd cut him with a scalpel if he ever heard his trigger word." He glanced to Alan. "That was the phone call. I simply uttered the magic word and hung up. Then I flicked on my monitor and enjoyed watching Clarkbridge's best flail about."

"Tolman and Krogman?" John asked.

"Much the same. I told Krogman to pretend his body was a carcass that needed separating before sale, and to be sure he had fun while doing it." The psychiatrist giggled. "I found Tolman's story quite entertaining. He had an abnormal fear of osteoporosis and bone fractures. I'm sure I laughed for an hour at the irony of a chiropractor fearing broken bones. The only thing better would have been a doctor of osteopathy." He turned back to John. "The work I put into those three was easy compared to developing your fake semen."

"You went through all that trouble just to create my semen?" John laughed. "You could have just asked."

Holbrook rolled his eyes. "How do you deal with someone so disgusting, Alan? Honestly."

"You call my brother disgusting?" Alan had held in the bulk of his emotions long enough. Rita would never know how much he'd loved her, or that he knew she still lived. Knowing Holbrook, she probably wouldn't outlive Alan for long. He was prepared for death. "You're too afraid to fight like a man so you drug us and tie us up. You had such a crush on your daddy that you thought you'd get revenge for his death. All you've done is prove how weak you are."

"That's enough out of you, Captain Reeves." Holbrook stood.

"You hide behind your intellect. You lie to yourself; tell yourself you're doing the right thing when you truly could have been great. Imagine what you could have accomplished had you not focused your entire damn life on this vendetta. Instead of healing or helping others, you hide in this basement with a child molester, cutting up women and children to establish your authority. You're a little, little man, Russell Holbrook, and you'll rot in Hell with your lunatic father!"

Holbrook shook. His hand glided into his pocket, his trembling fist outlined by the thin white linen. "I said I've heard enough—"

"I'll tell you when you've had enough," Alan snapped back. "You've already taken almost everything from me. The only thing I have left is the truth. And the truth is you're not half the man your father was, and he wasn't even half a man. I've seen farm animals with more common sense and morals than old Abe."

Holbrook ripped the mask from his head. He pulled his fist from his lab coat with a knuckle-white grip on the scalpel. He gestured behind him. "Cooper. Slide the sheet down on the child. The youngest. Let's see how long his heart beats after we remove it from his chest." He pointed the blade at Alan. "You've caused this, Alan. You alone."

"No!" Eddy screamed. "Stop. I'll do whatever you want. Please!"

The psychiatrist flew to Eddy's side, holding the blade to his neck and nicking the skin. "Shut your mouth, Eddy. If I have to tell you again, I'll sew it shut. Now sit here and watch what happens to those who cross a Holbrook."

Eddy wailed like a newborn baby, spit trailing from his mouth.

"You're a dead man, Coop!" John roared. "You both are. Don't touch that kid!"

Tears and snot dripped from Cooper's chin. He sobbed almost as hard as Eddy.

"Do it!" Holbrook yelled. "This is the moment we've been waiting for. This is why we're here. This is why I helped you. Do it!"

Cooper placed the blade at the edge of young Henry's shoulder, a bead of blood rising from the pressure.

Alan glanced to Eddy. The man's neck and arms shined red from exertion. "Turn your head, Eddy. Don't watch this. Just turn your head."

On the other side of Eddy, John alternated flexing and relaxing his limbs, battling the cuffs holding him in place. Fresh blood streamed in rivulets down his chest.

Alan stared at Cooper, begging and praying to every god he knew to stop the man.

The blade drew deeper, pulled against the flesh, and paused. Cooper's eyes closed, his chest heaved. His eyes flew open. He threw the scalpel against the back wall. "I can't do it."

Surprise showed on Holbrook's face, but only for a moment. He glared at the skinny man. He enunciated each word slowly and deliberately. "Do as I say, Cooper Eustace Forbes."

Cooper stepped away from the child and huddled against the wall, hands covering his face.

"Eustace!" Holbrook screeched. "Eustace! That is your trigger word. Remember, and do as I say!"

Cooper didn't move. He crouched with his back to the wall, crying and wailing like a child. Alan held his breath.

"Fine. I'll do it myself." Holbrook slammed his scalpel into John's uninjured thigh and started toward Henry.

John belted out a scream. "Stop, damn you!"

Eddy and Alan joined in, none of their words affecting Holbrook. Their ranting bellows echoed through the small basement room.

Holbrook stepped to his work desk and grabbed a fresh scalpel. He moved close to Henry and placed the blade in the same incision Cooper had begun at the child's bony shoulder. He paused and turned toward them, shouting over the babble. "Watch and watch carefully. Let's all count the heart beats together."

Cooper pushed away from the wall, wiping at his tears. He slid a hand into his pocket and paused. He turned away from the doctor.

Holbrook faced Henry again. His hand placed the blade just so. His jaw muscles clenched in unison with those in his hand.

Cooper spun back, a scalpel in both hands, ramming them into Holbrook's back. The gleaming blade slipped from Holbrook's hand onto the boy's chest. His mouth worked but no words escaped. He turned to the skinny man and coughed.

Tears streamed down Cooper's face. "I'm so sorry, my Savior. I just... not a child. I can't hurt a child."

Blood dribbled from the corner of Holbrook's mouth. One long rasp escaped his lips before his eyes glassed over. He fell limp into Cooper's waiting arms.

32. Late to the Party

Late to the Party

John couldn't believe it was over. Their deaths had almost been a certainty, and the blame thrown at his feet. Cooper shuddered. He'd been still so long John thought he'd fallen asleep. Cooper continued to murmur and rock Holbrook in his arms like a baby.

The moment Holbrook collapsed, his last breath rattling from his lungs, Eddy begged Cooper to unhook his children from the IVs. His begging quickly became forceful shouting.

John changed tactics. "Hey, Coop? Those kids have had their eyes taped open for hours. If Holbrook told the truth, they still feel everything. Why don't you at least help them?"

Cooper stood, eyes bloodshot, splotches of blood peppering his uniform. "I never wanted this."

Eddy's head popped up. "Cooper? Get my kids out of here!"

"Wait." John shushed Eddy. "Quiet down a second."

Alan added to the pleading. "Of course you didn't want this, Coop. You saved the children. It's time to finish saving them. We don't want them to be in pain any longer. Why don't you unhook them? Better yet, why don't you unhook me and I'll help?"

Something Alan said clicked. Cooper's eyes focused inward, somewhere far away, but he stepped forward as if by rote, pulling the tape from Alan's arm one piece at a time. The needles and straps next. He moved back to Henry's side and began the same.

Alan worked his limbs to regain the feeling. He rolled from the gurney and limped to John's side. "John, get Eddy up, but crank his bed back down first. He won't be able to walk with his Achilles like that."

"Gotcha." John grimaced when Alan yanked the scalpel from his thigh. "You get Eddy's family. No telling how long it'll take that crap to wear off."

John glanced to Cooper every few seconds to make sure he wasn't doing anything peculiar. The skinny cop had unhooked Henry from all the wires and sat down on the floor next to Holbrook with the child in his arms, humming a lullaby. John tore strips from his sheet and wrapped them around the open wounds on his legs, cringing with each tug. There wasn't much he could do for his chest at the moment. He pulled the rest of the sheet around him to cover up. Holbrook had never told them where their clothes were. He swung from the gurney and stood on unsteady legs.

The tape pulled from Eddy's eyelids with a rip. "Sorry about that, Eddy." John worked on the next piece.

"Just get me out of here, John. I need... my family needs me."

John nodded. "I know they do, Eddy. Alan's taking care of them now."

Alan crouched next to each bed in turn, cranking the lever beneath to lower the gurneys flat, ensuring the Bailey family wouldn't slide from the beds when they came around.

Before the last strap came off, Eddy stood and hopped on one foot, yanking his hand against the restraints.

"Wait a sec, Eddy. Almost got it." The strap snapped back and struck the puncture wound on John's thigh. He clenched his teeth against the pain.

Eddy made it a couple hops before losing his balance and careening over Holbrook's stool to the floor. John wobbled to Eddy's side and wrapped him in the sheet that had covered his friend moments before. He squatted down and hefted the man in his arms as he would a child. The pain was almost unbearable. He'd carry his friend as far as he had to, regardless of his own suffering.

When they reached Henry's bed, John sat Eddy down and clutched the edge to keep from collapsing.

"Give me my child," Eddy rasped at Cooper.

Cooper woke from his muttering stupor. He held Henry up. John slid his arms under the child and handed him to Eddy. It hadn't been more than a few days since he'd eaten grilled tacos with little Henry, yet it felt like a lifetime ago.

Eddy leaned from the gurney and thumped Cooper on the chin with a tight fist. Cooper turned away and fell to the concrete, sobbing again. Rather than rub his chin, he moved his fingers through the pool of Holbrook's blood, babbling, ignoring the fresh cut on his lip.

Alan unstrapped the three remaining Bailey children from the gurneys, Sandra as well, covering her with a sheet. The red door burst open and three Clarkbridge police officers poured into the basement.

"Sergeant Shaw." Her name tumbled from John's lips followed by an exhausted sigh. "How good of you to join us. That new hair color doesn't show as much when you have it pulled back like that."

Ruth Shaw, Corporal Gibbs, and Sergeant Clark, the huge officer he'd made friends with at the police station, eyed the room with horror on their sleep deprived faces. John followed their eyes around the gruesome scene. Bloodied sheets lay strewn about the room, hospital beds and medical equipment lined the walls, Cooper's vomit joined the puddles of water on the cement floor. The basement stank like a butcher shop.

Clark spoke into his shoulder radio. "Dispatch, this is Sergeant Clark. We need a bus at 1215 Rogers Road." He glanced around the room again. "Make that multiple buses and contact Detroit Forensics. Over."

"Alan!" Ruth rushed to Alan and wrapped her short arms around his waist. Despite the horror still surrounding them, a smile grew on his face. "Oh my God. I found your phone on my dash when Chief Burleson stopped at your house so I could grab my car."

Alan's eyebrows scrunched together. "You came here because you found my phone?"

She looked up into his eyes. "I used your spare key to get into the house. I thought I'd plug your phone in on the kitchen counter like I'd seen you do. When I powered it up, John's text came through. He said he and Eddy were over here for a barbecue."

John shrugged and showed a lop-sided grin. "I figured you'd know what I meant."

Gibbs crouched next to Holbrook and checked his pulse.

Ruth continued. "I assumed you got the message and came over here to check it out."

"That's not quite the way it happened," Alan said, "but what matters is that you're here now. I'm not sure any of us could have made it back to my house to call the police."

John grinned. "When did you two get so close?"

Alan's smile disappeared. He pushed Ruth to arms length. "I have to leave. Can you drive me to the hospital?"

Ruth looked up at him. "I can if you really want. Are you okay? What's the matter with your foot? Maybe you should wait for the ambulance?"

Sergeant Clark held his hand out for John to shake. "Good to see your ugly mug." He cleared his throat and spoke to Alan. "Are we all clear?"

Alan removed Ruth's arms. He gestured to Cooper. "Cooper here has some explaining to do. He won't put up much of a fight."

The huge cop's eyes grew wide. "Coop is part of this?"

Alan nodded. "He is. Or was. Don't go too rough on him. He was under Holbrook's control." He grasped Ruth by the shoulders and looked her in the eye. "I need you to take me to the hospital. Rita is alive."

"What?"

"It's true, Ruth. At least I believe it is. Lena wasn't the one who survived. It was Rita."

Wonderment fell across Ruth's features. "You mean, you've been visiting Rita this whole time?"

"I'll explain later. Let's get out of here." He turned to John and Clark. "You two got this?"

Alan no longer studied John as if he were a piece of evidence. They were brothers again. "We got it, Alan. Take care. I'll see you in a bit." He glanced at the V-shaped cut on his chest. "Getting this sewed up will be a bitch."

Sandra moaned behind them and sat up, holding the sheet to her chest. She swayed side to side. Gibbs ran over and caught her. She began to sob. The other three Bailey children responded as if their mother's cry had awoken them. Weeping and wailing cries began in unison.

John hefted the child closest to him, Holly. "It's okay, sweetheart. Uncle John's got ya. Let's set you right here with Daddy."

Gibbs helped Sandra stumble to the bed where Eddy had his arms around Holly and Henry. Maria and Edwin Junior joined Eddy on the small gurney, eyes wide, clinging to their parents.

Chief Burleson stepped into the room. His gaze shifted about the room. "Can somebody tell me what the hell happened here?"

John pointed to the camera still rolling on the tripod. "All your answers are right there on that camera, Chief."

He felt a tug at the sheet wrapped around his waist. He turned. Holly pulled at him from the gurney. "Uncle John?" She sniffled and wiped at her nose. "Daddy wants to tell you something."

"What I said about Alan," Eddy said, "and... you know, hurting him—"

"Never happened." John ran his hand through little Holly's hair.

Eddy nodded. "Thank you, John."

Mouthy

Blue and red lights danced across the farmhouse lawn. Ruth Shaw helped Alan hobble his way into her convertible. John sat on a hospital gurney behind a North Detroit General ambulance. He wasn't leaving until Eddy's family was taken care of.

Pain erupted in his chest. He smacked the EMT's hand away. "Take it easy, turbo."

"Sorry, Mr. Reeves."

"I get it. You're just trying to clean me up. You could be a little more gentle." He glanced at the woman tending his wound. A strand of her wavy blond hair stuck to her forehead. Her hands shook. He squinted at her name tag. "Katherine? Can I call you Katy?"

"That's what my friends call me."

"We're practically best friends already. My blood is on your fingers and I'm shirtless."

A nervous giggle escaped her tight lips.

"You're new at this, right?"

She continued to pat at the incision, nodding.

"Hey." He lifted her chin with a finger. "You're doing a great job. Don't pay too much attention to my attitude. I get a little ornery when someone tries to kill me."

Katherine smiled. "Does that happen often?"

"More than I'd like to admit." He grunted. "Any big plans for when this is over?"

"Really?" Sergeant Clark stepped up to the rear of the ambulance. "Not even a half hour and you're hitting on the next woman you see?"

"We only have one life to live, Clark. Besides," he nodded to Katherine, "She's beautiful, even with her hair tied back in a ponytail."

A deep laugh rumbled from Clark. "Whatever you say. So what are your plans?" He gestured around them. "When this is all done, I mean. You sticking around for a while?"

John glanced at the EMT. "I may. Though an old friend did call me from Chicago last week. Said there might be a job for me."

"Well, whatever you decide to do, let me buy you a drink before you go."

"Verbal contract," John said. Clark grinned and turned to walk away. John grabbed him by the shoulder. "What do you think? My chest is halfway to an autopsy and I had a psycho try to pop my thighs like balloons tonight. You might actually be able to take me now."

Clark laughed. "John Reeves, you are one mouthy son-of-a-bitch. You know that?"

33. Try it Again

Three Months Later

Alan sat across from Rita, her hands held in his own. The doctors said she'd walk again with months of physical therapy, but there was no waiting for her. The wooden chair he sat in wasn't comfortable, but it didn't bother him. The only thing that mattered was the woman who sat before him, wearing a smile still slightly crooked from the swelling.

Alan shifted forward in his chair and lifted the thin gauze veil. His fingertip traced the scar over her left eye, moved down her jawline and to her lips. A warm tear slipped from his cheek to her lap.

"You sure about this, old man?" Rita whispered past his finger.

"I've never been more sure about anything in my life."

The pastor spoke loud enough for everyone to hear. "You may kiss the bride."

THE END

Thank you so much for checking out the second stand-alone novel in the John Reeves series. If you enjoyed the read, please consider leaving a quick comment on the WRATH page at Amazon or other online retailers. I look forward to hearing what you think!

~ *Kirkus MacGowan*

Don't miss out on these other works by Kirkus MacGowan!

The Fall of Billy Hitchings
(A John Reeves Novel)
Top 5 Finalist in the Mystery/Thriller genre in the Best Indie Book of the Year contest at
The Kindle Book Review

In Search of Nectar
(A Short Story) - Humor

About the Author

Kirkus MacGowan wrote his first book at age eight about traveling to Mars to find the cure for cancer. He put his writing dreams on hold for twenty-five years and focused his energies on playing baseball. The day he found playing softball with friends more satisfying than baseball, he quit and never looked back.

Since then, he graduated with a B.S. in Psychology, married a woman too good to be true, and moved back to his hometown. He gave up an amazing career waiting tables and now stays at home with his two crazy children. He spends his time writing mystery, thrillers, and fantasy, playing softball with friends, enjoying the occasional computer game, and wrestling with his kids.

For book updates and future giveaway details, sign up for the Kirkus MacGowan Newsletter below:

http://www.kirkusmacgowan.info/newsletter/

Learn more at:

http://www.kirkusmacgowan.info/

Made in the USA
Lexington, KY
26 November 2012